"Sands's quirky sense of humor shines."
Romantic Times

"Vampire lovers will find themselves
laughing throughout."
Publishers Weekly

"A masterpiece of fast-paced, intelligent
action with hot and steamy relationships."
FreshFiction.com

Vampire Most Wanted

Marcus took the helmet she handed him and pulled it on as he watched her don her own. But his intention to do up the chinstrap died a quick death when she distracted him by bending forward. His eyes widened on her derriere as she caught the back of her skirt through her legs and drew the material tight as she pulled it forward. It wasn't until she straightened, with the cloth in hand, and tucked it into the front waistband of her skirt that he understood what she was doing. She then swung a leg over the motorcycle, started the engine, revved it, and then turned to peer at him. "Well?"

"Right," he muttered, quickly doing up the helmet she'd given him. It looked like she was driving. Hell. A motorcycle. He hoped she knew how to drive the damned thing.

By Lynsay Sands

VAMPIRE MOST WANTED
ONE LUCKY VAMPIRE
IMMORTAL EVER AFTER
THE LADY IS A VAMP
UNDER A VAMPIRE MOON
THE RELUCTANT VAMPIRE
HUNGRY FOR YOU
BORN TO BITE
THE RENEGADE HUNTER
THE IMMORTAL HUNTER
THE ROGUE HUNTER
VAMPIRE, INTERRUPTED
VAMPIRES ARE FOREVER
THE ACCIDENTAL VAMPIRE
BITE ME IF YOU CAN
A BITE TO REMEMBER
A QUICK BITE
TALL DARK & HUNGRY
SINGLE WHITE VAMPIRE
LOVE BITES

AN ENGLISH BRIDE IN SCOTLAND
THE HUSBAND HUNT
THE HEIRESS
THE COUNTESS
THE HELLION AND THE HIGHLANDER
TAMING THE HIGHLAND BRIDE
DEVIL OF THE HIGHLANDS

LYNSAY SANDS

VAMPIRE
MOST WANTED

AN ARGENEAU NOVEL

AVON

An Imprint of HarperCollinsPublishers

AVON BOOKS
An Imprint of HarperCollins*Publishers*
10 East 53rd Street
New York, New York 10022-5299

One

Divine saw her latest customer out, surprised to note that there was no one outside her door waiting for a reading. It was the first time that day that there was no line outside her RV. A glance at her watch explained why—it was dinnertime. That was the only time she ever had a lull in customers. Right now the food stalls would have ridiculously long line as everyone at the fairgrounds converged on them in search of greasy treats to power the rest of the evening's rides and fun. Which meant she had a few minutes to catch her breath and relax a bit.

She'd barely had the thought when she spotted a couple of women moving purposefully toward her trailer. After a brief hesitation, Divine quickly flipped the "Back in five minutes!" sign, let her screen door slide closed, and descended the few steps to the ground. Ignoring the fact that the women were looking alarmed

and rushing forward, she slipped around the side of her
RV. Most customers would have stopped then, sagged
with disappointment, and waited, probably impatiently,
but waited just the same, so Divine was a little surprised when her arm was grabbed from behind. She
was more surprised, however, by the strength in the
hand that latched on to her . . . until she turned and
noted that it wasn't one of the women at all, but a man.

A couple inches taller than she, dark-haired and
good-looking, he was built like a linebacker. He was
also looming over her, deliberately invading her space
in a threatening manner as he growled, "What the hell
did you say to my wife?"

Divine rolled her eyes with exasperation, wondering
how she was supposed to know since she didn't know
who his wife was. She was about to say as much, but
then realized that there was something familiar about
the man and quickly dipped into his thoughts. A heartbeat later she was relaxing.

"Allen Paulson," she murmured his name, getting an
almost childish satisfaction when his eyes widened incredulously.

"How do you—?"

"I told your wife that you were having an affair with
your buxom, blond, twenty-year-old secretary, Tiffany,"
Divine interrupted sharply, silencing him at once. "I
told her that this Tiffany was pushing for marriage and
that you, not wanting to lose her, but unwilling to give
up your wife's money, preferred widowhood to divorce.
I told her about your plans to bring about that widowhood on your upcoming vacation. I believe it was

either her drowning or suffering a fall while camping in Yosemite National Park?" She tilted her head. "As I recall, that trip was scheduled for this week, wasn't it?"

When his mouth dropped open and his hold on her arm eased, Divine added, "I'm guessing by the fact that you're here rather than in Yosemite, that she listened to my advice to make an appointment with her lawyer the next morning to change her will as well as remove you as the beneficiary on her life insurance."

His hand dropped away, falling limply by his side.

"No doubt she also listened to my advice and hired a private detective. I gather she sent him to get photographic proof of your infidelity at that cheap little motel you like to take your secretary to every day at lunchtime?" She slipped into his thoughts briefly, read the answer in the chaos there, and smiled with satisfaction. Not only had the wife done that, she'd then taken the proof straight to a good divorce lawyer. The woman was now safe and on her way to being single again. After that, though, the woman had told her dear hubby that the fortune-teller at the carnival was the one who had given her the heads-up and put her on this path and it had been the best twenty bucks she'd ever spent. Which was why Divine now had an irate and soon-to-be divorced and destitute husband on her hands.

Divine waited, braced for the man's anger. But instead of the explosive rage she expected, he asked in a small, frightened voice, "How did you know? No one knew. I didn't tell anyone what I planned. Not even Tiffany."

"Did you even bother to read the sign when you

walked your wife to my trailer that day two weeks ago in Pahrump?" she asked with amusement, and then reminded him, "Madame Divine. Let her do a reading and define your future," she reminded him.

"Yeah, but that's just . . . It's a scam," he protested. "You're a carnie. You just scam people out of their money for a laugh."

"Yes, of course," Divine agreed coldly, and then tilted her head. "So why aren't you laughing?"

Allen Paulson flinched as if she'd struck him, and then his awe and dismay gave way to the rage she'd expected earlier. Divine saw it roll over him, knew he was about to blow his top without the need to read him, but slipped into his thoughts anyway. It was like cutting through soft, half-melted butter with a ceramic knife. The man was so angry his thoughts were wide open. Divine wasn't terribly surprised to read that he'd brought a gun with him and planned to use it. She waited until he'd pulled the weapon from inside his jacket and raised it, though, before reacting. In fact, she let him get so far as to put his finger on the trigger before snapping her hand out, latching on to his throat, and lifting him off the ground. She then whirled and slammed him against her RV.

When the gun fell from his hand and he moaned in pain, she released him. The man fell like a rag doll. He landed on his ass with his legs splayed, a dazed expression on his face, and Divine immediately dropped to straddle his lap. Gravel ground painfully into her knees, but she ignored that, caught him by the hair at the nape of his neck, pulled his head to the side, and sank her fangs into his throat.

A little shiver of pleasure slid through Divine as thick warm blood began to gush from the wound, was collected by her teeth and passed into her body. It gave her an immediate rush as the nanos in her body swarmed, eager to collect this new supply of nourishment. The man had jerked in surprise when her teeth pierced his skin, and he'd raised his hands to try to push her off, but he never actually got around to exerting any pressure. Instead, he froze briefly, his mind overwhelmed as hers automatically began to transmit her own pleasure to him. In the next moment, he was moaning and tugging at her instead, pulling her closer with one hand, clasping her head with the other, and murmuring encouragingly, "Oh yeah, baby. Please."

He was also arching his body under her, rubbing a sudden hardness against her. Divine usually didn't cause pain in her victims, but this one deserved it. She also wasn't terribly eager to let a man who had planned to murder his own wife dry hump her there on the carnival grounds, so she deliberately withdrew the pleasure that she was experiencing and had unintentionally shared. But she also slipped into his mind to control his reaction to prevent him from screaming out in horror and pain as his mind cleared and he became aware of what was happening.

Divine was always careful not to kill her hosts. Why kill the cow that gave the milk? Besides, killing was wrong, no matter how despicable the person was, so while she drank more than she normally would have, she pulled back and freed him at the point when he was weak and woozy, but long before the man could come close to dying.

Smiling coldly at his horrified expression, Divine stood, lifting him as she went. Once they were both upright, she released him, leaving him to lean weakly against the RV rather than have to touch him anymore.

"Listen carefully, Allen Paulson," she said grimly. "You will not hurt your wife, or ever again consider harming or killing anyone for profit or any other reason. If you do, I'll find out, and then I'll find you . . ." She raised her hand to run one finger lightly over the wound on his neck. "And then I will finish this meal, cut your head off, and leave your cold dead body somewhere no one will ever find you. Do we understand each other?"

Allen Paulson nodded weakly. The man's face was as white as his T-shirt, his eyes almost sunken with horror, and he was sliding slowly along her RV, obviously eager to escape, but afraid to try and be stopped. Divine scowled. "And if you tell anyone about this, *about me*," she emphasized, "I'll do worse."

He began shaking his head frantically and whispered, "I won't. I swear."

She narrowed her eyes, and then her nose wrinkled as the acrid scent of urine wafted up between them. Glancing down, she saw the wet spot growing on the front of his trousers and stepped back with disgust. "Get out of here before I change *my* mind and wipe *yours*."

Allen Paulson didn't have a clue what she meant by

that—she could see it in his expression—but he didn't stick around to ask. He simply nodded wildly and sidled along the RV for a couple feet before finding the courage to turn his back to her and run.

"You should have wiped his mind."

Divine stiffened at those words from behind her, and then turned slowly. She peered at the tall, fair-haired man who had spoken. He was a greenie, an unskilled laborer and supposedly a local who had been hired to help out at the carnival while they were in town. The name he went by was Marco. Divine knew this second-hand, because while she was normally in on the hiring process, using her "special skills" to help Bob and Madge Hoskins, who owned and ran Hoskins Amusements, this time she hadn't been here. Family issues had kept her away and the hiring had been done by the time she'd caught up to the carnival. Had she been here to help weed out the troublemakers in the hiring process as she usually did, she never would have allowed Bob and Madge to hire the man. One, she couldn't read him, and that was usually a sign of insanity in a mortal. This led into the second reason she wouldn't have hired him; the man, like herself, was an immortal. She'd sensed that about him quite quickly. Divine wasn't sure how she'd known. She didn't run into a lot of immortals. In fact, she'd arranged her life so that she wouldn't. But there had been a frisson of awareness as she'd first passed him on returning to the carnival just before noon that day, as if the nanos in her body recognized and sent signals to those in his. She'd been avoiding him ever since.

But that hadn't stopped her from finding out all she could about him. Not that there had been much to learn. He went by Marco, last name Smith, of all things. The women all thought he was a hunk. The men thought he was practically a god because he was strong and could do the work of four men, and Bob and Madge were hoping he'd not just help out through their stay in this town, but travel with them to the next and the next and so on. For herself, Divine was wary. She had avoided other immortals for a reason and had been doing so for a very long time. She didn't like having one around. It made her anxious and she disliked feeling anxious.

"Don't you have something to do?" she asked, moving past the man and toward the back of her RV. The sign she'd turned had said back in five minutes and that time was up. Besides, she'd snacked on Allen Paulson and felt better for it. Break time was over.

"You should have wiped his mind," Marco repeated, falling into step with her.

"He'll keep his mouth shut," Divine muttered, annoyed, mostly because she knew he was right. The truth was she hadn't wiped Allen Paulson's mind because it was slimy, and she hadn't wanted to have to spend any more time inside his mind than necessary. Besides, he deserved to go through life terrified that she might someday revisit him should he set a foot wrong.

"And if he doesn't keep his mouth shut?" Marco asked as they neared the end of her RV. "What if he goes to the police?"

"If he goes to the police, *and* if they don't immediately lock him up as crazy but instead come to speak to me . . ." She shrugged. "I'll wipe his mind, the officer's mind, and leave this carnival for another."

"Is that how you landed at Hoskins Carnival?" Marco asked as they rounded the end of the vehicle. "You didn't wipe someone you should have and had to move on?"

Divine turned on him sharply, an angry retort on her lips, but just as quickly caught back the words that wanted to spill out and merely said with forced calm, "You're an inquisitive fellow, Marco. It's not healthy around here. Carnies mind their own business. I suggest you do the same."

Turning away from him, she smiled at the two women who were waiting in front of her door. Others had joined them. In fact, Divine now had a line-up of half a dozen people and it was growing by the minute, but she reserved her smile for the first two only and said, "Which of you would like to go first? Or shall I take you together?"

"Oh, me first," one of the women said eagerly. "This was my idea."

Divine nodded and led the woman inside, leaving Marco and all thought of him out on her stoop.

"Here, mister."

Marcus tore his gaze from the door Madame Divine had just ushered her client through and peered down at the small boy tugging at the top of his pant leg and holding out a half-eaten ball of cotton candy on a cardboard cone.

"Here," the boy repeated, holding it a little higher. "I don't feel good. You can have the rest."

Marcus arched an eyebrow, but took the cotton candy. He suspected the boy didn't feel good because he was stuffed full of cotton candy, something drenched in mustard, powdered elephant ears, and—he considered the last stain on the boy's shirt and then decided it had to be—ice cream. The kid was a walking menu of everything he'd eaten that day. At least, Marcus hoped it was all the kid had eaten that day. Otherwise he'd be wondering if Dante and Tomasso hadn't fathered the little tyke. They were the only two people he knew, mortal or immortal, who could have eaten like that as a boy.

"Danny! What are you doing? Get over here and leave that man alone."

Marcus glanced at the woman rushing toward them from the midway and offered a reassuring smile even as he slipped into her thoughts to ease her mind that he wasn't a child molester and nothing untoward was happening. By the time she reached them, she'd slowed to a fast walk, and was smiling in a relaxed manner.

"I hope he wasn't bothering you?" she said apologetically as she took the boy's hand.

"Not at all," Marcus assured her.

The young mother smiled again and then nodded and turned away with the boy, saying, "Come on, honey. Your daddy is waiting with your sister in the Ferris wheel line. They'll be worried."

Marcus watched them go and then turned his gaze back to Madame Divine's RV. The door was closed now as were the blinds. He couldn't see the woman anymore, except in his mind's eye, and he was definitely seeing her there. Madame Divine was more than memorable in her Gypsy getup. A white peasant blouse, worn off the shoulders, a crimson underskirt, a bright teal scarf skirt, an orange sash tied at the waist with gold chains hanging from it and tinkling merrily, a wide leather belt, and a crimson scarf around her head. Gold hoops had dangled from her ears, a gold chain hung around her neck, several gold bracelets dangled from her wrist, and knee-high black leather boots with stiletto heels strapped up the front of her legs had finished the outfit.

The woman looked damned sexy in the getup, so sexy in fact that when she'd straddled the would-be wife killer, Marcus had wanted to pull her off the man and onto his own lap. He'd been rather startled by that urge. Marcus hadn't been interested in women for a while. Okay, for a couple millennia. Still, he hadn't come across a woman like Madame Divine in quite a while either. The woman was walking sex in her getup, and his body was waking up and responding to it.

Obviously he had a Gypsy fetish, Marcus thought wryly. It made as much sense as anything else at the moment. Certainly more sense than his own life presently did. It appeared at the ripe old age of 2,548 he was having a midlife crisis of sorts. That was the only explanation for how he found himself doing a favor for Lucian Argeneau.

Marcus smiled wryly at the thought. Lucian Argeneau was not only the head of the powerful Argeneau clan, but also oversaw the Rogue Hunters and led the North American Immortal Council. Rogue Hunters were the immortal police force; they hunted down rogue immortals to be presented to the Immortal Council, who then passed judgment on them and sentenced them to whatever punishment they saw fit, often death.

As the head of those two organizations, Lucian could arguably be the most powerful immortal in North America. It was hard to imagine him needing anyone's help. But he did. He was searching for a family member, his niece Basha Argeneau, who had been thought to be dead for millennia, but who might now be alive after all . . . and who he feared had gone rogue.

Which was how Marcus had come to find himself at the carnival, eyeballing the trailer of a woman he couldn't read and found incredibly sexy. Not that his not being able to read her bothered him. If this was Basha Argeneau, she was even older than he was, and younger immortals usually couldn't read immortals older than themselves. It wasn't like any of the other signs of having met a life mate were cropping up, like renewed interest in food and such. Thank God, because if she *had* been a possible life mate and *was* Basha Argeneau . . . well, that would have been a doomed relationship from the start. Because Basha Argeneau was considered rogue . . . and rogues were executed. The last thing he needed at this point in his life was a rogue life mate.

"Hey! Marco! Are you going to stand around stuffing your face all night or help me with the pogo stall?"

Marcus glanced around with surprise to find Kevin Morrow walking toward him. The twenty-year-old carnie was tall and stick-thin, his face a collection of freckles so thick that from a distance it looked like a tan. Up close though you saw that his face was definitely freckled, and it was also presently scrunched up with displeasure, reminding Marcus that he was only supposed to take a fifteen-minute break from helping to man the food stall.

"I was—"

"Stuffing your face," the young carnie interrupted dryly and then turned away, gesturing for him to follow. "Come on. If you're hungry you can have a corn dog while you work. It's probably better for you than that sugary fluff anyway."

Marcus blinked and glanced down at the cone with the half-eaten cotton candy the boy had given him several minutes ago. Or what had been half-eaten cotton candy. There was nothing left of the sweet treat now. Surely he hadn't eaten it? He hadn't eaten in more than a millennium. He didn't remember eating it. But he did have a sweet taste in his mouth that was rather pleasant.

"Damn," he muttered, tossing the cardboard cone into a garbage bin as he headed after Kevin. He'd eaten it. Couldn't read Madame Divine, and was lusting after the woman. Oh, this wasn't good.

Two

Divine saw the last customer out of her trailer and then paused on the steps to peer along the midway. It was midnight, closing time, but the lights from the various attractions still glowed all along the midway. The tinny music still played too, but the rest of the sounds were dying down. The loud hawking by ride jockeys trying to lure people to their rides, and the agents trying to lure townies to the games, had died off. The laughter, chatter, and squealing of the townies enjoying the attractions were dying off too as the mad crush of people that had filled the area earlier dropped to a trickle of stragglers heading for the exit.

Without people filling every space, you could now see the mess that had been left behind. Discarded food and drink containers littered the midway, dropped and kicked to the side rather than placed in the garbage bins supplied at regular intervals. They were interspersed with half-eaten burgers, corn dogs, and ice cream cones left to melt on the tarmac where they fell. Among the mess she could see a pair of tiny running shoes and even a wrinkled T-shirt or two left behind and wondered how the owners had left without them. The shoes belonged to a child who might have been carried out, but hadn't the parent noticed the bare feet? As for the T-shirts, a lot of boys removed them and hung them through the loops of their shorts in the heat of the day, but shirts were required for rides and had to be re-donned if they wanted on. The only thing she could think was the owners of these particular T-shirts had lost them on the way out. It made her wonder how upset they would be when they got home and realized they were gone.

The music suddenly died and the Ferris wheel lights blinked out. Divine glanced toward it even as the lights on several other rides followed suit. Everything was beginning to shut down. Within moments the midway would be dark, the rides and stalls locked down for the night. The cleanup would be left for morning rather than waste the electricity to keep the lights on to do it now. It was more cost-efficient to do it in the bright light of day. Besides, by then some of the discarded foodstuff would have been gobbled up by local dogs or vermin, which would save a bit of cleanup time.

Divine's gaze swept the darkening midway, the structures mostly black shadows against the moonlit night. Within moments the first of the carnies would finish their shutdown and be headed for the back lot beyond the front of her RV where the trailers all were. There would be drinking and laughter as they unwound from their long day and the stress of dealing with the public. Divine sometimes joined them. Not to drink, since that did little for her. She went to enjoy the camaraderie. She usually sat and nursed a cup of tea outside Bob and Madge Hoskins's trailer on a nice night. If it was raining, they'd move inside to dissect the day and talk about how good or how poor the take had been.

Divine shifted her feet, briefly debating whether she should do so tonight. It was the greenie Marco who was making her hesitate. Most immortals, like mortals, considered carnies beneath them, not seeing the long, hard hours they worked, only seeing their shabby unkempt appearance, and bad teeth for lack of money and time to fix them. In fact, Marco was the only immortal besides herself that she knew of who had chosen to spend time with the traveling carnivals over the years, and his presence now was troubling.

She suspected Marco had to be rogue and hiding out to have found his way to the carnival. If that was the case . . . well, the last thing she needed was for a rogue to draw the attention of the Rogue Hunters to her carnival. Divine had managed to hide in this environment for a good hundred years. She didn't want someone like this new guy blowing that for her. The safest thing to do was to avoid the man, and since she couldn't guarantee he too wouldn't go to visit with the Hoskinses . . . well, she thought, perhaps she should bypass her usual routine of relaxing with the couple this night.

On the other hand, greenies often had homes to go to at night. If they didn't and stayed here with the carnies, they usually sat on the fringes, away from the owner and his wife. It might be okay for her to join the couple and unwind a bit. Certainly, she had no need to go hunting tonight. Allen Paulson had supplied her with dinner.

Decision made, Divine popped the lock on her RV door. She then headed around her vehicle for the back lot where Bob and Madge had parked their own private RV. The couple had several vehicles for business, including a trailer where they hired greenies and handled customer service issues. They also had several games and rides, but they never traveled without their own RV for living and sleeping in. After a long day dealing with carnies and customers alike, a private space to retreat to was a necessity.

The back lot was a large area, almost as large as the carnival itself. Here there were half a dozen RVs belonging to the better-off full-time carnies who had stalls, rides, or ran games, but there were also bunkhouse trailers with tiny rooms big enough for a bed or bunk beds and a small walking space. Divine suspected you'd have more room in a prison cell, but all it was for was sleeping so in that sense it served its purpose. There were usually four to six bunkrooms in each trailer; some bunkhouses had their own lavatory for the inhabitants to share, some didn't. For those without, there were other trailers with mobile lavatories in them. There was also a trailer that served as a schoolroom for those children traveling with carnie parents, as well as a laundry trailer and a couple of small trailers that acted like small markets, corner stores, or drugstores, depending on which one you used.

In effect, the carnival was a small traveling city carrying everything they might need with it. A carnie didn't really have to go into the towns they visited at all if they didn't want to unless there was some specialty item that wasn't available in the traveling stores.

"Miss Divine."

Slowing, she glanced to the side, nodding in greeting when she spotted Hal walking toward her with a slight limp. A lifelong carnie, Hal was short, wiry, bowlegged, and had more wrinkles, and fewer teeth, than an elephant. The man had one good tooth in his mouth—a nasty, brown thing that looked like it too should have been pulled or fallen out by now. Divine didn't like stereotypes, but some of the carnies lived up, or actually down, to those things said about them: hard drinking, fast living, rotten teeth, and old before their time. Hal fit every one of those stereotypes. Still, she liked the man.

From what Divine had read in his mind, Hal had earned every one of those wrinkles, and hadn't lost all his teeth to rot. In fact, it appeared he'd lost half of them to alcohol-fueled brawls over the years. He was also as honest as could be. He'd tell you flat-out to lock your stuff up or it would go walking. "Finders keepers," he'd add with a wink, making it more than obvious who would help it go walking. You couldn't fault the man for that. At least he gave fair warning. Few people did.

"Your limp is a bit better," Divine commented as she watched him close the last few feet between them.

"Ah-yep." He grinned at her, showing off his one good

tooth and a lot of gum. Running his fingers through his scraggly gray hair, he nodded his head and added, "All thanks to you. That remedy you gave me worked wonders. The gout's goin' away toot sweat."

Divine's lips twisted upward at the mispronunciation of "tout suite," but she didn't correct him.

"Another day and I won't be limping at all," he continued, beaming, and confided, "Haven't been limp-free in so long, I've forgotten how it feels. And I just wanted to thank ye kindly, Madame Divine. I haven't felt this good in more than a decade and it sure is nice."

"You're welcome," Divine said, smiling faintly. She'd noticed the man seemed to be doing more poorly than usual a couple of towns back. It hadn't taken mind reading to know he was suffering with his gout, and Divine had whipped up an old remedy for the ailment that she knew from her days running with the Gypsies. As he said, it appeared to be working relatively quickly. Of course, it would have worked quicker if he would refrain from red meat, coffee, and alcohol. But that was asking a bit much of the old man.

Divine could have slipped into his thoughts and controlled him, making him give up the booze and the other unhealthy food items that contributed to his problem, but she had no desire to control other people's lives. Animals like Allen Paulson were one thing; she had no qualms at all about preventing him or his ilk from harming or killing anyone for financial gain, but other than that, Divine was an advocate of the "live and let live" credo. She didn't want anyone controlling her actions and behaviors, and had no need or desire to con-

trol others. It was her opinion that people who did try
to control others were sadly lacking in self esteem . . .
and there seemed to be a lot of them. Judging by all
the people starting movements to try to get the gov-
ernment to stop this and ban that, they also seemed to
have a hell of a lot of time on their hands. She couldn't
help thinking that if they got a job, or a lover, friends, a
hobby, or—hell—even a life, they'd be a lot more ful-
filled and wouldn't look to control what others did as a
way to satisfy themselves.

"Well, I just wanted to thank you," Hal said again,
"And let you know your efforts worked before I head
out to celebrate with Carl." He hesitated and then
added tentatively, "And see if you maybe wouldn't
want to join us? We're going into town, McMurphy's
Irish Pub. I stopped there the last time we were in Bakersfield and they have the best ribs I ever tasted. Oak-
smoked I think the gal said they were. Real good," he
assured her.

"Tempting," Divine said gently. "But no thank you,
Hal. You and Carl have fun. No fighting, though," she
added firmly. "If you come back toothless I'll be
mighty annoyed with you."

"I've no great love for the hoosegow, so no fighting,"
he vowed, raising crossed fingers that suggested the opposite. The man was just too delightfully honest, she
thought as he added, "At least none we start. Now iffin'
someone in town starts something, we just can't let 'em
walk all over us, you know. But we won't be starting
them."

Shaking her head with amusement, Divine nodded

and turned to continue on her way, thinking she should keep her phone on. If Hal and Carl wound up in the "hoosegow" and needed bailing out tonight, she'd rather they call her than disturb Madge and Bob. The couple were getting up there in years, and the stressors and trials of running the carnival were beginning to show. If she could make things a little easier for the couple, she was happy to do it. Besides, it wasn't like she'd be sleeping. She generally only slept an hour or two a day now. Divine had no idea if that was a function of age or worry, and didn't care. It was just the way it was. Divine had learned over time not to sweat the small stuff. There was enough in life to worry about; the small stuff wasn't worth fretting over.

The light was on in the Hoskinses' RV, which meant that Madge, as usual, had left Bob to handle any last-minute issues that might crop up at closing and had returned to their RV to put on a pot of coffee and make a light snack for them to enjoy while they unwound. It was their usual routine. Madge opened and started the day and Bob closed at the end of the night. Teamwork at its best. At least, it seemed to work for them. The couple had been married thirty years and were still happy and affectionate with each other, which wasn't unheard of, but rare enough among mortals to be mentioned.

Of course, while it was unusual for mortals, that was the norm with immortals. Once they met their life mate they were set. Ten, a hundred, even a thousand years later that couple would still be solid and happy together. It was what every adult immortal looked forward to. Divine used to dream of it herself, but that was when she was much younger. She had soon come to realize that the way she lived, having to hide and avoid other immortals, made it pretty much impossible to meet her life mate. She would be alone always, and that was a very long time unless she either got lucky and had a fatal accident where she was decapitated or burned alive, or she went really rogue and got herself executed. Some days, when her Gypsy lifestyle and lack of home and family got to her, engineering such an accident actually seemed almost attractive. So far, though, those moods passed before she did anything stupid. So far.

Pushing the thought away as she reached the door to the Hoskinses' RV, Divine knocked briefly, waited for the "Come on in," that Madge called out, and then pulled the door open and stepped inside. But the smile that had started to lift the corners of her mouth and the greeting she'd been about to offer died as she nearly walked into the greenie, Marco.

"Oh, there you are, Divine, love," Madge said cheerfully. "I was just telling Marco all about you. I thought it would be nice if he joined us tonight you two could get to know each other. You have a lot in common. He's allergic to the sun too."

"You don't say," Divine murmured, peering solemnly at the man. *So much for avoiding the greenie.*

Marcus almost grinned at Divine's expression. She obviously wasn't happy to see him, but was trying hard to hide it rather than have Madge notice and have to explain why. He suspected what she wanted most in that moment was to turn and flee, but apparently she couldn't find a good excuse to do so because she was still standing there, sort of wavering in the doorway.

"Hi . . . Marco, is it?" Divine said finally. She offered an obviously forced smile before switching her gaze to Madge, where her smile became more natural as she said, "It would have been nice to visit, but Hal stopped me on my way here. His gout is much better and he asked me to join him and Carl in town to celebrate. I would hate to see the old guy lose his last tooth. I just stopped in to say I'm going to bypass our usual coffee klatch to go with them."

Correction, she'd come up with an excuse after all, Marcus thought. He didn't know how much of what she said was a lie. But he was pretty sure she hadn't planned to join this Hal and Carl in town when she'd first entered the RV. In fact, he was quite sure it was his presence that had decided her to go . . . Well . . . two could play at that game. Putting on an expression of feigned concern, he murmured, "Oh, I don't think you should accompany those two alone. I suspect once they get drinking, those two old codgers might be a bit hard to manage. Maybe I should go with the three of you."

"Oh, that's a wonderful idea," Madge interjected as Divine started to shake her head. "I'd worry about you otherwise, Divine, but with Marco there to look out for you, I'd feel a lot better."

For one moment, Marcus was sure Divine was going to refuse, but after a moment her shoulders sagged with defeat. Her expression wasn't defeated, however, but stiff with anger as she said, "Fine. Let's go."

"Stop in when you get back if the lights are still on," Madge called cheerfully, apparently completely unaware of the waves of anger and resentment rolling off of Divine as she muttered in the affirmative and turned to open the RV door again.

Marcus offered Madge an especially warm smile as he followed Divine out. He'd known at once that the carnival owner had matchmaking in mind when she'd invited him to the RV tonight. He could read her thoughts, after all, and after interviewing him that morning and watching him work today, she'd decided he seemed a decent enough fellow—good-looking, strapping, and hardworking . . . a good match for "our Divine" as she'd thought of the woman. He wasn't interested in a setup, of course, but it had worked well with his intention to get close to Divine and find out if she was Basha Argeneau, the woman he'd been asked to find.

Marcus found it hard to believe Divine could be the rogue Basha who ran with Leonius Livius. Not after reading Madge's thoughts. He'd found a lot of respect and affection for the fortune-teller there. But then he'd found that same thing in most of the minds he'd read that day. It seemed that Madame Divine, or Divine as most of the carnies thought of her, came across as a bit standoffish, but was always there to pitch in and help set up when they arrived in a new town, and assist with tear-down at the end of a run when she didn't have to, and was always there when someone needed help, even sometimes before the person himself knew he needed that help.

From what he'd learned that day, he knew Divine had been with this carnival for two years. In that time, she'd earned the respect and liking of most of the people here. The few who didn't like, or at least respect, her seemed to have grudges of one sort or another. One woman was jealous because she was sure the man she was interested in was interested in Divine, while another didn't like how everyone else thought so highly of Divine, which was something she wanted for herself.

There were also two men he'd come across today who didn't have very flattering thoughts toward the woman. One man was the carnival Romeo who had bedded nearly every woman in this outfit—all the single ones and several of the married women. But when he'd hit on Divine, she'd shot him down in no uncertain terms.

The other fellow he'd come across that day with unflattering thoughts of Divine was a man named Paul. He and his girlfriend Kathy had been with the carnival for a while. Paul had apparently been a good worker until recently when he'd started drinking. Unfortunately, he had a tendency to beat up Kathy whenever he got drunk, which was becoming a nightly routine. Divine had stopped him recently. She'd torn him off the girl, breaking his wrist in the process, probably deliberately in Marcus's humble opinion. Divine had then explained that if Paul hurt Kathy, or any of the other carnie females again, she'd break both his wrists. Paul had managed to refrain from beating Kathy ever since, but knew it was just a matter of time before he slipped and hit her . . . and then Divine would keep her promise . . . and that scared the hell out of him.

Paul didn't just dislike Divine, he was afraid of her, and that was a dangerous thing. In Marcus's experience, fear could make people do stupid things, and judging by the thoughts running through Paul's mind that day, he was going to end up doing something stupid sooner rather than later. The man had enjoyed several nasty fantasies that day while Marcus had worked with him, fantasies like catching Divine unawares one night, hitting her over the head with a bat to knock her out, and then beating her to death so she could never threaten him again. So long as they stayed fantasies, things would be all right. But fantasize about something often enough and you might get brave enough to try it in real life. Marcus suspected Paul would be in for a big surprise if he was ever stupid enough to carry out the fantasy. A beating would not kill Divine, and her fury at his attempt would be something to see, Marcus was sure. The man would be lucky to get away with his life. She'd probably break every bone in his body, and Marcus wouldn't blame her.

"Stop staring at my ass. I can feel your eyes drilling into my behind. If you're coming with me, walk beside me."

Marcus blinked at those words from Divine as she led him away from the Hoskinses' RV, and then blinked again as he realized he had indeed been staring at her behind. Huh, he thought. That was new . . . but then it was a fine view. He liked the way her skirts swung from side to side around her hips and behind with each step. And those boots. Damn, they—

His thoughts died abruptly as Divine paused, swung back, and scowled at him. She then pointed her finger to the ground at her side in silent demand. Repressing a smile, Marcus walked to her side and stopped, one eyebrow quirking. "I thought you liked attention. Isn't that why you wear the coins on your scarf skirt?"

"Not your attention," Divine assured him grimly, and then turned forward to walk again. A moment later he realized she was leading him to her RV. Surely she didn't intend to try to get the vehicle out of this mess? Good Lord, there was a ride on one side, a cotton candy trailer on the other, and the back lot at its front. The back lot was a maze of vehicles she couldn't possibly get through. He should tell her he had a vehicle and lead her to the SUV Lucian had given him, Marcus thought. It was presently parked in the lot outside the gates where he'd left it. Before he could make the suggestion, however, she stopped next to a large, slightly protruding rectangle along the side of the RV that he hadn't noticed until now. Divine flipped up a small flap, revealing a set of numbered buttons. She tapped out a code and then stepped back as a side panel immediately slid open, revealing a motorcycle.

While Marcus stood gaping, Divine unstrapped the two-wheeled vehicle, unflipped a narrow ramp on the end, and muscled the vehicle onto the dirt. Setting its kickstand in place to keep it upright, she then turned, retrieved two helmets from the inset, and then pressed the button again, closing the panel.

Marcus took the helmet she handed him, and pulled it on as he watched her don her own. But his intention to do up the chinstrap died a quick death when she distracted him by bending forward. His eyes widened on her derriere as she caught the back of her skirt through her legs and drew the material tight as she pulled it forward. It wasn't until she straightened with the cloth in hand and tucked it into the front waistband of her skirt that he understood what she was doing. She then swung a leg over the motorcycle, started the engine, revved it, and then turned to peer at him. "Well?"

"Right," he muttered, quickly doing up the helmet she'd given him. It looked like she was driving. Hell. A motorcycle. He hoped she knew how to drive the damned thing.

Three

The moment Marco settled on the motorcycle behind her and slid his arms around her waist, Divine knew she'd made a mistake. She'd had the occasional passenger on her motorcycle before, both men and women, but this time it felt uncomfortably intimate. The man had plastered his chest to her back, and Divine was very aware of his hands resting just below her breasts. She felt enveloped in his embrace, and that was something she hadn't experienced in quite a while, if ever. Short of elbowing him and perhaps catching him by surprise and sending him flying off the motorcycle, however, there was little she could do about it, so Divine did her best to ignore her own discomfort and concentrated on driving.

The Hoskins Carnival came to Bakersfield, California, every year. Divine had been in the town before, but not just with this carnival. She knew the place Hal had mentioned. McMurphy's had been around a long time. Not that Divine had dined in the establishment, but she had driven past it and had a good memory. Years ago it had been McMurphy's Tavern. It was now McMurphy's Irish Pub and Sports Bar, though. Whether it had changed hands and been renovated, or the owners had just changed the name, she didn't know. She *did* know where it was, though, and found it easily enough. Little more than ten minutes later she was relieved to be able to bring the motorcycle to a halt and wait a little impatiently for Marco to disembark before she set the kickstand in place and got off herself.

Divine avoided looking at Marco as she removed her helmet and quickly unhooked her skirt to let it fall around her legs again. She could still feel the warmth where his body had pressed against her back, and found herself annoyed by it. Sighing, she used the helmet lock to secure her helmet, then took the one Marco held out and secured it as well. Determinedly ignoring him then, Divine headed for the pub's entrance, but could hear him following.

The day had cooled once the sun had set, but was still hot at around eighty-five degrees. The pub was air-conditioned though, and the wave of cold air that hit them as they entered was a relief. Divine paused inside the doors and simply enjoyed the rush of cool air for a moment before turning her attention to trying to find Hal and Carl.

"I don't see them," Marco commented behind her, bending to speak by her ear to be heard over the cacophony of voices in the room.

Divine stifled a shiver as his breath blew across her skin. Ignoring the sensation, she simply peered around and then frowned. She didn't see them either. "Hal definitely said McMurphy's. He said he had their ribs last year and wanted them again."

"Hi. Can I help you? You look like you're looking for someone."

Divine glanced to the perky girl who had approached. She had long brown hair tied back in a ponytail and carried an empty tray, pressed against her chest. Divine couldn't help noticing she was also eyeing Marco appreciatively as she waited for an answer.

"We're looking for some friends of ours," Divine said, drawing the girl's reluctant attention. "A couple of older gentlemen. Kind of rough-looking, sun-weathered, one with no teeth, the other with no hair."

"Oh yeah." Smiling, the girl nodded her head, her ponytail waving as she turned her gaze back to Marco. "They're here. I sat them . . ." She had drawn her gaze from Marco to gesture to a table in the corner and frowned when she found it empty. "I sat them over there a couple minutes ago." She glanced around briefly and then smiled and shrugged. "They probably stepped out on the patio for a smoke."

"Probably," Divine agreed, remembering that Hal and Carl both smoked. Quite a few of the carnies did.

"Well, you can look for them on the patio, or sit down and wait for them if you're friends. They probably won't be long. I saw their waitress talking to them just after I sat them. They've probably ordered drinks and asked for menus, but haven't ordered their meals yet."

"We'll wait at the table," Marco announced, taking Divine's arm to lead her that way. She didn't protest. Divine had no desire to go out on the smoking patio. She didn't even really want to be here. She'd only come in an effort to avoid the man escorting her. Best-laid plans and all that. If not for this man, she could be sitting in Madge's trailer right now, relaxing to the buzz of conversation. Damned man, she thought with irritation.

Settling in the chair he pulled out for her, Divine picked up the menu to avoid looking at him.

"Do you eat?"

Stiffening, she glanced over the top of her menu to Marco as he settled in the chair across from her. Rather than answer, she asked, "Do you?"

He hesitated briefly, and then said, "On occasion."

Divine shrugged with disinterest and lowered her gaze to the menu again.

"So . . . you're an immortal . . ."

That got her attention; Divine peered at him sharply, and then glanced around to be sure no one had heard the comment. No one seemed to be paying any attention to them, but—

"And I'm an immortal," he continued.

"For heaven's sake," she snapped, glaring at him. "You know better than to talk about nonsense like that in public."

"No one's listening," Marco said soothingly, and then tilted his head and asked, "What are you running from?"

Divine stiffened in her seat. "What makes you think I'm running from anything?"

"Oh, I don't know," he said with amusement, "Maybe the fact that you're hiding out at the carnival?"

"If I were hiding out, I'd be working somewhere where hundreds of people didn't see me every day," she said dryly. "I work the carnival because I happen to make a very good living there."

"By reading people's futures?"

There was no judgment in his voice; still, Divine felt herself stiffening defensively. "I don't *read* their futures and I don't claim to."

"Right. You define their future," he said quietly.

Divine nodded. It was a fine distinction, but an important one to her. "I read their minds and define their futures. Or sometimes I read the minds of whoever accompanies them to my RV and use what I learn there to define the customer's future."

"Like the husband who planned to kill his wife for the insurance?" Marco asked. Expression becoming considering, he added, "The husband must have accompanied her to your stall when the carnival was in their town for you to know he planned to knock her off for the insurance."

Divine nodded.

"So you use your immortal abilities to help mortals," he said solemnly.

Divine felt herself relax. As much as she tried not to let it bother her, the attitudes she often ran into with "townies" about the carnies bothered her. Most people came to the carnivals just to have fun and didn't make judgments, but there were a large number of people who thought all carnies were scum, con artists, and thieves.

That *she* was a con artist and thief, scamming money off foolish people who believed in fortune-tellers and such nonsense.

Divine did not—and never claimed to—tell fortunes. She did, however, try to help whoever she was reading, in whatever way she could. It was rare to actually save a life as she had with Allen's wife, but she liked to think she had contributed to the health and well-being of others. She could quite often smell illness on a mortal. Undiagnosed diabetics had a sweet scent while cancer had the faint but distinct, sickly sweet stench of rot. She could also hear the rasp of lung or bronchial problems, a skipping or irregular heartbeat, a fast or slow pulse rate, etc. There were many health issues she could recognize and diagnose and advise the customer to have checked out.

Divine also did a quick read of the minds of whoever accompanied each customer, sometimes finding useful information there, like a cheating husband, a troubled friend, a child with a dangerous secret that needed revealing, or abuse they'd been warned to keep quiet. And then too, she could read the customer's mind and know when they were going to do something stupid, or illegal, or desperate and advise them against it. Often, their shock that she knew what they were thinking or planning was enough to return some sense to them.

Divine tried to help people in exchange for the money they paid. She did not simply take the money and give some spiel about meeting a tall, dark, handsome stranger and living the good life. She tried to help. She always had.

"Yes, I use our abilities to try to help mortals," Divine said finally. "And I get paid for it. I'm not ashamed of that."

Marco nodded, but then asked, "So you aren't hiding or running from something?"

Divine shifted impatiently at the question. She wanted to say no, but instead asked, "Is that why you joined the carnival? Because you're running or hiding from something?"

Marco grimaced and then sat back in his own seat with a smile. "Touché."

"You didn't answer the question," she pointed out.

"Neither did you," he responded at once.

They were both silent for a moment and then Marco sat forward and asked, "Will you at least tell me your real name?"

"Madame Divine to strangers and Divine to my friends," she answered at once and raised her menu again.

"Is Divine your real name?" he asked suspiciously.

"Is Marco yours?" she countered, staring blindly at the appetizer section.

After a pause he asked, "How old are you?"

Divine slapped the menu down with irritation. "Now that's just rude."

"Yes, it is," a laughing voice announced, drawing their attention to a cute little blonde who had just stopped at their table. Their waitress, it seemed. With twinkling eyes and a bright smile, she admonished Marco, "You *never* ask a lady her age. At least not if you enjoy your manhood and wish to keep it intact."

Divine's mouth twitched briefly and then eased into a smile when Marco's jaw dropped at the girl's cheek.

"Thank you," Divine said to the waitress. "You're going to get a big tip."

"Only if you're paying," Marco grumbled, but there was amusement in his eyes too now, and chagrin as he glanced to Divine and murmured, "My apologies. I wasn't thinking."

"Obviously," Divine said dryly, but was still smiling.

The waitress laughed and then tilted her head. "Can I get you folks something?"

"Ah." Divine's gaze dropped to the menu she'd been pretending to peruse. She really wanted to order something. She did plan to give the girl a tip. The problem was she didn't eat. At least she hadn't for eons. She didn't even drink except to nurse teas when in mortal company, and those she didn't drink so much as hold in front of her face, occasionally pressing the rim to her mouth as the steam gave her a mini facial of sorts. It was probably good for her pores, she thought, frowning at the menu. After another moment, she sighed and smiled apologetically at the girl. "Actually, maybe we'll wait for Hal and Carl to get back."

"Oh, you have friends coming?" the girl asked.

"Well, they're here already I think. Two older men, one bald and the other missing most of his teeth?" she said, hoping to prod the girl's memory. "The young lady who greeted us at the door said they had been seated here and thought they might have gone out to the patio."

"Oh no, they left," the blonde said, looking rather disappointed to pass this news on. "They wanted the oak-smoked ribs, but we only serve those on Sunday. They said they might as well come back on Sunday instead then and head back to their bottles and bunks now . . . Whatever that means," the girl added wryly.

Divine merely smiled faintly. It meant exactly what it sounded like; the two men had gone back to their bunks in the trailers and the bottles of booze waiting there. She didn't explain that though, but slipped her hand in her skirt pocket and pulled out a ten. Setting it on the table, she offered the girl a smile and stood. "Thank you."

"Oh, you don't have to—" the girl protested, picking up the ten-dollar bill to give back to her.

Divine waved it away. "I appreciate the information. We could have been here awhile waiting, and then I would have worried about what had become of our friends. Keep it."

Patting the girl's shoulder, she headed for the door, aware that Marco was following her.

"Bottles and bunks?" Marco asked. "I gather that means—"

"Back to the carnival," Divine finished with a nod. "Both Hal and Carl have bunks in the bunkhouses." She shrugged and added, "Dining out is expensive on their pay. If they want the ribs, they probably can't afford to spend money tonight too."

"Yeah, I noticed the pay is lousy in the carnival," Marco said dryly.

"Worse than lousy," Divine agreed with amusement. "Which makes me wonder why you'd bother with it. Surely you could find a job elsewhere?"

"Surely I could," he agreed evasively. "But this seemed like fun."

"Hmm," Divine said dubiously, doubting there was anything fun about hefting steel and hawking corn dogs.

"I gather you do better than the laborers?" Marco asked as they stepped outside into the humid night. It was like walking into a sauna, or slamming into a hot, wet towel. Honestly, the heat the last week or so had been terrible, but the humidity had been worse—a wall of misery that enveloped them everywhere they went. She would be glad when summer passed and fall returned with its milder temperatures.

"I suppose that's a rude question too," Marco muttered suddenly, and Divine realized he was still waiting for an answer. She debated just saying yes it was rude, but then changed her mind.

"I own my RV and don't need to hire setup guys," she said quietly as she led the way to her motorcycle. "Everything I make is my own."

"You don't have to pay Madge and Bob for rental space or anything?" he asked with surprise.

"I used to," she admitted. "But I've become a bit of a draw, and then I started helping them with things like hiring locals when we get to each town, steering them away from the troublemakers and criminals and things like that. The second year I did that, I prevented their hiring a fellow who turned out to be on the FBI's most wanted list. They were so grateful they decided to pass on making me pay rental anymore as a thank-you."

"Yeah, someone mentioned that this morning when I was hired," Marco said quietly. "Not that you'd prevented their hiring someone on a wanted list, but that you normally help with hires," he explained, and then added, "But you weren't there."

It was a question whether he couched it as one or not. As they reached the motorcycle Divine merely said, "I had personal business to attend to and didn't get back to the carnival until just before opening."

Marco wasn't rude enough to ask outright what that business was and remained silent as Divine unlocked the helmets and handed him one. She donned the other, then tucked her skirt up, mounted the motorcycle, and started it. This time she didn't have to tell him to get on. She'd barely got the engine started before Marco was sliding onto the seat behind her, his hands slipping around her waist.

"I could learn to like this," he said by her ear, speaking loudly to be heard over the engine.

Divine didn't comment, but simply revved the engine and headed for the carnival grounds. This trip had been a complete and utter bust. Not only had she not escaped his presence, but she didn't know much more about him than she had before. In fact, he'd learned more about her than the other way around. Not that he'd learned much either. At least she hoped he hadn't, and wondered if Marco could read her.

Divine definitely hoped he could not read her, and she was pretty sure he couldn't. Surely if he'd read who she was, he'd have said or done something by now? She fretted over that for the rest of the ride. By the time they reached the carnival grounds, she was eager to get away from the man and get a chance to think. Divine found it hard to concentrate with his hands on her and his body pressing up against hers. She supposed she just wasn't used to a lot of physical contact. It was distracting.

Divine steered the motorcycle up the empty midway, but didn't head for her RV, instead, turning off the midway between the Ferris wheel and one of the game stalls so that she could ride around to the opposite end of the back lot from her RV. It was where the bunkhouses were and where she presumed Marco was staying if he didn't have someplace in town.

She brought the motorcycle to a halt by the first of the bunkhouses and braced her feet on the ground on either side of the motorcycle to keep it upright, but left the motor running as she waited for Marco to get off. After a slight hesitation, he did, and relief immediately rushed through her. When he then moved up beside her and said something she couldn't hear, Divine decided it was probably thanks for the ride, or at least she wanted it to be. Eager to be off, she simply nodded and then sent the motorcycle shooting forward, driving along the outside of the back lot to reach her RV. Once there she dropped the kickstand and removed her helmet as she got off the motorcycle.

She was about to press the button to open the side panel to put the bike away when she heard a dull thud. It sounded like it came from inside her RV. Pausing, Divine listened briefly and heard a clinking sound. She set her helmet on the seat of her motorcycle and moved around to the door. She mounted the two steps, and slipped inside on silent feet.

There was no one in the curtained-off area where she saw clients. Divine eased across the floor, reached for the curtain, and tugged it to the side enough to peer through, but there was no one in the lounge and kitchenette area either. She wasn't terribly surprised. The panel where she kept her motorcycle was off the bedroom. Letting her breath out slowly, she moved through the lounge, reached for the accordion door to the bedroom, but paused as a rustle sounded behind her. Before she could turn, pain exploded inside her head and then the lights went out.

Four

Marcus shifted sideways to avoid a group of the younger carnies on their way to the bunkhouses. They'd obviously been celebrating the end of the first day in a new town. Every last one seemed to be three sheets to the wind. It hadn't been that long since closing, though, so they must have been hammering the drinks back. But then, it wasn't like they had hours to relax. It had been midnight when they closed, and morning came early.

With that last thought in mind, Marcus picked up speed as he headed for Divine's RV. Not only had the woman not answered him when he'd got off the motorcycle and asked if she was going back to Madge's, but she'd been in such a rush to get away from him, she'd left without taking back her helmet. Which was rather depressing when he thought of it, because while she appeared eager to escape his company, his feelings were the exact opposite. Marcus had enjoyed their outing to the restaurant, short as it had been. He'd enjoyed verbally sparring with her, but even more, he'd enjoyed the ride to the restaurant and back, having his hands on her, his chest pressing against her back. It had been an invigorating experience.

"Hey, Marco!"

Turning his head, he peered silently at the man approaching. As tall as he, and nearly as wide, Chapman was the owner of the Tilt-A-Whirl Marcus had helped set up on being hired that day, as well as the corn dog stand he'd then run for the rest of the day with Kevin. Technically, Chapman was his boss, although Bob Hoskins, the carnival owner, had actually done the hiring. Marcus had thought it a little strange that Hoskins would insist on doing the hiring for everyone, even the independent ride owners. At least he had until he'd read the man's mind. It seemed a local they'd hired to work the carnival in one of the towns some three years back had turned out to like children a little too much. He'd lured a little girl away from the midway while her mother was distracted and had led her to the bunks on the back lot. It was usually abandoned during the day. Fortunately, that day a full-time carnie had slid back to his own bunk on his break to grab something and had spotted the man ushering the little girl into one of the bunks. He'd intervened.

Unfortunately, he hadn't got her back to the midway before the mother had noticed the girl missing and raised a fuss. The police had been called, and while it was a carnie who rescued the little girl and beat up the local temp in the process, the carnival had taken the heat. It made the headlines as "Carnival Worker Kidnaps Local Child" not "Local Hired as a Temp by the Carnival Kidnaps Local Child."

Apparently, attendance had dropped right off after that, and Bob Hoskins and his wife, Madge, had nearly gone broke before the business had slowly bounced back. It was then that Bob Hoskins had insisted that from now on he would take over all hiring. It was also shortly after that that Madame Divine had joined their troop and offered her help in vetting the people applying. She had apparently weeded out some bad full-time carnies on joining the show, warning Bob and Madge' that this one was up to no good, or that one was stealing from then. But she'd also begun sitting in on all the interviews and Bob Hoskins made his decisions based on her opinion.

At least she'd done so until that morning. According to Bob's thoughts, personal business had taken her away shortly after their arriving at the carnival grounds at 4 A.M. She'd said she expected to be back by the time Bob started interviewing, but she wasn't. Bob had reluctantly started interviewing, thinking he'd weed out the worst and most obvious "don't hires," and ask the others to come back for a second interview when Divine did return.

At least that had been his intention. However, Marcus hadn't wanted the woman he suspected was Basha Argeneau reading his thoughts and knowing he was there to find out if she was the wanted rogue. So he'd slipped into the man's mind, put the rebellious thought that he didn't need her help, he'd worked in the business for years, he knew good people from bad. After all, he hadn't hired the man who had kidnapped that girl, he could make up his own mind . . . at least in Marcus's case.

Madge Hoskins had been a bit taken aback by her husband's decision to hire Marcus without Divine's seeing him first, but a little nudge from Marcus had helped her accept it and she'd gone through the paperwork with him and signed him up when Bob handed him over to her. According to what Marcus had read from Madge's mind this evening before Divine had shown up, Divine hadn't said a thing about Bob hiring Marcus. But then she hadn't had much chance to. She'd returned from her personal business just as the carnival had opened its gate and had rushed to her RV to set out her sign and change. Other than two or three breaks when she'd asked around about Marco, she'd pretty much worked straight through except for those few minutes when Mr. Kill-My-Wife-for-the-Insurance-So-I-Can-Run-Off-with-My-Secretary had attacked her.

"Earth to Marco? Have you even heard a damned word I've said?"

Marcus blinked as Chapman's hand waved in front of his face and then grimaced and shook his head with chagrin. "Sorry. I guess I'm a little tired."

"I'll say. It looked like you were sleeping on your feet," Chapman said with amusement, and then shrugged mildly and said with understanding, "We work long days. It can take some getting used to."

"Yeah. I can imagine," Marcus murmured.

"Why don't you go get some sleep. We need to check the rides before we open tomorrow, and I was thinking you're wasted on the corn dog stand. I think you should run the Tilt-A-Whirl tomorrow."

Marcus raised his eyebrows. "Isn't that Stan's job?"

"Yeah, well, I just got a call. Stan got rowdy in town and is in the clink. Not sure when they'll let him out," Chapman said grimly, and ran one weathered hand wearily through his thinning hair. Letting his hand drop back to his side, he shook his head. "I don't know the whole story yet, but Stan's a mean drunk. He probably popped the wrong person, the mayor's son or something. If so, he could be in for a day or two and that leaves me short. One of the girls is going to run the corn dog stand so you can help me on the Tilter tomorrow. I'll train you before we open." He smiled wryly. "You seem a smart one for a change, which is a blessing. Usually the greenies we hire are either stupid, lazy, or slow, and you're none of those. You shouldn't have any problem with the Tilt-A-Whirl. Now go get some sleep."

Marcus nodded, but the man was already walking away, his mind, no doubt, already on to the next problem. Chapman hadn't even really been talking to Marcus so much as telling him how it was going to be. He seemed to be a type A personality, always under stress. Marcus figured at that rate the man, who was apparently fifty, wouldn't make sixty, which was the age he already looked. That thought made Marcus glance around the back lot, noting the people making their way here or there. He'd noticed that most people here looked older than they were, men and women alike. If they looked fifty, they were probably forty. This life seemed hard on everyone, men and women alike. It made for interesting people though, he thought as he headed toward Divine's RV.

As he walked between her RV and the fence around the Tilt-A-Whirl, Marcus noted that her motorcycle was nowhere in sight. The panel was closed. She must already have put the bike away, he thought as he reached and mounted the stairs to knock on her door.

He turned to glance along the midway as he waited for her to answer. It was strange to see it so empty and silent. It was like a ghost town, the various rides and stalls just dark shadows against the night sky. It was kind of creepy, really. He turned back to knock at the door again, but paused as he noted that there was no light showing though the window in the upper part of the door.

Frowning, he backed off the steps, moved to the side, and peered along the RV. There were no lights at any of the windows. The woman hadn't only had enough time to get back and put her bike away, she'd already gone to bed too. That or she hadn't come back yet, he realized. Maybe she'd gone back to Madge's, he thought, and decided to wander over there and find out.

The sound of raised voices woke Divine and she opened her eyes, but immediately closed them again as pain shot through her pupils and into her throbbing head. Dear God, it felt like someone was using a saw on her skull.

For a moment, she was so caught up in the crushing agony that Divine wasn't paying attention to the yelling in the room. After a moment, though, the pain eased somewhat. It was still there, but a dull, throbbing ache that she could bear if she didn't move, open her eyes, or breathe too hard. Lying completely still and breathing shallowly, she waited for it to go away and slowly became aware of what was being said.

"—have to be reasonable. When the boys said she was cavorting with that Argeneau spy I had to order them to bring her in."

"She wasn't cavorting with him, Abby," a voice she recognized as her son, Damian, said, fury in his tone. "She was looking for some mortal friends with him along for the ride. She didn't want him along, and doesn't even know who he is! You told me that yourself."

"Yes, but I only know that because I read her," the first male voice reasoned. Abaddon, Divine thought as the man continued, "The boys can't read her, they're too young. I am the only one who can read your mother."

"So you told them to crush her skull and drag her back here?" Damian asked with disgust.

"I told them to knock her out and bring her back," he corrected calmly. "They were a little . . . enthusiastic in their efforts."

"They caved in her skull, Abby!"

"They are scared of her so hit her with a little more strength than necessary," the man said soothingly.

"A little more strength?" Damian gave a snort of disgust. "We've gone through three girls giving her enough blood to heal. Now we have to find others." There was a pause and then he demanded, "Which boys did you have spying on her? I want them punished."

"I sent them out to get more girls. It will be fine. Let me handle it," Abaddon urged.

"Like you handled this?" Damian asked sharply. He then snarled, "What the hell were they doing spying on her without my say-so? I won't have you and the boys doing things behind my back."

"You seemed to be enjoying that little blonde you were entertaining yourself with. I didn't want to interrupt and trouble you with it, so I took it upon myself to send a couple lads out to keep an eye on Basha. I was concerned," he added quickly. "With Lucian sending spies out to look for her, I thought it best to make sure there was someone nearby to help if she ran into trouble."

"Dragging her back here half dead is not helping her."

"She is immortal," Abaddon reminded him patiently. "She was nowhere near death. She will be fine."

"No thanks to you."

A long sigh sounded, and then Abaddon urged, "Come, you have been up with her all night. You should rest."

"I have been up all night with her because of *you*," Damian said resentfully, his voice moving away.

"Yes, and I am sorry for that," Abaddon said, his voice growing fainter as the two men apparently headed out of the room. "But at least we know she is not in cahoots with them."

"She is my mother, Abby. She would never act against me."

"I wouldn't be so sure. If she ever found out . . ."

Whatever came after that was too soft for Divine to hear. She instinctively opened her eyes and turned her head in an effort to be able to hear them again, but the instant she did, agony shot through her skull once more. This time it brought unconsciousness with it.

"**M**orning, Marco."

Marcus glanced up from the Tilt-A-Whirl's panel and offered a smile of greeting to Madge as she approached. He had gone to the Hoskinses' trailer last night after finding Divine's dark and quiet, but Divine hadn't been there. Still, Bob and Madge had been up and he'd sat and talked with them for a good hour before returning to his SUV and heading to a nearby motel to catch some sleep before returning to the carnival today.

He liked the Hoskinses, and they obviously liked Divine. Not only had they flat-out said as much while talking to him, but he'd read it in their thoughts as well. The couple hadn't been able to have children of their own and tended to unofficially adopt the younger members of their carnival. Divine was one of those they considered family. If they'd had a daughter, they would have been proud had she been like Divine.

While the couple had told him at least a hundred good deeds Divine had performed, and as many positive personality traits she possessed, Marcus hadn't learned a thing about Divine's past before coming to this carnival. She apparently didn't share much of that, and they, like most carnies, didn't pry. But what they knew of her from the last two years that she'd been with them had impressed them. She didn't drink, didn't do drugs, didn't mess around. She was quiet, did her work, and was always available to help others.

According to the older couple's thoughts, Divine might seem standoffish at first, but once you were around her for a while, it became clear she was thoughtful and kind. There was little for her to do in the way of setup for her fortune-telling gig, so she was always helping the others set up and tear down their own stalls or rides. She helped with the interviewing as he'd found out earlier, but she was also quick to help if labor was needed or something else, and she was handy as hell to have around. Bob didn't think there was anything she couldn't fix. "The gal was smart as a whip" by his reckoning. It was as if she had been in the business much longer than her years could possibly allow.

That thought had made Marcus smile. Divine might look twenty-five, but she was immortal, and while he didn't know how old she was exactly, she might have been "in the business" from the time of the first carnival. That would explain the knowledge and skill that so surprised the mortals here.

"What on earth did you do to our poor Divine when you two were out last night?" Madge asked, snapping his attention back to the fact that the older woman had reached him and that while she was smiling, there was concern in her eyes as well.

"What do you mean?" he asked with surprise.

"Well, she's usually up with the birds. I swear the girl doesn't sleep more than a couple hours a night. But as far as I can tell she isn't even up yet. We open in half an hour, but her RV's closed up tight, her sign isn't out, and I knocked and got no answer."

Marcus frowned and glanced toward Divine's RV.

"Maybe she's already up and out or something," Madge murmured, peering toward the RV too. "Although I don't know where she'd have got to. Being allergic to the sun like you, she usually sticks close to the RV when she isn't helping someone." The thought apparently reminded her of a concern she'd had for him and she glanced to the awning that had been set up over the Tilt-A-Whirl's controls and nodded with satisfaction. "I'm glad Chapman listened and set that up for you. Bob warned him he might lose you if he tried to make you work in the sun."

"Thanks," Marcus murmured. It had been a worry of his when Chapman had mentioned having him run the Tilt-A-Whirl. Well, okay, his head had been too wrapped up in thoughts of Divine to concern himself much with that last night, but it had definitely been on his mind when he'd walked out to the SUV that morning. Early as it was the sun had already been out and pounding its heat at the earth. He'd been glad to arrive and find Chapman had set up the awning for him.

"Have you seen her this morning?"

Drawn back to the issue at hand, Marcus shook his head slowly and then suggested, "Maybe she had to run into town for something."

"That's possible," Madge said with a sigh. "It's rare,

but she sometimes goes into the town in search of herbs and stuff for those natural remedies of hers."

Marcus hesitated. That was something else he'd learned last night. Divine was always offering natural remedies to the other carnies when they fell ill, which was much appreciated since most couldn't afford proper health care. Sometimes, though, she even seemed to know they were sick before the individual did, and they had all learned to listen if she said they needed to do something for their health. Everyone in the carnie either liked, or at least respected, her for it.

"That's probably where she is then," Marcus said to soothe the woman's worry.

"Yeah," Madge agreed, relaxing a little. "She'll probably come buzzing back on her motorcycle just before the gates open."

Marcus merely nodded, his gaze shifting over the RV again.

"Speaking of that, I guess I'd best get to the gate and help the ticket girls get ready." She turned away, adding, "You come on over after closing tonight and I'll feed you. We need to keep your strength up. Bob swears you work harder than three men put together here."

"Thanks," Marcus murmured, but his gaze was still on the RV, and after she left, he stepped away from the Tilt-A-Whirl control panel and headed for the vehicle. He knocked once on reaching the door, waited for the count of ten, and when there was no sound of movement from inside, tried the handle. It wasn't locked. Marcus hesitated, glanced around to be sure no one was paying attention, and then slid quickly inside.

"Hello?" he called as he waited for his eyes to adjust. With the curtains closed, there was no light in the room, but he had good night vision as all immortals did, and after a moment it kicked in and he glanced around the small consultation room Divine had set up. Everything was still and quiet and appeared in its place, so he moved to the curtain, tugged it aside, and looked around the lounge/kitchenette area as he started forward.

Marcus was perhaps halfway across the room when he noted the blood on the wall beside the door to the bedroom. Following the streaks down, he saw that they ended in an alarmingly large puddle on the floor. Hurrying forward now, he knelt and touched the puddle. The blood was drying, but the puddle was deep enough it was still wet in the middle. By his guess whatever had happened had happened hours ago . . . and it was immortal blood. He could tell that at once.

Cursing, he straightened and moved back outside to check the side panel where the motorcycle was kept. He'd been watching Divine the night before when she'd punched in the code to open it, and copied her actions now. When the panel slid open, it was empty. No motorcycle and no helmet. Marcus closed the panel and returned inside to search the RV.

Five

The rustle of clothing stirred Divine and then she blinked her eyes open with surprise when a cold cloth was laid across her forehead. She found herself peering up into her son's thin face. It was half obscured by strands of his long hair, making his expression inscrutable.

"You're awake. How do you feel?" Damian asked, sitting on the edge of the mattress she lay on.

Divine stared at him blankly, confusion rife in her thoughts. "Damian? What are you doing here?"

"You don't remember?"

Divine glanced past her son at that question, her eyes settling with dislike on the dark-haired man who had spoken. She couldn't prevent the scowl that claimed her lips. "Abaddon."

"Basha," he greeted with a condescending smile, and anger whipped up through her like a snake.

"I don't answer to that name, Abaddon, and well you know it. My name is Divine and has been for a good century. You should be used to it by now."

"You can call yourself what you like, but in your heart you will always be Basha," Abaddon said with a shrug.

That just made her furious, perhaps because in her heart she knew it was true. She could give herself any name she wished, but would always be Basha, daughter of Felix and Tisiphone, granddaughter of Alexandria and Ramses, and niece of the great and powerful Lucian Argeneau, a man she used to adore but had learned to fear. In her heart, she was still Basha, but she was trying hard not to be, and loathed that the young woman she'd been so long ago still clung to the woman she'd become.

Knowing he could and probably was reading her thoughts, Divine shifted her attention to the room she was in to clear her thoughts. She noted the torn, old-fashioned wallpaper and scarred hardwood floors. There were holes in the walls and a large one in the floor as well, telling her where she was—the derelict building on the edge of town that her son had settled in for his brief stay in California.

"I don't know why you choose to live in such horrible places, Damian," she said unhappily.

"Where should he live?" Abaddon asked dryly. "Should he run away? Join the carnival like you?"

"I didn't run away," she snapped.

"Basha, my sweet, you've been running from yourself since—"

"Get out of here, Abby," Damian interrupted. "You're just upsetting her."

Abaddon hesitated, but then nodded obsequiously. "As you wish."

"I don't know why you allow him in your life," Divine growled as she watched the man leave.

"He has his uses," Damian said mildly.

"He's an animal like his master was before him," Divine snapped, and then turned to her son and said with frustration, "It took me ten years to get us away from that man and remove his influence from your life, and then when you turned eighteen and set out on your own, you just welcomed him back in like a long-lost uncle."

"Do you really want to argue about this again? Now?" Damian asked.

Sighing, Divine shook her head and closed her eyes briefly. She'd given up arguing about Abaddon two and a half millennia ago . . . after more than two hundred years of useless attempts to get Damian away from the man, she'd acknowledged that it was his life, he could do what he wanted with it, and have who he wanted in it. That was also when she'd started spending less time around her son, leading her own life and leaving him to lead his.

"I don't want to argue, Damian," she said finally, "But he—"

"Saved your life," he interrupted, and then added chidingly, "Again. Surely you can cut him some slack?"

"He saved my life?" Divine asked with a frown, now trying to sort through her memories to find how she'd got here. She remembered coming back from town, dropping off Marco by the bunkhouses, returning to her RV intending to put the motorcycle away and . . . she'd heard a noise from inside the RV, Divine recalled. She'd gone in to investigate and— She raised a hand to feel her head as she recalled the pain crashing through it.

"Abby was concerned about this business of Lucian sending out spies to look for you."

Divine blinked her memories away and peered at her son when he said that. She'd found that out on her last visit here, the day before. Divine had been surprised to learn on arriving in town with the carnival that Damian was in the area. Even more surprising was that he'd wanted to see her. While they'd been close when he was a boy, he'd grown distant as he aged and she rarely saw him anymore . . . unless he needed something. This time he'd wanted to see her to warn her. Damian had got wind that her uncle Lucian wasn't only looking for him, he had sent spies out to look for her as well. It seemed he'd somehow learned that she lived. Their guess was that Damian's son Ernie had revealed it when he was caught and dragged up in front of the Council.

The little fool, Divine thought on a sigh. She'd raised Ernie for Damian, at least for the first five years. The immortal boy had been a sweet child, but somehow had grown into a weak and sometimes foolish adult. He'd always seemed to be trying to prove something to his father, and had apparently gone north to Canada with some harebrained scheme of performing some "derring-do" to earn his father's respect.

The little idiot had gone about it all wrong though. He'd kidnapped someone connected to the Argeneau family, Lord knew for what purpose, and then he'd got himself caught and executed for his efforts. If anything, Ernie had only made matters worse. Lucian had begun searching for her son in earnest then . . . as well as for her. Knowing that, Divine had suspected Marco might be a spy, but hadn't had a chance to find out for certain or do anything about it.

"Abby was worried about you all alone at the carnival, so he sent a couple of the boys to check on you and make sure you were okay," Damian continued, capturing her attention again. "They found you unconscious in your RV, with a head wound, and brought you back here. You're at the house."

Divine just nodded. She'd already worked out where she was and the knowledge was depressing. She loathed that her child had to live like this, always moving, always hiding, trying to evade her family. They both did, but she at least had the carnival and her RV. Damian refused to settle into such an existence and preferred avoiding mortals and immortals alike altogether, making do with abandoned houses and derelict buildings. He didn't have a real home and never had, really. They had always been running . . . because of her damned family.

"Abby has some suspicions about who knocked you out."

Divine glanced to him. "He does?"

Damian nodded. "One of Lucian's spies is working at your carnival."

"What?" she asked with surprise, and then her eyes widened as his mentioning the carnival recalled her to her responsibilities. Sitting up, she swung her legs off the bed. "What time is it? How long have I been here?"

"Mother, lay down. You took a bad blow to the head. A little rest—"

"I'm healed," Divine muttered, and glanced at her wristwatch. Dear God, it was almost noon. The carnival would be opening soon and she would be expected to be there. Saturdays they opened at 10 A.M., but weekdays and Sundays they didn't open until noon. It was too slow to bother before that on those days. But even when they didn't open until noon, they were up early, cleaning up from the night before and checking that everything was in working order and ready for the busy day ahead. She'd missed helping with that, but absolutely could not miss opening. "I have to get back."

"Mother," Damian said with exasperation as she stood up and peered down at her bloodstained blouse. She looked like she should be working the Haunted House ride rather than her own fortune-telling gig.

"How is your head?" he asked, catching her arm and drawing her attention away from her stained top.

"I'm fine," she assured him. "I heal quickly, we all do, and I have to get back. We open at noon."

"Yes, but I don't think you should go back," he protested. "You aren't safe there. One of Lucian's spies has joined your carnival. He must suspect you and we think he's the one who hurt you. If the boys hadn't found you . . ."

Divine paused to stare at him as his words sparked

a memory in her head. *When the boys said she was cavorting with that Argeneau spy I had to order them to bring her in.* The words played through her head in what she thought was Abaddon's voice.

"You see you can't go back there, don't you?" Damian asked.

Divine turned solemn eyes to her son. "The boys found me?"

"Yes. We think it was that Marco guy who hit you. He's one of the men Lucian sent to look for you."

"Marco?" Divine asked with surprise, though she supposed she shouldn't be surprised. She already knew that he was an immortal.

"Fortunately, the boys' arrival must have scared him off," Damian continued. "They found you and brought you back here to heal. I've been giving you blood all night. The worst of the healing is probably over, but you'll no doubt need extra blood for a while as it finishes."

Divine stared at him, other words playing in her head.

So you told them to crush her skull and drag her back here?

I told them to knock her out and bring her back. They were a little . . . enthusiastic in their efforts.

They caved in her skull, Abby!

They are scared of her so hit her with a little more strength than necessary.

A little more strength? We've gone through three girls giving her enough blood to heal. Now we have to find others. Which boys did you have spying on her? I want them punished.

"Mother?"

Divine forced her attention from the conversation replaying in her head and glanced at her son. He was frowning with concern.

"Maybe you should sit down," Damian said. "You've gone pale."

Divine sucked in a deep breath and turned to move toward the door rather than look at him. Her son was lying to her. "I have to get back."

"Mother—"

"Now that I know Marco is a spy I can be on guard around him," she said calmly. "But I have to go back. My RV is there." Pausing at the door she swung back. "It *is* still there?"

"Yes. The boys brought back your motorcycle but left the RV," he assured her, and then added quickly, "But we can send one of them to pick it up for you. There's no need for you to go back."

"Of course there is. If I just disappear, they'll know I'm the woman they're looking for," she argued. "Besides, it's always better to learn what you can about your enemy. I might be able to find out just what Lucian knows if I go back."

Divine didn't wait for him to respond to that, but turned and opened the door and hurried out. The hallway was empty, as was the front room when she reached it, and Divine supposed everyone was in bed by now. They tended to be night owls. While she was glad Abaddon wasn't around to read her chaotic thoughts just then, she would have liked to come across at least a couple of the boys. A quick butt kicking of one or two of them would have gotten her the truth of who had bashed her head in last night . . . which was probably why they weren't around at the moment. Damian obviously didn't want her to know that Abaddon had put her own grandchildren up to attacking her.

Divine spotted her motorcycle the moment she stepped out onto the dilapidated porch of the house. It would be a good thing to get away without running into Abaddon. She suspected if he read her and announced that she knew Damian was lying, she'd be stuck there for a while arguing with her son or kicking some ass, and she really didn't have time for either.

"All right, fine, go back," Damian said as she pulled on her helmet.

Divine managed not to grin at his tone. He said it as if he were giving her permission. She was the mother here, for pity's sake. She would go when and where she liked, and always had . . . and she would deal with him and his lie in her own time too.

"But be careful. Marcus Notte might not be the only spy that Lucian has there."

Divine had just pulled her helmet on, but paused in doing up the chinstrap to glance at him with a frown. "Marcus Notte?"

"That Marco guy at the carnival is Marcus Notte. The Nottes are in deep with the Argeneaus now. Marguerite is married to Julius Notte, and Christian is her son. He and his cousins are spending more and more time with the Argeneaus in Canada. They're getting tighter all the time. In fact, if you encounter a Notte, you may as well think of him or her as an Argeneau."

Divine digested this news, aware of the disappointment that pinched her at the news that Marco was really Marcus Notte, a spy for her uncle Lucian. Sighing, she shook her head, peered at her son, and asked slowly, "Where do you get all this information?"

"Abaddon has spies everywhere," Damian said with a grin. "How do you think I've managed to avoid your family all these years?"

The usual guilt slid through Divine at the reminder that her own family was hunting her son, that he'd been forced to live the way he did because of them. Mouth tightening, Divine merely nodded, did up her chinstrap, and mounted her motorcycle. The keys were in the ignition and she started the engine, and then glanced to her son and opened her arms when he stepped forward for a hug.

"Be careful," he admonished before stepping back, and Divine forced a smile and nodded, then set the bike in motion. Her mind was a whirl of confusion as she drove away though. Her brain was still healing from the attack that had apparently caved in her skull, and memory was returning quickly, including the conversation she'd heard on wakening the first time. The more she remembered of it, the more questions it raised in her mind. There were certain key phrases that bothered her.

They are scared of her so hit her with a little more strength than necessary.

The part about the boys being afraid of her didn't surprise her much. She'd had to knock a few heads recently when the boys did stupid things like taking too many risks and drawing attention to themselves. From what she understood, it was a couple of the boys acting up and getting caught by the Argeneaus that had forced Damian to try to rescue them, nearly getting him caught too.

It was Abaddon who had called her saying Damian needed her. The man had been pretty vague about what the boys had been doing to draw attention to themselves, but Divine hadn't worried too much about that at the time. She was a mother. She'd rushed north to save her baby and worried about the rest of it afterward. But afterward, no one would explain what had happened exactly. All of them had just kept saying they'd been stupid and acting up, and no amount of threatening or kicking butt had made them talk.

It was a great frustration to Divine that she couldn't read her son or grandsons. She didn't know why that was the case. Her own mother had been able to read her. The only thing she could think was that their being no-fangers rather than just immortals somehow hampered her ability to read them. Divine sighed inwardly. Her son being no-fanger hadn't been the first strike life had thrown at him, but it was a bad one. She didn't know why, but some immortals never developed the fangs others had. It meant he had to cut his victims to get the blood he needed to survive. Most of Damian's sons were the same way and while Divine had been able to read every one of them as children, once they'd hit puberty she'd lost the ability. It made her think that the lack of fangs wasn't the only difference in them.

Divine frowned over that, and then turned her atten-

tion to another thing that bothered her about the conversation she'd overheard. The bit about *We've gone
through three girls giving her enough blood to heal.
Now we have to find others. Which boys did you have
spying on her? I want them punished.*

That part of the conversation bothered her for two
reasons. For one thing, the bit about going through
three girls made her think . . . Well, frankly, it sounded
like he meant those girls had died. She had to be wrong
about that though. She'd raised Damian right. He fed
only when he had to, on the willing when he could, and
never to the point of death. She'd pounded that into his
head at an early age. It was how she was raised, and
how she'd raised him.

As troubling as that had been, Divine was more
concerned about Abaddon's response when Damian
had said that she was his mother and would never act
against him.

I wouldn't be so sure. If she ever found out . . .

Found out what? she wondered. What could Damian
have possibly done that would make her withdraw her
love and support of him? She didn't know, but Abaddon's words suggested he might have done something
that would cause that withdrawal, and the fact that he'd
flat-out lied to her about how she'd come to be injured
was disturbing, as was the fact that he'd been so convincing in the lie. It made her wonder how many other
lies he'd told her in the past.

Divine passed a billboard promoting the Kern County
fair, and her mind turned to another worry. Marco. So
his name was really Marcus Notte, and he was a spy

for Lucian Argeneau. It explained why he was at the carnival. The man wasn't rogue after all, and judging by the questions he'd asked last night, he might suspect she was Basha, but he wasn't sure. That was a good thing at least. She also thought it was probably a good thing that she'd started dying her hair a couple of years ago. Not that anyone probably had a clear idea of what she looked like anymore, except perhaps for her uncle and some of the other older immortals who had met her when she was young.

They hadn't had cameras back then, or portraits even, so wouldn't have an image to go by unless Lucian had arranged for one of those sketch artist pictures or something. He might very well have done that, but if he had, he would have been depending on his memory, which was admittedly good. Still, he hadn't seen her for more than two millennia. That was a long time. Besides, any sketch of her would show her as a blond which she presently wasn't. She'd started dying her hair dark auburn just before joining the Hoskins Carnival and was now glad she had. It might not have completely put Marcus off her trail, but it couldn't have hurt.

Divine spent a moment trying to sort out what to do about him. First she thought avoiding him would be best, but then that seemed useless. The man wasn't going to leave unless she convinced him she wasn't Basha and she couldn't do that by avoiding him. The problem was, she *was* the woman they all thought of as Basha. That being the case, how was she supposed to convince him she wasn't?

No ideas came to mind by the time she reached the

carnival, and Divine decided the best thing she could do was act natural around him. If she didn't act nervous or let on she knew anything, he might eventually decide she wasn't the woman he was looking for. Aside from that, perhaps by talking to the man as if he were a friend rather than an enemy, she could learn just what the Argeneaus knew about her and her son. Maybe even what those risky actions were that her son and grandsons had got up to when she'd had to save him from her uncle.

Several people greeted her as she rode through the carnival grounds. She returned the greetings, but didn't slow until she got to the RV. She made quick work of putting away the motorcycle and helmet and closing the panel, then turned and gasped, coming up short to avoid crashing into Marcus.

"How are you?" he asked.

Divine frowned briefly at the concern on his face. It was as if he knew— Dropping the thought there, she brushed past him, muttering, "I'm fine."

"There's blood on your clothes, and in your hair."

Divine had forgotten about it with everything else on her mind. The part about there being blood in her hair was news to her though. She reached up instinctively to feel the side of her head, mouth tightening as she felt the crusty collection of dried blood there. She didn't stop walking though, and as she mounted the steps to her RV, repeated, "I'm fine."

As she entered the RV, Divine flipped on the lights. Memories of the last time she'd entered slipped through her mind. She also recalled getting hit over the head outside the door to the bedroom and moved into the next section of the RV, flipping on that light too. Not that she needed it to see the dried blood on the wall, door, and floor.

Divine took a deep breath as she peered at it, and then moved into her bedroom to fetch fresh clothes from the closet. She headed into the compact bathroom next to shower. There wasn't much time to get ready. It was exactly three minutes before noon when she stepped under the shower; two minutes later she was out and pulling on her clothes. She towel-dried her hair, dropped the towel, and put the damp strands up in a ponytail as she walked back through the RV.

Snagging the A-frame sign from its resting spot beside the door as she went outside, Divine set it up on the dirt next to her steps and then glanced at her watch: 12:01. One minute late. Not bad, she decided, and peered along the midway to see that people were just starting to filter through the gate. Relaxing, she started to turn back to her door, her eyes sliding over and then pausing on Marcus. He was standing under an awning by the Tilt-A-Whirl controls, staring at her.

Divine finished her turn and went inside, leaving the door open so that she could see when the first customer arrived. She then settled in her chair facing the door to wait for another long day to begin. While they had been open from noon to midnight the day before, it was now Friday. They would be open until 2 A.M., and tomorrow they would be open from 10 A.M. to midnight. Sunday they would start at noon and close at six. Even so, it would be the longest day. Once the gates closed they would start tear-down. They'd pack up the carnival, which would take four to six hours, and then they'd drive to the next town on their schedule.

Divine couldn't remember the name of the town, but what she did remember was that it was a six-hour drive from Bakersfield. Even so, they wouldn't get to rest then, but would immediately have to set up all over again. If they were lucky they'd get done in time to catch a couple of hours sleep before opening, but sometimes they didn't. Truly, a lot of people bad-talked carnies, but they were some of the hardest-working people she'd ever encountered.

Her gaze found Marcus through the open door. He was still at the panel, but Chapman was with him now, no doubt giving him last-minute instructions.

Divine bit her lip. She had three days to convince Marcus that she wasn't Basha, or she suspected he'd follow them to the next town. Perhaps she needed to make up a fake backstory, a history and explanation for her being with the carnival. It would mean claiming a clan, and that could be checked though.

Alternately, she could claim she was turned by a rogue some centuries back and had fled before doing anything rogue herself. She'd have to name a rogue though, and give the name of a mortal with a birth date from the time she chose to back it up. They could always check on her stories.

Divine sighed and rubbed one hand along the side of her head. It was still throbbing a little, which meant the healing was still taking place. The major damage was taken care of, her skull repaired and reknitted into place and the majority of her brain obviously back in working order or she wouldn't be walking and talking. Now, she supposed the little arteries and bits of tissue and synapses were being repaired. Her body would be using blood like crazy to manage the task. She would need blood again soon.

"Hello?"

Divine glanced to the door and offered a smile of greeting. Her first customer had arrived.

Six

"You're a star, kid!" Chapman announced as he stopped at the Tilt-A-Whirl next to Marcus. "You handled the Tilter like you've worked it for years. And handled the kids like a pop star too. They were eating out of your hand. Never had a Friday night go by without some kind of push and shove war, or flat-out fights break out over girls or line cutters. Yes sirree, kid, you're a star."

Marcus straightened from collecting the empty cotton candy cones and disposable drink glasses that had been dropped carelessly around the Tilt-A-Whirl and smiled wryly at Chapman. He was often called kid, son, or young man by people in their forties or fifties and up. He was no longer surprised by it, but it still felt like he was being talked down to and it rankled a bit. "Thank you. Glad you are happy."

"Happy? Hell!" Chapman shook his head and spat

into the dirt. "How would you like a full-time job and come with us when we leave here?"

"What about Stan?" Marcus asked mildly.

"Stan," Chapman murmured on a sigh and scrubbed the back of his head with agitation. "Seems that scrap Stan got himself into in town wasn't a fight so much as a shoving match. He shoved harder, the other guy fell back and broke his neck on the bottom rung of a bar stool. Dead before he hit the floor." He let his hand drop wearily to his side. "Stan's been charged with manslaughter. He ain't gonna be available for a while."

"I'm sorry to hear that," Marcus said quietly. He'd seen too many stupid accidents like that happen over the centuries to be surprised by it.

"Yeah, so am I," Chapman said quietly, staring at the ground and shaking his head. "Stan's not a bad guy, and from what I hear the other guy started it. Didn't like a carnie talking to a local girl and decided to intervene, started shoving Stan around and when he shoved back—" He shrugged. Straightening, he shook his head again as if shaking off the thought of Stan's fate and turned away. "Well, you think on it. You have a job if you want to travel."

"I'll think about it," Marcus murmured, watching the man walk away looking tired and defeated. The sound of a screen door opening drew his gaze to the side to see Divine ushering a young woman out of her RV.

"Thank you so much," the brunette was saying earnestly as Divine walked her down the steps.

"You're welcome," Divine said solemnly, pausing at

the foot of the steps. "I hope everything works out for you."

"Thank you," the woman repeated, and then hurried away. Divine watched until the customer was halfway up the darkening midway, and then turned to pick up her A-frame sign.

Marcus frowned as he noted how pale she was, and that there were lines of pain around her mouth and eyes. It reminded him of the blood he'd found in her RV and the dried blood she'd had on her clothes and in her hair earlier. She'd obviously been injured at some point in the night, and judging by the amount of blood that had been in the RV, badly. She might even yet still be healing from it; he couldn't be sure. But he was quite sure she was in serious need of blood . . . and she didn't have any. He'd gone over that RV from stem to stern and not found anything but a small bar fridge with some old cream in it, presumably for those occasions when Madge came by for coffee.

Moving to the nearest trash bin, Marcus disposed of the garbage he'd gathered while waiting for Chapman to come tell him he could knock off. He then headed for the back lot where his SUV was now parked. He'd moved it there on his break. Finding the blood in her RV and seeing it on her had convinced him that it might be best to be close at hand, at least until he found out what had happened. Which meant he'd be sleeping in his SUV. It was probably for the best, he acknowledged. Staying at the hotel might raise suspicion among the carnies. No one on their wages could afford a motel room let alone a hotel. He wouldn't get any information at all if they were all suspicious and leery about him, so staying here had seemed the better choice.

Several people called out greetings as he passed and Marcus responded politely, but didn't slow. At his SUV he made sure no one was looking, then climbed in the back, unlocked the built-in fridge, and retrieved several bags of blood. He stuffed them inside his shirt, grimaced at how obvious it was he had something in there, and then tugged on the leather jacket he'd used as a pillow last night. It was too damned hot for the jacket, but the leather at least made the bulge in his shirt less obvious. Still, he moved quickly as he locked up and left the SUV, sticking to the shadows as much as possible on his way back to Divine's RV.

He knocked once on her door, but—afraid she'd turn him away—Marcus didn't wait for her to answer. He pulled the door open and stepped inside, barely ducking in time to avoid the mop that came swinging at his head.

"Whoa. It's me," he said quickly, holding up a hand as he straightened. Good thing he did too, or he would have taken the mop in the face. Damn, the woman was fast. "Divine, it's me, Marco."

"And what the hell makes you think that makes it okay to break into my RV?" she asked dryly, this time doing the unexpected and ramming the end of her mop into his groin.

Marcus's breath left him on a sound he didn't think he'd ever made before. It came out a whooshing "*eeeee-iiiii-owwwww*" and ended on a howl. He also dropped the bags of blood in favor of cupping his screaming genitals with one hand while grabbing the mop with the other to ensure she didn't do that again. He needn't have worried, Divine's hands had gone lax on the mop, her attention fixed on what he'd dropped.

"What the devil is that?" she asked with dismay, staring at the clear bags of dark crimson fluid lying on the floor of her RV.

"They're for you," Marcus muttered through gritted teeth. Damnnnn, the woman had nearly unmanned him . . . and the blow had hurt enough that he'd nearly passed out. He still might do so. Immortal women were stronger than mortal women, or mortal men for that matter, and she hadn't held back. It was all he could do not to cross his legs and hop around continuously howling like a sissy boy. Alternately, he wanted to rip his pants down and see if his balls were still intact. He suspected she'd crushed at least one of them with her blow, popping it like a balloon in his jeans.

That thought made Marcus cast a reluctant glance down. He groaned when he saw the blood beginning to blossom at his groin. Dammit, the woman *had* unmanned him.

"Well, what on earth do you expect me to do with these?" Divine asked, bending to pick up one of the bags and peer at it with distaste.

Marcus snatched it from her hand and slammed it to his mouth almost before his fangs had finished extending.

She stared at him wide-eyed as the bag quickly began to shrink. When the last drop of blood had been sucked up through his fangs into his body, he pulled the shriveled bag away with a gasp of pain and turned away to bang his forehead against the wall and then lean there trying to ignore the new pain now centered at his groin as the nanos in his blood began to make repairs. Damn, the fix was almost worse than the damage had felt when she'd hit him. Correction, he thought grimly, trying not to gnash his teeth. It *was* worse, because the blow had taken only a moment and the repairs were going to take much longer.

"Crap," Marcus groaned, pressing his forehead harder into the wall to try to distract himself from the pain in his lower regions. He followed that up with a lovely string of curses in both Italian and English that ended on an "Ah hell," when the world blurred around him and he felt himself sliding toward the floor and unconsciousness. It seemed the cure was going to knock him out where the actual blow hadn't.

Divine watched Marcus sprawl on her floor and sighed with exasperation. She really needed to control her temper. While she'd been annoyed that he would enter before she'd given him permission, all she'd managed to do was make more work for herself.

Clucking under her tongue, she shook her head, set aside the mop, and then squatted to turn the man over. He was white as a sheet, she saw, but didn't understand why until she gave him the once-over and noted the bloodstain around his groin.

"Oh damn," Divine muttered, guilt sliding through her. She hadn't meant to do real damage, just teach him a lesson about entering other people's homes without permission. Unfortunately, she used her strength so rarely that Divine forgot just how strong she was. This wasn't the first time she'd done more damage than intended. She'd once tossed a grandson through a wall when all she'd meant to do was slam him up against it. But she hadn't felt too bad about that. It had been Rufus, who she suspected didn't follow her rules about feeding. He was a mouthy piece of work, always sneering at the "stupidity and weakness of mortals." She'd heard him more than once declare they were stupid cattle and deserved to be slaughtered. He knew she hated it when he said things like that. She hated that he even thought like that, and blamed herself for it.

Divine didn't spend a lot of time around her son and his sons. She hadn't since he became a man and struck out on his own. She had visited with him more often at first. She'd even raised several of his boys in the early centuries when the birth mother didn't want to be bothered, but had found it too heart-wrenching when one or another of them had been caught by one of Uncle Lucian's scouts and killed. It had actually been a relief when Damian had stopped asking her to raise them.

The last time she'd spent more than a half hour or so with Damian had been when she'd had to rescue him from Uncle Lucian up in Canada. She'd moved as quickly as she could when she'd got the message from Abaddon that her son might need her. Fortunately, the carnival she'd been traveling with at the time had been in Michigan and she'd got to Toronto quickly enough. She'd checked into a hotel and had immediately tried to contact Damian. When she hadn't been able to reach him, she'd reluctantly tried to contact Abaddon with no success. She'd paced her hotel room for two days, trying repeatedly to reach either of the men. Just as she was about to give up and head back to Michigan, Abaddon had called in a panic. He'd told her Leo was holed up in a hotel in downtown Toronto and Lucian and his men were there searching for him.

Divine had ground her teeth at his calling Damian Leo, but had merely snapped out, "Which hotel? What room is he in?"

The hotel hadn't been far from her own. Still, by the time she'd arrived, slipped past the men her uncle seemed to have streaming through the building, and got to the floor Damian's room was on, she'd been too late. They'd found him, and Damian was lying on the floor in the hall, several bullets in his chest and an arrow protruding from his heart.

Shocked and horrified, Divine had scooped him up and started to turn away with him, but a small sound, perhaps a gasp, had made her swing back toward the room Damian had lain outside of. A petite brunette was trying to help a dark-haired man to his feet and had spotted her. The woman was opening her mouth to scream when Divine had taken control of her mind, stopped her from making a sound, wiped her mind, and put her to sleep. She'd then rushed off for the stairs with her son, carrying him up rather than down and then leaping from the rooftop of that building to the next, and then the next after that before stopping to remove the arrow from his heart. He hadn't miraculously gained consciousness right away, of course. Besides the arrow, he'd taken several bullet wounds and lost enough blood that he would be out for a while. She'd waited an hour, though, before moving.

Not knowing what else to do, Divine had left him there while she went for her RV. It hadn't taken long . . . even so, Damian was gone by the time she returned.

In a panic, she'd called his number only to have a strange voice answer. Suspecting it was one of Uncle Lucian's men, she'd hung up at once and called Abaddon instead, telling herself that just because they had the phone didn't mean they had her son. Her calls to Abaddon had again gone unanswered. Divine had stayed in town for another full day calling again and again, and then had packed up and headed for the border, intending to get as far away from Canada and her uncle as possible.

The next weeks had been stressful as she waited to learn whether her son had managed to drag himself off that roof on his own, or had been caught. She'd also changed carnivals at that point, moving to the Hoskins Amusements, and she'd dialed Abaddon's number so many times she'd started to dream about dialing it. And then she'd finally got a call, not from Abaddon, but from her son. He was alive, well, and wanted to thank her for saving his life. Seriously, that's what he'd said. Divine had flipped. All that anxiety and fear and he finally calls her up cheerful as a chimp to say thanks? Divine had demanded to know where he was and when she found out he was holed up not far from where the carnival was, she'd left at once to go see him.

Her temper hadn't improved any once she'd arrived at the dilapidated building he'd taken shelter in. He deserved better than the holes he chose to inhabit, and she didn't like his choice of companions either. Not the women. They were all emaciated drug addicts, every one of them high as kites, either passed out and blank-brained or so strung out their thoughts didn't make sense when she tried to read them. She hadn't been any more pleased to find her grandsons just as high from feeding on them. She'd ignored that at first, too intent on seeing for herself that Damian was all right to care what her grandsons got up to. Once she'd seen for herself that he was alive and well, Divine had demanded an explanation and Damian had explained that Abaddon had carried him off the roof and got him away when she'd left him there.

That last part had been said with a wounded note that suggested she'd abandoned him, and that was when Divine had let her temper rip. She'd explained in no uncertain terms that she'd left him to fetch the RV and came back to find him gone.

"Says you. You were probably off fetching the Rogue Hunters to come get Dad," Rufus had sneered, his words slurred with the effects of the drug-soaked blood he'd consumed. Divine hadn't even thought; she'd picked him up by the throat and thrown him up against the wall . . . only he'd gone right through it, crashing to the floor in the next room. Divine had followed to make sure he was all right, and then to warn him to watch his tongue if he didn't want to be tongueless as well as fangless. It had been an empty threat, but effective.

He'd said "Yes ma'am," and nodded repeatedly as she'd turned and stormed out.

Damian had followed her, but when she'd asked how Lucian Argeneau had tracked him down, he'd been infuriatingly vague about the whole ordeal. He'd claimed that a couple of the boys had taken some risks they shouldn't have and behaved stupidly, and that he'd tried to clean up their mess and got himself caught. Damian had refused to explain what those risks had been, however. He'd also avoided her eyes the whole time, which had made her suspect he was lying to her about something, though she couldn't tell which part of the tale was a lie.

"What risks?" she'd demanded. "What stupid things did they do?"

"They're my sons. I'll handle it," he'd said, refusing to explain.

Divine had let the matter go, too emotionally exhausted from weeks of worry to have the energy to fight with him. But she'd taken the time to warn him in no uncertain terms to lie low and avoid trouble for the next little while. Lucian didn't like to lose, wouldn't be happy about losing him, and would have his people out in force looking for him. She'd emphasized it by pounding at him until he'd assured her he'd lie low for a while.

The moment he'd made that promise, she'd mounted her motorcycle and left. Divine always came away from visits to Damian's chosen shelters feeling slightly dirty. She blamed it on Abaddon and some of her grandsons. She had always found Abaddon loathsome, but while she disliked admitting it, some of her grandsons left her feeling the same way. As a rule they avoided her as much as possible, and were mostly quiet and polite when they couldn't avoid her, but it didn't matter. Divine always left worried about what they were up to and feeling like she needed a bath. It was why she didn't go out of her way to see her son. In fact, she hadn't seen him more than half a dozen times over the last century, and four of those times had been over the last two or three years, twice when she'd had to save him from Lucian and then had visited him after, and twice the last couple of days.

Marcus moaned from the depths of his unconsciousness and Divine turned her attention to the man she was squatting over. She supposed she couldn't just leave him lying there on her floor. Well, she could, but it could get awkward if Madge or someone came along for a visit and peered through the window.

Clicking her tongue against her teeth, she picked up the man and carried him to the bedroom at the back of the RV. After laying him down there, she debated stripping him so he'd be more comfortable and then shook the thought away. Seeing the injury she'd done him would just make her feel guiltier and she resented feeling guilty at all. She shouldn't. He had entered uninvited. A man could get shot for something like that.

Mind you, Divine supposed he might prefer getting shot to whatever had happened in his pants when she'd hit him. She'd lived a long time and never seen a man actually turn the different colors he had with pain. At one point he'd actually turned green.

Grimacing, she quickly covered him with a blanket so that she didn't have to look at the evidence of what she'd done Divine then returned to the other room and surveyed the mess. After a sigh, she collected the remaining bags of blood and tossed them in her refrigerator, then set to the task of cleaning up the blood that had dried on her floor. Fortunately, she didn't favor carpet and her RV was floored with a laminate that looked like hardwood. Everything in her RV was easily cleanable, which came in handy at times like this. Not that there were many times like this. Actually, this was the first. But she had no doubt there would be others in the future before she traded this RV in for another. Life could get messy.

It didn't take long to finish her cleaning. Once done, Divine walked to the door to the bedroom and peered in at Marcus again. She'd nearly covered his head with the blanket when she'd tossed it on him, and he was lying as still as death under it, nowhere near regaining consciousness. In her experience, if he weren't very deeply under he'd be moaning and thrashing. Healing was often more painful than the injury that brought it on, which was something she'd learned well at an early age.

Not wanting to think about that, Divine turned away and headed for the door. She needed to head into town and find a meal. She needed blood. The throbbing in her head had got steadily worse as the day had progressed, and then it had begun to spread. A sure sign she needed blood. She wasn't too concerned about leaving Marcus here alone. There was nothing here for him to find that would tell him her identity. In fact, there was nothing here to tell him much of anything about her. Divine had learned long ago to travel lightly. She never knew when she might have to move again, and possibly do it with nothing but the clothes on her back. She'd done that many, many times over the years.

Stepping outside, she sucked in a breath of fresh air, peered up at the starlit night, and then went to get her motorcycle.

Seven

It was hunger that woke Marcus. His stomach was cramping with it. That awareness was followed by the realization that he was lying on a bed, under a blanket. A glance around told him where he was and reminded him what had happened. It also explained why he was so hungry. The one bag of blood hadn't been enough to make up for the blood his body had used healing his balls.

Grimacing at the thought of the injury he'd taken, Marcus reached down to feel gingerly around under the blanket. His jeans were hard and crusty with dry blood around the groin, but there was no longer any pain down there. He'd healed. Great. Now he just had to get up, get out of here without his oh-so-lovely hostess busting his balls again, literally, and get back to the SUV to find some blood. Unless, of course, the blood he'd brought here was still around. From the disgusted look on Divine's face, he doubted she'd consumed it. She'd acted like it was skanky week-old roadkill he'd offered her. Here he'd been trying to do something nice and she'd beaten the crap out of him and sneered at his offering.

"Women," he muttered under his breath, and was about to shift the blanket off himself and get up when a sound in the other room made him pause. He supposed he should have assumed it was Divine. It was her RV after all, but there had been something furtive about the sound. He lay still, ears straining, and then stiffened and closed his eyes to feign sleep as he heard the bedroom door slide open.

It was barely opened when it closed again, but the sound came with a smell that told him the person at the door wasn't Divine. She smelled like wild roses and vanilla, a surprisingly potent combination that made him think of cupcakes in the garden. It made him hungry.

However, the smell that had slid into the room when the door was opened was musk and male sweat. Marcus opened his eyes to find the room empty. Surprised by that, he eased the blankets aside and carefully sat up, relieved when the action didn't add to the pain his lack of blood was causing. He was weak though. He needed blood.

The distinct whoosh of the RV's screen door closing made Marcus get to his feet and head out of the room to investigate. Even if he only caught a glimpse of whoever was walking away from the RV, it was something, he thought.

Marcus was halfway across the lounge area when flames suddenly exploded outside the windows on either side of him. Freezing, he glanced from one window to the other and then continued forward, running now. He pushed through to the curtained-off area with the table where Divine did her fortune-telling, noting that there were flames outside those windows as well.

Muscles tightening, Marcus reached the door and tried to open it, not terribly surprised when the door-knob turned but the door didn't budge. Why set the RV on fire and leave the door open for the person inside to escape? And it had to have been deliberately set on fire. Flames were shooting up at every window. Natural fires did not start that way. Besides, he could smell gas. It must have been used as an accelerant. Put that together with the attack that had left Divine and the RV bloodied last night and it appeared someone was out to get her.

Grinding his teeth together as the doorknob grew hot in his hand, Marcus stepped back and then threw his weight at the solid panel. That would have done it on most doors he'd encountered, but all it did here was crack the solid inner door in a couple spots. The center held fast. They must have jammed something up against it inside the screen door, he realized.

The fire was growing quickly. Judging by the way the fire had erupted, they must have poured the gasoline all the way around the RV and then set it on fire. It was the only explanation for the way the flames had popped up at every window. But the fire was quickly taking hold now, eating into the fiberglass and whatever else the RV was made of, and the heat inside was quickly becoming like an oven on broil. Immortals tended to be highly flammable and Marcus knew he didn't have long.

Giving up on the door, he turned and glanced from one window to another and then hurried back into the lounge area. After a brief pause, he settled for the window above the couch. It was bigger and he could use the couch as a launching pad, he decided, and ran for it. When he hit the couch and leaped up, Marcus raised his legs, drawing them close to his chest even as he curled his head down and wrapped his arms around it, trying to make himself as small as possible as he crashed into and through the window. It was only as the glass cut into him that Marcus considered that he should have thrown one of the kitchen table chairs through it first to clear away the glass, and it was only as the flames licked at him that he thought he should have dampened the blanket on the bed and wrapped it around himself before leaping out.

Hindsight, however, was as useless as it was perfect, Marcus thought grimly as he felt his skin catch fire on his back and arms as he passed through the flames. He crashed to the ground with a jolting thud what seemed like hours, but must only have been seconds, later. Despite the pain radiating through every part of his body, Marcus began to roll away from the RV as soon as he hit dirt. He rolled once, twice, and then crashed into the cotton candy stand stationed on this side of Divine's home.

Pausing then on his back, Marcus raised his head

to peer along his body, relieved to see that he didn't appear to be on fire anymore. Sighing, he let his head drop briefly, took a deep breath, and then started to get up, only to groan and fall back as his body complained strenuously. He might not be on fire now, but he'd obviously not got away unburned. His skin was tight and painful in several places, his back, legs, and arms bearing the worst of it. Immortals were very flammable, human kindling. He was lucky that rolling had put out the flames.

Sighing, Marcus closed his eyes, but immediately blinked them open again as the sound of voices calling out in alarm told him that the fire had been noticed and the carnies were coming to investigate. He suspected that since he was a newcomer and no one had seen him crash through the window, he'd be suspect number one for who had set the fire. The thought was enough to make Marcus move, pain or no pain. He was in no shape to control the minds and thoughts of a large crowd of people. Hell, at peak health, he couldn't do it.

Pushing himself to his feet, he leaned against the cotton candy stall and stumbled forward along it, wincing as his shoulder and upper arm rubbed against the wooden surface. After a couple of feet, Marcus gave that up. He was moving too slowly and his legs were wobbling, threatening to collapse under him with every move. There was no way he was going to make it back to his SUV and the blood waiting there.

Marcus swallowed and took a deep breath, trying to clear his mind and figure out what to do. His brain was presently a chaotic mass of pain and confusion and his thinking was definitely less than optimal or it wouldn't have taken him as long as it did to notice the door next to him. Once he did notice it, however, hiding inside the cotton candy stand he was leaning against seemed the best option. If he'd had the energy, Marcus would have cursed at himself for being so slow. Instead, he merely turned to the door, closed his hand around the padlock, and pulled once, hard.

He was rather amazed when it jerked open. Marcus hadn't really thought he'd had the strength in him. But perhaps adrenaline was making the difference. There was definitely a ton of adrenaline coursing through him as he listened to the sounds of people rushing this way. Pushing the door open, Marcus slid inside the stall, closed the door, and then dropped to the floor like a stone, the last of his energy spent.

"What the hell," Divine breathed into her motorcycle helmet, automatically letting up on the motorcycle's throttle as she spotted the huge bonfire that had once been her RV at the end of the midway. She noted the silhouettes of people against it next, and at first wasn't sure what they were doing, but then realized several were rushing around throwing pails of water at the conflagration while others shot fire extinguishers at it. Still others were frantically screaming her name. They thought she was inside, Divine realized, and then remembered that while she wasn't, Marcus was.

Cursing, she sent the motorcycle racing forward, quickly crossing the distance to what had once been her home. At the edge of the group she didn't so much stop and dismount as step off as she let the motorcycle fall. The tires were still moving as it crashed onto its side. Divine undid and tugged her helmet off, dropping it by the bike as she hurried forward.

"Oh Divine! Thank God!" Madge cried, spotting her and rushing to her side.

"What happened?" she asked grimly, moving along the RV, checking the windows for movement and a way in.

"Nobody knows. It just went up like tinder," Madge said anxiously, following along behind her. "We've called the fire department, but weren't sure if you were inside. The men have been trying to beat the fire back from the door so someone could run in and try to get you out if you were in there."

"Tell them not to bother with the RV, but to start watering down or moving the nearby stalls and trailers," Divine said quietly, and then turned to peer at the woman, giving her a little mental nudge to ensure she did that, before turning and continuing around the RV.

She walked around the front of the vehicle. There was a door behind the driver and passenger's door that led into the closet in her bedroom, and she'd hoped she might get through to the living area that way, but the fire was worse here than anywhere else. Divine continued around the RV, pausing when she spotted the smashed window in the lounge area. The smell of burnt flesh surrounded her there. Divine ground her teeth together and started toward the window with some vague intention of jumping through it and inside.

But the moment she moved toward the RV the scent began to fade.

Pausing, she turned slowly, following her nose as the smell grew stronger. Firelight gleaming off of blood and burnt skin on the side of the cotton candy trailer caught her eye, and then she noticed that the padlock was broken. She was just stepping toward it when three men hurried around the burning RV toward her.

"The fire trucks just started up the midway."

"We're moving the cotton candy stand further away."

"Everyone else is watering down the Tilter to make sure it doesn't catch fire."

Divine blinked as each man contributed a comment, but they weren't done.

"We were going to back Roch's truck up to the cotton candy trailer, hook it up and pull it further away, but can't get it through the back lot."

"We'd have to move about a dozen other vehicles to get it here."

"No time for that, so the three of us are going to haul it. If we can."

The last man, a wiry little guy who was somewhat lacking in muscle, sounded pretty dubious about achieving that feat and Divine didn't blame him. While the stand was on wheels and Bevy was one of the men and a big brute, Mac and the thin kid she didn't know were the other two. She didn't think they'd be able to move it either.

"I'll help," she announced, moving up to the end where the trailer hitch was. "You guys push and I'll steer."

The men nodded and rushed around to the other end of the small trailer.

"Ready?" she asked, bending to slip one hand under the hitch to lift it off the bricks it rested on.

Grunts and groans answered her as the men put their backs into moving the trailer. She wasn't terribly surprised when it barely inched forward, in fact she was prepared for it and simply lifted the hitch upward and moved away from the RV, pulling the trailer behind her. Divine tugged it past the RV, weaved between a couple of other vehicles and into the center of the back lot before stopping and setting it down.

Walking back around the trailer, she grimaced to herself when she saw the three men standing a good twenty feet back, gaping at her and the trailer. Sighing, she moved toward them, quickly slipping into first one man's mind and then each of the other's and rearranging their memories a bit so that they recalled the hard, gut-wrenching, grunting work of pushing the trailer away from the RV.

"Good work," Divine praised them quietly when she was done. "Perhaps you should go see if they need help with the Tilt-A-Whirl."

The words were accompanied by a mental nudge that had them nodding, turning toward the RV, and heading away to find the others.

Shaking her head, Divine turned back to the trailer. The door was stuck, or appeared to be at first. After a moment, though, she got it open enough to realize that Marcus was lying in front of it. She called his name, but when he didn't respond, she forced the door open, pushing his body across the metal floor inside as she did. Once she could slip in, she did, and then let the door slide closed and bent to examine Marcus.

The smell of burnt flesh was overwhelming in the small space and Divine had to hold her breath as she examined him. Fire was one of the few things that could kill one of their kind, although it took special circumstances to succeed with it. Trapping someone inside a burning building or vehicle was special enough . . . so long as that someone didn't manage to escape before combusting. Marcus had managed to escape, badly burned but before the temperature had got so hot that he combusted.

Divine shook him gently, not really wanting to wake him to the pain he was no doubt in, but needing to know how bad he was. When he didn't rouse at all, she shifted him away from the door, straightened, and peered out. The night sky was lit up not just by the fire, but by both red flashing lights and bright white ones, and she could see water arcing into the air around her RV. The firemen were hard at work.

"Blood."

Divine glanced down at that word as Marcus suddenly caught her ankle in a hard grip. Easing the door closed, she knelt next to him again. "How bad is it?"

"Blood," Marcus repeated.

Divine sighed, but nodded. "I'll find someone."

"No." His hand tightened on her ankle. "My SUV."

"What about it?" she asked with confusion.

"Blood . . . there," he gasped.

Divine frowned, her confusion only deepening, and

then she recalled the bags he'd carried into her RV and that he had even slapped one to his mouth and drained it. She asked with amazement, "You mean that bagged stuff?"

He grunted and Divine shook her head.

"We can't survive on that, Marco. The nutrients die the moment it leaves the body. You need—"

"No," he hissed. "Bagged."

"Your bagged blood is in the refrigerator in my RV," she said, and then added dryly, "And I am not going in there to get it."

"More," he gasped. "SUV."

Divine clucked impatiently. Bagged blood would not help him through this. He needed live blood to give him strength and help him heal. However, she knew without question that the man was stubborn enough to refuse to feed from a mortal if she brought him one of the carnies. Besides, the trailer was tiny and hot and stank of burnt flesh. Getting him out of there and to his SUV was rather attractive just then. And once she had him in the SUV she could take him elsewhere to find donors to feed from. It was never a good idea to feed where you lived. Divine avoided that as a rule.

Decision made, she bent and scooped him up.

"What . . . doing?" he almost moaned the unfinished question, but Divine got his drift.

"Taking you to your SUV," she said grimly, turning to the door and cracking it open with the fingers of the hand at his shoulders so that she could peer out.

"Bring . . . here," he gasped.

Divine snorted at the very suggestion. "I'm not bringing anything here. You need blood to heal, but once you get it, you're going to scream your head off and thrash like a landed fish. I'm getting you the hell out of here and somewhere you can't alert the whole town to the agony you're going through."

Marcus groaned but didn't protest further so she supposed he thought that was the right decision. It didn't matter if he did or not, though; it was what she was doing, Divine thought grimly and slipped out of the trailer once she saw that the way was clear.

The first problem Divine encountered was that she had no idea where his SUV was. It took some hunting to find it and then she only knew she had the right vehicle because it had Canadian plates. That should have raised a lot of questions with the carnies. The only way it couldn't have was if Marcus had controlled some minds and such, she thought as she finally paused beside the vehicle.

"Keys?" she asked, glancing to the man in her arms.

"Pocket," he said, or at least she thought that was what he mumbled. Using the back of the SUV to help hold him up, she quickly patted him down until she found the keys in his pocket, his jeans pocket of course. Rolling her eyes, she slid her hand into the tight space to snatch the keys out, doing her best not to feel anything but the contents of his pockets. Dear God, she was an old woman, she shouldn't be shy about digging around inside a man's pocket . . . should she?

Shaking that worry away, Divine eyed the key fob on the chain with other keys and then pressed the broken lock symbol twice and heard the clicking as the locks were released. She then immediately slid the keys into her pocket, debated how to open the door she had leaned the man against, and then sighed to herself. There was nothing else she could do; she hefted him over her shoulder, wincing at his cry of pain, and then used her free hand to open the back door. She leaned forward then, easing him off her shoulder and onto the SUV floor, then shifted his legs inside and followed to close the door behind them.

There was a small refrigerator built into one corner of the back of the SUV. It was locked and she searched briefly through his keys until she found the right one and opened it, but then simply stared at the contents. Six bags of blood, almost ice-cold. Divine grimaced at the sight. Junk food for immortals. It held little in the way of nutrients, but it was what he wanted and she supposed at this point, even a small amount of nutrients were better than none.

Shaking her head, she grabbed a bag and turned to Marcus. He was still conscious and his fangs slid out as soon as he spotted the bag in her hand so Divine popped it to his mouth, waited for it to empty, and then replaced it with another. There were six bags in the refrigerator and Marcus went through them in maybe a little more than six minutes. He began to thrash and groan even before he finished the last bag. The healing was starting and it was obviously going to be nasty.

Divine peered at him with concern for a moment and then cursed under her breath and began to shift over the backseats to the driver's seat, his keys still clutched in her hand. They couldn't stay here. She had to get him the hell away from the carnies and anybody else if she didn't want him drawing attention to them.

That thought uppermost in her mind, she started the engine and managed to maneuver them out of the back lot and onto the road. Marcus began thrashing and shrieking in the back almost the moment she got the tires on blacktop.

Divine ground her teeth and did her best to ignore the tortured sounds, as well as the way the vehicle rocked with his wild thrashing. She needed to concentrate. She needed to find someplace secluded enough that his screams wouldn't be overheard.

Marcus was suffering. His entire body felt like it was on fire, from the tips of his toes to the ends of the hairs on his head. Everything seemed to be screaming in agony. He'd taken enough damage that the six bags in the truck hadn't been enough. He needed more.

"Divine," he croaked, writhing on whatever it was he lay on. He really had no idea, and didn't care. All he cared about in this world was making the pain stop. He'd give her Bastien's number and have her order more blood brought at once. He needed it. That was the only thing that would end this agony.

"Divine," he gasped, rolling his head back and around looking for her. He was in the SUV, he saw. Alone. Groaning, he curled into a ball on the vehicle floor and wept helplessly, overwhelmed by the pain thrashing him. But then he forced himself to drag himself closer to the door and reach for it. He needed blood.

Before he could even try to open it himself, the door was pulled open from outside, revealing Divine and a young mortal woman in a nightgown. He stared blankly for a moment, overwhelmed once again, this time by the smells and sounds coming from the blank-faced mortal woman. He could actually smell and hear the blood pumping through her body, and it was beautiful, he thought briefly and then lunged at the mortal, his fangs sliding out.

Eight

Divine tugged the leather jacket she'd donned a little tighter around herself and shifted uncomfortably in the front seat, and then opened her eyes on a little groan and rolled her head. She had a crick in her neck from sleeping upright in the driver's seat. Nice. That was something immortals didn't get if they had enough blood in their system, but then she already knew she didn't. She needed to feed.

Suddenly aware that the moaning and groaning that had been coming from the back of the SUV for what had seemed like hours had now died off, Divine twisted in the seat to peer back at Marcus. He was sleeping soundly, lying in the back amid the flakes of burnt flesh that his body had shed as he'd healed.

The truck would need to be hosed out, she thought with a grimace. It probably wouldn't help though.

Divine suspected the smell of burnt flesh would linger in the vehicle for a long time to come.

Turning back, she opened the driver's side door and slid out. Divine took a moment to stretch and crack a few bones before moving toward the door at the back of the SUV. Once there, she peered in at Marcus briefly, and then caught his legs and started to drag him toward her, but dropped them and quickly stepped back when he suddenly sat upright, his expression half asleep and half alarmed.

"Divine." He sighed her name with relief, lowering the fists he'd instinctively raised. Marcus slumped where he sat, letting his hands drop to the floor, only to raise them again and grimace with disgust as he peered at the ruined skin now clinging to his hands. "Gross."

"Yeah," Divine agreed with amusement. "I was going to get you settled next to a tree or something and sweep out the worst of it, then head into town and find somewhere to hose it out. Maybe hose you down too."

"I wouldn't say no to either suggestion," Marcus said dryly, sliding forward on the vehicle floor until he could get out of the SUV. Moving a few steps away from the vehicle, he then tried to shake off the worst of the flakes clinging to him. "I don't suppose there is a lake or anything near here?"

"Actually, we're about half an hour or forty-five minutes from the ocean," she admitted, and when he glanced at her in surprise, she shrugged. "I needed to take you somewhere no one would hear you screaming. I know the people who own this property. It's about forty minutes from San Bernardino, spans hundreds of acres, and they're out of town. I figured this was our safest bet."

Marcus glanced around then. They were parked on a dirt path near a copse of trees. He couldn't see the lights of civilization in any direction, although the copse could be blocking some.

"So you parked me here and went for a walk while I screamed my head off?" he asked with amusement.

"Actually I went for five or six walks," Divine informed him dryly, and then added, "But not here, on the edge of the nearest town, and each time to find you a host."

Marcus tilted his head uncertainly. "A host?"

"Someone to feed on," she said succinctly. "You needed blood to heal."

"You let me bite someone?" he asked, and she suspected he was having some memories of his feedings, because he looked horrified. She could understand that. The man had been in agony and out of control. If she hadn't been there, helping to control the situation, he probably would have killed every one of the mortals she'd brought to him. But she *had* been there.

"They are all alive and fine and back at home," Divine assured him solemnly. "I realized when you launched yourself at the first one that you weren't fully in your head. I controlled her mind while you fed, forced you to stop when you'd had enough, and then returned her to her bed and fetched another," she assured him, neglecting to mention that she hadn't been able to slip into his thoughts and stop him by controlling him, so had had to get physical with him.

"Hosts to feed on," Marcus muttered unhappily.

Divine didn't comment. Even after all these centuries, she disliked using the word *blood*. She didn't know if it was the need to hide what she was from the mortals she'd lived with over the years that made her avoid use of the word, but she found herself reluctant to say the word. *Hosts to feed on* just sounded less nasty to her.

Marcus turned back to the vehicle. Leaning in, he grabbed his duffel bag and straightened. He carried the bag around to the back passenger door, set it inside, and then turned to peer at her solemnly. "Thank you for getting me to the SUV and taking care of me."

Divine shrugged uncomfortably. "I couldn't just leave you in the stand for someone to find. You'd have attacked the first person who came along and drained them dry. Maybe the second person who came too."

"Yes," he agreed, sounding both weary and ashamed at once. Straightening his shoulders, he added, "Still, some would have left me anyway."

"I wouldn't," she said firmly.

"No," Marcus agreed quietly. "I know you wouldn't. You might be a ball buster—"

Divine glanced at him sharply, surprised when he grinned.

"But you're also the woman who does her best to help the mortals who come to you, as well as the carnies you travel with. You would not have left me screaming in a cotton candy stand at the carnival," he said with certainty.

Divine shrugged and glanced away, then sighed and

turned back, "Sorry about the . . . er . . . ball-busting thing. I—"

"I shouldn't have just walked in," Marcus interrupted quietly. "I gather that could get a man shot here in America. The truth is I walked right in because I didn't think you'd invite me in," he smiled wryly and admitted, "which probably means I deserved it, I guess."

"You deserved to get hit," Divine assured him. "But I didn't mean to do . . . what happened," she finished with a grimace. She really hadn't meant to do that kind of damage. She just didn't handle it well when people tried to take choice away from her. Now that he'd been through so much, she actually felt bad about her part in his suffering. Really, fate had over punished him.

"Well, fortunately, I healed. One of the benefits of being immortal," Marcus said with a shrug and then added grimly, "A benefit that is definitely appreciated after that fire."

Divine nodded solemnly. Healing was one very definite benefit of being immortal, but there were many; being stronger, faster, able to see in darkness, never getting sick . . . Some would say that never aging was an amazing benefit too, but that lost its charm after a couple centuries. At least it had for Divine. Actually, she would have been happy to die in her teens, but then she'd gone through something terrible at that time, a nightmare really. One whole year of her life had been hell. It had taken a long time to get over it, and she *had* got over it. But it was the kind of thing that had an impact on a person and shaped their personality. It would always be a part of her, but she had long ago got over the death wish it had inspired. The closest she'd got to that feeling since then was a deep weariness, a bone-deep boredom. She had been around long enough to have seen it all, well, at least when it came to human behavior. That boredom and weariness had begun to wane a bit the last couple of days though. Between the questions she suddenly had about her son, and the events that had taken place at the carnival, things had certainly turned interesting.

Her gaze slid to Marcus and she noted his pallor. She had seen him feed several times while he was going through the worst of the healing, but he obviously needed more. "You need to feed again."

"Yeah. The problem is there's no more blood in the refrigerator and it will take some time to get more delivered," he said, sounding weary.

Divine arched an eyebrow with disapproval. "You know bagged blood is like junk food for immortals, don't you?"

Marcus's eyes widened slightly. "Where did you hear that?"

"From Ab— a friend," she corrected quickly, and then shrugged. "Most of the nutrients are destroyed once they leave the body, and the longer it's refrigerated, the less good the blood does. It's like drinking from a dead person. Pretty much useless."

Marcus frowned. "I'm sorry, but your friend was misinformed, Divine. If what he said was true, mortals couldn't use bagged blood for transfusions and such. As long as the blood is kept at the proper temperature, it still holds on to its nutrients. It's as good as getting the blood straight from the source." He hesitated and then added solemnly, "That's why immortals are restricted to bagged blood now. It's just as nutritious, but doesn't carry the risk of discovery like biting mortals does."

"Immortals are restricted to bagged blood?" she asked with surprise.

He nodded and walked slowly back to join her behind the vehicle. "Except in cases of emergency, we aren't supposed to consume anything but bagged blood."

Divine frowned at this news. "And if they do?"

"They're considered rogue," he said quietly. "At least they are here in the U.S. and in Canada. Feeding off the hoof is still allowed in Europe and some other places, but even there it's frowned on more and more."

Divine sank to sit on the end of the SUV. She hadn't realized they had made that rule. She hadn't realized that bagged blood could even sustain them. Abaddon had said— Divine closed her eyes and bowed her head. She should have known better than to trust anything Abaddon said, and normally she was skeptical of everything he told her, but it had sounded so logical. Not that it would have made much difference. She didn't have access to blood banks and would have been forced to feed off the hoof anyway. That thought made her glance to him curiously. "So, what do immortals do? Rob blood banks or something?"

Marcus smiled crookedly at the question and shook his head. "They run their own blood banks. They collect the blood, and immortals purchase it like a mortal would buy steak or potatoes at a grocery store."

"They actually *sell* it in stores?" Divine asked with surprise.

"No, of course not. Immortals order it and it's delivered to their residence or where they're staying," he said with amusement.

"Oh," Divine murmured. "So how do you order it?"

"Argeneau Enterprises runs the blood banks and distribution of—"

"Of course they do," she said on a sigh and stood to walk around to the driver's seat. If the Argeneaus were involved in the distribution, she couldn't risk ordering it and drawing attention to herself. She would just have to continue on as she was going. It was a bit distressing to think that she was considered rogue now though.

Well, she'd been considered rogue before this, Divine supposed, but unfairly in her opinion. This, however . . . well, she knew the rule and could order the blood, but was choosing not to, so she supposed she truly was rogue now.

"Come on," she said, slipping into the driver's seat.

Marcus closed the back door and walked around to get in the front passenger side. "Where are we going?"

Divine paused, and then asked, "How long would it take you to get blood delivered to you?"

Marcus grimaced, and shook his head. "Bastien said to let him know when I was down to a couple days' supply because it would take him that long to get fresh blood to me."

Divine nodded and turned forward to start the engine, "Well then, we're going to find you donors. You can't wait two days for bagged blood, you're pale and sweating. I'd guess you're in pain too?"

He nodded reluctantly when she glanced over. "Yes, but—"

"There are no buts here, Marco. You need blood and this is an emergency. You haven't seen yourself. You've healed to the point of scarring, but the burn scars aren't going away. The nanos don't have enough blood to work with. They're obviously trying to find it though." She peered at him solemnly as he felt his face, and then leaned over to flip down the visor so that he could see himself in the mirror on the underside.

Marcus winced in shock at the sight of his own scarred flesh.

"It's an emergency," Divine repeated grimly. "The nanos still have a lot of work to do. You're going to be brainless with bloodlust pretty quickly if we don't get some blood into you." She flipped the visor back up again and shifted the car into gear. "So, we find you a donor."

"Yeah, all right," he agreed reluctantly. "But I should call that order in right now too."

"You must have lost your phone in the RV or while escaping it," Divine said as she noted him searching his pockets. "It's not on you."

"How do you know?" Marcus asked suspiciously.

"Because I searched your pockets for cash when I stopped for gas," she admitted quietly. "I didn't have enough on me to fill this gas guzzler and didn't want to steal the fuel. Fortunately, you had your wallet still. But I found it in the last pocket I searched and didn't come across a phone, so—" She shrugged as she turned off the dirt track and onto an actual road. "You don't have it on you."

"My wallet?" Marcus asked, suddenly looking wary, and Divine smiled.

"Afraid while looking for money I spotted your credit cards and driver's license and noticed that your name is Marcus Notte, not Marco Smith?" she asked with amusement. When he appeared at a loss as to how to address that, she shook her head and said lightly, "There's no need to look so guilty. Lots of people use fake names when they join the carnival."

Marcus grunted at that and seemed to relax in the seat, although his hands were still clenched as he battled the pain he was struggling with. After a moment, he offered a weary "Thank you again for taking care of me."

"It's not like I had anything better to do," Divine said wryly, her attention mostly on her driving. "My home and business were both destroyed in the fire, as was the money I keep at hand. I'll have to wait until Monday to get enough cash to buy another RV and start over." She glanced over with a touch of amusement curving her lips and added, "That means I'm at your disposal for the next day at least."

"Lucky me," Marcus said quietly, and it didn't sound like sarcasm. But then he probably was thinking it was lucky, Divine supposed. After all, his job was to discover if she was Basha Argeneau, and no doubt having her at his side for the next twenty-four hours could only help in that endeavor.

"Divine?"

"Hmm?" she murmured, her attention already split between driving and trying to decide where best to go to find him the blood he needed. It was Saturday night. Well, Sunday morning really, she acknowledged, glancing at the dashboard clock that read 12:30. A big city was always her preference. She could go to bars there and easily lure a man or three outside for a little bite, one at a time, of course. But big cities weren't always easily accessible from carnival locations that sometimes set up in mid-sized or even the occasional small town. No one, mortal and immortal alike, wanted to drive for hours for a meal, and she was sometimes forced to feed in more rural areas. In those cases, she tended to pick homes well away from the general population—farms that were mostly self-sufficient and where the inhabitants didn't have to go into town every single day. It made getting caught less likely.

That had been her trick with Marcus while he was healing. Leaving him in a bar parking lot while she went in to fetch out donors for him hadn't seemed practical. His screaming wouldn't allow for that. She'd had to find a nice healthy family out in the boonies. Actually, she'd ended up having to find two healthy families in the boonies. That was her fault. She obviously hadn't thought ahead when she'd brought the first donors to him. Marcus had been so desperate for blood he'd attacked with a speed and need that was disconcerting. Divine had controlled the girl's mind so she wouldn't feel the pain of the assault or even be aware of it, which was much easier than trying to erase the memory of it afterward.

However, when she'd judged that he'd taken enough from that first donor and tried to get Marcus to stop, he hadn't been able or willing to. Caught up in his blood-lust, Divine hadn't been able to pull him off. She'd ended up having to bash him over the head with a tire iron she'd found in the back of the vehicle to make him stop. That had happened three times before Divine had wised up. Fortunately that last time he'd managed to hurt himself while trying to hurt her and had knocked himself out. It had been Saturday morning by then and she'd driven into town to a huge hardware outlet to buy the thickest chain they had. Marcus had still been un-conscious when she'd returned to the SUV. Fortunately, the parking lot had been mostly empty, so she'd risked being seen and had chained him up to the refrigera-tor then before driving back out to the country to fetch another donor.

Marcus being chained had made it all much easier. Divine hadn't had to hit him with the tire iron again after that, which was definitely a good thing. Every time she'd hit him, she'd given the nanos in his body more damage to repair, which meant more blood needed. She'd been creating something of a vicious circle that way.

"I'm having some unpleasant memories," Marcus said tentatively.

Divine glanced to him at that comment, and then turned forward again. "I'm not surprised. Being broiled in an RV can't be pleasant."

"No, not about that," he said quietly. "These memo-ries are kind of fuzzy, but I—did I attack people?"

Divine grimaced. If he had switched to bagged blood when it first came out, it meant he hadn't hunted much since the advent of blood banks. She doubted he was used to it anymore. What was more, though, was that his feedings had been rather horrific. He really had been mindless. If he'd been aware of his donors as living beings, it had been hard to tell by the way he'd ripped into their flesh. She could hardly say that to him though, so said instead, "I brought you donors, and yes, you were a bit enthusiastic, but that was to be expected after what you'd gone through."

"So I didn't hurt anyone?" he asked with a frown.

"I controlled your donors for you. They won't remember anything," she assured him quietly.

"So I did hurt them," he said unhappily.

Divine hesitated. "They will all be fine. You took a little more blood than I was comfortable with from the first donor, but that was my fault. I should have expected that reaction. You were in serious need and a great deal of pain. Besides, when I couldn't get you to release her, I . . . er . . ." She sighed and admitted, "I bashed you over the head with a tire iron."

She sense rather than saw the sharp glance he turned on her.

"It worked," she said unapologetically. "You released her and it was in time. She is probably a little weak and anemic this morning, but otherwise fine."

Marcus cursed and sank unhappily back in his seat. When she glanced to him in question, he grimaced. "I remember it now. I acted like an animal." He stared out the window with dissatisfaction for a moment and then shifted uncomfortably and said, "It's disturbing to realize just how thin the veneer of civilization is. We're really just animals under the polite face we offer society."

"It isn't just us. Starve a mortal for a week or two and then give him a chicken leg and he'll eat like an animal too, tearing at the flesh, fluids running down his cheeks, hands soaked in grease," she said quietly. "Survival is a strong instinct . . . You didn't do anything to be ashamed of."

Marcus was silent for a moment and then sighed out the words, "Thank you."

Divine glanced at him with surprise. "For what now?"

"For . . . everything," he said with a weary smile.

"Even mopping you in the groin?" she asked with amusement.

"Well, that I could have done without," Marcus said with a crooked smile. "But I did deserve it." He turned to peer at her through the dark interior of the car. "Where were you when the fire started?"

"In town," she admitted, and her mouth tightened. "I came back to find the RV fully engulfed by flames and carnies running around trying to beat the fire back from the door far enough to get in and search for me."

"They would have done that?" Marcus asked with amazement.

"Carnies are like family," Divine said quietly, and then her lips tipped with a crooked smile and she added, "A totally dysfunctional one maybe, but—"

"So, your average family then," he teased, but she

could hear the pain in his voice. The man was suffering. She really needed to figure out where to find him blood. Divine could do with some herself. Marcus hadn't just attacked the donors she'd brought. When she'd tried to stop him feeding, and then gone about the business of chaining him up, he'd gotten rather aggressive with her. Divine hadn't taken it personally. She'd known he didn't know what he was doing. Still, she'd taken a couple of deep wounds in the process. They'd healed quickly enough, but it meant she was down a couple pints or four, and now she was in need of blood again too.

The problem was, now that Divine knew that feeding on mortals was against the rules, she was reluctant to do it, even in an emergency like this.

"So who is trying to kill you, Madame Divine?"

Nine

Divine stiffened.

He'd caught her by surprise with that question, so much so that she glanced at him sharply, turning the steering wheel as she did and sending the SUV swerving. Once she had the vehicle back under control, Divine forced herself to relax and asked, "What are you talking about?"

"You were attacked that first night after we returned from looking for Hal and Carl. Judging by the amount of blood and other matter in the RV and on your clothes, you were injured pretty badly too," he said quietly. "And now someone has set your RV on fire."

"The fire was set?" she asked quietly, a frown curving her lips.

"You thought it was an accident?" he asked dryly.

Divine blew out a long breath, and then admitted, "I haven't had much time to worry about it." She was now though. Frowning, she asked, "What happened?"

"I woke up, heard a noise, someone opened the door. I could smell it wasn't you." Marcus smiled faintly when she glanced to him with surprise. "You smell like roses and vanilla. They were more musky, male."

"Did you see them?" she asked worriedly.

"No," Marcus admitted. "By the time I realized it wasn't you and opened my eyes, they had already closed the door. I got up and started through the RV and I was in the lounge when there were suddenly flames outside the windows. He must have poured gas around it before coming inside. That or there was more than one and once culprit number one had assured him that you were inside, culprit number two lit it up."

"But I wasn't inside. You were," Divine pointed out.

"I was covered by the comforter, my head turned to the side. All they probably saw was fair hair sticking out of the top of the comforter. If he even saw that. All he could probably make out was that someone was in the bed. There were no lights on in the RV," he pointed out.

Divine nodded, but couldn't help thinking that if the he or they in question was an immortal, they would have seen more than Marcus thought.

"Do you think it could have been the husband?"

She glanced to him with surprise. "You mean Mr. Planned-to-Kill-His-Wife?"

Marcus nodded.

Divine thought about it. She hadn't considered that the little weasel might have the courage to do something like this. She still wasn't sure he had. It was possible though.

Spotting the lights of a gas station on the roadside ahead, Divine slowed.

"They have a vacuum station," Marcus pointed out.

"And a public washroom." Divine pulled in and slid to a halt next to the station entrance. "You can clean up and grab a snack while I vacuum out the back."

Marcus had reached into the back for the duffel bag on the bench seat, but paused at her comment.

"You need to feed," she said quietly. "Better that you do it while you still have it under control."

He let out a slow breath, and nodded solemnly as he finished grabbing his bag. "Leave the vacuuming. I'll do it when I come out."

"Sure," Divine said easily as he got out. He closed the door and went into the store, coming back out a moment later with the washroom key in hand. Divine watched until he slid into the bathroom, and then drove over to the vacuum station. There was change and small bills in the cup holder in the center of the SUV between the front seats, and Divine grabbed a handful of it and slid out. A moment later she had the back door open, the vacuum going, and was cleaning up the mess in the back of the SUV. There was a lot of mess. Divine was only halfway through the task when Marcus appeared beside her.

"I said I'd do this," Marcus said with exasperation, taking the vacuum hose from her.

"You can finish it while I use the restroom," she said with a shrug, and then turned to head for the gas station entrance to get the key he'd just returned. One look at the lone gas station attendant and Divine knew

Marcus hadn't fed. She supposed she could have fed on him herself, but found she just couldn't do it. If bagged blood was as good as getting it off the hoof . . . and if Marcus, who needed it more than she did, hadn't fed on the man . . .

It looked like they were going to have to find some bagged blood, she thought grimly as she headed around to the washroom door on the side of the building. Divine didn't have to go to the bathroom, but she did want to splash some water on her face and maybe wake herself up a bit. She was exhausted, but had a bit of a drive ahead. She had no idea where the nearest blood bank was, but suspected she'd have to drive into San Bernardino to find one.

Marcus was done with the vacuuming and on the pay phone outside the station when Divine came back around the building. She stiffened at the sight, but continued past him to return the key. He was hanging up when she came back out.

"We're in luck," he said, stepping away from the phone as she approached.

"Are we?" Divine asked mildly.

"Yeah. We aren't far from Los Angeles. There's a family friend who lives outside the city. His place is only about half an hour from here. He can give us some bagged blood to tide us over until Bastien can get more out to us."

"Us?" she queried carefully.

"I explained that the fire no doubt destroyed everything you had on hand too and you would need a fresh supply as well," Marcus said solemnly.

Divine merely nodded and turned to walk toward the RV. She hadn't had any blood in her RV, and he knew that. He had to know that from her reaction to just the sight of the bagged blood, but he'd covered for her. She wasn't sure what to make of that.

"I'll drive," Marcus said when she automatically headed for the driver's side. "You probably didn't get much sleep while watching over me, and I'm definitely not going to sleep. You may as well get some rest on the way. Besides, I know the way and you don't."

Divine merely nodded and shifted direction, heading for the passenger side instead. She was aware that Marcus was following her, and was confused by it until he opened the passenger door for her.

"Thank you," she murmured self-consciously, stepping up into the vehicle.

"My pleasure," Marcus murmured and closed the door.

Divine shook her head, and simply strapped on her seat belt. She wasn't used to being treated like . . . well, like a lady. She had been independent for so long, really living more like a man than a woman for most of her life. From the time she'd been able to lead her own life she'd . . . well, she'd been on her own. Carrying her own weight and sometimes the weight of others. She'd opened her own doors, found her own meals, paid her own way. She wasn't used to someone else arranging for her meals, and opening doors. She wasn't sure how to handle it.

"The seat adjusts," Marcus announced as he slid into the driver's seat. "It reclines, the lumbar support adjusts, and the head raises and lowers. Here I'll show you," he added when Divine glanced at him blankly.

She sucked in her breath and plastered herself backward into the seat when Marcus suddenly reached across her and down to the buttons on the outside of the passenger seat. Her seat slowly reclined, far too slowly in her opinion, since he remained draped across her the whole while. Once she was nearly flat on her back, he took her hand and led it down to the buttons.

"This one lifts and lowers the bottom part of your seat. This one raises and lowers your headrest. This one moves you back and forth if you shift it back and forth, but raises and lowers you if you turn it this—"

"I've got it," Divine gasped out, desperate to get him off her. The man must have done some serious cleaning up in the restroom at the gas station. He'd changed his clothes, but must also have performed a standing wash in the sink. That was her guess. Marcus smelled clean and masculine without even a whiff of the scorched skin smell of earlier and she found it a bit distressing for some reason.

Marcus raised an eyebrow at her breathy words, but straightened and did up his own seat belt. As he started the engine, he said, "Just relax. We'll be there in a jiffy and then both of us can feed and get some proper sleep."

Divine murmured in the affirmative, and then leaned back and closed her eyes. Despite that, she was positive she wouldn't sleep a wink. Despite the stress and exhaustion she'd been suffering for the last twenty-four hours, she was too wound up to sleep. The problem was, she couldn't figure out the reason for being wound up, except that it seemed to increase every time he got close to her. Weird, was Divine's last thought before that sleep she was sure she couldn't achieve overtook her.

Marcus found his gaze repeatedly shifting from the road to Divine as he drove. She'd fallen asleep quickly after heading out of the gas station, but then she'd looked exhausted when he'd woken up. He'd guess she hadn't slept at all since coming back to find her RV on fire. She'd been taking care of him instead and that was something Marcus wasn't used to. He'd spent most of his life looking out for others. As a boy, his grandfather had taken him aside and charged him with the task of looking out for his uncle Julius. Despite being his uncle, Julius was actually two years younger than he. The pair had grown up together and had already been as close as brothers when his grandfather had made the request, but Marcus had taken it seriously. His grandfather had never said why he should look out for Julius, or who might be a threat to him, but that hadn't mattered, Marcus had taken his charge to heart and acted as friend and bodyguard for centuries after that.

At least, he had until Julius's son, Christian, was born. There had been some nasty business when the boy was young, and Julius had asked Marcus to look out for his son. He hadn't had to ask twice. Marcus had then become Christian's confidant and guardian, accompanying him everywhere and helping to guide him through life, keeping him safe as he did. The necessity for that had ended when Julius had connected with his life mate, Marguerite. The dangers their grandfather had worried about for Julius, and that Julius had later worried about for his own son, had been revealed and taken care of. Neither Julius nor Christian needed protecting any longer. Marcus had suddenly found himself without a charge to look after . . . which had been incredibly strange for him. Marcus had felt a little lost and useless after that.

It was Marguerite Argeneau who had noticed his change in behavior and sudden lack of energy and had told him he was suffering what the mortals called "empty nest" syndrome. He was like a stay-at-home mother whose offspring have all grown up and left the nest, leaving him feeling unneeded. She'd then told him that Lucian had a personal issue he needed help with, a relative who might or might not be rogue that he was trying to find. Perhaps he could help Lucian find this individual, she'd said. At least it would give Marcus something to occupy his mind and time with while he adjusted to the change in situation.

Marcus had balked at the very suggestion that he was acting like a mortal housewife, but the idea of helping Lucian find this family member had held some appeal. Being useful to anyone at that point had seemed appealing. Not that he hadn't had a job. He always had a job when he wanted it. The family business, Notte Enterprises, had many arms and he could have worked in any one of them if he chose. In fact, he had filled in for Julius quite a bit the last few years as Julius had adjusted to life with his life mate, but Julius had adjusted quite well now, and Marcus wasn't really needed there.

Lucian, on the other hand, needed him, though he suspected the man would never say as much. This Basha Argeneau was someone he obviously very dearly wanted to find. He knew that because Lucian had been so cold in explaining things to him, and he'd found that with Lucian, the colder he was, the more important something was to him. It was like he had to divorce himself from all emotion to be able to deal with issues that touched closest to him. At least with issues where he feared the outcome wouldn't be a happy one. Lucian simply could not divorce himself from emotion when it came to his life mate, Leigh, but Marcus knew he'd done that with his brother Jeanne Claude, when he'd learned that the man was feeding off mortals . . . and he was doing it again with Basha. He was also keeping his cards close to the vest in this situation. All Marcus knew about Basha was that she was his niece by a deceased brother. That she'd gone missing a very long time ago, and that her name had popped up in relation to Leonius Livius II, a rogue no-fanger who liked to feed on living mortals rather than make do with bagged blood. Those mortals often didn't end up living when he was done with them.

As far as Marcus could tell, Lucian wasn't even sure if the Basha in question was the niece who had gone missing so long ago. But he feared she was from the information he'd been given by one of Leonius's sons, Ernie, and from Dee, a half-crazed mortal who had been traveling with Ernie.

Ernie had claimed she was Lucian's niece, but Lucian couldn't seem to believe the girl he knew would be tangled up with the likes of Leonius Livius II. Either way, he wanted the woman found and brought to him.

Marcus glanced to Divine again and wondered if she was the woman in question. It was hard to tell. There were no pictures of this Basha. They hadn't existed back in the days when she'd gone missing, and by the time someone had suggested getting a sketch artist to draw a rendition, Dee and Ernie were not available to help with it. The Council had had Dee's mind wiped, which had been the kindest thing to do for the girl, and Ernie . . . Well, the Council had already passed judgment and executed him.

In the end, it was Lucian who had worked with the sketch artist, but his memories of her were from more than two millennia ago. She'd been a young girl then, somewhere in her early teens by Marcus's guess. They'd found someone to age the image, made up copies of the new picture, and had sent them out with every delivery of blood Argeneau Enterprises had sent out. Attached to the picture had been a letter requesting that anyone spotting this woman should please contact Argeneau Enterprises. There had apparently been countless calls, and Lucian had several people checking out the information gathered. Marcus was one of them. The call he was following up on had come from an immortal in Nevada who had visited the carnival some years ago and had spotted a fortune-teller named "Madame something or other" there, who he thought looked "kind of like the image."

Marcus had gone to Nevada to interview the individual and find out what carnival, but the man didn't know the name. He'd never troubled himself to find out, but he did give Marcus the date he'd attended it. Armed with that and the town name, Marcus had been able to find out for himself. The only problem was, once he'd tracked down the carnival and caught up to them, he was told that their fortune-teller, Madame Divine, had left a couple years back to join another carnival and they didn't know the name of it.

This had forced Marcus to begin checking every carnival that had a fortune-teller. He'd been amazed at just how many carnival companies there were operating in the States, and had slowly been visiting each one. So far, he'd come across three immortals traveling with carnivals. One was a male who had been skittish as hell and had left the minute Marcus arrived, which made him think he should mention the man to Lucian. Traveling with a carnival would be a good way for a rogue to hide. The second immortal had been female. She also happened to be a fortune-teller like Divine, but had looked nothing like the sketch. Divine was the third immortal, also a fortune-teller. However, she did look a little like the sketch. At least, he thought she might if she was blond. He wasn't sure. Until he was, Marcus had to stick around and find out.

His gaze slid to her again and his mouth twisted with displeasure. At this point, he was really hoping she wasn't Basha. He liked Divine. He also found he wanted Divine. And he couldn't read or control her, but had started eating. He'd eaten that cotton candy the other day while distracted, and then a candy apple the afternoon of the fire when one of the girls, a greenie like himself, had stopped by the Tilt-A-Whirl to flirt and had offered it to him. The damned thing had looked delicious and his stomach had growled at the very sight, and before he'd known what he was doing Marcus had taken the apple with a muttered thank-you and bit into it.

That apple had been the most delicious damned thing he'd tasted in centuries. Juicy, sweet and tart all at once . . . Damn, he'd eaten it down to the core.

It was looking pretty certain that Divine was his life mate.

If she was Basha too . . . well, that was just a complication he didn't need.

Sighing, Marcus turned into Vincent Argeneau's driveway, stopped at the gate, and hit the switch to unroll his window. Rather than press the button announcing their arrival, however, Marcus reached over to gently nudge Divine.

"We're here," he announced quietly when she blinked her eyes open with confusion.

"I fell asleep." She sounded surprised, and Marcus smiled.

"You're exhausted. I could see that when I woke up. You need sleep."

"Thanks," she said dryly. "You really know how to charm a girl."

"Sorry," he muttered, realizing just how unflattering his words must have sounded. He hadn't meant them that way. The woman was beautiful to him, even with her hair a mess, her face pale, and huge black bags under her eyes. He suspected she could stand in front of him wearing a potato sack and covered in mud and he'd still think she was beautiful . . . and that was a bit alarming.

Turning, Marcus pushed the button on the intercom on a post several feet from the closed gate to the driveway and then waited.

"Yes?" It was a woman's voice. Probably Jackie, Vincent's wife and life mate, Marcus thought as he gave his name.

"Come on up! We're ready," Jackie said, sounding almost painfully cheerful. It seemed obvious that Bastien had warned them about his traveling companion. Jackie was a private investigator before she married Vincent Argeneau and still was as far as he knew. She would be all over this like white on rice, doing everything she could to sort out if Divine was this Basha that Lucian was looking for . . . and that thought worried Marcus.

Pushing the worry aside for now, he slid his foot from the brake to the gas as the gate began to slide open.

Ten

Divine peered curiously around as they headed up the driveway, her eyebrows rising as they got past the gate and she could actually see the house bathed in early morning sunlight. Two stories and huge, it was much more than she'd expected. This "family friend" was obviously the successful type. But then he hadn't been hampered by having to slide by under the radar, Divine told herself. Besides, she might not have a big house and such, but she had saved up quite a bit of money over the years. She wasn't exactly poor. She just couldn't afford to draw attention to herself by throwing money around, so lived conservatively.

It would have been nice to have a real home though, Divine acknowledged sadly as she peered over the curtained windows and well-tended gardens. The kind of home that had a plot of land rather than an RV that moved every couple days, always sitting on rented land.

But Divine had given up that dream long ago. Staying in one place was dangerous. Constant movement helped prevent capture.

Marcus pulled to a halt in front of the house, and turned off the engine. Glancing to her as he opened his door, he said, "Shall we?"

Divine's eyes widened with surprise. "I was just going to wait in the SUV while you went in to get the blood from your friends."

Marcus hesitated and then pulled his door closed. Turning to face her, he said solemnly, "Bastien is having the blood delivered here, but it won't get here until possibly tomorrow, tonight at the latest. Vincent and Jackie offered to put us up until then. They're going to feed us and give us rooms to sleep in."

Divine frowned at this news. She hadn't signed up for all of that. She wasn't used to depending on others, and wasn't comfortable doing so now. "I have to get back to the carnival, Marcus. Madge will be worried about me. I haven't had a chance to call yet. And I have to get money out of the bank, buy a new RV, and set it up for customers. They count on me to—"

"You can call or text Madge from the house. I'm sure Vincent will be happy to let you use the phone. And you can't buy a new RV until you can get to the money. It's Sunday. The banks are all closed. So that will have to wait until tomorrow anyway." Reaching out, he took her hands and said gently, "You need blood and a place to rest. Both of those are waiting just through that door."

Divine turned and peered at the door in question, but

still hesitated. Finally, she said, "Tell me about these friends of yours."

Marcus hesitated, and then said, "Well, their names are Vincent Argeneau and Jackie Morrisey Argeneau. They're life mates who found each other about four years ago."

Divine stiffened in her seat, her heart suddenly thumping like a scared rabbit's in her chest. Argeneau? He'd brought her to the home of an Argeneau? His family friends were Argeneaus? Who were they? How were they connected to her? Dear God, she was sitting outside the lion's den like a lamb waiting for slaughter.

"Jackie was born mortal and was turned less than five years ago . . . by a rogue," he added quietly. "Which was fortunate, because Vincent had used up his turn to save a cousin of mine."

Divine swallowed. Jackie was a mortal? That was good. Jackie wouldn't be able to read her, and wasn't likely to be a threat. However . . . "How old is Vincent?"

Marcus grimaced and then admitted, "I'm not sure. I think he's about four or five hundred years old."

"A baby," Divine murmured, relaxing a little. Neither of them would be able to read her. If she just continued to act as if there was nothing wrong, surely they wouldn't know who she was? She wondered though who his parents were, and if she'd ever met them. And she wondered if she'd even recall his parents if she had met them. It had been a long time ago that she'd lived with her grandparents. Uncle Lucian had been around a lot, and his twin too, though she couldn't remember his name. She hadn't much liked the man. She remembered an Aunt Marta or Martine, and a couple of other uncles visiting at one time or another, but those were not memories she had held on to. She'd done her best to forget that time of her life once she'd realized she could never return to it.

And yet, here she was, about to meet a relative, and Divine found herself oddly numb about the whole thing. This man was probably a cousin or something to her, but she didn't feel like she was about to meet family. He was a stranger to her whether he carried the same last name as she'd once had or not.

"Vincent has a company with diversified interests, but his main interest is in the theater," Marcus continued. "He produces plays. He used to act in them too, but I gather he's kind of dropped out of that since meeting Jackie."

An actor, Divine thought, relaxing a little more. Neither of them was sounding very threatening, and surely it couldn't hurt to stay here for one night? She was exhausted, and sleeping in a bed rather than the SUV was sounding mighty attractive. Sighing, Divine nodded and tugged her hands free of his hold. His touch was oddly disturbing.

"Fine. One night," she said quietly, reaching for her door. "But tomorrow, I have to visit a bank and someplace that sells RVs."

"I'll take you to both myself," he assured her, getting out on his side as she opened her own door and slid out.

"To both what?"

Divine turned at that cheerful question and found

herself peering at a well-dressed blond woman who was short and curvy, with intelligent eyes presently brimming with curiosity.

"Jackie," Marcus said with a nod of greeting as he came around the truck. Turning to Divine he said, "This is Jackie Morrisey Argeneau. Vincent's wife." Turning back to the woman, he added, "Jackie, this is Divine."

Jackie smiled and offered a hand in greeting, but asked, "Just Divine?"

"It's Madame Divine, but Divine will do," she said mildly.

"Right," Jackie said slowly, her eyes narrowing briefly. But then she smiled and turned to Marcus. "So what is this *both* you will take Divine to yourself?"

"Oh." He smiled crookedly. "Divine's RV burned up two nights ago and she needs to buy a new one. We'll have to hit a bank and RV place tomorrow,"

Divine noted the shock and dismay on Jackie's face as she took in what the fire had done to Marcus's face and found herself peering at him closely. She'd somehow forgotten that his face still bore the ravages of the fire. In the form of scars, but it was still ravaged.

"Dear God, Marcus." That comment, just as horrified as Jackie's expression, drew Divine's gaze to a male immortal just coming out of the house. He was as dark as the woman was fair, his face holding chiseled features and the striking silver-blue eyes of an Argeneau. He was also obviously aghast at the state of Marcus at the moment.

"You were in the RV at the time," Jackie said, and it

wasn't a question. Her gaze then turned to Divine and narrowed. "But you weren't."

"No. I wasn't," Divine said, her voice cool at the suspicion in the woman's eyes. "I was in town and returned to find the RV in flames and Marcus hiding in the cotton candy trailer."

"She helped me to the SUV and got me out of there," Marcus said quickly, drawing the couple's attention his way again. "She's been taking care of me for the last twenty-four hours, and managed to find me a couple of donors to help get the healing started. But I obviously need more blood to finish, and she needs blood too, but neither of us were comfortable feeding off the hoof once the worst of the healing was done."

Divine's gaze flickered at his words. She hadn't been uncomfortable with his feeding off the hoof, although she had found herself reluctant to feed that way now that she knew she wasn't supposed to. His neglecting to feed off the gas station attendant despite the agony she knew he must be in had made her reluctant to feed off the attendant herself despite the gnawing in her stomach. Still, she hadn't mentioned her reluctance to Marcus and wondered if he had been able to somehow recognize it, or was just saying that for the couple's benefit.

"Well, we had a fresh delivery yesterday so have lots of blood on hand at the moment," Vincent said cheerfully, drawing Divine's attention back to the couple in time to see Jackie peering at her intently. She wondered about that as Vincent continued, "So come on inside. It's bed and blood for the two of you. It looks like you both need it."

"Thank you," Marcus said solemnly, taking Divine's arm.

She was about to shake off his hold, but then realized he wasn't trying to control her, just taking her arm to walk her inside in what would be considered a gentlemanly fashion. She really wasn't used to this kind of treatment.

"Come, the kitchen is this way," Jackie said brightly, leading them down the hall as Vincent turned to lock the front door. It seemed they were security conscious, she noted, and wondered about that.

Marcus released Divine's arm and shifted his hand to her back as they followed the young woman. Divine had to grit her teeth to hold back the shiver the touch inspired.

"We have loads of blood, so don't be shy. Besides, Bastien is sending more, remember," Jackie reminded them as she led them into the large bright kitchen at the end of the hall.

Divine watched Jackie move to a refrigerator and open it to peer inside, but then turned her gaze over the kitchen. It was probably every mortal's dream kitchen; lots of cupboards, a kitchen table, a large island with stools around it, and one wall made up of large windows and French doors that overlooked a pool. She eyed the pool with interest. Divine had loved to swim since she was a small child and it had come naturally to her. They used to say she was swimming before she was walking, although she didn't know if that were true.

"Here you go."

Divine turned to see that Jackie had retrieved half a dozen bags of blood and was holding one out to her.

"Thank you," she murmured, accepting the offering. But she just held it. When she glanced to Marcus and saw that Jackie had already given him a bag, two in fact, and that he had opened his mouth and was raising one to his descending teeth, her eyes widened with alarm. "Wait. Marcus, maybe you should—"

She didn't bother to finish. The bag was already fastened to his teeth and draining so fast it would have been empty before she could finish speaking.

"Is something wrong?" Jackie asked as Vincent entered the kitchen.

"Oh dear," he murmured, taking in the situation.

"What?" Jackie asked with bewilderment as Marcus dragged the now empty bag from his teeth, alarm on his own face.

"I didn't think," he gasped apologetically, and had barely finished saying it when he cried out and dropped to his knees.

Divine sighed and handed her bag back to Jackie as she knelt next to Marcus. "Can you walk?"

His answer was a roar of pain as he reached for his face, both hands extended in claws.

Divine caught his hands before he could try to rip off his own face and looked to Vincent, yelling, "There's chain in the back of the SUV."

Nodding, he turned and rushed out of the kitchen.

"What's going on?" Jackie asked with alarm, shouting to be heard over Marcus. "He was fine a minute ago."

"That was before he had the blood," Divine snapped, blaming her for giving him the blood in the first place. But then recalling that the girl hadn't been an immortal long, and certainly situations like this didn't crop up every day, she dug deep for patience and as Marcus's screams dropped to a constant, ululating moan, explained, "The nanos are taking up the blood and rushing to try to finish their repairs. It will be excruciating. Marcus should have been chained or tied down before he was given blood."

"But then why did he drink it?" Jackie asked with dismay.

"He obviously wasn't thinking clearly," she said grimly.

"But he seemed fine," Jackie argued sounding a little shaky. "He was talking fine, and thinking fine . . . and you let him drive here," she pointed out, sounding accusatory.

"He *was* fine," Divine assured her grimly. "I wouldn't have let him drive otherwise, but—" Marcus managed to get one hand free of her hold, and she took a moment to grab it up again, before saying, "Look, when he woke up the last time it was because he was no longer in danger medically speaking, and the nanos needed more blood to finish healing him. They back off then, buzzing around inside the body, attacking nonessential organs like the bladder and kidneys in search of more blood—"

"Those are hardly nonessential organs," Jackie protested.

"They are for an immortal. Any damage done to

them will be reversed the moment the immortal gets more blood. In the meantime, the pain serves to tell the host that they need that blood. The nanos mostly leave the mind and limbs alone, though, until the necessary blood arrives. They are usually healed first anyway."

"Why?" Jackie asked at once.

"I presume because the brain and mobility may be needed for the host to get the blood the nanos need," Divine said through gritted teeth as she dragged Marcus's hands to clasp them against her chest and press them there. He'd nearly slipped her hold again, and she had no doubt that if he got loose he'd try to rip his own face off in a desperate bid to end the pain he was presently enduring. It wouldn't work, of course, but he wasn't exactly thinking clearly right now. All Marcus would be aware of at this point was the agony he was going through as the nanos set to work repairing the newly formed scars on his face. It probably felt like the flesh was on fire, or like they'd pressed red-hot frying pans to his face. Basically, a million little nanos were tearing away the damaged skin in tiny pieces and re-building fresh, baby-soft skin in its place.

"So the pain went away long enough for him to get the blood?" Jackie asked, sounding almost fascinated.

"Oh, he was still in pain, but it was a different kind of pain to this," she said, and spotting her expression, Divine sighed. "The pain when you're low on blood feels unbearable, right?"

Jackie nodded.

"Well, it isn't. We bear it, but it certainly inspires us to make sure we feed and that's the point. It's like a toothache or a really loud blaring alarm screaming nonstop. It's painful, constant, urging you to do something. In this case, feed. And it's distracting enough that you will feed no matter the pain you know it will cause once you do. Or maybe the pain is there to ensure you can't think clearly enough to recall the pain that will follow once you feed," she muttered. She knew all this only from experience after having lived so long. Divine did not have any scientific knowledge to back it up.

Shrugging, she said, "While the pain caused by the need to feed *feels* unbearable, the pain of healing actually *is* unbearable. Marcus won't be able to withstand it for long before he—" She paused abruptly as Marcus's moan turned into another long, loud shriek. His whole body vibrated briefly in her arms, his teeth snapping like a cornered dog in pain, and then he went abruptly limp as if someone had flipped a switch turning him off.

Divine stared down at his pale, scarred face and released a little sigh. Marcus had passed out, but who knew how long that would last. The pain would probably wake him in a bit and have him thrashing and screaming again. They had to move quickly to get him tied down so he wouldn't hurt himself. He'd simply prolong the healing if that happened. That concern uppermost in her mind, Divine shifted her hold on Marcus, and then stood up with him cradled in her arms.

Jackie stepped back, expression incredulous, and for a minute Divine thought the girl was such a newbie as an immortal that she didn't yet know her own strength now. She realized that wasn't the case though when Jackie said, "Your chest."

Divine glanced down and took brief note of the bloody rivulets in her chest where she'd trapped Marcus's hands. He'd clawed at her, digging into her chest to try to make her release him. She'd been aware of it at the time, but had ignored it. Sighing, she shrugged, "He did worse in the back of the SUV. I'll heal."

Swinging away toward the door, she asked, "Can you show me to the room you prepared for him?"

"Of course." Jackie hurried around her to get the door, held it for her, and then rushed past her again to lead her to and up the stairs. They were halfway up when Vincent hurried back through the front door, chains in hand.

"You should have told me he'd stashed them under the front seat. I looked everywhere before I found them there," Vincent reprimanded as he hurried toward the stairs.

"Sorry," Divine murmured, not bothering to explain that she had hid them there, not Marcus. She hadn't wanted him to wake up and see them and be reminded of the unpleasantness he'd suffered.

"Here, let me take him for you," Vincent offered, rushing up the stairs behind them.

"I'm—" Divine had meant to say she was good, but didn't get the chance to finish. Vincent had already handed the chains to Jackie and then took Marcus from her. He then hurried up the stairs, Jackie hard on his heels. Divine was left to follow.

Eleven

"You're awake."

Marcus had barely stirred when Vincent's overly cheerful voice finished rousing him from sleep. Opening his eyes, he stared briefly at the man standing beside the bed he lay in before glancing around the room. It was disturbingly cheerful, a bright yellow room lined with a wallpaper border of sunflowers. He closed his eyes with a sigh. "Yeah."

"How do you feel?" Vincent asked.

Marcus popped his eyes open again as his brain began to function. He was in a room in Vincent and Jackie's home, healing after a fire that had torched Divine's RV, he recalled.

"Where's Divine?" he asked abruptly, trying to sit up, only to have Vincent force him back down with one hand on his chest.

"Slow down, buddy. She's fine. Resting in her own

room. Now, tell me how you feel," Vincent insisted, withdrawing his restraining hand and straightening when Marcus stopped struggling to sit up.

Marcus almost barked out *Fine* as an automatic reply, but then thought better of it and took inventory. Nothing hurt, which was a relief. He had a serious case of dry mouth though, and while he wasn't suffering the pain of blood hunger, he was hungry . . . which was truly weird. He hadn't experienced that in quite a while.

"Hungry," he said finally.

Vincent nodded as if that were to be expected. "We could tell you were on the verge of waking up so Jackie went down to fetch you a drink and something to eat. She should be back in a minute."

"How could you tell I was on the verge of waking up?" Marcus asked curiously.

"You stopped moaning and thrashing hours ago and lay still as death since then," Vincent said dryly. "But about ten minutes ago you started shifting restlessly and talking in your sleep."

Marcus stiffened at this news. "Talking? What was I saying?"

"Something about ball busters," Vincent said with amusement. "It wasn't very intelligible for the most part."

Marcus grimaced and relaxed in the bed.

"I gather Divine did some damage to the old baby makers, huh?"

Marcus stiffened again, eyes sharp on the younger man. "Did Divine tell you that?"

Vincent shook his head solemnly. "I read the memory from your thoughts."

Marcus stared at him silently for a moment, his mind in an uproar. Vincent shouldn't be able to read him. The man was younger than he. The fact that Vincent could read him . . . well, that was another symptom of finding a life mate. Hunger, sex drive, and the inability to block your thoughts were all signs of a life mate's presence. Divine *was* his life mate.

"Damn," Marcus muttered finally, letting his head fall back and eyes close. "I was afraid of that."

"Yeah, I know."

Marcus scowled at the sympathetic words and opened his eyes again. "So? Can you read her too?"

"Yes," Vincent admitted, but Marcus didn't miss the reluctance in his voice.

"Yes, you can read her, and . . . what?" he asked quietly. When Vincent hesitated, he guessed, "She's Basha?"

"We're not sure one way or the other," Vincent admitted.

"What?" Marcus asked with disbelief, sitting up again.

Vincent pushed him back down almost automatically, his attention on his thoughts and trying to express them. "She has a very . . ." He paused, hesitated, and then tried again, "Her mind is rather . . ."

"Rather what?" Marcus snapped impatiently, sitting up again, only to have Vincent absently push him back flat in bed again as if it were little effort at all. He might be healed, but he obviously hadn't regained full strength yet if Vincent could handle him so easily, he thought with disgust, and then glanced sharply at Vincent as the man started to speak again.

"I've never been able to read someone as old as Divine appears to be," he said finally. "Her mind is . . ." Vincent grimaced and then said, "Well, frankly, it's a weird combination of almost anal organization and complete disorganization at the same time."

"How could she be both organized and disorganized?" Marcus demanded impatiently, sitting up again.

"It's weird, I'll admit," Vincent said, pushing him back in the bed once more, and then sitting down on the edge of the bed beside him and leaning his weight on his elbow on Marcus's stomach as if it were a pillow. The move ensured Marcus wouldn't rear up again, which was apparently the man's intent. But he looked damned pleased with himself as he did it. "But I think it might be a result of the length of her life."

"The length?" Marcus asked with a frown. "How old is she?"

Vincent shook his head. "Not sure, but she's old. There are memories in her head dating way back. She's spent her life always moving from one place to another, always amongst nomadic, mortal tribes. She's traveled with the Wu Hu, Huns, Magyars, Romani, carnies." He gave a crooked shrug, his elbow digging into Marcus's stomach. "There are far too many to list them all."

"Try," Marcus said dryly.

"What's more interesting," Vincent went on as if he hadn't spoken, "is that in every section or chapter of her life, she's had a different name that *was her name*. Now, and since she began traveling with carnies, it's been Madame Divine and the moment she became

Divine, she was no longer whoever she was in the previous chapter of her life. With the Romani it was Nuri, which means Gypsy, which is what the Romani are and how she's lived her whole life as far as I can tell."

"Nuri," Marcus murmured.

Vincent nodded. "As far as she was concerned that was her name while she traveled with the Romani and her previous name and life no longer existed." He pursed his lips and then commented, "It's almost dissociative."

Marcus scowled at the comment. "When did you get your psychology degree, Dr. Freud?"

"No degree yet," Vincent admitted cheerfully. "But I've been taking some night courses the last year or two and have a little psychology under my belt."

"There's nothing more dangerous in this world than 'a little' knowledge," Marcus growled.

Vincent heaved a dramatic sigh, showing his acting roots, and then perched his chin on the heel of his palm and arched one eyebrow. "Since you're obviously cranky, I shall skip to just the facts. She's in the next bedroom sleeping after her own bout with healing."

"What?" Marcus sat up abruptly, despite Vincent's weight on him. "Healing from what?"

"You shouldn't be up yet," Vincent said with a scowl as Marcus tossed his sheets and blankets aside and sat up on the side of the bed.

"Screw you," Marcus snapped, looking around for his clothes. "What is she healing from?"

"The wounds you gave her," Vincent said grimly as Marcus stood up.

That brought him up short and Marcus turned to stare at him wide-eyed as Vincent walked around the bed toward him. "Wounds I gave her?"

Nodding, the younger man gave him a push that sent him toppling to sit on the side of the bed again. Bending then, Vincent grabbed his now unresisting legs and lifted them onto the bed, turning him on it as he did. He then covered him up and announced. "You gouged out some nice striations on her chest after drinking the blood when you got here. I gather from what I read of her mind, those weren't the first injuries you gave her. While you were out of your head healing in the SUV, you did some serious damage. She was suffering and in serious need of blood herself, though we didn't realize that at first."

Finished tucking him in, Vincent sat on the side of the bed again, eyed him solemnly, and said, "The woman is very good at hiding her pain. And judging by some of the memories I caught glimpses of, it comes from practice."

"What does that mean?" Marcus asked with concern. "What did you see?"

The door opened then and they both glanced toward it to see Jackie walking in with a tray in hand. Marcus raised his head, his nose sniffing the air.

"I thought you'd be awake by now, I—" She paused abruptly, her gaze shooting to her husband as an alarm suddenly sounded in the house.

"What's that?" Marcus asked, sitting up abruptly.

"The security alarm. Someone's breached the gate," Jackie said grimly, turning toward the dresser with her burden.

Marcus didn't stay to watch her set it down, but leaped off the bed, and strode out of the room with Vincent hard on his heels.

"Where is she?" he growled, once in the hall.

"This one," Vincent said, leading him to the next door on the right. The man wasn't stupid enough to get between him and the woman in the room. He merely turned the knob and pushed the door open. Vincent then stepped back to allow Marcus to enter. It was a good thing too, since Marcus would have charged right over him in his bid to see that Divine was okay.

"Stay with her," Vincent said after glancing to the unconscious woman in the bed. "Jackie and I will check out the breach. We'll come back either when we catch someone or when it's all clear."

Marcus merely grunted, his attention on the restless woman in the bed. She wasn't screaming or thrashing, but she wasn't still either. Soft moans and murmurs of pain were leaving her lips and she was shifting this way and that in the bed, obviously still healing.

Vincent had said Marcus had hurt her, and the knowledge made him peer carefully over her face. When he didn't see anything there, he reached for the top of the blanket covering her and tugged it down, revealing the peasant blouse she still wore. Like the one from that morning, this one was stained with dry blood, but more disturbing to him were the scars on her chest. They were fading even as he watched, but were obviously from deep scoring. It was as if he'd tried to dig deep trenches in her chest. Marcus could only imagine how much pain he'd caused her. It made him wonder about the other injuries Vincent had mentioned his having caused her. What had he done to the poor woman while out of his head after the fire?

The question made him tug the blanket lower. He'd intended to get a look at her arms that rested at her sides under the blanket, but instead his attention was caught by an even larger bloodstain below her left breast. It was dry now but had blossomed around a hole through the material there. She'd obviously been stabbed with something.

How the hell had he missed this earlier and not questioned her? he wondered with dismay, and then, thinking back, recalled that she'd been wearing a leather jacket over the top when he'd woken up. *His* leather jacket, he thought now. The desert got chilly at night and she may have donned it for that reason, but it had done a fine job of hiding all of this too.

"All clear," Jackie announced, suddenly appearing in the door.

"Video shows two men climbing the fence and then fleeing when the alarm sounded. Good thing Jackie insisted on alarming the fence and yard as well as the house after that business when she was turned," Vincent added, pausing behind her, one hand on her shoulder.

Marcus glanced to the couple and nodded. He had been there for "that business" and wasn't surprised that Jackie had ramped up the security since then. The culprit who had attacked her might now be caught and taken care of, but an experience like that could haunt a person and make him more cautious. His gaze slid back to Divine, and he asked, "Did I do this to her?"

"You were out of your head," Vincent said at once, slipping past Jackie to move to his side. "She doesn't hold you responsible."

She might not, but he felt guilty as hell for it and asked grimly, "What did I stab her with?"

"I gather it was an arrow, or a bolt I guess," Vincent said, peering at the wound and then bending to tug the peasant blouse out of her skirt and up so that he could get a look at the wound. It was further along in healing than the striations in her chest.

"Where the hell did I get— Oh," Marcus ended on a mutter as he recalled the weapons box built into the floor beside the refrigerator. Every SUV had one; his held a gun, knife, and bows with specially made bolts, the tips painted with a drug strong enough to knock out an immortal, if only temporarily.

"I gather the two of you were struggling and you opened the weapons box, grabbed the first thing, and stabbed her. Fortunately, you stabbed her with the wrong end, and accidentally stuck yourself with the drugged tip while doing it," Vincent announced, straightening. "Which is probably a good thing. You passed out and she was able to get into town and buy chains, then chain you down before you came to."

Marcus grunted, and then muttered, "I'm surprised she didn't use them to stake and bake me out in the desert if I did all of this to her."

Vincent actually smiled faintly at the suggestion, but shook his head. "She doesn't seem the type."

"No, she doesn't," Jackie agreed, and when Marcus glanced to her, the woman added, "She was very caring with you when you passed out and we brought you up here. And the memories we can read suggest she's like that with everyone. Divine's a mothering type, taking care of and helping everyone she encounters." She paused briefly to peer at Divine's face and then frowned. "If she *is* Basha Argeneau, than I think Lucian must be wrong about her being rogue."

Marcus had been coming to the same conclusion himself, but had feared his decisions were biased by the fact that she was probably his life mate. Still, a woman who did what she could to help pretty much every mortal she encountered just didn't seem to be the type to hang out with and harbor an animal like Leonius Livius. She wouldn't align herself with a man who brutally sliced up and slaughtered whole families. Perhaps she wasn't Basha. That was a good thing.

They were all silent for a moment, each of them peering at Divine, and then Jackie said quietly, almost apologetically, "We need to sort out what is going on here. Who set the RV on fire? Were they after you or her? Is it likely it was the same people who broke in here? Could they have followed you?"

When Marcus frowned but didn't respond, Vincent said. "She's right, my friend. We need to know what we're dealing with here. Whether we need more people, more security, more weapons."

"Yes, yes, and yes," Marcus said at once. He definitely wanted anything and everything they could get here to keep Divine safe. Running one hand through his sleep-ruffled hair, he dropped to sit on the side of the bed and quickly began to recount everything that had happened since arriving at the carnival. He faltered, however, when he got to the part about his taking bagged blood to Divine, and barging into her RV with his offering without waiting for her to invite him. Just recalling what had happened then was enough to make him want to moan in remembered agony.

It was Vincent who said what he couldn't. "But she went at you with a mop for not waiting for permission to enter and burst one of your baby makers."

Marcus winced at the memory. "Yeah. Hurt like hell too."

"I can imagine," Vincent said, and Marcus noticed that he unconsciously squeezed his legs together as if his own baby makers were shriveling in sympathy.

A choked sound, suspiciously like a laugh, came from Jackie, and both men turned to glance at her with matching expressions of outrage.

"Having your ball busted is no laughing matter, Jackie," Vincent said with a frown.

"I'm sorry," she said at once, her expression truly apologetic, but then that expression slipped away and she gave a little laugh and said, "It's just—I mean, men are always calling women ball busters, and usually when they don't deserve it, and now Divine has actually *earned* the title and it's just . . . not funny at all," Jackie ended solemnly when she noted their expressions. Shaking her head, she added, "Definitely not funny."

"Hmm," Vincent muttered, not appearing mollified.

Jackie cleared her throat and said, "But she didn't mean to . . . er . . . bust your ball."

"No," Marcus acknowledged. "I don't think she did."

"And she took care of you afterward, putting you in her bed to heal," she pointed out.

"Yes, she did," Marcus agreed. "And that's where I was when a man entered the RV. At first I thought it was Divine and just laid there waiting for her to say or do something, but then I caught a whiff of the person and knew it definitely wasn't Divine."

"Did you see who it was?" Jackie asked, moving closer to the bed.

Marcus shook his head. "I opened my eyes when the door closed but they had gone. I got up to go after them then, intending to find out who it had been, and that's when the RV went up in flames."

"But they saw that it was you in the bed not Divine?" Jackie asked with a frown.

"I don't think so," Marcus said at once. "I was burrowed into the covers, most of my face even under it. Only my forehead and hair stuck out a bit and it was dark in there." He shook his head. "I'm pretty sure they didn't know who was in the bed. They probably noted the lump under the covers, presumed it was her, and left to set the fire."

"So two attacks on her in one day?" Vincent said thoughtfully.

"Two attacks in two nights," Marcus corrected. "I'm pretty sure she must have taken the head wound right after we returned from town Thursday night."

Jackie didn't look certain about this. "So you think what? That she was attacked on returning and somehow rode off on her motorcycle? You said she returned on it the next day, right?"

"Yeah." Marcus knew it didn't make sense. The amount of blood in the RV and dried in her hair had suggested a terrible wound. One she wouldn't have been able to walk away from, let alone jump on a motorcycle and ride away from. Besides, where had her attacker gone? What had they done while she was escaping? The motorcycle had been gone and the RV dark and silent when he'd got to it intending to return her helmet. It couldn't have taken him more than ten or fifteen minutes to get to her RV after she'd dropped him off. That wasn't a lot of time. Whatever had happened, had happened quickly. Glancing from Jackie to Vincent he asked, "Did you see anything about the attack in her memories?"

"No," Vincent admitted. "But then I wasn't really looking for anything specific, and as I said, her thoughts and memories are sort of organized and disorganized at the same time. She . . ."

When his voice trailed off, Marcus followed the man's gaze to Jackie to find her staring hard at Divine with concentration. She was reading her now, he realized and almost protested, but the donning horror on Jackie's face stopped him. He watched with a sickening knot growing in his stomach as Jackie paled, then flushed, then paled again, this time actually going a bloodless gray before she suddenly turned away and rushed for the bathroom.

"Well, that can't be good," Vincent muttered, hurrying after her as they heard her retching.

Marcus glanced back to Divine and then followed the couple. He watched silently as Vincent held Jackie's hair back as she lost whatever meal she'd last eaten. He waited as Vincent murmured soothing words and dampened a cloth to wash her now flushed face, then just as he was about to ask what she'd seen, Jackie glanced to him, swallowed, and, voice husky, said, "She isn't harboring Leonius. She's one of his victims and the man is an animal. Worse, a monster. The things he did to her, at least the little bit I saw . . ." She shook her head. "She'd never harbor someone like that. He—"

The rest of what she would have said was lost as she turned and retched into the toilet again.

Vincent immediately dropped the cloth he'd used to wipe her face, slid his arm around her shoulders again, and murmured soothingly as he held her hair back. Marcus turned away from the scene to peer at Divine in the bed, wondering what the hell Jackie had seen.

Twelve

Divine woke up making a strangled sound she recognized at once as a scream caught in her throat. She'd woken up like that many times over the years. She used to wake up like that daily, surfacing from nightmares that claimed her while she slept. But they'd waned over the centuries and millennia. She rarely had them anymore. She supposed it was the pain of healing that had brought them back now.

Pushing the dark memories determinedly from her consciousness, Divine concentrated on the here and now instead, taking careful note of the room she was in. It was the same rose-colored room Jackie and Vincent had shown her to before chaining her down so she wouldn't hurt herself and giving her the bagged blood. The chains were gone now, she noted, probably removed once the worst of the healing had ended.

That was a good sign, she decided. It meant they

had no idea she was the Basha Argeneau they were looking for.

Sighing, Divine sat up, pushed the sheets aside and grimaced at her bloodstained clothes. She looked like a two-year-old wearing her last meal. Wrinkling her nose with distaste at the nasty dry stuff, she slid out of bed and then headed for the bathroom Jackie had pointed out earlier. She'd considered showering and stripping then, but it had seemed a waste of time at that point when she knew that the healing would leave her feeling slimy and dirty anyway. It always did as impurities and damaged tissue were broken down and pushed out through the pores.

Jackie and Vincent would probably have to throw out the linens and beds she and Marcus had lain in while healing . . . unless they had really good bed protectors. She hoped they did. She'd hate to think she'd cost them anything. Maybe she should give them money for their trouble, Divine thought as she turned on the shower and stripped off her clothes.

The warm water pounding down on her head and body went a long way toward clearing away the last of the darkness at the corners of her mind. Divine hated the nightmares that occasionally plagued her. It was bad enough to have suffered what she had once; having nightmares about it just seemed to her like her own mind continuing the torture originally visited on her by Leonius Livius. She didn't deserve that. No one did. That being the case, she'd learned to give the nightmares as little room as possible in her waking mind. On waking, she always pushed them back into an imagined closet in her head and firmly closed the door. To her mind it was the only way to handle it.

Divine felt pretty good after her shower, even better when she walked back out into the bedroom and spotted the clean clothes folded neatly and placed on the end of the bed. The fact that the blankets she'd tossed aside on waking lay half over them told her they'd been there when she'd got up and hadn't been brought in while she'd showered. Jackie was obviously not only thoughtful, but the organized type, figuring out what needed doing and doing it before it was needed. Divine appreciated that.

Dropping her towel, she picked up the clothes and began to pull them on, surprised to find there were still tags on everything. Pretty pink panties, a matching bra, a flowy skirt in deep red similar to one of her own skirts that had probably gone up in flames, and a white peasant blouse with red stitching along the neckline that suggested it was Mexican in origin. There was a large skirt scarf too, but without the coins that she'd sewn onto her own scarf. There was also a pair of high-heeled, knee-high black boots.

It wasn't as elaborate as the costumes she usually wore as Madame Divine, but it would do and she appreciated the effort put into the outfit.

Once dressed, Divine grabbed the towel and returned to the bathroom to hang it over the shower door to dry. She then looked around in the drawers and found a brand-new toothbrush in its wrapper, toothpaste, and a brush. She used all three items to make herself more presentable, and then walked back out to strip the bed.

There *was* a mattress protector, she saw with relief. So only the linens would have to be thrown out. No amount of washing would remove the stench and stains from a healing. After a glance at the windows showed her that it was early evening, the sun just setting, Divine rolled the pillowcases inside the sheets, picked up the bundle, and headed out of the room in search of Marcus and her hosts, sure that if they weren't already up, they would be soon.

The murmur of voices coming from below as she descended the stairs told her someone was up. Divine followed the sound up the hallway toward the kitchen, but slowed as she reached the door when she heard Marcus ask, "Lucian said he was coming here? Why? We don't know that she's Basha."

"I presume that's why," Vincent said, and she could imagine him shrugging as he said it. "To find out if she is."

There was a brief silence and then Jackie said, "Don't worry, Marcus. Whether she is Basha or not, there is no way she is in league with Leonius. Lucian will see that. He got the wrong information. She would never be in league with him after the things he did to her."

"What the hell did he do to her?" Marcus growled, and the frustration in his voice suggested it wasn't the first time he'd asked the question.

"I told you, that's not for me to say. You'll have to ask Divine," Jackie responded solemnly.

Divine turned slowly away from the door and moved silently back up the hall. She carried the sheets all the way back up to the room she'd woken in, set them on the bed, and then simply stood there for a moment, her mind racing.

Lucian was coming.

The thought terrified her despite Vincent and Jackie's reassurances to Marcus that everything would be well. The man was as much of a monster as Leonius had been. While Leonius had haunted her nightmares, Lucian had haunted her waking hours. The fear of his finding her, of his killing her and Damian. She'd been hiding from the man for more than two millennia. It was ingrained now and her mind was screaming at her to run and hide. But a lifetime of training kept her from simply running willy-nilly. That rarely led to good results.

Stop, think, plan, Divine told herself. He wasn't here yet. She had time. She had to do this all carefully, figure out where to run to, and where she could hide.

Carnivals wouldn't be safe anymore, they'd look for her there. She'd have to give up that life, but then she'd seen the end of that coming anyway. Hoskins was one of a dwindling number of self-owned carnivals left in the industry. Big corporations were moving in, buying them up, and taking them over as they did everything else.

Divine knew that Bob and Madge themselves had been approached twice now about selling. She also knew that they had seriously considered accepting the offer and retiring. They hadn't said as much, but she'd read it in their minds. The couple were both in their late fifties, carnie life was hard, and the offer got better each time they were approached. The only thing holding them back was the carnies themselves.

Bob and Madge thought of most of their people as family. Many of the carnies had been with them from the start, others for nearly as long. Bob and Madge felt like they'd be betraying kin by retiring, but Divine knew it would take only one bad thing to change their minds, another greenie trying to lure a child away from the midway, or finding out someone they trusted was robbing them. It was why Divine had got in on the hiring and helped clean house when she'd joined the carnival. Well, that and because she had genuinely wanted to help the couple.

Divine glanced to the bundled sheets on the bed and frowned as it suddenly occurred to her that the RV fire might be the one bad thing to change their minds and make them accept that next offer. Certainly it could be if they learned the fire had been deliberately set. She'd smelled the gasoline around the burning RV. Had they? She wasn't sure if mortals would have been able to, but certainly their fire inspector or whoever it was who investigated such things would be able to tell an accelerant had been used.

"Crap," she muttered, and spun to pull open the door to reveal a startled Marcus standing in the hall, one hand raised and curled to knock.

"Oh. Good. You're up," he said after a pause. He shifted from one foot to another and then gave her a crooked smile and asked, "How do you feel?"

"We have to go," Divine announced, pushing past him into the hall.

"What?" Marcus said with surprise, and then hurried to follow her. "I don't think that's a good idea, Divine.

You've just woken up. You aren't really through with healing yet. You should rest a bit and—"

"What day is it?" she asked as she started down the stairs.

"It's Tuesday evening. About 4 P.M.," he answered helpfully.

"Damn, I'll never make it to a bank before it closes," she muttered and then shrugged. She would worry about that later. Right now, she had to get to Madge and Bob and see what was going on.

"Divine." Marcus was sounding less caught out, and more exasperated. He was regaining his footing after his initial surprise. The fact that it had taken this long, though, told her that he, at least, still wasn't fully healed. She supposed she probably wasn't either, but she felt fine. A little thirsty, maybe, but the marks from his stabbing her with the arrow and clawing at her chest were gone. There wasn't even the faintest scarring any-more. Any healing still taking place would be inside.

"Dammit, Divine, stop!" Marcus suddenly barked, catching her arm as she stepped off the stairs and headed for the front door.

"What's going on?" Vincent asked, drawing their attention as he started up the hall toward them with Jackie at his side.

Marcus opened his mouth to answer, but Divine quickly said, "Thank you so much for everything you've done for us. But I have to go now."

She sensed rather than saw Marcus's head swiveling sharply in her direction. "A minute ago it was 'We have to go,'" he growled, sounding annoyed.

Divine shrugged. "Well, I do. You don't though, so I understand if you want to stay here with your friends. I can always take a taxi back to the carnival grounds."

"You are not taking a taxi—" He stopped suddenly, realization on his face. "The carnival won't be there anymore. They were moving on to the next town on Sunday night."

"They might have been held up by the fire, it being arson and all," Divine said quietly. "If they were, I'll clear things up so they can continue with their schedule. If not, then I'll still clear things up with the local firemen and police and what have you, and then I'll follow them to the next town."

She wasn't sure if that last part was true. Divine had no idea what she would do. She might catch up to the carnival just long enough to see how Bob and Madge were taking things and to assure them she was all right. After all, she'd disappeared rather abruptly. But after that, she'd have to move on to something else. The problem was, she wasn't sure just what she'd move on to.

"Divine's right," Jackie said thoughtfully.

"She is?" Marcus asked with amazement.

"About what exactly?" Vincent asked.

"Well, we've been so busy worrying about whether she was . . . er . . ."

Divine raised her eyebrows and simply watched as the woman floundered. She knew the ending to that sentence had been "whether she was Basha or not." However, she also knew Jackie wasn't going to say it now that she'd caught herself. The question was, what would she use in its place?

As it turned out, Jackie didn't say anything. It was Vincent who saved her bacon by suggesting, "Whether she was healing all right?"

"Yes," Jackie breathed on a relieved sigh and even managed to smile. "We've been so worried about these two healing that we didn't consider what would be going on with the local authorities." She glanced to Marcus. "You said you could smell gas and that the flames erupted all around the RV at once? Filling every window?" She barely waited for Marcus to nod before saying, "Well, it won't take long at all for the authorities to decide the fire was deliberately set, and since you two disappeared directly afterward . . ."

Marcus blinked in surprise. "You think they'll think Divine and I set the fire?"

"More likely they'll think you set the fire since Divine wasn't there," Vincent commented, looking thoughtful. "But the two of you disappearing after that will probably make them think you set the fire and maybe kidnapped her or something when you realized she wasn't caught in the fire."

"What?" Marcus squawked with dismay.

"It's all right. We can fix this," Jackie said at once and then gave her head a shake and admitted, "Although I'm a little embarrassed that we didn't think of this when you first arrived. The sooner we'd tended to it, the less fixing there would have been. By now, a lot of people are probably involved and every one of them will need mind wiping and such." She clucked with irritation and then suddenly said, "Who are you calling?"

Divine didn't bother glancing around from the phone she'd picked up, but punched in numbers as she answered, "Information. I need the number for a taxi service."

Marcus immediately snatched the phone from her hand. "You don't need a taxi. I'll take you back. I'm certainly not letting you go back alone with people bashing you over the head and setting your home on fire."

"We'll all go," Vincent said, suddenly sounding cheerful. "In fact that was the plan all along. Marcus was sure you'd want to return to the carnival as soon as you were up and about, so I called the office and had a couple of our vehicles sent over."

Vincent moved past her to the front door, and threw it open with a dramatic gesture that was punctuated by the house alarm suddenly blaring all around them. Cursing, he rushed to a panel on the wall and began punching in numbers to silence it.

"Forgot about the . . . er . . ." Vincent gestured toward the panel with a grimace and then moved back to take her arm. "Close your eyes," he ordered as he ushered her toward the door.

Divine reluctantly did as he asked, and allowed him to lead her outside. When he said, "Okay, open," she blinked her eyes open to find him standing in front of her grinning like an idiot and blocking her view. Just as she started to arch an eyebrow, he waved his arms about like a magician and then stepped aside with a loud singsong of "Ta-daaaa!"

Divine stared in surprise. There were two RVs parked

in front of the house, both of them at least as large if not larger than her own had been. She stared at them briefly and then said, "They look new."

"Newish," Vincent admitted. "We have older ones, but I like to travel in comfort so told them to send the newer ones."

Divine frowned. "I understood you were in the theater business."

"Among other things," Vincent agreed. "We use these sometimes for dressing rooms for the more demanding stars in our plays. Or for stakeouts."

"More for stakeouts than demanding stars," Jackie said dryly. "Vincent doesn't seem to understand that stakeout means being unobtrusive and drawing as little attention to yourself as possible, and that parking a big old boat of a recreational vehicle out in the street is the opposite of unobtrusive."

"Nonsense," Vincent said at once. "We've never once been pegged as being on a stakeout."

"Only because no one with any sense would imagine a detective would be stupid enough to drive such a ridiculously large and noticeable vehicle around on a stakeout," Jackie said with exasperation.

"See. It works then," Vincent said with a pleased smile.

Jackie shook her head, but then smiled and even gave a short laugh as she admitted, "Yes, it does."

"And we enjoy the comforts of home while spying on the ne'er-do-wells of the world," he said with satisfaction.

Divine narrowed her eyes and turned to Marcus.

"Jackie was a private detective before she turned," Marcus explained quietly, and then added, "Well, she still is obviously, and Vincent helps her out from time to time."

Divine let her breath out on a small sigh. Great. So the two she'd thought were a baby immortal and a flaky artsy type were just another pair of detectives out to find her. Great. She turned back to Vincent. "Why two?"

"One for us," Vincent said, slipping his arm around Jackie. "And one for you two."

"You can change that to one for you two and one for Marcus. I am not sleeping in either of those with him," she said firmly, and then shifted impatiently. "Actually, I don't know why you two are even coming. You have no business at the carnival. Marcus and I can handle the authorities."

"But you need protection," Jackie said firmly. "You've already been attacked twice. We don't want it to happen a third time. Vincent and I will help with the authorities and then stick close to help sort out who set the fire and who attacked you the first time."

Divine almost said, "Don't you have to wait here for Lucian to show up?" but caught the question back. She had no intention of revealing that she knew about that. Her main concern at that moment was to get to the carnival, let Bob and Madge know she was healthy and well, and make sure they weren't being held up by the authorities looking into the RV fire. After that, she could slip away and disappear and start yet another new life. First, she had to get to the carnival though, and it was looking like if she wanted to get there, she'd have company. It would have been a lot easier if they'd let her call a taxi, but that obviously wasn't going to happen.

"Fine," she snapped, and then forced herself to smile and added, "Thank you. For . . . everything," she ended on a sigh, and then asked, "Can we go now?"

Jackie and Vincent exchanged a glance and then turned toward the house. "Just give us a couple minutes to pack our bags. Why don't you two raid the fridge and pantry for food?"

"There's a cooler in the pantry for cold stuff," Jackie added, glancing back to them as they started into the house. "And bags to put the canned and dried goods in."

"Don't worry about blood. I'll take care of that," Vincent added before the two disappeared inside.

"Shall we?" Marcus asked.

Divine wanted to say no and make a run for it, but suspected she wouldn't get far. While she'd got the better of the man when she'd gone after him with the mop, she suspected that the element of surprise had played a big factor in that. The man was immortal. He was as fast as or faster than she, and probably stronger, if only because men were physically stronger by nature.

Although it looked to her like he might be physically stronger than most male immortals too, she decided, her gaze sliding over his chest in the very tight and obviously borrowed T-shirt he was wearing. The man really had a very large, very nice physique. Funny she hadn't really noticed that until now.

"Who bought my clothes?" Divine asked curiously as she let him lead her inside.

"Vincent had one of his people buy them," Marcus admitted. "He asked what you normally wear and I said pretty much what you had on when we got here. That I'd never seen you in anything else, and he made a couple calls and . . ." He shrugged.

"And voilà," she finished wryly, thinking it must be nice to have "people" to do things for you.

"He had them pick up clothes for me too, but—" Marcus glanced down at himself with a grimace.

"But he was a little off on size for you," Divine said with amusement, and then said, "Either you pissed him off at some time in the past, or Vincent only has an eye for size when it comes to women."

"Jackie helped him with that," Marcus assured her.

"Oh good," Divine murmured, and when he glanced at her in question, admitted, "Well, it would be a little alarming to think he could guess my bra size at a glance."

His gaze slid over her bare shoulders where she'd tugged the peasant blouse to the side to ride her upper arms and she explained, "It's strapless."

"Oh." He nodded.

As they entered the kitchen, Divine added, "Pretty pink with white lace trim along the bottom. I'm wearing matching panties too."

Marcus stopped dead in the doorway as if he'd been shot and after a couple steps, Divine glanced back at him and almost smiled at the expression on his face. She didn't know what little devil had made her say that.

Really, it had surprised her as well when the words had slipped out, but the expression on his face . . .

Goodness, the man looked like he'd swallowed his tongue. He was also looking at her as if he could see the undergarments she'd described right through her clothes. For some reason that sent a thrill of excitement through her.

"Yo! Marcus?"

Divine glanced past Marcus to the stairs. Vincent was halfway down, hanging over the railing to peer into the kitchen at them through the kitchen door Marcus held open with his body.

Marcus turned to peer at the man and then cleared his throat. "Yeah?"

"Make sure you throw some ice cream in the cooler too. I want to make us some of my famous super-duper sundaes later while we're relaxing."

"Right. Ice cream." Marcus nodded.

"And the fixings," Vincent added.

"Right. Fixings." Marcus nodded again.

Divine couldn't see his expression, but whatever it was made Vincent suddenly frown. "You do know what fixings are needed for sundaes, right?"

When Marcus didn't respond Vincent clucked impatiently and yelled upstairs, "Honey, can you throw a couple pairs of shorts and some T-shirts in a bag for me? Marcus hasn't eaten in more than two millennia. If we leave it up to him we'll be stuck with Puppy Chow or something."

"You have a puppy?" Divine asked curiously.

Vincent lowered his gaze back to them and grinned.

"Yeah. We dropped her at the vet's last night. She was being operated on this morning. Spayed," he added and then frowned. "We were supposed to pick her up at four." Raising his head he yelled, "Jackie, we forgot to pick up Little One at four."

"Crap," they heard from upstairs. "I think they're open until eight. I'll call."

Divine raised an eyebrow. "You don't plan on bringing her along to, do you? I mean, what if they set the RV on fire again or blow it up this time or something?"

Vincent stiffened and then raised his head and yelled, "I'll call the office and have someone pick her up if they're open. They can take her to the kennel tomorrow until we get back."

"Oh, but—"

"It's safer for her," Vincent interrupted.

There was a pause and then Jackie sighed. "Okay."

Vincent nodded, but didn't look pleased himself as he came down the rest of the stairs to join them in the kitchen. Once there he commented, "You know, Bastien should really have some of his scientists look into developing nanos for dogs."

"Why not just give our nanos to the dog and see if it takes?" Divine suggested, crossing the kitchen to a set of double doors she suspected was the pantry. She was right, she saw once she opened them.

"Because that wouldn't work," Marcus said with a laugh.

"Why?" Divine asked absently as she flipped on a switch, lighting up the small room lined with shelves. A survey of the contents on the shelves left her a little bewildered. There were fruits and vegetables. She recognized those, but there were a ton of other items she didn't recognize. What the devil was Spam? she wondered.

"You're kidding, right?"

Divine glanced over her shoulder to see Marcus in the doorway, peering at her with wide, disbelieving eyes. Shifting uncomfortably, she asked, "About what?"

"About why our nanos wouldn't work for dogs," he said. "I mean, they were made to work with the human anatomy and chemistry only. The scientists who made them programmed them that way. They—"

"Scientists?" Divine interrupted with surprise before she could catch herself. She hadn't realized the nanos that made her so strong and gave her such a long life were man-made. She'd thought . . . well, she supposed she'd just assumed they were a part of every immortal, as natural as gills on a fish. That immortals were maybe a different species to humans or something.

Divine hadn't been educated on the origin of immortals before she'd been kidnapped, and certainly Leonius hadn't had any desire to teach her anything that didn't have to do with horror and pain. Once she was free of him, her time had been taken up with running and hiding and constantly moving to avoid the great and monstrous Lucian Argeneau. It had left little time to ponder the origins of her people or the source of their nanos.

"Divine," Marcus said slowly. "Did no one teach you about—?"

"Of course they did," she interrupted sharply. Turning away, she picked up a can of Spam as she added, "I was just pulling your leg."

A long silence passed, and then Vincent said, "Marcus, come help me with this, will you?"

Divine remained completely still until he moved away and then let her breath out on a sigh. She should have just admitted that she didn't know, but she hadn't wanted to look stupid in front of Marcus. Divine had no idea why that should be the case. She wasn't stupid. She knew that, and not knowing something didn't make her stupid. It just meant *she didn't know something.* It did not take away from all the things she *did* know. No one could know everything there was to know on this vast planet, no matter how many years or centuries they'd lived. For instance, she had no clue what Spam was and didn't care who knew that. So why did not knowing their origins bother her and make her feel ignorant?

Sighing, Divine set the can of Spam back on the shelf. She wasn't packing anything she didn't recognize . . . which was pretty much everything in a can or box in the pantry. Shaking her head, she grabbed a folded bag from the shelf, opened it, and began to place vegetables into it.

Thirteen

"I'm just so glad that you're both all right," Madge said, beaming on both Divine and Marcus.

"Yes." Managing a smile, Divine nodded and then changed her expression to an apologetic one. "I'm really sorry, Madge. I thought I'd left a note to let you know that Marco was taking me to get a new RV. I guess in all the excitement and chaos I just forgot. Or maybe it just got mislaid. I was sure I left that note."

It was at least the twelfth time Divine had told that lie. She was beginning to find it hard to keep her smile in place as she repeated it, but then the past eight hours had been a bit harried. They'd arrived at the carnival site to find it empty The only evidence that it had ever even been there was some yellow police crime scene tape that had caught in the branches of a tree at the edge of the grounds and was fluttering in the hot, dry breeze.

Divine, Marcus, Vincent, and Jackie had headed
straight to the police station from there and then the
fire department. As Vincent had suggested, the arson
investigator had quickly recognized the fire as deliberately set. Divine had apparently been the number one
suspect at first. At least until they learned from various
witnesses, both carnies and townies alike, that she had
been in town when it started, had returned to find it in
flames, and was now missing. When Marcus's absence
had then been noted, he had become the prime suspect
for both the arson and her kidnapping.

There had been no other choice but for Divine,
Marcus, Vincent, and Jackie to use a combination of
finessing memories, influencing thoughts, and even a
touch of mind wiping to turn the situation around. By
the time they'd finished, the whole ordeal had turned
from arson and kidnapping to nothing more than an
accidental fire with no insurance claim, no one injured,
and nothing of real note about the entire episode.
They'd then ensured the file went missing, both hard
copy and digital.

After that had been taken care of, they'd followed
the carnival to its next scheduled stop. They'd arrived
at the fairgrounds where the carnival was set up to find
the midway silent and dark, and the carnies relaxing in
the back lot after a long, hot day.

Divine had headed straight for Madge and Bob's RV
with Vincent, Jackie, and Marcus following her. But
by the time she'd arrived at the older couple's home
on wheels, most of the carnies were following as well,
every single one of them eyeing Marcus suspiciously

and asking if she was all right, but leaving any other questions until she reached Madge and Bob.

There was a pecking order in carnivals and as the owners, Madge and Bob were Ma and Pop, King and Queen. The others left it up to them to get the answers they wanted and merely surrounded Divine and the three strangers accompanying her as they made their way to the Hoskinses' RV.

Well, most of them had. Someone had obviously run ahead to tell Madge and Bob that she was back because the couple had been coming out of the RV when Divine led Marcus, Vincent, and Jackie to it. The mortal couple had greeted Divine with relief, ignoring the three people with her, even Marcus, until she'd explained that while the arson investigator had first mistaken the fire for arson, he had now determined it had been accidental, an electrical fire that had ended with the propane tank blowing up. She'd then explained that Marco had found her distraught after she'd stumbled away from her burning RV, had comforted her, and then had offered to help her replace the vehicle so that she could get back to work and that's what they'd been doing the last couple days; visiting used RV lots and the bank to arrange for a replacement.

"Well, I'm just glad the fire inspector realized his mistake and informed the police it was an accident before they arrested poor Marco," Madge said now.

Bob snorted at his wife's words. "He'd have been lucky to have been arrested. If Marco had returned to us alone instead of with Divine alive and well at his side, our boys would have strung him up, no questions asked."

"Yes," Madge agreed solemnly, and then patted Marcus's arm as if to soothe him. "Well, fortunately, he didn't. He brought her back, and with friends too to help us."

Divine's smile became decidedly forced at this comment. Vincent had quite caught her by surprise when he'd informed Madge and Bob that he and Jackie were friends of hers who had come to help in any way they could, and who wanted to set up a gourmet candy apple stall with another couple, Tiny and Mirabeau, right next to Divine's fortune-telling spot. She had been just as surprised when Madge and Bob had embraced the idea with enthusiasm, until she'd realized that Vincent and Jackie were using their special skills to influence the couple and ensure they thought it was a good idea.

It seemed that so long as she stayed with the carnival, Divine was going to have a trio of bodyguards/babysitters on her butt. Actually, a quintet of bodyguards/babysitters, she thought, recalling this unknown Tiny and Mirabeau.

"And your timing couldn't be better," Bob announced. "Jack's submarine ride died on him today. We'll move it out in the morning and you can park your RVs side by side where it was."

"Oh yes," Madge said happily. "That worked out well."

"Not for Jack," Divine muttered and then asked. "Can't he fix it?"

"Divine honey, that ride is more than fifty years old," Bob said dryly. "Jack has fixed and fixed it, but frankly I think this time it's done in."

"He had a technician out today, but he said the parts

would cost a good couple thousand dollars by themselves," Madge told her solemnly. "And Jack just
doesn't make any money on that ride anymore."

Bob grunted and nodded. "It's a kiddie ride that even
the kiddies find boring. A bunch of yellow tubs that go
round and round." He wrinkled his nose. "Not much of
a thrill. He'll probably either sell it for scrap or as an
antique online or something."

Madge nodded in agreement. "We were just going to
put an 'Out of Order' sign on it and leave it in place so
we didn't have a hole on the midway where it had been
positioned," she admitted, and then added brightly,
"But now that you and your friends are here, we'll have
the boys take it down so you can pull the RVs in for the
night."

"Oh no," Divine protested as several of the men
moved forward, apparently volunteering for the duty.
"I don't want the boys to have to trouble themselves at
this hour."

"Oh now, Miss Divine, it's no trouble," Jack said,
moving through the crowd to join them. "It's trailer
mounted. We just have to take the fencing down around
it and haul the trailer off. It won't take more than a
couple minutes. Besides," he added dryly. "I can't stand
to look at the damned thing. It's given me nothing but
grief for years now. I'll be glad to get it out of my sight,
and then out of my hair. I'm happy to move it."

"Great," Divine said dryly as Jack headed away with
several men following him.

"Why don't you take your friends and go get your
RVs," Madge suggested. "By the time you walk there

and drive back, I guarantee the submarine ride will be gone and you can pull right in."

"Great," Divine repeated weakly as Marcus took her arm to urge her away. She'd been rather hoping that they'd have to split up the RVs and park them in different spots along the midway. Or that they wouldn't have been able to fit them both in at all and the second RV, with Marcus, Vincent, and Jackie in it, would have had to be parked somewhere in the back lot, well away from the one she intended to use. That would have given her at least a little space to maneuver and manage her escape. She certainly needed to get away from her bodyguards/babysitters before Lucian arrived. But it seemed even fate was against her in this endeavor. Seriously, what were the chances that the submarine ride would drop dead, leaving a space just big enough for two RVs to park side by side in its place?

Pretty good, actually, Divine acknowledged. The damned thing seemed to break down pretty regularly. Although this was the first time the breakdown had been something that Jack couldn't repair himself.

"Oh darn, Divine!" Madge called suddenly.

Divine paused abruptly and turned to see the woman waving her back. After a hesitation, she turned to Marcus and suggested, "Why don't the three of you go ahead? I'll catch up. She probably just forgot to tell me something."

He didn't even hesitate, but said at once, "I'll come with you."

"Are you going to join me in the toilet too when I have to use it?" Divine asked sweetly, and when his eyes widened in surprise, she said in a firm voice, "I've been taking care of myself for a very long time, Marcus. I don't need an escort to walk over and talk to Madge, and I don't like tripping over people every time I move. I'd appreciate a little space. You can either wait here while I see what she wants, or go get the RV, but you are not going to follow me around like a guard dog."

Marcus eyed her solemnly for a moment and then nodded his head and said, "As you wish."

Divine had no idea what that meant. Was he going to go get the RV or wait here? And why the hell was Vincent now chuckling softly? Shaking her head with bewilderment at the pair of them, Divine turned and headed back toward Madge. She'd taken only a couple steps though when she heard Jackie say softly, "Tiny loves that movie."

The comment was just as bewildering to her as the men's behavior was, but Divine merely rolled her eyes with exasperation and continued on to Madge. Honestly, she didn't know what to make of the three of them. They had been kind; had given her blood, a bed, and clothes; and had taken care of her while she'd healed. They also appeared sincere in their intention of finding out who was behind the attacks on her and her RV. But she'd heard them talking. She knew they suspected she was Basha, and she knew Lucian was coming. Why hadn't they just kept her chained to the bed and held her there until he arrived? Why this charade of friendship and caring?

Divine didn't understand and didn't have time to

figure it out. She needed to lose the trio, leave the carnival, and start the next chapter in her life of running and hiding.

"Come," Madge said when Divine reached her. Catching her hand, she then turned to lead her back toward her RV. "I almost forgot."

"Almost forgot what?" Divine asked, following the woman.

Madge didn't answer, but led her to the small enclosed trailer they always kept attached to the back of their RV. She quickly unlocked the door, pulled it open, and then beamed at Divine. "I bet you thought it was gone forever."

Divine raised her eyebrows at the comment and shifted closer to the woman to peer inside the trailer, a smile pulling her lips apart when she saw the motorcycle inside. She'd forgotten all about the vehicle she'd left lying in the dirt in front of her burning RV the night Marcus had been injured.

"Madge, you're an angel," she said, stepping forward to run one hand gently over the handlebar. This was her ticket to freedom. It was how she was going to escape. All she had to do was give the trio waiting for her the slip for even five minutes, hop on the bike, and ride away. Turning, she gave Madge a quick hug. "Thank you. Can I leave it with you for now?"

The woman's eyebrows rose in surprise, but she nodded readily enough. "If you like. I suppose the new RV doesn't have a built-in storage space to keep it like your old one did."

"No, it doesn't," Divine agreed, and then admitted,

"But the RV I'm using right now is just borrowed. I'll have to wait on a custom made one for special storage spaces like that. But I won't make you hold on to the bike for that long," she assured her. "I'd just rather leave it here for now. Tomorrow or the next day I'll probably swing by to pick it up. If that's all right with you?"

"Of course," Madge assured her, closing the door. "It's no problem at all."

"Good," Divine murmured as she watched her attach the lock once more, and it *was* good. She really hadn't wanted to dip into the woman's mind and make her agree to keeping it for her. But she would have. She needed the motorcycle, and she needed Marcus and the others not to know about it.

"**W**hat do you think she was showing her in the trailer?" Marcus asked, eyes narrowed on the women as they turned to walk back toward them.

"A motorcycle," Jackie announced. "Divine's motorcycle. She apparently abandoned it here when she took you away in the SUV the night of the fire and Madge had Bob put it in the trailer to keep for her until she returned."

"Hmm." Marcus nodded. He had fond memories of that motorcycle and riding behind Divine on it. He was actually surprised he'd forgotten about it until now. "We could store it in the RV to keep it safe yet handy. Why isn't she bringing it with her?"

"Because she doesn't want us to know she has it," Jackie announced, and then pointed out, "It would be easier for her to slip away and escape on it if we don't know it exists."

"Escape?" Marcus asked with surprise. "Why would she want to escape? I'm her life mate."

"I don't think she knows that yet," Vincent said thoughtfully.

"Well then maybe it's time I helped her with that," Marcus muttered.

"You'll have to help her with more than that," he said solemnly, and when Marcus glanced to him in question, added, "She has no idea what nanos are or how they work. She really didn't know they were man-made by scientists back in Atlantis."

"What?" Marcus peered at him with surprise. "How could she not know something like that?"

Vincent shook his head. "I'm not sure. I guess you'll have to ask her to find out."

Marcus frowned and turned to peer at Divine. She was confident, caring, beautiful to him, and seemed so savvy on so many subjects that it was hard to believe she didn't know what were basically the immortal facts of life. He hoped that she at least knew what the symptoms of immortals finding their life mates were. That thought made him ask, "Do you think she knows about life mates?"

The question obviously surprised Vincent and he blinked twice before saying, "For your sake, I hope so."

Divine saw Marcus give her the thumbs-up in the rearview mirror, brought the RV to a full halt, and then slipped it into park and turned off the engine. Much to her surprise he'd suggested that perhaps she should be the one who parked the RV in the tight space left over once Vincent had parked the other RV. She'd been surprised because most men seemed to prefer to take the wheel when it came to driving. Apparently, Marcus wasn't most men. He'd merely shrugged at her surprise and pointed out that he'd never driven an RV before while she had years of experience at it. She seemed the better choice for the job. Divine found she had a great deal of respect for him for that and was a bit ashamed that she hadn't admitted her own lack of knowledge when it came to the origins of nanos.

Marcus didn't mind admitting she knew or had more experience and skill than he did at something. Yet she'd been too embarrassed to do the same.

Ah well, Divine thought as she opened her door to get out. No one was perfect.

"Nice job," Marcus complimented, meeting her halfway up the side of the RV.

"Thanks," Divine murmured and went to move past him, but he caught her arm to stop her. Pausing, she raised her eyebrows. "What?"

"I wanted to ask you a couple of questions," Marcus said quietly.

Divine hesitated, but then forced herself to at least appear relaxed and nodded slowly. "Okay."

Marcus took a breath, considered her briefly and then asked, "Do you know about life mates?"

Divine tilted her head a little surprised by the question. "Of course." She smiled faintly and admitted, "A visiting cousin and I used to play at being life mates when I was eleven. She was always the girl," she added dryly and shrugged. "Don't all immortal children chatter and dream about finding their life mate one day?"

"What do you know about them?" he pressed.

Divine shrugged. "They are an immortal's one true mate, the one who can't read or control them and whom they can't read or control. They bond for life."

"Do you know the symptoms of finding a life mate?"

She frowned now. "Why are you asking me this?"

"Because I'm 2,548 years old," Marcus announced. "And I can't read you."

Divine blinked. He was old . . . but she was older. His not being able to read her, therefore, was no great surprise. However, as the older one, she should have been able to read him . . . and couldn't. She hadn't enjoyed any of the other symptoms of meeting a life mate though, at least not that she'd noticed. She wasn't hungering for food, but then she hadn't really been around any unless you counted the canned and boxed goods in Vincent and Jackie's pantry.

"And neither Jackie nor Vincent should be able to read me, but they can for the first time since I've known them," Marcus added solemnly, and then pointed out, "The inability to block younger immortals from reading your thoughts is another symptom of finding a life mate."

Divine swallowed, her mind beginning to whirl.

"And," he added, "while I can't read you, Jackie and Vincent can."

Divine actually felt the blood leave her face as this news struck her. This was . . . Cripes, Vincent and

Jackie could read her? Two babies like them? Impossible. But if they could . . . Was Marcus her . . . ?

What had they read? She worried, suddenly. What did they know? Was all of this true? Was Marcus her life mate? She remembered the sensations that she got whenever their bodies touched, brushed, or accidentally rubbed together and had to shake her head. She couldn't handle that just then. She couldn't handle Marcus being her life mate either. This was some cosmic joke. One of Lucian's spies her life mate?

Dear God, Divine thought with dismay and then her mind circled back around to wondering what Vincent and Jackie had read in her thoughts. What did they know? What had she given away?

Marcus was her life mate, her mind screamed, and Divine raised her hands to rub her temples. Her thoughts were too chaotic. She couldn't deal with all of this right now. Couldn't even consider him being her life mate. He was Lucian's spy, for God's sake, and her son might be in jeopardy from whatever Vincent and Jackie had read in her thoughts.

"Divine?" he asked with concern.

"I have to—" Divine shook her head and tried to move past him, but was so shaken up she stumbled over her own feet and would have fallen if he hadn't caught her arm. Marcus saved her from falling, but her momentum swung her around and she slammed up against his chest with a surprised gasp. Swallowing, she stared at his chest briefly, but then closed her eyes as his scent wafted up to her nose. His scent was definitely male, something woodsy but with a hint of citrus. It was incredibly . . . tempting. She wanted to press her nose into the crook of his neck and just inhale deeply. Instead, she stopped breathing altogether and tried to gather herself to step away.

"Divine?" His voice had dropped, becoming this sexy, husky murmur of sound. That combined with his warm breath brushing her ear made a small groan slip from her lips.

"Did you hurt yourself?" Marcus asked with concern, urging her back slightly to try to see her face. The action pressed their lower bodies tighter together, nestling her groin against his, and Divine bit her lip at the sensation that sent rushing through her. Dear God.

"Divine? What's wrong? Look at me," he insisted.

Tipping her head back, Divine reluctantly opened her eyes and then simply stared. His eyes were a black glowing with silver streaks through it. They were fascinating, hypnotic. In fact, they so had her attention she didn't notice that they were moving closer until a heartbeat before his lips covered hers. Divine had that heartbeat to pull away, and should have, but instead she hesitated and that was her undoing. Once his mouth brushed over hers she was lost.

Fourteen

It started with a tingling that erupted where their lips met, like a sparkler spitting out little flames of heat. Then Marcus's arms slid around her back, pulling her closer, and his mouth opened over hers and the night exploded inside Divine's head. That was the only way to describe it; heat and light and color all seemed to explode behind her eyes, and fire licked up her body as his tongue slid out to spread her lips and plunge between them.

At first they clung to each other as if each were the other's lifeline in a stormy sea, but then Divine was left to cling to him alone as his hands began to move. Anywhere Marcus's fingers roamed, her body burst into flame . . . and his hands were everywhere, moving with a swiftness that was almost dizzying, as if he wanted to ensure she had all the necessary parts, or he wanted to touch all of her at once.

Divine gasped and moaned by turn, unconsciously thrusting her hips closer when his hands covered and squeezed her breasts, then tugging desperately at his shoulders and rising up on her toes when he dropped one hand to cup her between the legs and pressed upward, the thin material of her skirt and panties the only thing between them. That caress made her a little crazy and Divine began to suck almost viciously at his tongue, one of her own hands finally giving up its hold on his shoulder to scrape its way down his chest, clawing at the thin cloth of the tight T-shirt he wore. Already strained, the cloth gave way like film, the material spreading where it tore open and leaving a large opening over one side of his chest. Feeling the coarse hair under her palm, and the nub of a nipple, Divine tore her mouth from Marcus's and lowered her head to his chest instead, eager to taste his skin.

Her mind was filled with an insatiable hunger that had her licking his skin and then closing her lips around his nipple and drawing on it eagerly. She barely heard the startled curse Marcus uttered, but she felt his surprised pleasure wing its way from his body to hers.

Shared pleasure, another symptom of life mates, she recalled, and the thought was an electrifying one that gave her a boldness Divine hadn't known she possessed in this area. Even she was startled when she suddenly reached down and clasped the hardness pressing against his tight black jeans. The sensations that sent through both of them had her tearing her mouth from his chest and seeking out his mouth again for an almost violently demanding kiss.

Divine felt the material of her skirt moving against the backs of her legs, and then his hands were there, sliding upward and pushing the material ahead of them. Still, her eyes blinked open with surprise when he suddenly caught her by the backs of the thighs and pulled them up around his hips. Instinct kicked in and she crossed her ankles behind his back to keep from falling. She also withdrew her caressing hand from his trapped erection to clutch at his shoulders again. The moment she did, he suddenly turned with her.

Divine gasped into his mouth with surprise as her back slammed into the side of the RV.

Marcus immediately tore his mouth away then to mutter an apology against her cheek. He took several deep breaths as well, then pulled his head back to ask breathlessly, "Are you all right?"

His words were mumbled and slurred as if he'd been drinking when she knew he hadn't. Marcus was obviously as overcome by the passion as she was. Divine grunted in the affirmative for answer and then clasped his face and pulled it back so that she could cover his mouth with hers again.

Damn the man could kiss. At least she thought he could. She wasn't positive though. Maybe it was just the chemical reaction of life mate sex. It was supposed to be mind-blowing and that seemed a good description. Divine had never experienced anything like this. Even bloodlust had never been this all-consuming for her. She wanted him on her and in her and around her. She wanted it all and she wanted it right then, right there.

Much to her relief, Marcus's moment of concern passed quickly under the influence of her kiss and he began kissing and touching her again. He pressed her against the RV, holding her there with his lower body, and pulled back his upper body so that he could tug at her peasant blouse. It was a damned handy blouse for a situation like this and Divine grunted with relief when he tugged it down, revealing her breasts to the hot night air. She then groaned deeply with pleasure when he both raised her a little higher against the RV and lowered his head to claim one already erect nipple.

It was as if his lips were tugging on a fuse that ran from breast to groin and that contact with his mouth had set it alight. Gasping, she threw her head back, nearly knocking herself out when it crashed into the RV wall. Marcus's hand was immediately there, rubbing the spot on her head where she'd hit the wall, and then cupping her head to prevent her doing it again, but his mouth never left her breast, never stopped drawing and suckling, his tongue flicking the nipple the whole while.

It was enough to drive her crazy. Divine moaned and groaned, her hands caught in his hair and tugging, her hips moving and thrusting against his stomach now. And then she reached for her free breast with her own hand and began to squeeze and knead the excited flesh that was being neglected.

Everything he was doing was incredible, mind-numbingly exciting. Her entire body was humming with excitement and need. She was actually aching between her legs with it . . . and it wasn't enough. She wanted him inside her, wanted to feel his hot, hard body pressing into her. The thought made her reach down now, trying to find that hardness again. But he was holding her too high. She unhooked her ankles and kicked her feet in frustration, grunting with satisfaction when he lifted his mouth from her breast and let her slide down along the RV wall until her hand could find the top of his jeans. As he began to kiss her again, Divine pressed her palm to his stomach and then slid her hand down between the material and his skin until she could cup him without the material of his jeans or underwear in the way. Not that he appeared to be wearing any underwear. The man was commando, and she was grateful for it. She doubted her hand would have fit with the added material in the tight space.

Divine couldn't have got more reaction out of Marcus if she'd lit a match where her fingers clasped him. Excitement shot through him in a tsunami of sensation that damned near knocked Divine out when it vibrated across their connection and blew through her. When he then slid one hand under her skirt in response, and slid it along her thigh to slip beneath the edge of her panties to touch her, Divine was already wet for him, soaking in fact, her body weeping for him to fill it.

She moaned in protest when he broke their kiss, and really didn't understand what he was trying to say when he gasped, "We shouldn't—not here—but I can't—I need . . ."

Divine gasped and jerked in his arms as his touch became more intimate, his fingers sliding between her warm wet skin to find the center of her excitement. He strummed her once, twice, and then slid a finger inside her and Divine bit his shoulder to muffle the scream that tore from her as her body shuddered and shook with release. In the next moment, her teeth released him and a sigh was slipping from her lips as darkness rolled over her.

A shout followed by a drunken laugh stirred Marcus. He blinked his eyes open, confused at first as to where he was. It was the head resting on his chest and the warm body on his legs that brought his memory back to him. Damn . . . he'd just experienced his first bout with life mate sex . . . and it had been . . .

Damn, he thought. There was no way to describe it. He'd heard it called mind-blowing and incredible and it had certainly been both those things, but that was like calling a tornado a light breeze, or saying a tsunami was the tide coming in. What he'd experienced had been mind-bending and life altering and he definitely never wanted to let it go.

Another laugh, this one closer, claimed his attention again and Marcus glanced around, quickly taking in their situation. They'd passed out and were outside, lying on the ground next to her RV . . . and someone was coming, stumbling drunkenly toward them . . . more than one someone.

Marcus swept the area in both directions, but didn't yet see whoever was approaching. Marcus then briefly debated just waiting there and trying to control the person or people when they got close enough for him to see them. He could take control, ensure they didn't see him and Divine, and send them in another direction . . .

if there weren't more than two. Two would be tricky, but more than that would be pretty much impossible.

He'd just had the thought when he caught movement out of the corner of his eye and glanced to the side and down. He was lying on his back between the two RVs with his feet toward the back of the RVs and the midway, and his head toward the front of the RVs and the back lot where the bunkhouses were. The movement he'd glimpsed was several pairs of feet, maybe a half a dozen, walking along the back of the RV. Within half a dozen steps the owners of those feet would be at the opening of the space between the two RVs and able to see them.

Marcus moved quickly then, shifting to the side to slide under the RV that Divine was supposed to use, and dragging her with him through the dirt. He tried not to think about what the action must be doing to her new clothes, more concerned with getting them both under the cover of the vehicle before they could be spotted. And they would have been spotted for certain, he thought grimly as the six pairs of feet turned down the row between the RVs to make their way to the back lot.

"These are new," someone said, the words slightly slurred.

A group of the young carnies returning from celebrating the end of a long workday, Marcus thought and didn't doubt that was the case. He didn't know where they got the energy though. They worked like dogs all day in the heat and should have been sacked out, exhausted in their beds when midnight came and the carnival closed.

"Maybe Divine got a new trailer and is back," another voice suggested. The first had been female. This one was male.

"That'd be awesome," another male voice said. "Divine's hot."

"Hot?" another female demanded in sulky tones. "She's old. She has to be at least twenty-five."

"Yeah? Well, I'm twenty-four, so I guess I'm old too. Too old for you at least. What are you anyway? Twelve?" he taunted as they passed the spot where Marcus and Divine lay.

"Eighteen," the girl snapped with irritation. "Bob and Madge would hardly hire a twelve-year-old."

"Whatever," the fellow laughed, his voice growing fainter.

Marcus tipped his head to watch the group reach the front of the RV and turn left to walk along the back lot. He waited a moment, and then glanced around, checking under the RVs in all directions to be sure no one else was approaching. Only then did he slide out from under the RV, taking Divine with him again. Once he had them both in the lane between vehicles, Marcus quickly stood and then stooped to scoop up Divine.

She wasn't sleeping. Divine didn't even stir. She was definitely unconscious, which was another sign of life mates; they usually passed out during or after life mate sex. The thought made him cuddle her closer against his chest. She was his. His life mate, his partner, the light that would stave off the darkness over the next two millennia or more of his life. She would be his reason for rising in the morning and she would be why he went to bed at night at peace with his world . . . so long as she wasn't Basha Argeneau.

That thought made Marcus frown. She couldn't be Basha. She was Divine.

"Divine," he murmured softly, tasting the name on his lips. She had certainly chosen the right name for herself. She was divine, in every way.

Marcus was still smiling at that thought as he carried her around the RV to the door halfway down the passenger side. This RV was not custom-made. It was your standard setup. Rather than a door at the back, the door was on the side and led directly into a combined kitchenette and lounge, though the kitchenette was on the left and the lounge on the right with a curtain that could be drawn between the two as it had been in Divine's RV. Beyond the kitchenette was where the bedroom was, and behind it, running from one side of the RV to the other, was the tiny bathroom with a shower at one end, the toilet at the other, and a sink in the middle.

Divine had parked the RV next to the fencing around a ride called the Zipper. She'd parked it with the back end a little farther out than the back end of Vincent's RV so that the side door was visible and easily accessible where the fence around the Zipper curved back.

Marcus stopped at the door and shifted Divine a bit to be able to open it, but paused and glanced around at the sound of footsteps rushing toward him.

"What happened?" Jackie gasped as she reached them. Her worried gaze slid over Divine. "Was she attacked again?"

Marcus grimaced. He supposed that depended on

how you looked at it. He certainly hadn't been overly gentle or careful in what had passed between them. Although he didn't think it would be classified as an attack, unless you wanted to say she attacked him too. They'd both behaved like animals really . . . and it had been awesome!

"She's fine," he assured her as Jackie pulled the screen door out of the way and reached to open the inner wooden door for him. "She just . . . fainted."

"Does she need blood?" Jackie asked with concern, following him as he carried Divine inside.

"No. She's fine," he repeated as she flipped on the lights. "A little rest and she'll be as right as rain."

"But what—?"

The way she stopped so abruptly made him glance her way to see that she was staring wide-eyed down at Divine. Marcus followed her gaze, biting his lip when he saw that Divine's peasant blouse was still pulled down from when he'd been lavishing her breasts with attention. They were on full view and her nipples were still erect. When Jackie then glanced to his ripped shirt and he switched his own gaze there to see that his own nipples were also still erect, he sighed with resignation.

"Oh," she said with sudden understanding and then arched an eyebrow as she looked them both over again more fully, taking in their filthy state. "Outside in the dirt?"

Marcus grimaced and merely said, "We're definitely life mates. One kiss and we both lost all sense."

"Yeah." Jackie sighed the word with a little smile and warned, "It's going to happen again and again, and don't think good intentions will stop it. One touch, a kiss . . ." She shrugged helplessly. "You two might as well just lock yourselves up in here for the next year and have fun, because you'll be useless for anything else."

"Somehow I don't think Divine would go for that," Marcus said dryly, carrying her through the RV to the bedroom at the back.

"No, perhaps not," Jackie agreed, following, flicking on lights as she went. She paused in the doorway to the bedroom, turned on that light as well, and then watched him set Divine on the bed before saying, "Okay, so . . . then you might want to avoid certain situations."

Marcus straightened next to the bed and raised an eyebrow. "What situations?"

Jackie pursed her lips and then began to list things off on her fingers. "Public elevators, movie theaters, moving vehicles unless someone else is driving—"

"You're kidding," Marcus interrupted with amusement. "Moving vehicles?"

"She's not kidding," Vincent said, appearing behind his wife. Slipping his arm around her waist, he tugged her back against his chest and kissed the top of her head before saying, "You haven't lived until you find yourself flying down the highway at top speed with your life mate bouncing around on your lap, shrieking with pleasure like a crazed baboon."

Jackie flushed with embarrassment and elbowed her husband in the stomach, making him release her as she muttered, "*You* were the one shrieking like a crazed baboon."

"Perhaps I was," Vincent agreed with a grin as Jackie pushed past him to get out of the confined space.

"I've seen your car," Marcus said dryly. "I wouldn't think there was enough room in that little Lexus to—"

"It's a convertible," Vincent interrupted. "The top was down."

"Dear God," Marcus muttered as he got the visual. He was surprised there hadn't been a pile-up, or a video caught and put on YouTube.

"It was the middle of the night," Vincent said with a shrug, and then added, "Thank God. I wasn't much good for steering, and I damned near passed out before I could pull over to the shoulder and get us stopped."

"You passed out on the side of the highway?" Marcus asked with disbelief. That seemed damned risky.

"Yeah. It was," Vincent said as if he'd spoken the thought aloud. "We got lucky, but I wouldn't recommend it."

Marcus shook his head and then turned to peer down at Divine, quickly tugging her blouse back into place when he realized she was still on view. Only then did Vincent leave the door to join him.

"How did she take finding out you're her life mate?"

Marcus grimaced. "She seemed a bit upset before I kissed her."

"Hmm." Vincent nodded, not appearing surprised. "Did she say anything useful before you two got too caught up?"

"Do grunts and moans count?" Marcus asked dryly. "It came over us pretty quickly."

"Yeah, it does," Vincent acknowledged. "Jackie

wasn't kidding about places to stay away from. She's probably making a list as we speak."

They both chuckled at that, but then Vincent sobered and said, "But in case she forgets it, definitely stay away from any grocery shopping at night. And the store freezer is not a good spot to drag her to if things get hot and heavy."

When Marcus turned to peer at him with disbelief, he nodded solemnly. "I must have fallen off of her as I passed out. When I woke up three of the night crew were standing there gawking at us like idiots and my dick was frozen to a metal shelf." He winced at the memory and muttered, "Nasty."

Marcus shook his head with a sort of horror, and then grabbed him by the shoulders, turned Vincent toward the door and gave him a push to get him moving. "Get out of here. I don't want to hear any more of this."

"Just trying to give you some helpful advice," Vincent said with a shrug, but he did leave the room.

Marcus walked over and was about to close the door when Vincent appeared again and announced, "I ran a hose to the water supply while you two were making out between the RVs. Since you were busy I hooked you guys up too and then plugged both RVs into the power supply. You have power and water if you want to take a shower and wash away some of that dirt."

Marcus glanced down at himself, able to see just how filthy he was in the lit room. He was covered with a layer of dust so thick his black jeans looked almost beige.

"You're welcome," Vincent added as he turned and headed away.

"Thanks," Marcus called out belatedly, but was frowning as he did. What had Vincent meant when he'd said *while you two were making out between the RVs*? Had he actually seen them? Or was he just guessing?

Marcus sighed and closed the bedroom door. It didn't really matter what Vincent had meant. If the man had seen them . . . well, Marcus could hardly make him unsee what he'd witnessed, so he might as well just forget about it, Marcus told himself as he crossed the bedroom to the door to the bathroom.

He grimaced when he saw the size of the room. It was little better than an airplane bathroom with a shower on the end, Marcus thought, but knew that wasn't true. It was a little roomier than that, but would still be a bit confining for a man his size.

Shrugging, he turned on the water and quickly stripped his clothes.

Fifteen

Divine woke up with a terrible need to relieve herself. That was her first and only thought as she sat up in bed and swung her feet to the floor. She hurried to the door, thrust it open, and then paused abruptly as she recognized Vincent and Jackie's borrowed RV. She'd forgotten for a moment that this wasn't her RV. In her RV, the bathroom had been along the sidewall outside the bedroom. In this one . . .

She turned and hurried back across the room, rushing into the bathroom there. Divine hiked up her skirt, tugged down her panties, and settled on the toilet so quickly she probably would have been a blur to anyone watching. Immortal speed rocked, she thought on a little sigh of relief as she proceeded to—as a carnie she once knew would have put it—piss like a racehorse. She'd *really* had to go. Probably all the blood they'd given her for the healing, Divine thought, and wondered

that the noise she was making wasn't drowning out the
sound of the rain outside. She'd been vaguely aware of
the sound of splashing water as she woke up, but hadn't
paid it much attention. Now, however, it seemed louder
to her, almost like the water was actually falling—

Her bowed head jerking up, Divine peered at the
shower across from her, noted the figure inside, and
couldn't hold back a muttered "Oh crap."

"Please don't."

Marcus was in the shower with his very bare back to
her, but she could hear the amusement in his voice as
he said those words and knew he was teasing her. She
wanted to give a light chuckle and say something witty.
After all this wasn't the first time she'd been caught
out in a situation like this. She'd lived too damned long
not to have experienced this or a similar scenario a
hundred times over. But none of those scenarios had
included Marcus, and rather than handle it with the
insouciance she wanted to, Divine groaned and closed
her eyes as her face flamed what she suspected was a
violent red.

"I guess this means the romance phase of our relationship is over, huh?" he teased.

Divine's eyes popped open at the sudden silence as
the sound of running water suddenly stopped. He'd
turned off the shower. That meant he'd be getting out,
she thought with dismay.

"I mean they say once a couple starts doing these
kinds of things in front of each other, the honeymoon
stage is done and they're into the relationship phase."
Marcus stepped out of the very tiny shower, into the

tiny room just inches away, and grabbed a towel to quickly dry himself, elbows banging into the wall as he did.

Divine bit her lip and belatedly dropped her skirt, letting it settle around her. She then tried to sit there, pretending she was sitting on a chair rather than the porcelain throne, all while avoiding looking at a very big, very naked Marcus standing just inches away from her.

"Stop staring at my cock, you're making it grow."

Divine blinked at those growled words, mortified to realize she *had* been staring. So much for avoiding looking . . . and damn, it *was* growing.

"You're still staring," he warned.

"Well, stop waving it around in front of me if you don't like it," she snapped, forcing her eyes away. "Cover it up or something."

Marcus chuckled and then caught her face with one hand, to turn it back and up so he could press a kiss to her lips. She suspected he'd meant it to be a quick peck. It didn't end up that way. Fire leaped between them at the first touch, both mouths opened, tongues were engaged, and Divine so forgot herself she was about to wrap her arms around his shoulders and climb him like a telephone pole when he suddenly broke the kiss and straightened.

They were both panting and simply stared at each other briefly, then Marcus growled, "I'm going to go lay down. Naked."

Divine's eyes widened and she watched silently as he snatched his clothes off the floor, turned, and slid out of the room, tugging the door closed. She sat there for one more moment, before moved to action. She finished her business, and almost raced out of the bathroom after him, but then caught a glimpse of herself in the mirror over the sink as she washed her hands. She was a mess, hair mussy, skin filthy . . .

Turning to the shower she opened the door and twisted the knobs to get the water running, then quickly stripped her clothes.

Divine spent much longer in the shower than she normally would have, mostly because once she was in there she started to think of all the reasons why she shouldn't have done what she had, and shouldn't do it again. The main reason was that she was a wanted woman, hunted by the man Marcus apparently worked for. Not that he'd admitted as much yet.

What she needed to do was to learn what she could from Marcus, find out what he knew, what Lucian knew, and what she could do to keep her son and herself safe. That thought firmly in mind, Divine finished her shower and stepped out to quickly dry herself. She then eyed her clothes with distaste. They were filthy, but it didn't seem smart to walk out of the bathroom in a towel, not if she wanted to actually talk to Marcus and not end up naked and unconscious in the bed.

Grimacing, she picked up her blouse and gave it a shake, then donned it and used the towel to brush away what she could of the dust and dirt clinging to it. Once satisfied she'd done the best she could with the item, Divine did the same with the skirt. She just couldn't bring herself to re-don her panties and bra though.

This would have to do, she decided, took a deep breath, pinned a smile on her face, and left the bathroom.

Divine had expected Marcus to be waiting for her in the bedroom, so was a bit startled to find it empty. After a hesitation, she moved to the bedroom door and opened it to peer out into the rest of the RV, surprised to find him working busily in the kitchenette. He was even dressed. Sort of. The man had his jeans on, but was shirtless. He was a beautiful sight like that, his still-damp hair slicked back, chest muscles glistening in the overhead light and rippling as he sliced cheese on a cutting board on the table.

"Stop looking at me like that or we aren't going to get to eat this lovely fare Jackie made for us," he said without glancing up, his voice light.

Divine relaxed and even managed a smile. Moving toward the table, she said just as lightly, "It looks to me like you're the one making this lovely fare."

"I washed the fruit, took the salad out and put it in bowls, and am now cutting cheese, but Jackie made the casserole that smells so delicious," he assured her and then finally glanced up. His eyes began to glow as they slid over her in her still slightly dusty clothes and then he lowered them again to what he was doing. "Damn, I was sure I was hungry for food when I smelled it, but now—"

"Now *I'm* hungry," Divine said firmly and sat down at the place setting across from him. She also forced herself to stop gawping at his chest like some lovesick calf and, instead, focused on examining the contents of the table.

The casserole did smell delicious and everything else looked good too. Still, Divine was surprised when her stomach suddenly grumbled. It was a sound she hadn't heard since . . . well, she couldn't remember when she'd last heard her body make that sound. It had been a long time since she'd last eaten food, and just as long since she'd felt hunger. Like most immortals she'd stopped eating after a hundred years or so of living. Eating had grown tiresome and food had seemed tasteless and boring.

It didn't smell boring or tasteless now.

"Here." Marcus picked up the cutting board and used the knife to slide several pieces of cheese onto her plate. He then set that down and scooped up some casserole to add to her plate as well before pushing the bowl holding the grapes and strawberries next to the bowl of salad he'd set beside her plate. "We have a couple of dressings to choose from. Apparently it goes on the salad, but I don't know what's good and what's not."

Divine shrugged. "I guess we'll find out," she said, reaching for a grape from the bowl. She popped it into her mouth, bit into it, and closed her eyes as the sweet juice burst across her tongue. Dear God it was . . . luscious, lovely, sweet, wet.

"Try the strawberries," Marcus suggested when she reached toward the bowl again. "They're even better."

Divine immediately changed direction, reaching for the red fruit instead of the green, seedless balls of juice called grapes. She popped one of the berries in her mouth and bit down and found he was right. The strawberries were—

Marcus glanced up from his cutting with surprise when Divine grimaced and spat out the slightly chewed strawberry. He glanced at it briefly and then wrinkled his nose. "I don't believe you're supposed to eat the stem and leafy bits. I've seen others eat them and they leave that part."

"Oh," Divine muttered, using the napkin he'd set beside her plate to wipe her mouth.

"Try another," he suggested, picking up a large plump one and holding it out. "Just bite the fruit off though; I'll hold on to the stem and leafy bit."

Divine hesitated and then leaned forward and carefully bit into the strawberry, avoiding getting too close to the leafy end. She started out watching Marcus's face as she did, but the sudden flaring of silver in his eyes made her lower her eyes. It was a relief when she finished the action and sat back.

"Well?" Marcus asked, and she didn't miss the husky note in his voice.

Divine was silent for a minute as she concentrated on chewing up the fruit and then swallowing, but she smiled then and nodded. "Yes. They're lovely. Much better without the stem and leafy bits."

Marcus grinned and settled in the seat across from her. They were silent for several minutes as they began to eat. All of it was good, but the casserole was amazing. What had Marcus called it? A sausage, potato, and cheese casserole? The various flavors blended beautifully in her mouth. They hadn't had food like this the last time she'd eaten.

"Divine?"

"Hmmm?" she asked, trying the salad next. Not sure which dressing she'd like, Divine had put a creamy concoction called ranch dressing on half her salad and another one called balsamic something or other on the other half. She tried the ranch first and found it surprisingly tasty. But it made her wonder what the balsamic one tasted like and she scooped up a bit of salad from that side to try next.

"Would you tell me a little about your life?"

The question made her pause with the salad halfway to her mouth. Setting the loaded fork back, she peered at him silently.

"Anything," he said quietly. "How long have you traveled with carnivals for instance?"

Divine relaxed a little and contemplated her fork. She didn't suppose answering that would be a problem or reveal anything she shouldn't. "Pretty much since carnivals began," she said, and then added, "Well, I think the first one was around for a couple years before I joined a competitor in 1901."

Marcus nodded and took a bite of casserole.

Relaxing even more, Divine slipped the balsamic salad into her mouth and felt her eyebrows rise. She thought she might like this better than the creamy one. It had a bit of tang to it that she enjoyed.

"And before the carnival?"

Divine swallowed her salad and took a drink as she thought, and then set down her glass and admitted, "Before turning to carnivals I rode and lived with the Comanches."

Marcus's eyes widened incredulously. "Seriously?"

She smiled faintly at his expression and nodded. "They called me Naduah."

"Naduah," he murmured. "That's pretty. What does it mean?"

"That depends on who you ask," she admitted with amusement. "I was told by the chief who gave me the name that it meant 'she who carries herself with dignity and grace.' However, a rather nasty and jealous maiden once told me it means 'she who keeps warm with us,' and the way she said it suggested I did so in a rather X-rated fashion."

Divine grinned at the scowl this brought to Marcus's face and shrugged. "As I said she was jealous. The chief listened to me when I advised him and allowed me to ride into battle with the men. I suppose she thought I'd slept my way into the chief's good graces to be allowed to do so." She smiled and then added, "Even if the chief was wrong and it did mean 'she who keeps warm with us,' it would be true. I shared their fire of a night."

"You couldn't have stayed with them for long. They would have noticed your not aging," he said.

"There were different tribes of Comanche; the Yamparikas, the Jupes, and the Kotsotekas, and they all had different bands." She shrugged. "I moved around the various bands for a while, but no, I wasn't with them for as long as I've moved around with carnivals."

"And before them?"

Divine sighed and set her fork down. "Marcus—"

"Tell me . . . please," he added softly, and then offered, "If you do I'll tell you about myself."

She stared at him briefly, then nodded and picked

up her fork again; gathering some casserole on it, she took a bite, chewed and swallowed and then admitted, "Before the Comanches I was with the Romani."

"Gypsies," he said softly and she nodded.

Divine smiled crookedly. "They called me Nuri. It means Gypsy."

"So even to the Gypsies you were considered a Gypsy?" he asked with amusement.

She smiled wryly. "Well, I moved around even more than they did. I'd travel with a group for five or ten years and then leave and find another. I traveled most of Europe with different Romani groups before sailing to America."

"I'm surprised they let you travel with them," he said quietly. "I understood the Romani didn't embrace out-siders."

Divine smiled with amusement and reminded him, "I'm immortal, and we can be very persuasive."

"Ah." Marcus nodded. "A little mind control, a little influence and bibbidi-bobbidi-boo, you're in."

"Bibbidi-bobbidi-boo?" she echoed, eyes wide with disbelief.

Marcus flushed. "There's a little girl named Livy who was staying with a friend while I was there and she had a thing for Disney movies."

"Ah," Divine said solemnly, but she suddenly had an image in her mind of Marcus watching a Disney car-toon with a little girl in pigtails. She had no idea if this Livy wore pigtails, but that was the image that sprang to mind. It was a beautiful image. She thought he'd be good with children. What would their children look like, she wondered, and then pushed the fantasy aside. He might be her life mate, but she could never claim him as one so long as he worked with Lucian.

"And before the Romani?" Marcus asked now.

Divine considered him briefly, and then said, "Isn't it time you told me a little about yourself?"

Marcus paused and then set his own fork down with a nod. "Fair enough."

She was glad he didn't argue the point . . . for two reasons. She really did want to learn more about him, but she also wanted to eat more of the delicious food on her plate, which was hard to do while she was talking.

Marcus took a sip of the water beside his plate and then set the glass down saying, "Okay. My grandparents are Marzzia and Nicodemus Notte. They were a part of the group of original immortals, the survivors of Atlantis."

"Atlantis?" she asked with bewilderment.

Marcus stilled and tilted his head. "Has no one taught you the history of our origins, Divine?"

She almost lied again and said yes rather than look ignorant, but then sighed and admitted, "No. I'm afraid not. My childhood was rather . . ." She frowned and glanced away.

"Unconventional?" he suggested gently, and the word made her snort indelicately.

Covering her mouth and nose quickly, she peered wide-eyed at him over her hand and then suddenly lost patience with herself. She was no shrinking violet. She had taken care of herself for millennia, and would be damned if encountering a life mate she couldn't claim, and recalling a childhood that had been a horror all around, was going to reduce her to the state of a blithering idiot afraid to say what she felt or meant or wanted. Her history was her history and that was that. She couldn't change it, and he could accept it, deal with it, or just get the hell out of her life if he didn't like it.

Letting her hand drop she said, "Unconventional does not begin to describe my childhood. For one thing, my parents were not true life mates." His eyebrows rose at that and she nodded. "My mother, Tisiphone, was older than my father, Felix, and she wanted a child. My father was apparently very likable and easygoing and so she decided he would do."

Divine paused to take a drink of water before continuing, "While my father couldn't read Tisiphone, he knew she was older so thought nothing of it." She grimaced and added, "Until Tisiphone claimed she couldn't read him either and they therefore must be life mates."

"She was lying?" Marcus asked.

Divine nodded. "Yes. She could read him . . . and control him too. She used both skills, plus manipulation and drugs, to make him think he was experiencing the infamous life mate sex."

Marcus frowned. "Was your father young enough to still eat?"

Divine shook her head. "I gather she used mind control, or perhaps drugs too, to make him think he was hungry and that the food was the most delicious he'd ever had and whatnot."

"And she did all this for a baby?" he asked with a

frown. "Why not just manipulate a mortal into impregnating her? Hell, she wouldn't even have had to manipulate one. They'd have been lining up to sleep with her."

When Divine raised her eyebrows at that, he explained, "We apparently give off some chemical mix of hormones that makes us seem ultra attractive to mortals."

"Really?" she asked with interest. Divine hadn't known that. But it explained why mortal men seemed always to be making nuisances of themselves around her.

"Yes," Marcus said, and then added. "Even if that hadn't worked, she could have easily influenced any mortal to think she was gorgeous. Although, if you got your looks from her, she must have already been gorgeous."

Divine felt her face heat up at the compliment and rolled her eyes at her own reaction. Seriously? Blushing? She was too damned old to blush, she thought, and then said, "Yes, she could have. But apparently my mother didn't want just any baby. She wanted the baby of a man from a powerful family."

"And your father, Felix? He was from a powerful family?"

Divine almost bit off her tongue as she realized that she'd given something away that might be dangerous. Trying to act as if she hadn't, she shrugged. "Apparently, although I only heard all of this from a servant. And my mother had been a servant herself before she tricked my father into thinking he was her life mate."

"Your mother was older than your father, immortal, and yet a servant?" Marcus asked with surprise.

Divine shrugged. "That's what I was told."

Marcus sat back and shook his head at this news, apparently finding it hard to believe. She could understand why. As an immortal Tisiphone could have controlled and influenced any number of wealthy mortals into marrying her, and with them under her control, they would have let her do whatever she wanted with their wealth. Heck, she could even have just used mind control to make them give her their wealth if she'd been of a mind to. That was certainly no less dastardly than what she'd done to Divine's poor father. But the truth was she'd needed the power of Divine's father's family to get her out of servitude. Because she'd been a servant to another powerful, immortal family to pay a debt she owed for causing the death of one of their children.

Marcus cleared his throat suddenly and Divine glanced to him. He was about to ask a question, and she knew exactly what it would be. What was the name of her father's powerful family? She couldn't answer that, so quickly said, "Of course, her lies and manipulations couldn't hold up forever. I was four when my father eventually figured out that she'd used him. Once he realized that, he apparently snuck out a message explaining the situation and asking for help with one of the servants, who was ordered to take it to one of his brothers."

"She could still control him," Marcus realized with slow dawning horror at the predicament her father had been in.

Divine nodded. "And she could still read him, which she must have done. The night after the servant slipped away with the message, she barricaded the doors and windows of our home and set it on fire."

"And then took you with her when she fled?" Marcus asked.

"Oh, she didn't flee," Divine corrected him. "She barricaded all of us in the house while we slept: myself, my father, the rest of the servants, and herself. She meant for all of us to die."

"How did you get out?" Marcus asked at once.

"The servants," Divine said quietly. "They slept on the main floor and woke first. She tried to control them and make them just sit down and let themselves burn, but there were apparently four of them, too many to control all at once. I gather she gave it a good try though," she added dryly. "She kept them busy long enough that by the time my father woke to their cries, the fire was raging."

"He rushed downstairs, sent one of the servants up to get me, and tried to battle with my mother, but she could still control him. When Aegle, the mortal servant my father had sent to fetch me, returned to the top of the stairs with me in her arms, two of the remaining servants were dead and the third was rushing up the stairs while my mother and father struggled below, the pair of them engulfed in flames."

Divine paused, more to let Marcus digest everything she'd just said than for her own sake. To her, this was an old story, one she'd lived with her whole life. She had no more tears for her long-lost parents and felt only sadness for her father who had been used so poorly and then had died trying to save her and the servants.

"The servants got you out," Marcus said finally.

It wasn't a question, but Divine nodded in response anyway. "They managed to unblock an upstairs window and jump out with me." She turned her fork absently on her plate and said, "I don't know what became of the other servant. I think Aegle said she left us, planning to return to her own family, but Aegle stayed in the area for three days waiting for my father's brother to come before giving up and setting out to try to find my family herself." She glanced to him and grimaced before explaining, "Aegle was actually my nanny, though I don't think they called it that back then. She'd cared for me since birth and had been trusted with our secrets. She knew that I was an immortal and needed blood to survive and did her best to help me get it. But I was young and couldn't yet control the minds of donors which made matters difficult."

"How the devil did she see you fed then?" he asked with amazement.

"I don't remember it, but I was later told that she lured men to a secluded area and then knocked them out so that I could feed on them." Divine smiled faintly. "Aegle was a very intelligent and creative woman."

"No wonder she had to move after a couple of days then," Marcus said with amusement. "I'm actually surprised she stayed in the area as long as she did with those men no doubt out looking for her."

Divine nodded.

"So she was able to find your family and reunite you

with them?" he asked after a moment when Divine didn't continue.

"Eventually."

Marcus's eyes narrowed. "How eventually?"

Divine sighed. "I was eleven when we kind of stumbled across an uncle who read my mind, realized who I was, and took us to my grandparents."

"Do you mean to tell me it took seven years for—"

"Yes," Divine interrupted. "I'm afraid the way we were forced to live didn't help. Actually, it hampered it greatly. We could never stay anywhere long with her having to knock out people for me to feed on."

Marcus dropped back in his chair with dismay. "You had no one to teach you to read or control their minds so she could stop knocking them out."

"No," Divine admitted.

For some reason her answer made him frown, and he said slowly, "But surely you began to learn to do so on your own? It is a natural skill. Training helps, but with enough time around mortals you should have begun to pick up on their thoughts, and then started to be able to begin to control them."

"But I wasn't spending time around mortals other than Aegle," she told him. "We were constantly moving, traveling mostly at night to avoid the sun's damage and the need to feed even more often. And then the stories of Aegle's attacks on men became almost legendary and we had to avoid people in case they had heard of her and had been given a description."

"Hmmm." Marcus shook his head. "It's a wonder you found your uncle at all."

"That was pure luck," she admitted. "He happened to be in the same area as us on business. Aegle spotted him while she was looking for a likely man to lure away for my next meal. She noticed that he looked similar to my father, and then she saw his eyes and knew he must be an immortal like me because of the metallic silver in the blue, and she approached him. But when she asked if he knew Felix, he eyed her suspiciously and asked, "Who wants to know?"

Divine smiled softly. "Despite all she did for me and the chances she made herself take to help me survive, Aegle didn't consider herself a brave woman and his reaction frightened her. My father had been such a charming and easygoing man that she felt sure she'd made a mistake and rather than say anything, simply scurried away and hurried back to me. But she'd caught his attention with my father's name, and he apparently read her mind, and followed her back to me."

Her smile faded. "He was a hard man. Taciturn by nature and not very . . ." She hesitated, searching for the right word, and finally said, "He wasn't very sympathetic. He gave us quite a fright when he strode into our little camp, and then simply started barking orders. When we didn't move fast enough for him, he bundled us both up on his horse, grabbed the reins, and simply led us back to the village where Aegle had run into him. It was only then he said that he was my uncle, the one my father had sent a message to. That the family had been looking for me for years and he was taking us to them."

"Aegle went with you?" Marcus asked with a smile.

"Of course. She was the closest thing to a mother I knew at that point. I wouldn't have gone without her," Divine said solemnly.

Marcus nodded in understanding, and then asked, "And your grandparents? Were they happy to see you when your uncle took you to them?"

"Oh yes." Divine smiled. "They welcomed me with open arms. They were both very sweet and loving. They were kind to Aegle too. They offered her a position in the household as my guardian so that we wouldn't be separated, and paid her very generously, promising her a home and enough wealth to retire on when she was ready. We both suddenly had beautiful clothes and plenty of food and my grandparents taught me how to read and control minds. Everything was perfect. It was all like a fairy tale really," she said sadly, and thought that every fairy tale had a monster.

"But they didn't teach you about our heritage?" he asked with a frown.

Divine shook her head. "They spent the next year not only teaching me how to use and control my abilities, but catching me up on all the things I'd missed as possible while wandering around with Aegle. I was eleven years old with no education at all other than how to hide and survive," she pointed out. "I had to learn to read and write and do math and . . ." She shrugged helplessly.

"And after that?" Marcus asked. "Why didn't they teach you once you'd learned the necessities?"

"They didn't get the chance," she said woodenly, and

then took another drink of water, set it down, peered at him and said, "I guess you'll have to teach me about Atlantis."

"Oh," Marcus looked surprised by the suggestion.

"After you tell me more about yourself," she added firmly. "All you've told me so far is that your grandparents were Marzzia and Nicodemus Notte and that they were survivors of Atlantis."

"Right," Marcus muttered and then made a face. "I'm afraid my history isn't nearly as interesting as yours. My mother was my grandparents' third daughter, Claudia. Her life mate was a mortal male she turned. My father, Cyrus, died, beheaded in battle shortly before I was born, and my mother returned to her parents to have me. They helped her raise me."

"And then?" Divine prompted, unwilling to let him stop there.

"A few years later my grandparents had their first and, so far, only son, and—"

"So far?" Divine interrupted with surprise. "They're still alive?"

Marcus smiled wryly and nodded. "They're a pair of tough old birds. Nothing short of an apocalypse will take them out."

"Oh," she said faintly and wondered if she'd ever meet them . . . or if she ever had.

"Anyway, they had a son, Julius," Marcus continued. "While he was my uncle, I was a bit older. Still the two of us were close enough in age that we became fast friends. Then one day my grandfather sat me down and told me there was a threat to Julius's well-being. Someone meant him harm and he wanted me to keep an eye out for him and watch Julius's back."

Divine raised her eyebrows at this, but didn't interrupt again.

"I loved Julius like a brother, so of course I agreed to the request," Marcus said. "And spent most of my life working and playing at his side."

"What kind of work?" Divine asked curiously, trying to imagine what it would be. He was very strong and well built, which suggested physical labor, but he was also smart.

"Back in the beginning it was many things; sword for hire, courier, etc."

"Warrior," Divine said, nodding. She wouldn't have expected anything less. He had the body of a warrior who had to wield large weapons.

"Later it changed to other concerns," Marcus continued, "And now we have an umbrella company that shelters several different industries. The main one right now though is an international construction company."

Divine smiled. She could see him in construction. Shirt off, tight jeans clinging to his hips, construction boots, and his body dripping with sweat as he wielded a sledgehammer. A fantasy, she knew. If he helped run the company, it was doubtful he wielded anything more than a pen, but she was enjoying the fantasy.

"Most of the family works for or has shares in the family company," Marcus continued, drawing Divine's reluctant attention away from her pleasant little daydream. "As have I off and on over the centuries."

"Why off and on?" she asked curiously.

Marcus shrugged. "Julius had his moments of rebellion over the centuries and since I was supposed to be watching his back—"

"You had to go where he went," she finished for him.

Marcus nodded. "And then a little over five hundred years ago Julius met his life mate and they had a son, Christian." He smiled wryly and said, "And then a similar situation arose with Christian, a threat to his life, and Julius asked me to—"

"No," Divine interrupted on a half laugh. "Surely he didn't ask you to watch out for his son's well-being and guard his back?"

"Yes, he did," Marcus said with shared amusement.

"What did you do?" she asked curiously.

Marcus shrugged. "What could I do? Julius was all grown up and whatever threat there had been hadn't seemed to manifest itself, but Christian was just a babe and the threat to him was very real."

"What was the threat to him?" Divine asked curiously.

Marcus hesitated and then said, "Julius was away when Christian was born and his mother bore him while away from the house. A servant then brought the boy back in a panic, claiming the mother had ordered him killed."

"Had she?" Divine asked.

"Yes," Marcus said solemnly. "She did give the order, though there was more to it than that. However, we didn't find that out at the time. All we knew was that she'd ordered him killed. He needed protecting."

"From his own mother," Divine said with a shake of the head. It seemed her mother hadn't been the only cold, heartless, crazed bitch out there. At least she wasn't alone in that.

"So you protected and guarded him," she murmured.

"Yes," Marcus said solemnly.

"For how long?" she asked.

Marcus considered the question and then seemed to do some figuring in his head. "Everything was resolved about three years ago."

"And what did you do after that?" she prompted. They were getting closer to the now. Had he started working for Lucian then?

"Well, Julius connected with his life mate at about that time and was a bit distracted so I stepped in and took on the job of running the family company until he got past that, which took a couple or three years."

"And once he was back running the company full-time?" Divine prodded.

"Well, he didn't really come back full-time. Marguerite—his life mate," he explained with a fond smile that suggested he liked the woman—"she and her family live in Canada, so Julius spends a great deal of time traveling back and forth between Italy and Canada."

"Italy," Divine breathed, sitting back in her seat as her gaze swam over his face. She should have known by the name and his looks that he hailed from there. He even had a bit of an accent, although it seemed to have been watered down and distorted, probably by his living in a lot of different places. Divine doubted he'd spent his whole life in Italy. He seemed to have French inflections, German, Spanish, and even English sounds to his speech . . . as she did. That being the case, she supposed she would have classified his accent as simply being European in origin.

Realizing that he was peering at her in question, she shook her head. "Sorry. Go ahead. Julius travels between Italy and Canada so . . . ?" She tilted her head and suggested, "So you run the company when he's not there and step down when he is?"

"I did," Marcus said wryly. "But thanks to developments in technology even that isn't necessary anymore. So long as he has a computer and cell phone handy, Julius can run the company from anywhere in the world. He can bank online, conference call meetings . . ." Marcus shrugged. "It took him a couple years to get a handle on the new technology, but now that he has, he doesn't really need me anymore. And now that Christian has met his life mate . . ." He shrugged and admitted wryly, "I'm pretty much at loose ends."

Divine considered him solemnly. He wasn't going to admit to spying for Lucian and she supposed she couldn't blame him for that. What kind of a spy would admit they were spying?

"Why stay here in North America?" she asked abruptly, wanting to know how he'd explain that away. "Why not return to Italy? Surely they could find a position for you in the family business?"

"I considered that," Marcus admitted quietly. "And certainly they have many things for me to do there, but I found myself too restless to go back to the family company once Julius took over again. It just didn't sound appealing."

"So you just suddenly decided to fly to America and join the carnival?" she asked quietly.

Marcus hesitated, toying with his silverware and avoiding her eyes as he did. After a moment, though, he raised his head to offer her a crooked smile and said, "Actually I drove here and joined the carnival. I was in Canada until a couple days ago."

"I see." Divine stood and began gathering dishes. "I guess we should call it a night."

Despite refusing to look directly at him, Divine caught glimpses of the worried frown suddenly on Marcus's face, so wasn't surprised when he said, "But what about explaining Atlantis?"

"That will have to wait," she said, unable to keep the stiffness out of her voice. "We've been talking most of the night as it is and it's nearly dawn. Morning comes early at the carnival."

"Right," Marcus murmured, and began to gather the salad dressings, and then stopped and frowned as he asked, "Did I say something wrong?"

"It's what you didn't say," she muttered, suddenly angry. He was her life mate. He wasn't supposed to lie to her, was he? Even by omission?

"What do you mean?" he asked at once. "What didn't I say?"

"Oh, I don't know. Why don't *you* tell *me*?" Divine suggested dryly as she turned to scrape her plate into the pull-out garbage pail under the sink. She then dropped the plate in the garbage to scoot desperately to the side in an effort to avoid his touch when he went to grab her arm. No doubt he'd merely intended to pull her around to face him, but she couldn't risk his touching her. One touch and they'd both go up like tinder. She was pretty sure of that.

"Divine," he said with exasperation, moving to close the space between them. "I'm not going to hurt you. I could never hurt you. You're my life mate."

"Really?" she asked, backing away from him. "I'm not so sure of that. How do I know you're not just like my mother? You could be lying about being younger than me. You could really be older than me and able to read and control me. Maybe you're just claiming to be my life mate to lull me into a false sense of security or something."

"How could I lie about being younger than you? I never said I was. All I did was tell you how old I am. I don't know how old you are," he said reasonably. "And why would I want to lull you into a false sense of security?"

Because you're Uncle Lucian's spy.

Divine so wanted to say that, but she bit back the words and stared at him.

"Besides, there is no way what we experienced out there beside the RV tonight wasn't life mate sex," he said firmly. "I felt every shaft of pleasure that went through your body, every quiver of excitement my touch raised. And you felt mine. Didn't you."

It wasn't a question but a statement. And he was right, she *had* experienced his pleasure with him . . . or she thought she had. Either he really was her life mate, or he was one hell of a good faker. And the man was just standing there, so bloody beautiful with his bare chest, bare feet, and tight jeans. His hair was dry now, but lay ruffled around his head. She could remember how damned soft it had felt under her fingers, as soft as the rest of him had been hard.

She'd wanted to feel all that hardness against her softness, Divine recalled. She'd wanted his naked skin against hers. She'd wanted him filling her with the bulging erection she'd felt with her hand . . . and she'd never got the chance. Might never get the chance if she found the opportunity to slip away today, reclaim her motorcycle, and escape.

"Divine?"

She shifted her gaze to his face and noted that his eyes were sliding over her body more silver than black. Muttering, "Ah hell," she closed the small space between them and basically plastered herself against his chest, her hands reaching to draw his head down to hers. Divine didn't have to do much drawing. His head lowered eagerly to let his mouth claim hers and then they were on that lovely roller coaster called life mate sex again. Only this ride had a bunch of highs and exciting turns and only one low, the one that waited to drag them under at the end.

That low on her mind, Divine began to move slowly backward, drawing Marcus with her toward the door to the bedroom. He went willingly enough, but didn't stop kissing her and began touching her as well as they went.

His hands slid up her arms, partway down, then simply moved around to claim her breasts through the cotton of her blouse. Divine bit into his lip in reaction, then immediately reached up to tug at her blouse, pulling it down and out from under his fingers so that they were against her naked flesh.

The moment she did, Marcus stopped walking to bend and lash first one nipple and then the other with his tongue. The man had a very talented tongue, she decided faintly, clutching at his head with one hand and his shoulder with the other to keep her feet beneath her as pleasure washed through her.

Divine felt his hand drop to her behind and start to squeeze and then he suddenly dropped to kneel before her, his mouth never ceasing in the attention it was giving her breasts. But when he began to urge her skirt up her legs, she gasped and shook her head as she grabbed for the wandering hand. They were still a foot from the door to the bedroom.

"Oh, no, no, no," she managed to get out. "The bedroom."

"Okay." He rumbled the word around one excited nipple. Then he let that nipple slip from his mouth.

Divine was torn between disappointment that he was no longer suckling her and relief that they were going to move this to the bedroom, but before she could move, he suddenly lowered himself to sit on his feet before her.

"What—?" she began with confusion and then nearly bit her tongue off when he suddenly pushed up her skirt and pressed his mouth to the inside of her left thigh.

"Oh God no," she gasped and would have tried to push his mouth away, but couldn't seem to make her hands do her bidding. They did reach for his head, but instead of pushing, they caught in his hair and tugged encouragingly as he ran his tongue upward. His tongue was a bare inch from the top of her leg, when he suddenly let go of her skirt with one hand and instead clasped her leg to draw it over his shoulder. Before it had even settled there, his tongue had found the nub at the core of her excitement and proceeded to show her just how talented it was.

Divine struggled briefly to keep herself upright, but when his finger then found the center of her and slid in and out even as his lips plucked at her nub and tongue flicked it at the same time . . . Well, she cried out and threw her head back, managing to completely lose her balance. In the next moment she was falling. Fortunately, darkness claimed her before she hit her head on the bedroom door frame.

Sixteen

"Really, he's not as bad as you seem to be reading in your crystal ball. He can be sweet."

Divine blinked her eyes open at those strained words and stared at the door frame overhead, her mind a complete blank for a moment.

"Kiddo, he's an uneducated, unemployed, pothead thief who treats you like crap. You really need to cut him loose and find someone else."

That was Jackie's voice, she realized. Who the devil was she talking to? *And where the devil am I?* Divine lifted her head to glance around, then let it drop back down as she realized she was lying in the bedroom doorway of the borrowed trailer. At least her head was, the rest of her was sprawled on the floor of the kitchenette with Marcus lying half on top of her, his head in her lap . . . under her skirt. Dear God, they had—

"I told you, he just *borrowed* his dad's girlfriend's car.

He didn't steal it. He borrowed it for the day and then took it back a little after midnight. He's not a thief."

Divine didn't recognize that voice but it sounded like a young female, a rather desperate young female. And she sounded close. Turning her head to try to find the source of the voice, Divine took note of the fact that the curtain had been drawn between the lounging area and the kitchenette where she and Marcus now lay. The voices seemed to be coming from the lounge beyond it.

That curtain had not been closed last night. But then Jackie hadn't been there last night either. Her gaze swiveled to the small clock hanging over the sink and Divine almost groaned aloud. It was almost three o'clock in the afternoon. They'd passed out on the floor and slept right through what had remained of morning and a good portion of the afternoon to boot. Jackie must have come searching for them when they hadn't shown up that morning and—

Divine sat up abruptly, horror sliding through her as she realized that the woman must have seen them like this. She peered down at the skirt-covered lump in her lap that was Marcus's head, noted that the collar of her top was sitting down under her breasts, and closed her eyes. Wow. Well, this was embarrassing.

"Taking without right or permission is the definition of stealing," Jackie said firmly from the other side of the curtain. "It doesn't matter that he brought the car back. Taking it in the first place was theft."

"God, you're being as hard on him about this as his dad and the girlfriend are." The younger woman sounded resentful.

"Of course they're being hard on him," Jackie responded at once. "Theft is a serious business." .

"He *brought it back*," the girl stressed.

"Right," Jackie said sounding unimpressed. "And did he bring back the money he took from your purse to buy his pot?"

Divine's eyebrows rose. The girl had a real winner there. Shaking her head, she tugged her skirt up, eased Marcus's head off her lap to rest on the floor, and then got silently to her feet.

"You can see that in your crystal ball too?" the younger woman cried with dismay. "What else can you see? Is he screwing around on me? If he is, he's out of my apartment."

Divine rolled her eyes as she brushed the worst of the wrinkles out of her skirts. So his being an uneducated, unemployed pothead who treated her like crap and apparently not only stole from her, but sponged off her as well wasn't enough to convince the girl to leave. But if he was messing around he was done?

At least the girl had some limits on what she would put up with, Divine thought wryly as she turned and slid through the bedroom to the bathroom door. She'd encountered too many mortal women who hadn't seemed to have any limits at all on the bad behavior they would take from a partner. They didn't seem to recognize their own value and that they deserved so much more, which was such a shame. Mortals had such short lives, so little time to enjoy all that life and the world had to offer. Why would they waste even a moment of their precious time on someone who didn't appreciate and treat them well?

Divine shook her head over that as she slipped into the bathroom and pulled the door closed, blocking out the voices from the other side of the curtain. She was in and out of the tiny room quickly, only taking the time to rinse her face and run a brush through her hair. She would have liked to stop to change her clothes then too, but when she slid out of the bathroom and stuck her head out of the bedroom to check, the sounds coming from the other side of the curtain suggested Jackie was wrapping up the session and preparing to see the girl out.

Straightening her shoulders, Divine forced her head up and moved to the curtain to tug the end of it a few inches away from the wall. She noted that they'd set up a small round table between the sofa and chairs in the lounge, covering it with an antique tablecloth, and then placing what looked like an honest-to-God crystal ball in the middle. It was probably a prop, but still . . . Divine had never bothered with such stage setting, merely taking the client's hand as if reading the future through some strange energy emanating from them. Which was really what she did. She read their thoughts and helped them clarify the situation they already knew about but were possibly ignoring, or lying to themselves about.

Shrugging, Divine glanced to the women in the room. A petite blonde in jeans and T-shirt was just rising from one of two folding chairs set on either side of the table as Jackie got up from the other.

Her eyebrows rose at the sight of the woman. Vincent's mate was wearing a long flowing skirt, a peasant blouse, a red scarf around her head, the most god-awful gaudy jewelry she'd ever seen, and ridiculously dramatic makeup. Probably Vincent's doing, Divine decided. Jackie looked like a theater version of a Gypsy rather that the real thing.

She'd barely had the thought when Jackie glanced her way as she ushered the girl to the door. She paused at once, a smile curling her lips.

"Good morning," she said, smiling widely. "You look well rested."

Divine grimaced at the words as she pulled the curtain further open. She normally didn't sleep more than a couple of hours a day, but she'd certainly got more than a couple of hours of sleep this morning. It had been just before 6 A.M. when she and Marcus had— Well, anyway, that couldn't have taken more than a couple minutes so she must have slept a good nine hours straight. Strange for her.

"Who's she?"

Divine glanced to the blonde at that curious question, but it was Jackie who answered.

"Don't worry about it. Go on now. Have a good day," she said cheerfully, and then pushed the girl out the door, adding grimly, "And dump that loser you call a boyfriend."

Closing the door, Jackie turned to Divine and said wryly, "I don't know how you do it. I swear I've wanted to slap some sense into half the people who have come in here this morning."

"That's about par for the course," Divine said with amusement.

"Hmmm." Jackie wrinkled her nose at this news and then asked, "Is Marcus up?"

"He is now."

Divine gave a start at that announcement and glanced over her shoulder as Marcus pushed himself to his feet and walked toward her.

"Is that Jackie?" he asked as he approached.

Realizing she'd only opened the curtain enough to frame herself, she pushed it further open now so that he could see the other woman. "Yes. She opened shop while we slept. Thank you for that, by the way," Divine added, turning back to offer a grateful smile to the woman.

Jackie smiled in return and shrugged. "It's fun."

Divine snorted at the claim, knowing it was sometimes interesting, sometimes rewarding, and sometimes just plain frustrating, but not really ever fun.

"Well, I appreciate it," she said sincerely, stiffening a little with surprise when Marcus slipped an arm around her waist. Smile a little forced now, she eased out from under Marcus's arm and turned back into the kitchenette saying, "You go ahead and find that husband of yours and I'll quick-change and take over now."

"Don't be silly, I'll continue here for the afternoon," Jackie said at once, bringing her to a reluctant halt. When Divine turned back, she added, "You need to eat, feed, shower, and change. Just grab some clothes and head to our RV, you can shower and everything else there."

Divine shook her head at once. "Oh, I can't make you—"

"You aren't making me do anything," Jackie said firmly, moving into the kitchenette to catch her by the shoulders and urge her toward the bedroom door. "Besides, I want you to meet Tiny and Mirabeau."

"Are they here already?" Marcus asked, trailing after them as they entered the bedroom.

"Got in early this morning. Arrived with half the apples grown in California and enough caramel and chocolate to cover the state," Jackie announced dryly, and then squeezed Divine's shoulders and said, "You're going to love Tiny. He's been my best friend for ages. He's a sweetie. And his partner, Mirabeau, is lovely too."

Divine murmured noncommittally, hardly noticing when Jackie left her by the end of the bed and moved to the closet. Her mind was busy trying to find a way to get rid of Jackie and Marcus and reclaim her position as Madame Divine. The arrival of the other couple was only going to complicate matters and make escaping more difficult. She needed to think and found it difficult to do so with Marcus nearby.

"I hope you don't mind, but I slipped in and borrowed one of your outfits this morning when I realized you two weren't going to make opening. But there is plenty more here to choose from," Jackie announced, beginning to slide clothes along the rod in the small closet.

"Of course I don't mind." Divine smiled wryly as she took in the blue skirt and peasant blouse Jackie wore. How could she mind the woman wearing them when they weren't really hers anyway? Vincent had arranged for the clothes Jackie was now calling hers.

"I think the forest green skirt," Jackie decided, pulling out the skirt in question. "It will look great with your coloring."

Nodding, Divine walked over to take the skirt the woman was holding out. Then she reached past her and grabbed several scarves as well. She'd need them to add some color, Divine thought, and then glanced to the floor of the closet and the row of boots lined up there. She bent and picked up a pair of dark red-brown ones and then turned away with her booty, pausing briefly when she noted that Marcus was dragging clothes out of the closet on the opposite side of the bed.

"Vincent put Marcus's clothes in here," Jackie explained quickly. "There are only the two tiny closets in each of the RVs and we were using both of ours."

"Of course," Divine murmured and simply turned to head out of the room. But as she entered the kitchenette area, she frowned and said, "Maybe I should shower and change here. That way Marcus can use the shower in your RV and—"

"The sound of the shower would be distracting for the people wanting a reading," Jackie pointed out and shook her head. "No. It's better you use the other RV. You'll like it better anyway. It has a bigger shower," she added in tempting tones, and then smiled wryly and added, "Everything about it is bigger. It's the 'luxury' RV Vincent had made for our stakeouts and he insists everything should be bigger and better. The man is spoiled rotten."

Divine couldn't help smiling at the claim. Especially since Jackie made it with a combination of exasperation, amusement, love, and something that sounded very much like pride.

"All set," Marcus announced, coming out of the bedroom. He'd pulled on a T-shirt and boots and looked ready for the day. His gaze slid to Divine. "Don't worry about the shower. It's yours. I have to get to work before Chapman or Mac come looking for me."

"They won't. Vincent filled in for you today," Jackie announced.

That sent Marcus's eyebrows shooting upward. "Vincent? Work?"

"He's just running the Tilt-A-Whirl, it's not like he's slinging steel or something," Jackie said with amusement. "And actually, I think he's enjoying himself. He's surprisingly good at luring in riders with his patter. Must be the theater in him."

"Must be," Divine said with a smile.

"You two go on next door," Jackie said, ushering them into the lounge area. "I should get back to work. The natives are probably getting restless out there."

"No doubt," Divine murmured and then stepped outside when Marcus pushed the door open for her. She paused after one step though, her hand instinctively rising to block out the worst of the sun as the day slapped her. It was the hottest part of the afternoon. The sun was high in the sky and the heat was a wave that plastered itself to her skin like thin, clinging plastic. It stole Divine's breath, even as the glare of the sun blinded her.

She sucked in a lungful of stifling air and blinked several times to get her eyes to adjust and then let her breath out on a sigh as the blurry glare subsided into the shapes and color that made up the midway. People of all shapes and sizes milled everywhere, rides turned and whirled in motion, various songs and sounds rose from the different rides clashing in the air with the sound of laughter, the patter of ride jockeys and game agents, and the excited screams of the people on the rides. And all of it accompanied by the smells of popcorn and food grilling under the burning Death Valley sun. Carnival life.

"Okay?" Marcus asked, resting a hand on her shoulder.

Forcing a smile, Divine nodded and descended the stairs to weave her way through the line outside her door to get to the RV next to this one. Like hers the door on Jackie and Vincent's RV was on the side, so she had to walk around the back of their RV to get to it. Divine was shifting the bundle of clothes she carried so that she could open the door when Marcus reached past her to do it for her.

Murmuring a thank-you, Divine slid inside and was brought up short again.

This RV was set up much the same as the one she was using, except that both the kitchenette and lounge were a bit bigger. They were also both presently filled with apples; baskets of the sweet red fruit filled every space on the floor as well as the couch and the chairs in both the lounge and kitchenette. Meantime the countertops and kitchen table were covered with trays of apples, each with a Popsicle stick poking out of it. They were also all coated with some variation of chocolate or caramel or both, and then had been rolled in various toppings ranging from crushed peanuts to tiny marshmallows. The stove was the only place free of apples. Instead it held four large, simmering pots that a huge man was stirring by turn as he hummed.

"Hi, you must be Marcus and Divine. Awake at last, huh?"

Divine turned to peer blankly at the woman who had spoken. Tall and curvaceous with short, dark hair highlighted with streaks of fuchsia, the woman wore an apron reading "Did you hug the chef today?" Under it were tight, faded jeans and a T-shirt. She was definitely interesting-looking, Divine decided, accepting the hand the woman extended in greeting as Marcus said, "Yes, I'm Marcus, and she is definitely Divine."

The way he said it suggested he wasn't talking about her name. She wasn't the only one to think so though, because the man at the stove looked amused as he murmured, "I'm sure she is."

Flushing, Divine peered at the man with curiosity. He really was a big fellow. Huge. Marcus was a big man, but not like this guy. She'd never seen shoulders quite as wide and muscular as this man had.

"This is my life mate and husband, Tiny," Mirabeau announced.

Moving to stand behind the man, Mirabeau slid one hand up and down the center of his broad back.

Tiny shivered and arched under the touch briefly before growling, "Woman, unless you want me to spill this fudge all over both of us, I suggest you cut that out."

Mirabeau grinned and leaned up to kiss his ear, murmuring, "That might be fun."

"Yeah," he agreed, bending to kiss the tip of her nose. Then he glanced past her to Divine and Marcus. "You two must be hungry. I'll whip you up some breakfast while you shower and change."

"Oh, that's not—"

"Thank you, Tiny. That'd be great," Marcus interrupted, urging Divine toward the door to the bedroom. "Go ahead, take a shower and get ready," he said, pushing her gently into the room. "I'll be out here with Tiny and Mirabeau."

Divine watched him close the door, stared at it for a minute, and then shrugged and headed into the bathroom.

Marcus stood by the door for a moment until he heard sounds that suggested Divine was actually going to do as he'd suggested, and then relaxed and turned to Tiny. "Good to see you again."

"You two know each other?" Mirabeau asked with surprise.

"That business with Vincent and Jackie," Tiny said solemnly.

"Oh yes." Mirabeau nodded at once and smiled apologetically at Marcus. "You and Christian arrived in time to help with the turn and what followed."

Marcus nodded. "I saw the two of you at the big multiwedding as well, but you were both a bit distracted and then gone, of course, on your secret mission. I'm glad that worked out all right."

"There were a couple of close moments, but it turned out better than all right in the end," Tiny said with a grin, slipping his free hand through Mirabeau's.

Marcus nodded as they shared a smile and muttered, "I should be so lucky."

Mirabeau glanced to him quickly. "Jackie told us about you and Divine. She might be Basha, but no one's sure."

Marcus grimaced and nodded.

"But Jackie says she's pretty sure that if Divine is Basha, she can't be rogue like Lucian thinks," Tiny added solemnly. "And I've never known Jackie to be wrong. Things will work out."

"From your mouth to God's ear," Marcus said, running a weary hand through his hair. He shouldn't be tired, he'd just woken up for God's sake, but he was as exhausted as if he hadn't slept at all.

"It's the situation," Mirabeau said sympathetically, as if he'd spoken his thoughts aloud. And he might as well have, he supposed. His mind was apparently an open book right now to everyone.

"Yeah, well, we've all been there, so can sympathize," Tiny said gently.

"Yeah," Marcus drew out the word and then asked wryly, "Do you think you could stop doing that and maybe only address things I say out loud?"

"We could try," Mirabeau said with amusement.

"I'd appreciate that," Marcus assured her.

"Why don't you come over here and stick some Popsicle sticks in apples and we'll try to sort out how you can convince Divine that she is your life mate and should accept you as hers," Tiny suggested, waving him over.

"She knows she's my life mate," Marcus muttered, accepting the bag of Popsicle sticks Tiny held out to him and then moving in front of an empty tray with a basket of apples beside it. "At least she should after last night."

"I'm afraid the issue isn't that she hasn't accepted that he is her life mate," Mirabeau commented, taking a stick from his bag and showing him how to stick it in the apple and place it on the tray. It was a pretty simple procedure. Still, examples were always good.

"No," Tiny agreed, moving back to stirring his pots. "It's convincing her that she can have him."

"She can have me," Marcus assured them, stabbing an apple. "Anytime, anywhere, anyhow."

"Yeah. I feel you, buddy," Tiny said with amusement.

Mirabeau rolled her eyes as the men shared a wry smile, and then said seriously, "But she doesn't think you'll want her for a life mate once you know she's Basha Argeneau."

Marcus stiffened, his head slowly turning to the woman. It was Tiny who said with surprise, "You're sure she's Basha?"

Mirabeau nodded solemnly. "It's right there in her thoughts, plain as day."

"I didn't get that," Tiny said with a frown.

"You haven't been an immortal for long, sweetheart. You might not be reading everything clearly."

"Yeah, but Jackie and Vincent didn't read that and Vincent is four or five hundred years old," Tiny pointed out.

"But I'm older," Mirabeau pointed out quietly. "And it's possible that wasn't on the top of her list of concerns when she arrived at Jackie and Vincent's. After all, Marcus was hurting, she was hurting . . ." Mirabeau shrugged.

"But it is now?" Marcus asked with a frown. "On the top of her list of concerns, I mean."

Mirabeau nodded. "She wants you as her lover and life mate. That's on the top of her mind right now. That she wants you, but doesn't think she can have you. That she has to escape. That you would turn from her anyway if you knew she was Basha. She knows you're a spy for Lucian."

"How the hell did she find that out?" Marcus growled, stabbing another apple, a little too enthusiastically this time. He snapped the stick.

Mirabeau took the apple from him to remove the stick and replace it. "I'm not sure. I guess she could have read Jackie and Vincent, but I don't think that's it." She was silent for a minute, and then shrugged and said, "It doesn't matter. The point is she knows you were sent here by Lucian to find her. She also knows Lucian is on the way here and she's desperate to escape."

"What do I do?" Marcus asked quietly.

Mirabeau shrugged. "You two need to spend time together doing more than fighting or having sex. You need to gain her trust, Marcus. I think Jackie's right and she isn't rogue, or at least not intentionally. But you need to get her to trust you so you can find out what's what."

Marcus was silent for a minute. He knew Divine—

Basha, he corrected himself, had been feeding off the hoof despite the Council's banning it. But she hadn't known about the ban. He wasn't sure that was enough to get her off the hook for it, but surely it had to be a consideration. He couldn't imagine she'd done anything else that would label her a rogue.

"About that," Mirabeau said, and Marcus peered at her blankly. He hadn't said anything. Oh right, he recalled, she could read his thoughts.

"About what?" he asked finally.

"The rogue thing," she said with a grimace.

"What about it?" he asked warily, suspecting by the way she was avoiding his eyes that he wouldn't like what she was about to say.

Mirabeau hesitated and then heaved a deep sigh. "Well, Lucian and the boys had Leonius sometime back. About two years ago. They raided a hotel in Toronto, and caught Leonius. Well, actually, they shot him," she corrected herself. "Through the heart with an arrow. He wasn't going anywhere."

Marcus narrowed his eyes when she paused again. He knew the story, but asked anyway, "And?"

"And someone took him. Just picked him up and carried him off while everyone was busy with his victims."

"Someone?" Marcus questioned grimly.

"Yeah, well, they didn't know who at first, but Mortimer, the head of Lucian's Rogue Hunters—"

"I know who Mortimer is," Marcus interrupted impatiently.

"Right. Well, he reviewed all of the hotel security tapes and it was a woman. Cameras in the stairwells showed a blond woman carrying Leonius up to the roof. I saw them. There were no really good pictures of her face, but from what I saw, it could have been Divine. A blond Divine."

Marcus didn't comment, but his heart was sinking. He'd discovered last night, while his head was under Divine's skirt, that her hair was not naturally the color she presently wore. Her hair was dyed.

"And then there's Dee," Mirabeau added.

"Dee?" Marcus asked. "The mortal victim and kind of co-conspirator to one of Leonius's sons?"

Mirabeau nodded. "She described a woman connected to Leonius named Basha, an ice blonde . . . who was his mother," she finished apologetically.

Marcus was so startled by that one that not only did he stab at the next apple with enough enthusiasm to break the stick, but he missed the apple entirely and broke the stick in his own hand. Cursing, he dropped the apple and jumped back, holding his injured hand by the wrist.

"Okay. No problem," Tiny said soothingly, at his side at once. The big man took his injured hand, quickly removed the stick, and wrapped a dish towel around the wound, then turned to open the small bar-sized fridge and retrieved a bag of blood for him.

Marcus slapped the bag to his mouth the moment Tiny handed it over, and then he just stood there, his head swimming. Divine was Basha . . . Leonius's *mother*?

"Wait a minute," he muttered, tearing the bag from his mouth. Fortunately, the damned thing had already emptied or it would have made one hell of a mess. "Divine can't be this Basha the mother of Leonius. It's not possible. She's immortal. He's no-fanger. The child gets their blood from their mother, whether they are mortal, immortal, or no-fanger. An immortal woman can't have a no-fanger child."

Tiny's eyebrows rose and then he glanced to Mirabeau in question.

"He's right," Mirabeau confirmed at once. "And while I did find a son in Divine's thoughts, his name is Damian not Leonius, but—"

"So she can't be this Basha who is Leonius's mother," Marcus said with relief.

Mirabeau shook her head. "But I read it in her mind. She *is* Basha Argeneau."

"So?" Marcus asked with irritation. "The other Basha could be Basha Smith or even Livius or something. They could both just have the same first name. I'm sure you're not the only Mirabeau in the world and I'm certainly not the only Marcus."

Mirabeau remained silent for a minute, and then shook her head. "I don't know. She looks an awful lot like the woman on the security footage and *she* thinks she's rogue or wanted for some reason."

Tiny peered from one of them to the other and then settled his gaze on Marcus. "I don't know either, but I think you'd better find out and do it quickly, before Lucian gets here."

Marcus sighed and ran his good hand through his hair with frustration. "How the hell am I supposed to do that?"

"Like Mirabeau said, you have to spend time with her and gain her trust," Tiny said simply.

"If only it was as simple as you make it sound," Marcus muttered.

"It is," Tiny assured him. "If you do what I say . . . and we have to have a quick chat with Jackie, Vincent, and Madge before Divine comes out."

Seventeen

Divine had meant to be quick about her shower and she would have been if she could have shut off her brain. Sadly, the moment she was standing under the shower, her mind returned to that morning and what had happened with Marcus. The man was definitely her life mate. Or he could have been, she thought unhappily. She suspected he wouldn't want her for a life mate if he knew who she was, and Divine couldn't help thinking how ironic it was that after more than twenty-seven hundred years she met her life mate and he was the enemy.

And she was so pathetic her mind was doing somersaults trying to figure out how she could have him . . . which was impossible. She knew it was. Still, her mind was running in circles trying to work it out. Maybe if she explained what had happened. Maybe if she could make him understand . . .

Of course there was no way of doing that. She couldn't be honest with him without risking . . . Well, she wasn't sure what she'd be risking. What would he do if she admitted she was Basha Argeneau? Would he restrain her until Uncle Lucian could get there? Or maybe he'd just kill her as other spies and scouts and so-called Rogue Hunters had been killing her grandsons for the last two thousand and seven hundred years, most of them under the age of ten, innocent children who had done nothing but been unlucky enough to be born her grandchildren.

Divine sighed and pressed her forehead against the cool tiles of the shower wall, suddenly ashamed that she'd even let Marcus touch her, or shared a smile or laugh with Vincent and Jackie. She was consorting with the enemy. People she'd feared and loathed most of her life.

On the other hand, her mind argued, her own grandsons had knocked her out and dragged her away from her RV and possibly later set it on fire, although she wasn't sure about that. It could have been Allen Paulson, or some other mortal she'd angered over the years by foiling their less-than-pleasant plans.

And her son was lying to her, Divine recalled. Damian had claimed that Marcus had knocked her out and the boys had saved her and brought her to him, when she knew he knew that wasn't true. She could understand his reluctance to tell her that his sons had done it and turn her against them, but this made her wonder . . . What other lies had he told her over the years?

More importantly, what had Damian done that Abaddon thought she might turn from her own son? That concern troubled her more than anything else. It made her suspicious and want to avoid him, and it made her frustrated that she couldn't read him. If she just knew . . . well, not knowing, she was imagining all sorts of things, all of them horrible, because it would take a lot to turn her from the boy she'd given birth to. She already knew that. Divine wasn't happy with the way he lived his life, or the people he surrounded himself with. She wasn't happy with how he raised his boys or his insistence on having so many of them. But he was her son. It would take breaking her rules on feeding and harming a mortal, or even an immortal to turn her from him. Surely he hadn't done that, though? She had raised him with the rules she'd been taught. He knew better than that . . . didn't he?

Sighing, Divine turned off the shower and stepped out to dry herself. It seemed to her that there was only one thing for her to do. She needed to slip away from the others, reclaim her motorcycle, and disappear. She needed to leave America and head somewhere else, perhaps somewhere in Asia this time. North America was too risky now. And leaving the country had the added benefit of putting some distance between herself and her son.

This wouldn't be the first time Divine had done that. She'd left Europe to put distance between them because of the way he lived, only he'd followed. This time she would have to ensure she didn't leave a trail. She would be alone again, but Divine was used to that, or she should have been, but somehow this time was different. The idea was wearying beyond belief. Perhaps because this time she would be leaving behind a life mate and any chance of ever having one. It had taken her 2,758 years to find Marcus; she wasn't foolish enough to imagine she'd find another possible life mate around the next corner. Once she walked away from him, that dream, one she'd never dared to dream before this, was dead. It made the future seem unbearably bleak.

Pushing these depressing thoughts firmly away, Divine concentrated on dressing. She'd found it was always best to live in the here and now rather than waste time with past events or what she couldn't have and what could have been. Mind you, living in the here and now wasn't always easy, but she did her best.

When Divine made her way out to the kitchenette, Marcus was standing at the counter, poking Popsicle sticks into apples. Mirabeau then dipped them in the pots of chocolate or caramel and rolled them in the peanuts and/or marshmallows before setting them on a tray to harden.

While they did that, Tiny was manning a frying pan that was putting out the most amazing smells Divine had encountered in her many years.

"Is there something I can do to help?" Divine asked after watching for a moment.

All three glanced around and smiled at her in greeting, but Tiny immediately opened a cupboard door and retrieved two plates to hold out to her, saying, "Perfect timing. The omelet is done. Take these."

Divine moved up beside the big man and took the empty plates. The moment she did, Tiny cut his masterpiece in half and slid each portion onto one of the plates. She peered down at the steaming plates with interest, unsure what she was looking at and knowing only that it smelled lovely.

"And here," Tiny added, reaching into the oven with an oven mitt to retrieve a plate with four slices of buttered toast on it that he'd apparently stored there to keep warm. He slid two slices of the golden toast on each plate. He then paused to consider his handiwork before nodding with satisfaction. "Enjoy."

"Thank you," Divine murmured.

"Don't thank me until you taste it," he said with a smile, and then glanced around the kitchen, pursed his lips, and muttered, "I'm not sure where you're going to eat though. I'm afraid we've sort of taken over everywhere with our apple making."

"No problem," Marcus said stabbing one last stick into an apple and then reaching to take the plates from Divine. "We'll eat in the front cab."

"The front cab?" Divine asked uncertainly as he started to turn away.

"Yeah. Come on," he said, heading for the lounge.

"Hang on, you'll need these," Tiny said, and when Divine turned back he was holding out a tray with silverware, two cups of coffee, cream and sugar.

"Thanks." Divine took the tray and turned away to follow Marcus.

He led her through the lounge to the curtained off front of the RV and held the curtain aside for her to pass. Divine slipped by him and then hesitated before choosing the passenger seat. She then glanced to the center console between the two front seats, happy to see that like on hers, a flap could slide forward to make it a table of sorts.

"The seats turn too," Marcus said, settling in the driver's seat.

Divine merely nodded and set the tray on the console, then leaned to the side a bit to adjust her seat so that it would turn toward the center console. She then took both plates from Marcus so that he could do the same.

"Thanks," he murmured, taking back one of the plates. After a hesitation, he turned the tray so that it only took half the console. That left just enough room for their plates to rest next to it and they both set their plates down.

"It smells good," Divine murmured, peering over the folded-over flap of something pale yellow on her plate. "Tiny called it an omelet?"

"Egg folded over—" Marcus lifted part of the upper flap to see what was inside. "—cheese, onion, green pepper, and sausage."

Divine lifted the top corner of her half to peer inside. It looked a bit of a mess inside, but smelled divine.

"Christian loves these. Caro makes them for him all the time," Marcus commented, cutting off a piece. "I've never been tempted to even try one before this, but now . . ." He paused and smiled wryly as his stomach rumbled, then shrugged and popped the bite of omelet into his mouth.

Divine watched him chew and swallow and then raised an eyebrow. "Well?"

"Mmmm, amazing," Marcus announced, cutting off another piece.

"Thank you," Tiny called out from the other side of the curtain.

Divine chuckled and cut a piece for herself. She was more tentative about putting it in her mouth though. This eating business was really quite new to her still. She shifted the food around inside her mouth, chewed experimentally, and then smiled as she swallowed. Turning to the curtain, she called out, "He's right. Amazing."

"Thank you," Tiny repeated cheerfully.

They ate in silence for a bit, but it had been so long since she'd eaten that Divine was full before she'd eaten a third of her omelet. She hadn't eaten much last night either, she recalled as she set her plate down and turned her attention to the coffees on the tray. Madge and Bob drank coffee all the time. Divine had never tried it. Now she peered at the dark liquid uncertainly.

"Bob drinks his with cream and sugar, but Madge takes it black. Less calories she says," Divine commented.

"You don't have to worry about calories," Marcus said with amusement. "But if you aren't sure how you'll like it, try it black and then add cream and sugar and try it again."

"Good idea," she said, and picked up the nearest cup to take a sip, grimacing at the flavor. Good God it was bitter and . . . well, she didn't even know how to describe it. Swallowing the bit she'd taken, Divine set the cup back and put two teaspoons of sugar in, and then poured some cream in as well until it was a pretty caramel color. She stirred it for quite a while before risking tasting it again.

"Well?" Marcus asked.

Divine shrugged a bit. "Better."

He chuckled at her lack of enthusiasm and fixed his coffee the same way, then took a sip and sighed. "I like it."

She smiled at his expression. He looked . . . satisfied, she decided, and sipped at her coffee again.

"Shall I tell you about Atlantis now?"

Divine glanced up with surprise at the question. "Now?"

"You have anything better to do?" he asked.

Smiling wryly, she shook her head. She could hardly escape just now, unless she could come up with an excuse to slip his presence for a bit.

"Maybe you should tell me what you know about our . . . state?"

"Our state?" she asked with amusement.

"Well, why we're different than mortals. Do you know about nanos?"

Divine nodded. "Yes. My nanny only told me that I was different than others and needed blood to survive, but my gran told me once that I was different because I had nanos and they were what needed the extra blood." She smiled faintly at the memory. "When I asked what nanos were she said they were basically little tiny miracle workers in our blood that kept us healthy and well."

"That's it?" Marcus asked with a frown.

"It was bedtime and she was trying to get me to sleep," Divine explained and then sighed and added, "I did ask once or twice about the nanos, but we were usually in the middle of something when I thought of it;

teaching me to control minds, or how to stalk prey . . ." She shrugged. "Grandfather promised they'd teach me everything eventually, but the priority was to ensure I knew how to survive and knew the rules about feeding. After that they could teach me our history."

"The rules about feeding?" Marcus asked, eyes intent.

"Grandfather had rules," Divine explained and listed them off, "I was never to draw attention to myself, my people, or what we are. When feeding, I was to always treat my host with the respect they deserved and never cause them pain or distress. And never *ever* was I to feed to the point of harming the health of, or killing, my host."

Marcus sat back, expression thoughtful. When several moments passed like that, Divine asked, "So what are the nanos? And what has Atlantis to do with us?"

He hesitated and then said, "I'm going to give you the short answer."

"Okay," she said.

"Atlantis is where our ancestors came from. It was somewhat isolated from the rest of the world, and technologically advanced. While humans outside Atlantis were still wielding spears and sleeping around fires, our ancestors' technology was beyond what we have even now today. One of the areas where their science was strongest was in health. Their scientists set out to develop a way to repair the human body internally, to mend wounds and fight infection without the need for invasive surgery or antibiotics and such. Nanos were their answer. Minuscule little . . ." Marcus hesitated and then said helplessly, "I'm no scientist, I'm not sure what they are exactly. I know they're partially made up of human tissue or blood. They use blood to propel and reproduce themselves and they've been programmed like computers, with the human anatomy and whatnot and with the task of keeping their host at their peak condition."

She arched her eyebrows. "So our needing blood is because the nanos use blood to reproduce themselves?"

"And to make repairs and fight infections, etc.," Marcus said. "They also repair damage from the sun, pollution, illness, injuries, poisons, toxins . . . basically anything. And apparently it takes a lot more blood than we can produce to do all that."

"Okay," Divine murmured. She considered it briefly and then said, "So we were human once?"

"We *are* human," he corrected. "We are not a different species. The nanos simply make us stronger, faster, and able to live longer."

"And the fangs?" she asked.

"Ah, well, see—" Marcus grimaced and admitted, "I guess I skipped a part."

"Okay," Divine said patiently.

"You see the nanos were originally developed as a short-term aid. They were supposed to be injected into the host—a sick or injured human—where they would heal the wound, or surround and destroy the viral cells of illness or what have you. Once their job was done the nanos were programmed to then destroy themselves and be flushed from the body. But as it turns out, what the scientists didn't take into account was that the human body is constantly under attack by sun, pollution, and even simple aging. There is always something to repair or heal, so the nanos never broke down as expected."

"Ah," Divine said slowly. That made sense.

"And then Atlantis fell. Nearly every Atlantean died that day. The only survivors were the ones carrying the nanos. They crawled out of the ruins and over the mountains and joined a society much less developed than their homeland had been. While they'd had blood transfusions in Atlantis to help feed the nanos, those were no longer available. Some survivors died, but in others, the nanos followed their programming to keep their host at their peak condition and basically forced the necessary evolution on us to ensure that happened. They made immortals stronger and faster, gave them better night vision, and the ability to read and control the minds of other humans, and they gave us fangs. Every extra skill or strength they gave us was to make us better able to hunt and successfully feed off of mortal humans. It was so we could get the blood we needed to ensure their continued ability to fulfill their programming and keep us at our peak condition."

Divine nodded slowly, and then asked, "Is there anything else I should know?"

Marcus frowned and considered it briefly, and then said, "I think that covers it."

"Okay. Thanks," Divine said, standing up.

"Okay thanks?" Marcus echoed with disbelief, jumping up to follow when she carried her plate out through the lounge to the kitchenette. "That's it?"

Pausing at the sink, Divine glanced over her shoulder

with surprise. "You were expecting something else?"

"Well . . . yeah," he said dryly as she opened the cupboard door under the sink and began to scrape the remains of her omelet into the garbage there.

"What were you expecting?" Divine asked curiously as she closed the door and began to rinse the plate in the sink.

"Well . . . I don't know," he admitted with a frown. "I gather most people react with shock and amazement to finding out the source of nanos."

"Really?" she asked, and considered that as she set her plate and fork in the tiny dishwasher next to the sink. Vincent really did like his luxuries, she thought, and then turned to Marcus and shook her head. "I suspect if they're shocked and amazed it's more by the fact that vampires truly exist than by their source being scientific. I already knew about us, just not the mechanics of what made us this way so there's nothing for me to be shocked and amazed at."

"She's probably right," Tiny commented.

Marcus glanced to him, then back to her, and then relaxed and smiled wryly. "Yeah. She probably is."

Divine turned to Tiny and Mirabeau then to offer them both smiles and said, "Thank you very much for breakfast. I appreciate it."

"Tiny did all the work. He's the cook in the family," Mirabeau admitted with a smile. "All I did was make the toast."

"And it was delicious too," Divine assured her, and then hesitated before saying, "Now, I suppose I'd best go relieve Jackie."

"Actually . . ."

Divine had started to turn toward the door, but paused at that one word from Mirabeau. Turning slowly back, she arched an eyebrow in question.

"We've arranged a play day for you," Mirabeau blurted.

"What?" Divine asked on a half laugh.

"Well, half a play day now," Tiny put in wryly. "A play evening, I guess."

Divine peered at them with bewilderment. "A play evening?"

Tiny nodded. "What with one thing and another you two have had a rough couple of days. Both of you. So, we got together with Jackie, Vincent, and Madge and arranged a play day for you. Madge gave us these passes for you." He turned to pick up two passes off the counter and held them out and she glanced at them curiously as Marcus took them. They were VIP passes, allowing them on all the rides. "Jackie is going to continue at your readings, Vincent is going to continue at the Tilt-A-Whirl, and you two get to have fun for the evening."

Divine frowned and started to shake her head.

"Oh come on," Mirabeau chided. "I bet you've never ridden on the rides. From what I've heard you're always trapped inside with a long line of customers outside the door waiting for their readings. Madge says they keep you going from the time you open, usually until several minutes after closing. But tonight you'll have the freedom to go where you want and do what you want. You can have a little fun for a change."

Divine stopped shaking her head. Mirabeau's use of the word *trapped* had caught her attention, and the comment about being free to go where she wanted and do what she wanted had too. Both made her realize that if she took over reading customers she would be trapped inside the RV until after closing. But taking them up on this offer would give her some freedom. She wouldn't have five babysitters watching her, she'd only have Marcus, and surely it would be easier to give him the slip than to try to get away from all of them? It was suddenly sounding like a really good idea.

"Okay," she said finally. "A play evening it is."

"Great," Mirabeau said and then suddenly held up a bottle of lotion. "SPF 100," she announced. "The sun is still out and it's better to be safe than sorry. Fortunately, it's spray-on, so easier to apply. But we'd better do it in the bedroom or the apples will all taste like lotion."

"Right," Divine said wryly, and turned to lead the way into the bedroom.

Eighteen

"Who gets the rip cord?"

"She does," Marcus said at once and when Divine glanced to him with surprise, he added, "Well, I'm sure not pulling it. I hate heights. We'd be sitting up there forever if it was left to me."

"You don't hate heights," she said on a laugh as the two girls attached their harnesses to the rig for the bungee drop. Divine and Marcus had been on the Zipper, the Yo-Yo, and every other high ride available and both of them had laughed their way through them as everyone else screamed. Divine hadn't known what she was missing never bothering with the rides at the carnival. Honest to God they were incredible; exhilarating, exciting, fun as fun could be. She'd been having a blast all evening, and Marcus had seemed to be too. The two of them had done the Zipper three times, the third time at his insistence. Divine felt like a kid again, or maybe for the first time, since she'd missed out on anything resembling a normal childhood when she'd actually been a child.

"I do hate heights," Marcus assured her, laughing even as he said it. "I mean I know I'd probably survive a fall even from incredible heights, but the healing . . ." He grimaced and shook his head.

"Well, why didn't you say so?" she said with exasperation. "We don't have to—"

Her words ended on a gasp as their legs were suddenly swept out from under them, leaving them dangling in the air Superman-style.

"Okay, I'm going to count to three and then say pull. When I say pull, you pull the rip cord, Divine," Kathy Walters instructed, drawing her attention. "When I say pull, you pull. Got it?"

"Yes, but—" Divine let her words die as they started to rise, pulled back and up by the cord the girls had attached to their connected harnesses. She glanced to Marcus uncertainly. "I could slip into her head and have her bring us down. I can do this alone."

Marcus just smiled and shook his head, reaching out with his left hand to rub her left arm where it was linked with his right arm. "Nah. I'm with you. If you go down, I do too."

"Hold on to your wrists," Kathy yelled from below. "Don't break the hold."

Marcus smiled wryly and returned to clasping his wrists with his hands as Divine was doing before muttering, "Let's just hope we land safely."

"I'm sure we will," Divine said. "They've never had an accident yet since I joined two years ago."

"So what you're saying is, they're due for an accident."

"No," Divine laughed. "I—"

"One!" Kathy shouted from below.

"Oh, are we up all the way already?" Divine asked with surprise, glancing around. Yep, they were up, pretty damned high too.

"Two!"

"Oh, look I can see Vincent at the Tilt-A-Whirl," she said brightly.

"Three!"

"Yeah, he looks like a bug from here. Just how far up are we?"

"Pull!"

Rather than answer, Divine released her wrist long enough to pull the cord and then quickly caught her wrist again as they suddenly plummeted downward. Despite his claim that he didn't like heights, Marcus laughed his head off as they dropped, but Divine didn't join him at first. For those first five seconds it felt like they were going to plummet to the earth. It wasn't until their cord pulled tight and they suddenly swung forward, swinging on their stomachs in their harnesses, that she began to smile and then laugh. This was madness, crazy, awesome!

They were allowed three swings that took them out over the midway and then back above the back lot, before Kathy shouted at them to grab a rope she was holding up on a pole.

"Is she kidding?" Marcus asked with disbelief. "We'll pull her right off that stand she's on."

Divine shrugged and—trusting that the girl knew what she was doing—grabbed for the looped rope as they flew past. Marcus caught it first. It didn't jerk them to a halt or drag Kathy off the stand, instead the loop pulled out, showing that it was attached to a chain. It came out more slowly than they would have gone had they not held it and slowed them to a stop after thirty or forty feet, then began to pull them back toward the takeoff pad.

"Well," Marcus said and then grinned at her. "That was fun. Want to do it again?"

Divine laughed at him. "I thought you were afraid of heights?"

"Not afraid. I just don't like them," he corrected. "But I find with you there are a lot of things I didn't used to like or didn't care about that are suddenly interesting and fun."

"Same here," she acknowledged, her voice husky as she thought of some of those things.

Marcus's arm tightened on hers where they were linked at the elbows and he tugged her closer, his face moving in. She knew he was going to kiss her and closed her eyes as her body began to tingle at the very idea and then she blinked them open again in surprise as they suddenly jerked to a halt.

"How was that?" Kathy asked by her ear, and Divine tore her eyes from Marcus's and glanced around to see that Kathy and the greenie working with her had caught and positioned them over the landing pad. Even as she noted that, the back of their harness was released and they both swung to a standing position again.

"It was great," Divine said with a grin as the girls worked to unhook them.

"Want to do it again?" Kathy asked, pausing in unhooking them.

"It's up to you," Marcus said when she glanced his way. "I'm game if you are."

Divine hesitated, but then glanced to the line-up the girls had. "No. Thanks, Kathy, but you have a heck of a line-up there. Besides, I'm kind of hungry."

"Yeah, so am I," Marcus announced as the girls continued unhooking them. "We can always do this again later if you want."

"Come by at closing," Kathy suggested. "Lots of us take turns at it after the carnival closes."

"Sounds good," Marcus said, stepping out of his harness. He then turned to hold Divine's hands as she stepped out of hers and slid his arm around her waist to lead her away. "What do you feel like eating?"

"I'm not sure," Divine said with amusement. "That omelet this morning and last night's casserole are the only things I've eaten in ages."

"Me too," he acknowledged, and then let his hand drop from her waist to catch her fingers and said, "Come on. I have an idea."

She followed, surprised when he led them back to the trailers. He released her hand, then said, "Wait here," and slipped inside.

Divine stared at the trailer for a moment before it suddenly occurred to her that this was her chance. She was alone. She could slip away and make her escape now, go somewhere and start her new life . . . alone. Again.

She let that thought settle in her head and didn't have to wonder why that wasn't at all appealing. She'd been having fun with Marcus. They hadn't talked much or had long, deep conversations, mostly they'd run from ride to ride, laughing like children and basically just having fun. They had cracked the occasional joke, or commented on things they saw. A mother shrieking at a weeping child for dropping his ice cream had angered them both. Children dropped things, accidents happened. The child was already upset by it and the mother standing there yelling at the little boy that he was stupid and clumsy and useless hadn't impressed either of them. Marcus slipping into the mother's head and giving her an attitude adjustment had made Divine smile. She knew it wouldn't last long, but the boy's smile as the mother had suddenly hugged him and told him she loved him, that accidents happened and he was a good boy and she would buy him a new ice cream . . . well, at least he'd have one good night at the carnival to remember when he grew up.

They'd both grinned when they'd spotted a couple of plump teenagers making out on the Ferris wheel as they passed. The pair had been pretty into it and it was Marcus who noticed that Carl let their car swing by without making them get out.

"Our Carl's an old romantic," Divine had told him with amusement when he'd commented. "He'll let them go around two or three times before ending their ride."

They'd smiled and laughed over several things since coming out for their play evening three hours ago, and Divine had enjoyed every moment of it. She had gathered memories she could pull out and look at over the years ahead, she told herself. But now playtime was over. She had to go.

Sighing, she turned away and started around the RV, intending to slip up the opposite side of it to reach the back lot rather than risk Marcus coming out and spotting her slipping away between the two vehicles. She was about to turn down the far side and head for the back lot when Marcus suddenly said, "You aren't trying to escape me, are you?"

Divine turned quickly to see him jogging toward her, a smile on his face that looked a little concerned and even forced. Managing a smile of her own, she shook her head. "I just thought I'd—" She glanced around for an excuse, and finished, "—try my hand at the balloon game while I waited."

Marcus glanced to the game a few stalls ahead and then took her hand. "We'll both try it before we go."

"Go?" Divine asked with a frown. "Go where?"

"You'll see," Marcus said, squeezing her hand. "It's a surprise."

Divine frowned over that as they arrived at the balloon game stall. Marcus gave the game agent tickets for darts and they both began tossing them at the balloons. She had always considered herself a good aim, and she was, but the balloons weren't fully blown up and the darts sometimes just bounced off them until she began to put more strength in the throw. Marcus didn't miss a single balloon with his darts, and he was fast. He was working on his third round of darts by the time she finished her first. She stood back and just watched then, waiting for him to tire. Divine didn't realize he was working toward a goal until he suddenly stopped and put his head together with the game agent who nodded, turned, and retrieved a little brown bear with a heart on its stomach and handed it over.

Marcus turned and offered it to her at once. "For you."

Divine stared at the offering and then slowly reached for it. She couldn't say how many times she'd witnessed this scene, or something like it on the midway; a male winning a prize for his girl. She'd always thought it was sweet and had felt a pang of envy. Now she had her own prize, won for her by Marcus.

"We'll find someone to sew 'Marcus and Basha' on it with the year," he announced with a crooked smile, and when she blushed, caught her hand and led her along the midway.

They were heading through the gates to the parking lot when Divine suddenly registered what he'd said. She came to an abrupt halt, sure she was as pale as a sheet. It certainly felt like all the blood had left her face.

"What?" Marcus asked with concern when he glanced around and saw her expression.

"Marcus and Basha?" she asked, trying not to panic.

He nodded. "Vincent, Jackie, Tiny, and Mirabeau can all read you, Divine. They can read both of us. But Mirabeau was the first one to pick up on your real name being Basha."

She tried to tug her hand free of his, but he held her fast.

"I know Madge has your motorcycle and you planned to run away on it, but I can't allow that," he said quietly, and then caught her other hand as she swung it at him. When she then tried a front kick, he turned her abruptly and slammed her up against a van they stood beside. "I can't allow that because there isn't room for me on the motorcycle and I'm going with you."

"What?" Divine asked with disbelief, suddenly going still.

"You're my life mate, Basha—"

"Don't call me that," she interrupted sharply.

"All right," he said patiently, "Then you're my life mate, Divine," Marcus corrected solemnly and then added, "Where you go, I go. Your future is my future. Your fate my own." Releasing her hands, he cupped her face gently and whispered, "I'm running away with you. That's the surprise. I borrowed the SUV Tiny and Mirabeau came here in. They think I'm taking you to dinner, and I am, but then we're running away together. We can go to Italy. My family is powerful. They can protect you from Lucian if necessary. Or we can go somewhere else if you want. But you aren't going alone."

Divine stared at him wide-eyed for a moment. In all the scenarios she'd imagined with Marcus, not once had she dared imagine this one. For a moment it seemed like she held the brass ring in her hand, but then her conscience kicked in. She'd be sentencing him to life as a Gypsy, always moving, never still, no home. And she'd be sentencing him to a life without children too, because she would never bring another child into the life she'd been forced to lead. She couldn't do that to an innocent baby, and she couldn't do it to Marcus either. No one should have to live the life she did, always running and hiding, always looking over their shoulder, always scared.

Sighing, Divine lowered her head and shook it sadly. "That's sweet, Marcus. But I can't ask you to do that."

"You're not asking," Marcus said, taking her hand and drawing her away from the van to lead her through the parking lot before adding, "I'm telling you how it's going to be. I've waited twenty-five hundred years for a life mate, Divine. I'm not letting you slip away now."

"You don't know what you're saying," she said quietly. "You don't even know who I am."

"I just told you who you were not minutes ago, Basha Argeneau, remember," he said dryly, pausing beside an SUV. He opened the door for her to get in.

Divine stopped beside him though and faced him grimly. "I'm a rogue."

"You're thought to possibly be a rogue," Marcus corrected firmly. "I don't think you are. But," he added quickly when she started to speak, "if you are, you must have had a good reason for whatever you did, or you were confused, or . . . something," he finished weakly and then shook his head and said with more certainty, "Whatever it is, we'll deal with it."

"Marcus, I—"

"Lucian is expected here this evening," he interrupted, drawing her up short. "I'm not sure what time he'll get here, but I'd rather we were gone before he arrived. You can tell me everything you want to. I want to hear it, just not right here, right now. Okay? Please? Just get into the SUV. We'll go have dinner and you can tell me whatever you want."

Divine hesitated one more moment, but then got into

the SUV. Lucian was an old bogeyman for her; avoiding him was kind of priority number one. She remained silent as Marcus walked around and got in the driver's seat, but once he'd started the engine and steered them out of the lot and onto the road, she said, "This isn't a conversation we should have in a public place."

"Okay," Marcus said calmly. "Where?"

Divine hesitated briefly, considering their options. A hotel would work, but she wanted to be somewhere crowded and busy. It would help her slip away quickly and quietly. "How far are we from Vegas?"

"A little more than two hours I think," Marcus said quietly. "Did you want to go there?"

"Yes, please," Divine murmured, trying to make plans and contingency plans in her head. There was no way she was letting Marcus throw away his life to be with her, and the only way to stop that was by telling him everything. Once he knew the truth, he wouldn't want anything to do with her, she was sure. The problem was, he might then want to turn her behind in to Lucian to redeem himself. She needed a plan to avoid that. As depressing as the future seemed to her without Marcus in it, she wasn't suicidal quite yet.

"Vegas it is then," Marcus said, relaxing in his seat. "It'll be handy, actually. We can talk, sort things out, then visit one of those little chapels and get married while in town."

Divine blinked as those words hit her, and then simply closed her eyes. The man might know her name, but he hadn't accepted who she was. He'd be singing a different song once he knew the truth.

Nineteen

"Why the Luxor?" Marcus asked as he unlocked the door to their room and ushered her inside. "It's not exactly in the thick of things here."

"That's why," Divine said, sounding amused as she glanced around the room and then moved into the bathroom to look it over.

Marcus glanced around as well, and managed not to wrinkle his nose. The room was in need of refurbishing. The carpet was worn, the furniture too, and the wallpaper had to be a good thirty years old. If this was the state of the rooms, he wasn't sure he wanted to try the food.

"I picked it because it's near the end of the strip and less busy," Divine explained, coming out of the bathroom. "And it reminds me of my youth."

He arched an eyebrow at that. The Luxor was a huge pyramid with a one-hundred-and-ten-foot re-creation of the Great Sphinx of Giza. "You were in Egypt during your youth? Did your parents live in Egypt?"

Divine grinned at the question. "Youth is a relative term. I guess I was two hundred, maybe almost three hundred years old when I accompanied the Persians there."

Marcus arched his eyebrows. "The Persians conquered Egypt, didn't they?"

"But good," she agreed dryly.

"Hmmm." He watched her cross the room to a binder on the table and open it to glance through the contents. They'd grabbed a couple of donuts and coffees from a drive-through coffee shop to tide them over on the way here, but he was starved now. It looked like she was too.

"This room service menu . . ." Divine frowned and shook her head. "It might as well be in Greek. What are buffalo chicken wings? Are there buffalo chickens? I thought buffalo were wild ox or cows or something."

"So did I," Marcus said with a shrug. "We could always bypass the menu and order pizza delivered. Dante and Tomasso seem to really like that and order it delivered all the time."

"Would they deliver to a hotel room?" she asked with interest.

"Why not?" Marcus said and pulled out the cell phone Vincent had loaned him. He quickly looked up pizza delivery in Las Vegas. He found one close to the hotel, looked up the menu, and pursed his lips.

"Problem?" Divine asked, snapping her binder closed.

Marcus shook his head. "I'm just not sure what's good on pizza. The boys usually order something called a meat eater's or something and— Oh good, they have a meat lover's pizza that should be similar . . . It has pepperoni, sausage, bacon, and meatballs," he read off, and glanced at her in question. "Is that okay with you?"

"Sounds fine," Divine said and stood up to head for the bathroom. "I'm going to take a quick bath while you order."

"Take your time," Marcus murmured, distracted by punching in the restaurant phone number from memory. "It usually takes a while for pizzas to arrive after ordering. Anywhere from half an hour to an hour in Canada."

"Okay."

He heard the door close, but his attention was on the ringing from his phone. It wasn't until he placed the order and ended the call that Marcus realized that Divine was taking a *bath*. He could hear the running water and supposed she was stripping and—

Realizing that he'd somehow moved across the room without intending to and that his hand was now on the doorknob, Marcus caught himself. She wanted a bath. If she'd wanted something else she wouldn't be shut up in the bathroom running water, she'd be stripping out here in front of him.

He couldn't blame her for wanting a bath, Marcus thought as he turned away from the door. While it had probably been in the nineties when they'd started their play evening at five, it had cooled off a little as the night had progressed, but had still been in the high eighties and humid as they'd rushed around from ride to ride. He was feeling a little in need of a bath himself and his clothes were grimy and sweaty, Marcus noted, wrinkling his nose as he raised an arm and sniffed himself.

He definitely needed a change of clothes, and Divine would no doubt appreciate fresh clothes when she got out of her bath too, Marcus thought, and headed for the door.

The plan was for him to just quickly nip out and pick up a couple of things, then hurry back. It didn't end up that way. Divine was the problem. Marcus wasn't sure on size or even what she'd like. It wasn't like Gypsy outfits were easy to find in hotel gift shops. Actually, while there were lots of T-shirts, jackets, etc. with the Luxor logo on them, there wasn't much in the way of bottoms. Not that he thought Divine would want to walk around with "Luxor" on her ass.

In the end, Marcus asked the concierge for a suggestion of somewhere nearby to shop and then grabbed a taxi out in front of the hotel to the place the guy suggested. What followed was several panicked moments, maybe even half an hour, of picking up and discarding items until he just gathered a bunch of items together and rushed to the till. He had to be back in time to accept the pizza. Marcus wasn't sure Divine had any money on her, if she was even out of the tub to answer the door.

He was weighed down with half a dozen bags heavy with clothes when he got back to the Luxor. Marcus rushed to the elevators, conscious of the passing time and afraid he'd missed the pizza delivery. That worry in mind, he made a run for it when he saw that one of the elevators was on the ground floor, the doors just closing. Even so, he wouldn't have made it if the young guy inside, the only occupant, hadn't grabbed the door to stop it from closing.

"Thanks," Marcus murmured with relief as he slid inside.

"No problem," the young man said easily as Marcus glanced to the numbered buttons on the wall.

Finding the button for the floor the room he shared with Divine, Marcus noted it was already lit up and let out a little sigh as he leaned against the wall for the ride. He'd barely done so when the scents in the elevator drew his attention back to his companion. The kid who had held the door for him smiled and nodded when Marcus's gaze zeroed in on the wide flat insulated bag he carried on one raised hand like a waiter carrying a tray.

"Smells good, huh?" the fellow asked.

"Yeah," Marcus agreed and completely relaxed as he read the room number on the sales slip taped to the top of the six-pack of Coke in the guy's other hand. He hadn't missed the delivery. This was it. Marcus didn't say anything to the delivery boy, though, simply rode up with him, stepped out, and headed down the hall, aware that the boy was following.

"Figures," the kid said with a laugh when Marcus stopped to unlock his room door.

"Yeah," Marcus agreed. "I was afraid I wouldn't be back in time. Good thing you held the elevator door for me. Thanks again for that."

"My pleasure. Saved me a trip back and forth for nothing," he said with amusement, moving forward when Marcus gestured for him to follow. He didn't come all the way into the room, but stopped just inside, his body keeping the door open as he waited for Marcus to drop all his bags and pull out his wallet to pay him.

Marcus gave him a good-sized tip, took the pizza and pop and wished the kid a good night, then let the door close and turned into the room just as Divine came out of the bathroom. Her hair was damp and slicked back from her head, and she wore a hotel robe. She looked shiny and clean and sexy as hell in the oversized robe and for a minute Marcus considered leaving the pizza until later and just—

"Mmmm, that smells delicious," Divine said, smiling widely.

"Right," Marcus murmured, and gave his head a shake. Food first, he told himself firmly and carried the pizza and Coke to the small round table between two chairs. Setting them there, he then snatched up the ice bucket and headed for the door. "You go ahead and start eating. I'm going to grab us some ice."

Marcus didn't wait for a response, but hurried out. He'd spotted the ice room on his way up the hall and hurried there now to fill the bucket. When he got back, Divine had found little packaged coffee packets with a spoon, sugar, cream sweetener, and napkins in them. She'd opened a couple and taken out the napkins for them to use. She'd also collected the two glasses from the bathroom counter and set them out on either side of the pizza box on the table.

"Go ahead and start, I'm going to wash my hands," Marcus said, setting the bucket on the table and heading for the bathroom. The room was still a little steamy from her bath and smelled good from the shampoo and soap, he noted as he walked up to the sink. He turned the tap on, but one glance at himself and Marcus grimaced. He was filthy. He didn't know how, all they'd done was ride the rides and then drive for a couple hours, but he was coated with a fine dust of dirt, that had pathways through it from where sweat had run.

Turning the tap off, he spun to the shower and turned that on instead, and then quickly stripped. What followed was possibly the fastest shower ever. It couldn't have been more than five minutes later that he walked out of the room with a towel wrapped around his waist.

"There's another robe in the closet," Divine announced on seeing him, and Marcus stopped to find the item, and then drew it on over his towel.

"Feel better?" Divine asked as he joined her.

"Yeah. Sorry about that," Marcus said as he settled in his chair and noted that she'd put ice in both glasses and poured them both pop . . . and the pizza box was still closed. "You didn't have to wait."

Divine shrugged. "I only finished pouring the soda a minute ago. I was debating starting without you when I heard the water shut off so I waited."

"Well, thank you for pouring the pop," Marcus murmured, and opened the pizza box and then glanced around with a grimace. "No plates. Didn't think of that. I guess we'll have to eat out of the box. The boys do that sometimes."

"The Dante and Tomasso you mentioned who like pizza?" Divine asked with amusement, reaching for a piece of pizza.

"Yeah." Marcus smiled faintly as he picked up a slice for himself as well. "They aren't the only ones who like pizza though. Actually, I can't think of anyone in the family who eats who doesn't like pizza."

"Then it has to be good," Divine said, lifting her piece to her mouth, but only sniffing. "It smells good."

Marcus took a bite of his slice and stilled, savoring the various flavors that assaulted his tongue.

"Good?" Divine asked curiously. When he moaned aloud with pleasure and nodded, she finally took a bite of her own. Her eyes immediately widened. After chewing and swallowing, she said, "Oh yeah. It's good."

It was the last thing either of them said for several minutes as they concentrated on eating. Marcus hadn't been sure what size to order. Dante and Tomasso could demolish too large apiece, but Christian and Caro tended to order one large only so that's what he'd ordered, a large for them to share. However, since he and Divine were both still new to eating and stretching out their stomachs, a large was too much. He managed two pieces, Divine only got down one. It left most of the pizza still in the box.

Marcus closed the pizza box with regret, wondering if it would keep for a snack later, and then sat back with a little satisfied sigh and glanced to Divine. She was curled up in the opposite chair, looking relaxed and sipping at her drink. His gaze slid slowly over her in the robe. It was big, white, and fluffy. It had also parted above the knees, leaving her lower legs on display. Marcus couldn't help thinking she had the cutest little feet he'd ever seen. He wanted to kiss each of her little toes and play that "This little piggy went to market" game, and when he got to "This little piggy went wee wee wee all the way home," he'd tickle his way up her legs to—

"You have the strangest smile on your face," Divine said suddenly. "What are you thinking?"

Marcus blinked and then sat up abruptly. Sexually, he wanted Divine like crazy, but more than that, he wanted her in his life. But he had to sort out if she was rogue, and if so, why. He needed that knowledge to sort out a way to keep her safe. So, instead of answering, he said, "Tell me about your family."

Divine stilled, wariness crossing her face, "My family? I told you about my family."

"Yes, you did, but—" Pausing, he leaned forward and said, "Divine, the Basha that Lucian is looking for is the mother of Leonius Livius."

"His mother?" she asked with a start. "I didn't think she was alive. I thought she died long before he did." And then with sudden alarm, Divine asked, "He is dead, isn't he? I was told he died back during the immortal/ no-fanger war."

"Leonius Livius I is dead," Marcus assured her, noting the way she'd paled. "I'm talking about Leonius Livius II."

She blanched as if he'd slapped her. "There's another one?"

"Yes," he said gently, concerned by her obvious upset. "Apparently one son escaped during the immortal/

no-fanger war." His eyes narrowed when she suddenly seemed to stop breathing.

After a moment, she let her breath out and said bitterly, "So one of his sons survived and you call him Leonius Livius II." Before Marcus could respond, she asked sharply, "Why? Because he's his father's son?"

"No, because that's what he calls himself," Marcus said patiently and then explained, "He calls himself Leonius Livius II and has named all his sons Leonius as well. They go by numbers though. At least, Leonius the twenty-first was called Twenty-one, Leonius the thirteenth was Thirteen, and the others the Rogue Hunters have caught all went by a number. Except for Ernie," he added with a frown.

"Ernie?" Divine asked sharply.

"Another son of his, but an immortal rather than a no-fanger," Marcus explained. "For some reason he was named Ernie instead of Leonius . . . Perhaps because he was immortal rather than no-fanger," Marcus thought aloud and considered that briefly before shaking his head. "Anyway, I'm off topic. The point is that Leonius was captured two years ago or so and a woman apparently whisked him away, and that woman according to Mirabeau looks like you but with blond hair. And then Ernie and this girl named Dee were captured, and from Dee they learned about a blonde named Basha who was Leo's mother."

Divine stood up and started slowly across the room.

Marcus frowned and said, "Now we know your son's name is Damian so you can't be the Basha who is Leonius's mother. And Jackie said you were actually Leonius's victim. But Mirabeau said there was still something in your thoughts about you being rogue or wanted. So just tell me why you think you would be—" He stopped abruptly, nearly swallowing his tongue when Divine suddenly stopped at the side of the bed, turned to face him with the robe undone, and shrugged it off her shoulders. All Marcus could do was sit and gawk as the robe hit the ground and pooled around her bare feet.

He swallowed, opened his mouth to speak, and then closed his mouth again, unsure what he'd been about to say. What had they been talking about?

Turning away, Divine climbed onto the bed, crawled to the center of it on her hands and knees, and then shifted to lounge on it, legs together, knees raised, feet and palms flat on the bed, arms back a bit, holding her upright at an angle that thrust her breasts into the air. It was about the sexiest damned pose he'd ever seen, or maybe it was just the woman. Marcus didn't know which and didn't care; without actually giving his body the order to move, he found himself standing at the side of the bed.

Disappointment slipped through Marcus when Divine immediately shifted to sit on the edge of the bed in front of him, but that died when she reached out, undid his robe, and then pulled it open. His erection, which had sprung into existence the moment her robe had dropped, bounced upward without the heavy terry cloth to hold it down and nearly poked her in the eye. Divine took that in stride though and simply caught it in her hand.

Marcus sucked in a breath, eyes squeezing shut as her cool hand closed around his hot member. His eyes blinked open again, though, on a shocked grunt when her hot, wet mouth suddenly closed around it.

Oh dear God, no, Marcus thought. This was too much, too fast. He'd lose control and— Oh hell, he thought as his hands reached for her head, his fingers tangling in her drying hair. She seemed to know exactly how much pressure to exert, just where to flick with her tongue, when to suck hard and when to ease up. It was like she was psychic.

Or a life mate experiencing what he was along with him, Marcus realized as his pleasure seemed to grow inside him in waves that rolled out, seemed to gather steam, rolled back in to gather more, and rolled out again.

Marcus moaned as a particularly strong wave of passion hit him, and heard Divine's answering moan, and then just as he reached and started to fall over the edge of that cliff their pleasure had built, he was suddenly alone. It was as if they were back on that bungee drop ride, harnessed in together, and when she pulled the rip cord, he was suddenly whipped away from her, riding it out alone. Marcus instinctively tried to stop his own fall, but couldn't, and found himself tumbling helplessly into the abyss where darkness closed over him.

Twenty

Divine straightened with a little sigh, and then paused to contemplate the man she'd just finished tying to the bed. The robe ties and torn-up jeans she'd used to tie up Marcus wouldn't hold long, but they weren't meant to. She didn't want to leave him here helpless until room service came to see why he hadn't checked out, she just wanted to keep him from following her too quickly should he wake up sooner than expected.

Unfortunately, she'd kind of mistimed things. Divine had meant to try to shut her mind off from his sooner than she had, but had got wrapped up in the passion she'd so carefully stirred to life in them both and left it just that one second or two too long. Instead of remaining conscious as she'd hoped, she'd ended up passing out with him. Or perhaps that hope had been a lost cause from the start. Divine had never had a life mate before to try it with, so hadn't been sure that shutting him out of her head at the last minute would prevent the passing-out business. Fortunately, while she'd passed out with him, she'd woken first. Hence the reason he was now tied to the bed.

Turning, she moved to the bags Marcus had brought back from his shopping trip and went through them again. She'd already gone through them once in search of something to tie him up with; now Divine went through in search of clean clothes. She'd noted that he'd bought them both clothes. Now she quickly picked out a pair of jeans and a T-shirt and pulled both on, only to peer down at herself with a grimace.

Divine normally wore dresses. Actually, she'd never worn pants, so wasn't sure how they were supposed to fit exactly, but they certainly weren't comfortable compared to the Gypsy outfits she'd been wearing for the last hundred years or so. The jeans were close fitting, barely reaching her hipbone at the top, or her calves at the bottom. As for the T-shirt, well, that had a similar problem; it was a scoop neck, but tight, stopping short of the top of her jeans, the sleeves stopping just past her elbows. If she hadn't seen young women wearing similar outfits at the carnival, she would have thought Marcus had mistakenly bought them from the children's section or something.

Shaking her head, Divine glanced to the bags, considering finding something else to wear, but just as quickly changed her mind. She didn't know how long she had before he might wake up. It was better just to get out while she could, Divine thought, and headed for the door.

She was almost out the door when she recalled that she'd need the SUV keys. Turning back, Divine let the door close and quickly searched the room for Marcus's keys. It wasn't until she recalled his showering that she thought to look in the bathroom. His jeans were on the bathroom floor, and a quick rifling through the pockets revealed them in the front right pocket.

Sighing with relief, Divine hurried out of the bathroom, headed for the door again. This time, though, she only got as far as clasping the doorknob before she was stopped again. This time by Marcus muttering, "What the hell?"

Pausing, she glanced back just as he turned his attention from his tied hands to her and said with confusion, "Divine?"

"It's better this way, Marcus," she said quickly. "You don't want to give up everything and everyone you know for me."

"Don't tell me what I want. I— Wait!" he barked as she opened the door.

Divine hesitated and that was her undoing.

"At least give me an explanation. You owe me that much, don't you think? You're my life mate, Divine. Just help me understand. That's all I ask."

Divine bit her lip and stared for a moment at the doorknob she was holding, trying to make herself leave. But her mind was throwing up reasons why she shouldn't. One of which was that she had questions of her own she needed answers to. Sighing, she released the door and turned back, frowning when she saw that he was eyeing the ties on his hands with intent.

"Only if you promise not to try to free yourself until I'm gone," she said sharply.

Marcus shifted his gaze to her, hesitated for the count of perhaps ten, and then relaxed back on the bed. Staring at the ceiling he said, "Okay. We'll do this your way."

Divine breathed a little sigh of relief and then just stood there for a moment before admitting, "I don't know where to start."

"The beginning is—" He'd lifted his head to see her as he spoke, but paused to ask, "Can I at least sit up for this talk without you running out the door? Please?" Marcus added dryly.

"Oh, yes, of course," she said, moving forward. "Do you need help?"

Since he was seated upright, his hands now hanging down and out to the sides where they were tied, by the time she got to the bed, Divine supposed he didn't.

"As I was saying, the beginning is usually a good place," he said solemnly. Leaning back against the headboard, he then prompted, "You told me that after your uncle found you, he took you home to his parents and they taught you to read and control mortal minds and feed safely. But you said they never got the chance to teach you about Atlantis, our history, and the origin of nanos?"

"Right," Divine murmured, but didn't speak right away. Instead she paced the room once, slowly, and then paused in front of the dresser, leaned against it, and crossed her arms.

"Your name is Basha Argeneau," Marcus prompted when she didn't say anything.

"I was *born* Basha Argeneau," she corrected, and then added, "Alexandria and Ramses were my father's parents, my grandparents. Lucian Argeneau is my uncle and is the one who found Aegle and me, and took us to my grandparents."

"And it was like a fairy tale, you said," Marcus reminded her.

Divine nodded, but unconsciously tightened her arms around her waist, and then said, "My grandparents were great, but Uncle Lucian was a bit scary at first; gruff and . . . well, scary to a kid. But Gran assured me was a marshmallow underneath."

When Marcus raised his eyebrows at this assessment, Divine nodded with amusement. "Yeah, I think she may have been a little delusional on that score, but at the time I believed her and lost a little fear around him." She smiled sadly at the memories sliding over her and then shook her head and admitted, "I basically followed him around like a puppy . . . and he put up with it. He also helped with my training, taking me out to stalk mortals, control minds, and feed. He said I was a fast learner and smart," she admitted, remembering how happy she'd been when he'd said that. How she'd glowed under the praise.

"It sounds like you looked up to him," Marcus said quietly.

Divine grimaced. "Actually, I think I kind of— I guess he was a kind of replacement father for me."

Marcus merely nodded.

Letting her arms drop, Divine peered down at her bare feet, and said, "Everything was good. I was happy,

Aegle was happy. I was safe and warm and fed and loved. Grandmother and Grandfather were very kind, but it was always Uncle Lucian I looked to for . . . I don't know what," she finished unhappily, and then rushed on, "Everything was great until one evening I got up and Uncle Lucian was gone. Gran said he'd had to go away on business, but . . ." She wrinkled her nose. "Before that he'd taken me with him on his trips, and the one time he hadn't, he'd at least come to wake me up and told me he was leaving, and for how long, as well as when he'd be back. This time I got up and he was just gone."

"You were hurt," Marcus murmured.

"I guess so," Divine said on a shrug.

"What happened?" he asked, obviously recognizing that the story didn't end there.

"We lived in what is now called Tuscany," Divine told him. "Grandfather had a large tract of land on the Tiber River and I used to like to play and swim in the river, sometimes with my cousin when she visited, but always with Gran or Aegle or Uncle Lucian accompanying. That night, though, Aegle was suffering some mortal bug and didn't feel up to going. She said to ask my gran, but Gran had company, and Uncle Lucian wasn't there, so I just decided to go alone."

Divine sighed and glanced to him to admit, "I guess I was a bit out of sorts that he left without saying goodbye, and . . ."

"And rebelliously did what you knew you shouldn't," Marcus suggested softly.

She nodded and was alarmed to feel tears glaze her

eyes. She hadn't cried in ages, especially over this, and had no idea why telling Marcus about it would bring back those ancient tears now.

Wiping them impatiently away, she took on a more matter-of-fact tone and said, "I picked the wrong day to do it, and then to add to my folly, I spotted a hare, and gave chase. I planned to catch it and take it home to show Uncle Lucian when he got back, but the damned thing was quick and led me quite a chase. I was so intent on catching it I didn't even notice when I followed it off our property." She snorted. "Hell, I ran right into the center of a group of men and horses before I even noticed they were there."

Divine closed her eyes briefly as she recalled crashing into Abaddon's horse and bouncing off. She'd landed on her behind and then had simply stared wide-eyed up at the laughing men standing or mounted around her.

"What have we here?" one of the men had crowed, bending to catch her by the collar and lift her to her feet. Peering at her closely then, his ugly yellow-gold eyes had widened. "Why, you're an immortal. Such a shame. I was hoping for a snack."

He'd then laughed when she immediately started struggling and kicking.

"Put her down," someone had growled, and Basha had turned to stare at a man on horseback with long, lank, dirty blond hair, and ugly yellow-gold eyes. It was Leonius Livius, though she hadn't known it at the time. Despite not knowing, he'd frightened her from the first look she had of him and she'd stared at him wide-eyed until the dark-haired man on the horse beside him had ridden forward and bent to pick her up and set her on the horse before him. Turning her to face him, Abaddon had looked her over and said, "If I'm not mistaken this little immortal is an Argeneau. She has the Argeneau silver-blue eyes. Am I right, little one? Are you an Argeneau?"

Basha had glared at him, refusing to speak. But he didn't need her to speak. He'd easily read her mind. "Ah, little Basha Argeneau. The long-lost daughter of Felix, so newly restored to the family." The words had sounded light, but there had been a look in his eyes that had frightened the child she'd been then.

"Divine?"

Marcus's voice drew her from her memories and she forced a wry smile. "I was duly repaid for my stupidity. The group of men I charged into the middle of was Leonius, his sons, and his right hand man Abaddon. They captured me and took me back to their camp . . . And there I stayed for a year."

Marcus cursed. "He was trying to build an army of his own sons. He tortured and raped any woman he got his hands on, mortal, immortal, and no-fanger alike."

"Yes, I know," she said succinctly and he blanched.

"He didn't . . . ?"

Divine stared at him unflinching and he shook his head.

"But you were just a child. Just eleven years old."

"I turned twelve a week after I was taken," Divine said, feeling as empty as her words sounded . . . which she didn't understand at all. She'd cried a river of tears over this during her first two or three hundred years, but eventually she'd cried herself out. Divine had thought when she could remember it without an emotional reaction that she had finally got over that period in her life. Yet, here she was now having to shut down emotionally to avoid a rage of pain, shame, and remembered terror.

"The first couple of months were unbearable," Divine found herself saying, and while she was surprised to hear the words leave her mouth, they were true. Leonius was a no-fanger, which meant exactly what it sounded like. While he was immortal, he had never developed fangs to feed with. He had to cut his victims. Like immortals he could control his victim's minds and keep them from feeling the pain of his cutting if he so chose, but Leonius's mind had been sick and twisted beyond comprehension. He'd enjoyed the suffering of others. He'd cut and cut and slice and dice the mortals he fed on, feeding as much on their agony as on their blood until he drank them dry. But while it was bad for mortals, it was worse for immortals, because he couldn't feed off their blood, so those cuts were purely for pleasure. At least mortals could die and escape him. Immortals healed . . . and then he'd start in on them all over again, raping, cutting, raping, slicing, sometimes slowly cutting a limb almost completely off just to see if it would heal and reknit itself.

"But then I learned how to shut him out," Divine breathed.

"Shut him out?" Marcus asked, eyes narrowing.

"He enjoyed the pain and suffering. I thought if I stopped giving him that, he might tire of me and just kill me," she admitted. "So I started trying to close my mind to him. Eventually I succeeded."

"Is that what you did to me?" Marcus asked quietly, and when she blinked and glanced to him with surprise, he said, "At the end, just before I passed out, it was as if you suddenly weren't there anymore."

Divine swallowed and nodded solemnly. "Yes. I tried to use the same technique with you. I didn't want to pass out."

"You wanted to stay awake and tie me up," he said dryly and glanced resentfully to his bound wrists. "And obviously it worked."

"Actually, no it didn't. Not as well as I'd hoped," she confessed. "I left it too long before shutting down and I briefly passed out as well."

Marcus looked only slightly mollified, but grudgingly said, "Go on. You learned to shut him out. I doubt he was pleased."

"No," Divine acknowledged. "It was no fun if he couldn't feel my suffering. But rather than stop, it just seemed to make him redouble his efforts."

"I'm sorry," Marcus said quietly.

"Well, fortunately before he tired of that and killed me, I became pregnant."

Marcus stiffened. "Your son . . ."

"Damian is a son of Leonius Livius I, yes," Divine said wearily.

"Damian," he breathed with seeming relief and then frowned. "You say fortunately, as if that was a good thing? I mean, some women—"

"Some women would loathe carrying the child of their rapist and torturer and giving it life," she said quietly. "I understand that, but . . ." Divine swallowed and peered down at her feet, realizing only then that she'd been going to leave without shoes. She was barefoot. Sighing, she raised her head and said, "You have to understand, being pregnant meant an end to the torture and rape for us. Some of us couldn't bear to carry the child of our captor, but some saw it as a blessing, a gift. So long as we were pregnant or breast-feeding afterward, we held no interest for Leonius. So that baby was precious and we fed as often as they'd let us, desperate to consume enough blood to keep the pregnancy safe."

"How many of you were there?" Marcus asked with a frown. "I mean, I've heard the stories, a hundred women kept locked up in cages, released only to rape, torture, or feed on, but I always thought it an exaggeration."

"It wasn't," Divine said quietly. "I would guess when the immortals attacked, he had about fifty mortal women for feeding on; twenty or so no-fangers he'd turned and was raping and torturing; along with four immortal women, all of whom he was hoping to breed with; and another twenty-four no-fangers plus myself who were pregnant or breast-feeding."

Marcus breathed out slowly and then asked, "Which were you? Pregnant or breast-feeding?"

"I gave birth the morning of the attack," she said quietly. "Actually, looking back I think it was an induced labor."

"Induced?" Marcus asked.

Divine nodded. "We received word the night before that the immortals had formed an army under my grandfather, as well as Uncle Lucian and some others, and that they were marching on Leonius's camp. The women were all aflutter, half hoping for rescue, half terrified of it."

"And you?" Marcus asked. "Were you hoping or terrified?"

"I was just confused," Divine said unhappily. "They were saying all sorts of things. Some thought that the immortals would rescue the women, but purge the pregnancies rather than risk bringing another Leonius into the world. Others thought they might just slaughter everyone, Leonius, his men and the women—"

"Why the women?" Marcus asked with a frown. "They were victims in all of this."

"We'd been tainted," she said simply. "A lot of women thought we would be considered damaged goods."

"What did you think?" Marcus asked with a frown.

Divine shook her head. "I didn't know what to think."

They were both silent for a minute, and then Divine continued, "Anyway, I didn't think I'd sleep that night I was so distressed by everything, but I must have because I remember that Abaddon had to shake me to get me to wake up. It was the middle of the night and I was confused at his waking me, and even more confused when he gave me a tincture to drink. When I asked what it was he simply took control of me and made me drink it. Shortly afterward I went into labor."

Divine closed her eyes briefly and grimaced. "Damian was born quickly. It all happened much faster than anyone expected. Dima, the mortal who acted as my midwife, said if I had been mortal, I wouldn't have survived. I was torn up pretty badly."

"But you survived, and so did the baby?" he asked.

Divine nodded. "Yes. He was fine. He had no fangs but he was a strong healthy baby."

"Wait, what?" Marcus said with confusion.

"He was strong and healthy," Divine repeated, and then said wryly, "I wish the same could have been said for me. As I mentioned, I was ripped up pretty badly during the birth and I wasn't allowed the time to heal afterward. Leonius ordered Abaddon to smuggle my baby and me out of camp through a secret tunnel before the immortals breached the camp, and he did so minutes after Damian was born."

"Were other mothers and their babies smuggled out too?" Marcus asked at once.

"No," Divine said quietly. "At least, Abaddon said I was the only one and they were all there when he hustled me out of—"

"Why did he want you smuggled out?" Marcus asked.

Divine hesitated, a little startled by his sharp tone and his interrupting her, but after a minute she sighed and said, "Abaddon said that Leonius thought my uncle might let the others live, but felt sure he'd cut me down where I stood and kill Damian as well when he learned that I'd dishonored my family like that."

"Like what?" he asked with confusion. "How did you dishonor your family?"

"By having Leonius's child," she pointed out softly.

Marcus shook his head. "Divine, you were a child yourself, raped and tortured. Lucian would hardly have held you responsible for the resulting child, and he wouldn't have killed an innocent baby."

"He killed all the other women and children they found in the camp," she pointed out sadly, recalling the women she'd lived and suffered with.

"The immortals did not kill those women and children," Marcus said firmly. "When Leonius realized he was going to lose the battle, he retreated to camp with six of his eldest sons. They rounded up all the women and children and killed them. The few immortals were tied up with the no-fanger females and set on fire, and while they screamed and burned, he and his oldest sons visited an orgy of blood on the remaining mortals, drinking every last mortal woman dry."

"But Abaddon said . . ." Her voice trailed off. She'd known all her life that Abaddon could not be trusted. She should have held everything he'd ever told her suspect. But he'd been her only source of news back then, and he'd pretended that she was important, given into his care to be looked after and protected. His lord's dying wish.

"What happened after this Abaddon smuggled you out of camp?" Marcus asked. "Where did you go?"

Divine shrugged wearily. "The first part of the journey after leaving is something of a blur in my memory. I was weak and in pain from the labor, never given a chance to heal, or even to feed. We had to run and hide and run again."

"Why?" Marcus demanded. "To keep you and your son safe from your uncle?"

Divine nodded.

He stared at her for a minute, and then said, "You mean to tell me that your whole life has been spent hiding and running from your family because you believed they would kill your son?"

"And me," she added solemnly.

"Divine," he said slowly. "Lucian wouldn't have done that. He would not kill an innocent child."

"But he was no-fanger like his father," she pointed out. "And my grandfather and uncle were out to destroy all no-fangers."

"Your son can't be—" He shook his head and muttered something about dealing with that later, then said, "Yes, the immortals were determined to put down no-fangers back then. But not edentates."

"Edentates?" she echoed uncertainly.

"That is an immortal without fangs. They are called edentate. Any child born fangless is considered edentate unless and until they go crazy and show the tendencies of no-fangers, a liking for torturing and killing, etc. But not all edentates turn no-fanger. Your son would not have been killed. And you certainly wouldn't have been."

"But I didn't kill myself," Divine pointed out.

"What?" he asked with bewilderment.

"The reason there were so few immortal women in the camp was because they usually killed themselves rather than suffer Leonius's raping and impregnating them. I saw two of them do it during the year I was there. One got free and when the guard pulled his sword, she just threw her head over it, decapitating herself. Another threw herself in the fire and burned to death. Abaddon said they had honor and their families would have been shamed had they not done it. That their families probably would have cut them down themselves had they found them in Leo's camp alive and well, never having tried to escape or kill themselves. He said Uncle Lucian was the same, arrogant, cold, hard . . ."

"Abaddon again," Marcus interrupted angrily. "Divine, he was lying to you. He lied to you about what happened to the women in the camp, and he lied to you about this. How long did he pound those tales into your head?"

"I don't know. Ten years, I guess," Divine said, staring at him wide-eyed. It was the first time she'd seen him really angry.

"You were with him for ten years after he smuggled you out of camp?"

She nodded. "At first I needed him. I had Damian, I was breast-feeding, I—"

"You were a child," he added grimly. "You needed someone to find you hosts to feed on while you breast-fed, and you needed someone who could provide a roof over both your heads."

"Yes," she said, bowing her head.

"There is no shame in that," Marcus said, his tone less angry. "Besides, as I said, I suspect he was using mind control on you. You seem to see Lucian as some kind of bogeyman, and for him to go from a substitute father to bogeyman like that, mind control must definitely have been involved."

Divine rubbed her eyes wearily. She suspected Marcus was right and wondered how she hadn't seen that for herself centuries ago.

"How did you eventually get away from him?"

"He was away looking for hosts to bring back one night and I . . ." She shrugged helplessly. "I just packed up Damian and ran with him."

"Just like that?" Marcus asked with a frown.

Divine nodded.

"What happened to bring it about?" he asked after a pause.

"I'm not sure I understand what you mean," she said slowly.

"You thought you needed him to survive. Why suddenly did it seem better to be away from him?"

Divine bit her lip and then reluctantly admitted, "I caught him calling Damian by the name Leonius."

Twenty-one

Marcus dropped his head back against the headboard and closed his eyes. Divine might have named her son Damian and taught him the rules about not harming mortals, but Abaddon had busily been undoing all her good work from the boy's birth. It was obvious to him that Damian and Leonius were one and the same son of Leonius Livius I.

"It infuriated me," Divine admitted, drawing his attention again. "And scared me. I was suddenly desperate to get Damian away from him."

"He called him Leonius," Marcus murmured, and then lifted his head to peer at her and simply asked, "Did you take Leonius from that hotel in Toronto two years ago?"

"No," Divine said firmly, and he felt a moment's relief, until she added, "I took my son, Damian, from it."

"Ah crap," Marcus muttered, closing his eyes again.

"He is not like his father," Divine said quickly. "My uncle has been hounding and hunting him ever since the immortal/no-fanger war just because he carries his father's blood, but Damian's not like Leonius. I brought him up with the same rules my grandfather taught me. He knows not to harm or kill mortals. Yet Uncle Lucian has hunted him, killing Damian's sons in the process, innocent little boys, most of them under ten."

"What?" Marcus asked, shocked at the very suggestion. When Divine nodded her head, he stared at her blankly for a minute and then said, "Divine, I don't know what happened to your grandsons, but I guarantee you that Lucian would not kill little boys. At least not unless they were no-fanger and killing mortals willy-nilly."

"They weren't no-fangers. Most of them hadn't turned yet and were mortal still," she responded.

"Mortal still?" he queried blankly.

Divine shrugged. "Some of the boys seemed to be mortal and then turned when they were somewhere between five or ten."

"That's not possible," Marcus said at once. "What's more, if Damian is no-fanger, he is not your son."

She blinked in surprise at that comment, and gave a short laugh. "I'm sorry, Marcus, but you're the one mistaken this time. Damian *is* no-fanger and he is *definitely* my son. I gave birth to him."

"You couldn't have," Marcus said firmly. "Divine, I explained about nanos. They are carried in the blood. A mother passes them down to her child."

"Or the father does," she said with certainty.

"No," Marcus said stoutly. "He doesn't. He can't. It's in the blood, not in the sperm."

"Well, that still doesn't mean an immortal mother can't have a no-fang— edentate child," she corrected herself. "No-fangers and edentates are immortal too, aren't they? We all have the same nanos."

"Ah, damn," he whispered suddenly with realization. "I didn't explain that part to you in the RV."

"What part?" Divine asked uncertainly.

Marcus breathed out a sigh and then explained, "No-fangers and edentates don't carry the same nanos as immortals. The first no-fangers and their prodigy carry the nanos from the first batch the scientists came up with. But those nanos turned out to be somehow flawed. A third of the subjects died when given them, and a third went crazy. The other third were fine. And then when Atlantis fell, none of them produced fangs and they had to cut to feed. The crazy immortals without fangs were called no-fangers. The noncrazy immortals without fangs were called edentates to differentiate them.

"Immortals," he continued, "are the result of the scientists going back and tweaking the nanos. I don't know what they did, or how they changed the programming, but the second batch of nanos produced the immortals that simply go by the name immortal. None of them died or went crazy when the nanos were introduced to their bodies. And when Atlantis fell, it was only in the immortals with the second batch of nanos that the fangs developed."

"Oh," Divine said with a frown.

Marcus sighed and then continued, "Because the

nanos are carried in the blood, the child becomes what his mother is. A mortal mother will have a mortal child every time no matter what the father is, and the same is true of an immortal. An immortal mother with the second batch of nanos can only produce an immortal child. But both a no-fanger and edentate mother with the first batch of nanos will pass those on to her child and produce an edentate who has a thirty-three percent chance of remaining edentate, a thirty-three percent chance of turning no-fanger, and a thirty-three percent chance of dying.

"You carry the second batch of nanos, Divine. The child you gave birth to in that camp, and any children you produce in the future, can only be immortal. If Damian isn't an Immortal, with fangs, then he is not your birth child."

"But . . ." She shook her head, confusion rife on her face. "I gave birth to him."

"Is it possible your child was switched for Damian?" he asked gently. That seemed the only explanation. "Was the baby you gave birth to ever out of your sight?"

"No, I . . ." Divine paused and frowned. "Well, Abaddon did take him out of the room briefly to clean him up, but . . . he was only gone moments before returning with him bundled up in swaddling."

"This Abaddon must have switched Damian for your child then. Damian must have been the child of Leonius and a no-fanger woman." He raised his eyebrows in question. "Were there any no-fanger women who gave birth around that time too?"

"Yes," Divine murmured, looking defeated. "One of them had a child the day before."

Marcus nodded. "Damian is probably her child."

"Yes," Divine agreed, and then she suddenly straightened. "But he is still my son, Marcus. I raised him, I breast-fed him, I cared for him, taught him, kissed his scraped knees and boo-boos. I *raised* Damian. He *is* my son."

"I'm sorry you feel that way," he said sadly, and she glanced to him with surprise.

"Why?"

"Because if Damian is the man who was shot several times, including an arrow through the heart, and was picked up outside the hotel room in Toronto, then he's a stone-cold killer, and a no-fanger, not edentate."

Divine was shaking her head before he'd even finished. "No. He's not a killer. I taught him—"

"If the man you whisked away from the hotel is Damian, then Damian *is* a killer," Marcus said firmly. "He and a handful of his sons killed several women in northern Ontario, and then kidnapped a doctor and her sister. The doctor was rescued right away, but one of the sons, Twenty-one I believe he was called, got away with the sister. The man you whisked away was captured at the site where the dead women were found, but he too got away."

He saw Divine close her eyes at this news, but continued, "The sister, who was a teenage girl by the way, was rescued, along with a couple of other victims, from the hotel room you whisked your son away from as well as from the room next door to it. And he was going by the name Leonius."

"You said that earlier," she muttered unhappily, and

then said, "But Damian said he was only there because a couple of the boys got up to some risky business and he had to go get them out of trouble."

"Risky business?" he interrupted with amazement. "They cut those women up like kindling . . . and he bragged about at least one of his kills to the doctor they took. And," he added heavily, "one of their victims, a young woman named Dee, told us how Leonius and his boys slaughtered her family. He wasn't there to get them out of trouble. He was leading them into it."

Marcus gave her a moment to digest that, and then said, "Everything I've said is true, Divine. I wouldn't lie to you. You're my life mate . . . and believe me I wish this wasn't true. Because this *does* mean you're rogue and we are going to spend the rest of our lives running and hiding."

Divine stared at him blankly for a minute, and then suddenly turned and headed for the door.

"Wait! Where are you going?" he called, struggling with the ties on his wrists.

Divine didn't answer, simply slipped out of the room and let the door close behind her. Cursing, Marcus gave up trying to tug his hands free of the ties at his wrists and began to jerk at them, trying to snap the cloth. Instead, on the fourth pull, he snapped the bed headboard clean off the bed. That was good enough. Marcus tugged the ties off of the snapped wood, and quickly removed the cloth from his wrists as he slid off the bed. He then rushed for the door, but when he hurried out into the hall and looked both ways, it was empty.

Marcus cursed and turned back to the room, intending to dress and go after her, only to find that the door had closed behind him . . . and locked.

"Brilliant," he muttered, slamming one fist on the wooden panel with fury.

Divine kept expecting Marcus to rush up behind her and stop her as she made her way out to the hotel parking lot where the SUV was parked. She didn't know if she was relieved or disappointed when that didn't happen. A little of both, Divine supposed as she slipped into the driver's seat and started the vehicle. However, it was probably for the best. She knew it was. That didn't make it any easier. But then there was very little in her life that had seemed to be easy.

While Marcus had wanted to learn more about her from their talk, in the end she'd learned more from him than he had from her. All he'd learned was that she was indeed the rogue he'd been sent to find. She'd learned that her son wasn't her son, that he was a killer, and that Abaddon had probably been using mind control on her from the get-go to get his way.

Divine really couldn't believe that she hadn't picked up on it before this. Now that Marcus had said it, it seemed so obvious. Her fear of her uncle had been so solid and deep with little in the way of doubt . . . and so constant. Abaddon must have been feeding that into her thoughts day in and day out for those first ten years and then reinforcing it every time she'd encountered him.

Of course, the fact that he'd played on her own fears had probably helped. She'd admired and envied those two immortal women who had chosen death over Leonius's abuse. She'd even wondered if that wasn't the more honorable choice. They had escaped, after all, if only into death. They needn't suffer the pain and humiliation he'd visited on her and the others. They were free. Their family honor safe . . . While she had quavered and wept and screamed in pain and terror, begging him not to hurt her, groveling at his feet like a pathetic—

Divine gave her head an angry shake as she started the SUV engine. She might have done all of that for nearly four months, but then she'd become pregnant and life had been more bearable . . . and she had survived. She had lived more than two thousand years since then. She'd met millions of people over the years, some shining stars of brilliance, others individuals in need of a little guidance to find that brilliance.

Divine had spent her life helping others. Surely that made up for any shame her family might have suffered? And surely that made what she'd suffered, if not worthwhile, at least bearable?

Her life had been long, with many quiet joys, moments of satisfaction, or peace. They might have been quiet, hidden moments in comparison to the bright and fiery moments she'd shared with Marcus these last days, but they were moments nonetheless and every single one of them had taken place away from Abaddon. She hadn't enjoyed even a second of peace or enjoyment in Abaddon's presence. It was part of the reason she'd finally taken Damian and run from the man, and why she'd spent so little time with her son after learning he'd welcomed the man back into his life.

Now Divine wondered if all of this was her fault. Damian might not be her child by blood, but she had raised him, he *was* her son. And he had been a sweet child growing up. Always smiling, always eager to please. It was after they'd left Abaddon that Damian had changed, becoming secretive and moody.

At first Divine had thought he just missed the man and would get over it, and then she'd blamed it on puberty. All teenagers were like that, weren't they?

At twelve he'd started wandering the woods or cities depending on where they lived, taking off for hours at a time despite her haranguing him to stay close to home. At sixteen he'd begun disappearing for days at a time. On returning he'd always been manic with happiness; laughing, chatting a mile a minute, telling her tales of his adventures while away. She'd allowed it at the time because he was considered a man in that time period.

Damian was eighteen when he'd been gone a week rather than the usual day or two. Worried that Lucian— who Abaddon had assured her was still looking for them—had finally found her son, Divine had gone looking for him and found him holed up in an abandoned hut. He'd been outside, laughing and chatting by a fire with, of all people, Abaddon. And Abaddon had been calling him Leo, she recalled now. She'd been so furious to find him with the man she'd kind of let that slip her mind at the time.

Divine had tried to send Abaddon away, but Damian had protested. Abaddon was his friend.

"Abaddon is no friend of ours," she'd said furiously. "He was Leonius Livius's lapdog."

"You mean my father?" Damian had asked.

Divine had simply gaped at him. She had never told him about his father. How could she tell her son that he was a child of rape? That his father was a man she loathed who had tortured and raped her for months before he'd been conceived? She hadn't told him before that, and couldn't tell him then. Instead, she had drawn herself up and said, "You are old enough to do what you wish and live where you want now. But I will have nothing to do with this man. Never bring him to my home when you visit."

She had turned and left then. Damian hadn't followed. And Divine had simply continued with her life. He had visited often during the first fifty years or so, relatively speaking. It had been only a year after that when Damian had come to her with her first grandson. When she'd asked his name, he'd said the mother hadn't given him one and didn't want the boy. She'd offered to raise him, which she suspected he'd counted on at the time.

Divine had named the boy Luc and had loved him like her own. She'd been heartbroken when Damian had come to visit on the boy's tenth birthday and decided he needed a father and should go with him. She'd been absolutely devastated, though, when she'd gone to visit Damian and the boy some months later only to learn that their camp had been raided by Lucian's scouts and the boy hadn't got away. He was dead.

Her old fears of her family had immediately resurfaced and the first wave of her anger with them had been born. Luc had been only the first of her grandsons that Divine had raised. Damian had brought her eight of them in all during those first two centuries. She'd raised each as her own, with all the love she could give them, and then had been forced to stand by as her son took them away to finish their upbringing himself. Some had become no-fanger after leaving her, some had not, which Abaddon had said was normal. He had claimed that some children were like that, their no-fanger needs simply not kicking in until puberty.

Of course, now that Marcus had explained nanos to her, she realized that couldn't be the case at all. Those boys must have been birthed by mortal women. If they became no-fangers later, it was because Damian must have tried to turn them. She now wondered if that was the real cause of their death, because not one of the grandsons she'd cared for had survived to adulthood. Each of them had died, supposedly slaughtered by Argeneau spies or hunters. And then Damian had stopped bringing her the children he spawned, claiming that she made them weak.

Once he'd stopped bringing her children, Damian's visits had grown more sparse. Some centuries she'd seen him more often than others, but they had gone as much as eight decades between visits at times. In fact, Divine had often been amazed that he was able to find her when he did come around or send for her. She was constantly moving, after all.

Divine sighed and dashed irritably at her eyes. Thoughts of her grandsons always made her teary. But it was more than that right now. Looking back with the new information she had, she was seeing a lot of the lies that had been told her and wondering just what in her life had been true. She was also wishing she hadn't been quite so gullible and accepted what Abaddon had said. In fact, she really didn't understand why she had. She'd loathed the man. Shouldn't she have doubted every word out of his mouth?

Influence seemed the obvious answer. All she could think was that he'd used mind control, influence, and mental nudging to ensure she believed him. It didn't matter though, whether he'd used influence and such, or she'd just been blind and stupid, the end result was the same. Divine was left with the ruins of a life; no home, no family, no friends, and unable to claim her life mate. It also left her with a son who, if Marcus was to be believed, was a killer like his father. And so were his sons.

Divine shook her head. She'd never seen any evidence of that. The women who had been around when she'd visited had— Frankly, she'd not thought much of them. They'd all looked unkempt and emaciated, and had always been high as kites when she'd visited, as had her grandsons. Now she had to wonder about that too. Were they druggies, or just kept drugged up when she was around so that she couldn't read fear or terror from their minds? Narcotics muddied the thoughts enough to make them incomprehensible when read.

Were those poor women really victims like she had been to Damian's father, Leonius? Divine's mouth tightened. Marcus had said that Damian went by his father's name and named his sons Leonius as well so that he had to call them each by their birth order number. She had heard him call them by numbers over the centuries. For instance he'd called Rufus, the rude grandson she usually wanted to swat, Four on more than one occasion, although in front of her he usually just called them all boy.

Her thoughts returned to the women. Divine couldn't bear to think her son was treating those women as his father had treated her. She intended to find out and set them free if that was the case. She intended on finding out the truth of everything if she could.

Spotting a gas station, Divine slowed and pulled in.

As she'd hoped there was a pay phone here, against the side of the building. She needed to call Damian and find out where he was. She didn't want to drive all the way to the last place he'd been only to find he had moved on.

Divine had always had a good memory. She suspected it had something to do with the nanos. Certainly she didn't recall Damian's number because she used it excessively. She usually called him once a month or so. At least she had until a couple days ago when he'd suddenly called saying he was in the area and needed to see her.

The phone barely rang once before it was picked up, but it wasn't Damian who answered, it was Abaddon. The sound of his voice immediately set her teeth on edge. "I want to speak to my son."

"I'm sorry, Basha, he's playing with one of his little female friends right now," Abaddon said sweetly. "Can I take a message?"

Divine didn't bother insisting he use the name Divine, but simply growled, "Are you still at the house I woke up in the other day?"

"No," Abaddon said at once. "We've moved. I felt like seeing the Cirque du Soleil perform, and your son was amenable, so we headed to Vegas. We're about half an hour outside that city."

Divine went still. That seemed a happy coincidence, but she doubted if it was. After all, she knew Abaddon had some of Damian's sons watching her. They'd probably told him that she and Marcus were in Vegas, and that was the real reason he was here. The only question was why? The boys could call in their reports. He didn't have to remain close by.

Grinding her teeth, she asked, "What's the address?"

When he finished rattling it off, Divine hung up without a good-bye and returned to the SUV to check the GPS. The address he'd given her was half an hour out of the city, but on the other side from where she was now. And it looked like it was in the middle of nowhere, she noted, making the GPS image bigger.

Setting that address as the destination, Divine started the SUV and shifted into gear. She would return it to the hotel parking lot after confronting her son. If she survived the confrontation. Divine suspected one of them wouldn't. If he was killing people, Damian was a menace, and while she hadn't technically brought him into this world, she'd raised him, was responsible for him, and would take him out if she had to.

Twenty-two

Divine brought the SUV to a halt and shifted it into park, but didn't get out. Instead, she simply sat and stared at the building the GPS had brought her to. It looked like an old abandoned warehouse, though why anyone would store anything way the heck out here in the middle of nowhere, she didn't know. The only thing she could think was that the land was probably cheap as spit. Although, from the looks of it, even that hadn't been enough to make it worthwhile once the gas prices had started to skyrocket. By her guess, no one had used the building in at least thirty years . . . until now.

Another palace for her son, Divine thought grimly. In the past, she would have blamed her uncle for Damian's having to live like this. Now she wondered if Damian didn't actually choose places like this because of the lack of neighbors. There would be no one to hear the screams if he really had followed in his father's footsteps and was torturing women in that building.

Mouth tightening, Divine finally got out of the SUV and headed for the building. There were several doors to choose from, half a dozen bay doors that trucks would have backed up to, and one door customers and employees would have used to enter on foot. She chose the latter.

Divine didn't bother knocking, but simply reached out and turned the knob, not surprised when it opened unimpeded. Damian had never been overly concerned about security . . . something that had always frustrated her since she'd thought perhaps her grandsons' murders might have been prevented had he troubled himself with even a modicum of security.

Pushing that thought aside, Divine stepped inside. This was obviously where customers would have been received when it had still been in use. It was a large reception area with a long counter running from one end, almost to the other. Beyond it was an old desk, some filing cabinets, and the door to another room. Despite the fact that it was bright daylight and the front of the offices were faced with large windows, this room was dim. A good cleaning of the grime that coated the windows would have fixed that, but Divine wasn't here to perform housekeeping for her son. Besides, avoiding sunlight was always a good thing. The damage from sunlight meant more blood was needed and more frequent feeding was necessary.

Divine moved around the counter, her eyes shifting over everything as she crossed to the second door. There wasn't much more to see, a few bits of old yellowed paper on the floor along with years of built-up dust and grime. Through the door though, she found a room that was nearly pitch-black.

"You made good time."

Divine narrowed her eyes at the sound of Abaddon's voice and waited for her night vision to kick in. Once it had, she saw that she was in a large room with a long table and several chairs. There was also a kitchenette of sorts at one end with a tired old white fridge and kitchen cupboards, half of them missing their doors. As for Abaddon, he was seated at a chair at the table, as comfortable as you please. His eyes glowed gold in the darkness.

Reaching to the side, Divine searched the wall for a switch, found it, and turned it on, but nothing happened.

"No electricity," Abaddon said helpfully.

A rustling drew her attention back to him as he lifted what appeared to be a lantern onto the table. He turned a knob and the lantern gave off a weak glow that barely lit up a small circle around where he sat.

"Solar," Abaddon explained. "Much cheaper than gas or oil lanterns and the like. Leave these outside during the day while we sleep and they can light up the night for us. I'm a great proponent of solar power," he said with a smile, and the shadows cast by the light made him look like the devil himself.

The devil in a powder blue jogging suit, Divine thought, eyeing the man with disgust. Where she and

Leo were fair-haired, Abaddon had dark hair, brown eyes with gold flecks in them, and a clean-shaven face. All in all he looked unremarkable; average build, average looks, totally nonthreatening. Most people would have mistaken him for a businessman on his way to working out after a busy day . . . until it was too late.

"Where's Damian?" she asked shortly.

"On his way. You beat him here. But then, as I said, you made very good time."

"I was in Vegas," Divine said coldly. "But then you knew that."

"Did I?" he asked mildly.

"If you didn't then your spies are slipping."

"Oh," Abaddon said softly. "So you know."

"That you've been jerking me around for two millennia?" Divine asked grimly.

"Two millennia plus seven hundred and forty-seven years," Abaddon corrected. "I'm rather proud of that so you should give me every day I'm due."

Divine stared at him. There was no shame or dismay at being caught, not that she'd expected any, but she'd expected *something*, and there was no apparent reaction in his face at all. She eyed him with loathing for a minute and then said, "If Damian is really coming, I'll just wait to speak to him."

"He isn't coming," Abaddon said at once. "In fact he doesn't know about this place, or this meeting even. I told him I had some personal business to attend to, and suggested he just relax today and play. He took my advice," Abaddon added with pleasure, and smiled when she cursed. "I gather you're disappointed?"

"Only that he takes your advice on anything," she snapped.

"He always takes my advice, Basha. He sees me as more of a parent than you could ever be," Abaddon said, his voice dripping with feigned pity. "Because while he had to hide his true nature from you, he could always be himself with me. I know and accept him for what he is rather than try to turn him into what I want him to be."

"Oh, stuff it, Abaddon," she snarled, furious. "You were never a parent to him. He likes you because you always let him have his way. I was the parent, telling him no, punishing him when he was bad, and teaching him right from wrong."

"Hmmm." Abaddon nodded. "That must be why he confessed to me when he started torturing and killing small animals and children as a boy."

Divine stiffened and felt herself pale at this news. Her son had tortured and killed animals and small children? Animals were bad enough, but small *children*? How could she not have known—?

"Because when he wept and fretted that you would be angry if you found out, I helped him hide it," Abaddon said as if she had spoken her thoughts aloud. Smiling, he added, "Leo was worried for a while that it was naughty and there was something wrong with him, but I explained it was simply in his nature. Like a bee stings and a lion stalks, he was born to be like that. His father was like that before him and he was just as he was meant to be. That's when I started calling him Leonius . . . and he liked it."

"Bastard," she growled, launching herself at him. Divine wanted to scratch his eyes out, choke him, and twist his head off in that moment, but she didn't even get to touch him. Divine had barely taken two steps when she was grabbed from behind.

Cursing, she twisted her head from side to side to see that she'd been grabbed by two of her grandsons. No doubt the ones who had been sent to spy on her, Divine realized, and wondered how she could have forgotten about them.

"Sit her in the chair and chain her up," Abaddon ordered, standing, and Divine found herself strong-armed across the room and set in the chair he'd just vacated. One of her grandsons—one of Damian's sons, she corrected herself—then moved to the refrigerator, opened it, and retrieved some chain and several padlocks from a stack of them inside. It appeared they'd come prepared. Divine only wished she had. She'd been so determined to talk to her son, she hadn't considered a scenario like this.

She remained silent as the two young no-fangers worked. Abaddon watched them, checked the chains afterward, and nodded his satisfaction. He then murmured something to one of the men. Despite her immortal hearing, all Divine caught were the words "I want you to go wait for—" as Abaddon walked the man out of the room. He returned alone a moment later, but didn't even cast a glance toward Divine before beginning to pace, head down, expression thoughtful.

Divine frowned, her gaze sliding to the young no-fanger still behind her. He'd moved to lean against the wall, a bored expression on his face. Her gaze slid back to Abaddon, still pacing. "What are we waiting for?"

"Your life mate," Abaddon answered absently, continuing to pace.

"Well then you're wasting your time," she said at once. "Marcus won't come here. He doesn't know where I am."

"Yes he does. I left a message for him at the hotel with this address," Abaddon murmured, taking out his phone when it made the sound of a foghorn. It was obviously a text message, and one that annoyed him, because he began tapping out a message in response, his mouth twisted with displeasure. He finished his message, started to slip the phone back in his pocket, only to pause and draw it back out when it made that foghorn sound again. He muttered with exasperation at whatever the latest incoming message said, and quickly typed another response. This time as he returned the phone he glanced to Divine and announced with irritation, "Your son is bored."

"Not my son," Divine said coldly. "You're the one who encouraged him to be the way he is."

"Well, yes, because that's what a parent does, Basha," he said with exasperation. "A parent is supposed to encourage the child."

"He wasn't your son to encourage," she growled.

"No, but then neither was his father, and I encouraged him and helped him find his full potential too," Abaddon said with a shrug.

"You helped Leonius Livius find his true potential?" she echoed dubiously.

"Of course. Do you really think he came up with the idea of creating an army of his own sons all by himself?" he asked dryly. "The man didn't think past his next pleasure, let alone the next day. He wasn't concerned about the other Atlantean refugees getting wind of what he was doing and rising up against him."

Divine merely stared at him. She'd always thought that Abaddon was just another follower of the man. That he'd shown up on the scene after Leonius Livius was well into the plan. Now he was suggesting he'd been there at the start of it.

"Most no-fangers are mad, but not really naturally cruel," he lectured, apparently determined to convince her and lay claim to the dubious honor of being the puppet master behind the monster. "Mostly they just seem to be lacking a conscience and don't care who or how they hurt others to get what they want. The cruelty Leo has and his father had before him, though? That had to be nurtured and helped to grow in them and I did that for both of them, Leonius Livius I and the son you raised."

Divine stared at him with horror. "You ruined Damian."

He snorted at the claim. "Nonsense! I didn't put the knife in his hand the first time he chopped up a child. I just helped him develop to his full potential once he revealed it."

She was shaking her head in denial before he even finished speaking. "He had a conscience, you said yourself he was weeping and fretting over what he'd done. He knew it was wrong. If I had known and—"

"He was weeping and fretting at the possibility of getting caught and the consequences of it," Abaddon corrected sharply. "He was afraid his *mommy* would be angry and not love him anymore." Lips pursing with disgust, he added, "The boy has some serious mommy issues, Basha. Despite everything I've done for him, he will listen to you over me when he feels he has to, to appease you . . . and he doesn't want you hurt or angered either." He scowled and added, "Mind you, he might worry less about that if he knew his precious *mommy* was thinking of turning him in to her uncle Lucian. What kind of mother does that make you?"

"He's torturing and raping innocent mortals," she barked defensively, stung at the accusation that wanting to stop Damian made her a bad mother.

"And killing. Don't forget that," Abaddon added with a grin. "But innocent, bah!" he sneered, and then said with disgust, "Most of them are runaways, whores, and junkies who had a short life expectancy anyway."

"Made even shorter by my son's arrival in their life," Divine growled. "And you said *most* of them are; what about the others? How many lives has he brought to an early end? How many women has he tortured before killing?"

"Women *and men*," he corrected. "Unlike his father, Leo has a liking for family picnics. Something you instilled in him, by the way."

"Family picnics?" she asked with bewilderment.

"Yes, you know, finding a nice wholesome family out on a farm and taking them all out to the barn for a meal. Although I believe you used to take them one at a time, and generally on the back porch or behind the barn. Of course, you never let him hurt or kill them, making him take just enough blood to get by before putting them back in their beds. Still, those are fond memories for him and he likes to relive them."

"Relive them?" she echoed uncertainly.

"Yes. Mind you, Leo likes to do things on a much grander scale."

"Grander how?" she asked, sure she wouldn't like the answer.

Abaddon considered her briefly, but apparently couldn't resist and rushed over to claim the chair across from her. Leaning on the table, he smiled enthusiastically and explained, "See, he gets half a dozen or so of the boys together, and they find an isolated farmhouse with a nice big family. But that's where his feedings differ from the ones you took him on. Instead of taking one member at a time, he and the boys roust everyone from their beds and take the whole family down to the barn together. Now, they're still in their pajamas, mind, and Mommy and the kids are huddled together with a couple of boys keeping them from running or looking away, and they get to watch while Daddy is strung up by his feet like a pig for slaughter, and then . . ." He shrugged. "Well, they slaughter him."

Divine closed her eyes against the images he was painting, but they continued to play across her mind as he added, "It's really something to see, the boys all working together with their dad as they slice and dice their prey. They do it slowly, of course, to draw out the pleasure."

"Shut up," Divine whispered.

"Sometimes they get thirsty and stop to chug blood from the pails they set out beneath him to catch the precious liquid, but other times—although this is only toward the end," he assured her, "one of them will hit a major artery like a carotid, or—and this is cool—the ulnar or radial in one of the arms hanging down, and then they just stand there and let it squirt and flow into their mouth from his arm like it's the spout of a teapot."

"Shut up," Divine repeated, her voice stronger but raspy. It felt like her throat was closing up.

"Oh, I'm sorry, am I making you thirsty?" he asked solicitously.

"Thirsty?" she echoed with disbelief. "You're making me sick."

"Oh," Abaddon said with feigned surprise and then tsked and shook his head. "You always did have a weak stomach, didn't you? Ah well." He shrugged and then said, "Anyway, that usually finishes off the dad and then they string up Mom next to him, also upside down, which is handy for getting her nightgown out of the way if she's wearing one, and then they do it all over again. Of course, she's followed by the eldest child and so on."

Unable to kill him chained to the chair as she was, Divine just bowed her head, trying to shut him out as he finished, "So there's the bonfire, the blood, the screaming, and fun is had by all. The boys love it. They get all excited when Leo says they're going on a family picnic."

"Dear God," Divine breathed.

"Oh, don't be like that," Abaddon chided. "You should be proud of your son. He's at least equaled, if not surpassed, his father when it comes to acts of depravity. And that was despite having you for a mother, which was certainly a handicap, what with your goody-two-shoes ways."

"He's not my child," she said coldly, raising her head and staring through the man.

"No," Abaddon said sympathetically. "Your child was a girl with big silver-blue eyes and ice blond hair like yours is under that nasty dye. She—" He paused as his phone made another sound, this time a twitter. Pulling it out, he peered at the message and smiled. "Well, Marcus made good time too. He's just pulling in."

Divine felt her heart sink at this news. Despite his saying they were waiting for Marcus, she'd hoped he was just lying to her or that Marcus would have the sense to not come in the end. She would even have been happy did he hate her now that he knew she was the woman who had unknowingly rescued a monster when she'd swept her son up and carried him away that day in the hotel. She hated herself for it now that she'd heard what he'd been up to all these years.

Divine couldn't imagine the blood the man she'd thought of as her son, Damian, had on his hands. But she knew every drop of it was on her hands too. She'd failed him as a parent. She should have escaped Abaddon the moment they were out of the camp. She should have . . . Well, truly, she didn't know what else she could have done to prevent this, but she was sure there was something.

Marcus stopped the rented sedan next to the SUV Divine had taken and surveyed the building ahead, wondering how many people there were inside. He was walking into the lion's den, and doing so willingly. Why? Because the message left for him at the hotel had said that if he came and forfeited his life, Basha's would be spared.

As far as Marcus was concerned, that had left him little choice. She was his life mate. It was that simple. He'd rather cut off his own head than see her hurt in any way. He just didn't know if giving up his life would save hers in the end. He wasn't foolish enough to trust that this Abaddon who had left the message would really let Divine walk away.

Marcus also didn't know how long they had before Lucian and the others would track them down. They'd been expected back at the carnival last night. He'd called while in the taxi on the way to buy clothes last night to tell Vincent that they were going to be a little later than expected, that Divine had agreed to tell him everything, but it would take time. However, it was now noon of the following day and he hadn't called again, nor had he answered any of the many calls from them this morning. First he'd been tied up and talking with Divine in the bedroom while his phone had been in the pocket of his jeans in the bathroom and he hadn't heard the first of the calls, and then he'd been desperate to get to her so ignored the rest. Besides, he hadn't known what to say, whether to call them in to help or not. Marcus wasn't sure Divine was any safer in their hands than she was with the man she'd raised as her son.

The sound of a car drew his gaze to the rearview mirror. Marcus wasn't terribly surprised to see the car that came to a halt behind his rental. It had followed him all the way from the hotel in Vegas. But now that it was no longer keeping a safe distance between them, he could see the two men inside. They could have been twins despite the fact that one had a shaved head and the other had long, stringy unkempt hair. They were definitely sons of Leonius Livius II. All his sons seemed to take after him in looks.

The men got out of their vehicle, but simply leaned against it, patiently waiting, both dressed in jeans and T-shirts. Neither looked too bothered by the fact that they were standing out under the noonday sun and would have to feed more because of it later. Marcus was though, because he knew they would feed on some poor mortal they snatched from her bed or off the street.

Mouth tightening, he got out of the car and headed for the main door of the building, not even bothering to glance around to see if the men were following. Marcus knew they were. He would have known even if he couldn't hear the crunch of the sand and stone under their Doc Martens.

Twenty-three

"**A**h, here you are. Thank you for coming so speedily."

Divine pulled herself from her thoughts and glanced to the door as Abaddon said those words. Her heart leaped and then sank when she saw Marcus walking calmly into the room, two more of Damian's sons on his heels.

Leonius, she corrected herself. They were Leonius's sons. He might have been Damian as a boy, but he was no longer. He had chosen his path, and he had chosen his name. He was Leonius Livius II now, and she could never let herself forget that.

"Come, sit down," Abaddon said jovially, gesturing to the chair he'd vacated just moments ago.

Marcus crossed to the chair, his eyes moving over Divine with concern as he settled across from her.

"I'm fine," she whispered sadly, really wishing he hadn't come.

"Of course she's fine, Marcus. Do you mind if I call you Marcus," Abaddon asked, gesturing to the men, who immediately retrieved more chain and began to padlock Marcus to the chair. "And you, of course, should call me Abaddon. Or Abby if you like."

Marcus ignored him, as well as the men chaining him up, and merely stared into Divine's eyes as if she was the only one there. She could see the silver swirling through the black of his eyes and was sure his emotions were a tumultuous mix of anger, worry, and some softer feeling she didn't dare call love. But she didn't know if he was angry at her or Abaddon. Probably both, she thought unhappily and then glanced toward Abaddon as he ordered the two newly arrived men to go out and keep an eye out for company. The two men left, leaving just Abaddon and the grandson who had stayed behind her all this time. He had remained leaning against the wall, looking bored, since she'd been chained to the chair.

"Well," Abaddon said, settling into the seat at the end of the table. "We have just been sitting here chatting about the good old days."

Marcus finally tore his eyes from Divine to acknowledge the other man by saying, "Divine told me you were one of the first Leonius's men."

"His friend," Abaddon corrected. "We were great friends."

"I'm surprised you had anything in common. You're immortal, not no-fanger, aren't you?" Marcus murmured, narrowing his eyes as he peered at the other man.

"Oh, yes, well that's true, but despite that we had a lot in common," Abaddon assured him.

"You like raping and torturing women too, do you?" Marcus asked grimly.

"I'm more of a watcher than a doer," Abaddon admitted with a little laugh. "Leo liked to cut them up, and I liked to watch them scream and squirm. It worked out very nicely."

Divine glanced at him sharply. She'd always thought she was alone with Leonius when he'd done the things he did. Now she wondered if Abaddon had been there somewhere, watching through a peephole the entire time. The thought just added to her humiliation.

"Only the first time," Abaddon said suddenly, apparently reading her mind. "And he threw me out after the first few minutes, which he never did with any of the other women," he added resentfully, and then forced a smile and said, "Leo was oddly jealous of you . . . which I can understand completely, of course," he added, running a lascivious gaze down her body. "He and I always had similar taste in women."

Despite his ogling her, all Divine felt was relief that Abaddon hadn't witnessed her humiliation, at least not past the first few minutes of it. Although she supposed it was silly to feel that way when all he had to do was read her mind to enjoy every second of it.

"Enough of that though," Abaddon said suddenly, sitting back in his chair and turning his gaze to Marcus. "Before you got here we were talking about Basha's baby. I was telling her how pretty she was, and that she looked just like a mini version of her, but kind of plump and roundish as babies are." His gaze shifted back to Divine. "You should have seen her, Basha. She really was adorable."

"What happened to her?" Marcus growled.

Abaddon addressed the answer to Divine. "I cut off her head outside the tent while you were still inside panting from the exertion of birthing her. Leonius had no use for daughters."

Divine closed her eyes, but Marcus growled and tugged uselessly at his chains. "You—"

"And you gave me Damian in her place?" Divine said quickly, interrupting Marcus. Abaddon might claim he enjoyed watching rather than doling out torture, but he was just as cruel in his way, and had been known to lash out. She wouldn't have him lashing out at an incapacitated Marcus.

Abaddon's expression was amused when he turned to her. He knew exactly what she was doing, but all he said was "I know you like to think you named him Damian, but really, Basha, he was a day old and already named Leonius II when I placed him in your arms."

He let that sink in and then laughed and added, "Although, I must say it's ironic. Your name choice, I mean. Don't you find it ironic . . . especially now? I mean, you must think he's the devil's spawn."

When Divine just stared at him with bewilderment, he sighed with disappointment. "Of course, you don't do anything as plebian as go to movies or watch television, do you? So you've never seen *The Omen*? No?" He shook his head. "Such a shame. I think you'd really enjoy it."

Divine had no idea what he was talking about and

no interest in movies at that point. She did have a lot of questions though. "Why?" she asked grimly. "Why give me the boy in my daughter's place? Why rush me out of there with a child that wasn't my own? Why not take the mother of the boy instead?"

"To give him a better chance at survival," he said simply. "You are an Argeneau, the boy's mother was just some mortal Leonius turned edentate. With you in her place, if we were caught making our escape, your uncle would have taken you both under his wing and home to his parents, and Leonius's son would have been raised in the bosom of the very family who brought about his father's downfall."

Divine shook her head at once. "They would have known he wasn't my son. He's edentate, an immortal woman can only produce immortals."

Abaddon glanced to Marcus. "I'm guessing you clarified the science for her? You must have. She was never around immortals before you. I made sure of that." Smiling faintly, he sat back and suggested, "Perhaps you should tell her why they would have believed he could be her son."

Marcus was silent for a moment, and Divine was just beginning to think he would refuse, but then he turned to her and said, "He's right. They might have believed he was yours back then. Immortals tended not to mate with no-fangers so there wasn't a lot of experience to go on. Besides, none of the scientists made it out of Atlantis, and it's only been the last couple of centuries that mortal science has progressed enough for us to learn those kinds of things."

"Exactly," Abaddon said triumphantly. "Lucian would have accepted Damian as your son and probably would have helped you raise him too." He sat back with a little sigh and said, "Wouldn't that have been grand?"

"That's what Leonius wanted, wasn't it?" Divine said with sudden understanding, sure the bastard would have enjoyed the irony of that.

"Hmmm," Abaddon murmured with a nod. "And I'm sure he died happily, thinking that would happen. Sadly for him, I had a change of heart as I led you out of the camp and decided not being caught was preferred."

"Why?" she asked at once.

"You mean aside from the fact that I would have been killed on the spot if we'd been caught?" Abaddon asked dryly and shook his head. "I'm afraid I wasn't *that* loyal to Leonius. I found his behavior entertaining, certainly, but dying for him and his cause was just that one step beyond the call of duty in my mind."

"Then why not just leave us and flee on your own once you were out of camp?" Divine asked at once, thinking how different things would have been had that happened. She would have had family, a home . . . Damian might even have turned out better.

"That's why," Abaddon said.

Divine blinked her thoughts away and peered at him with confusion, but it was Marcus who asked, "What's why?"

Staring Divine in the eye, Abaddon said, "You would have had family, a home . . ." He stopped listing off the thoughts she'd been having and shrugged. "As ashamed as I am to admit it, I'm a vengeful prick. Even my mother used to say that."

"You had a mother?" Divine snapped. "And here I was sure you were hatched like the rest of the snakes."

"Name calling?" he asked with a laugh. "Really? That's the best you can do?"

"Remove these chains and I'll do better for her," Marcus said silkily, drawing his gaze.

Abaddon smiled. "Now why would I do that? I have you both where I want you and I'm truly enjoying this."

"Torturing her, you mean?" Marcus asked grimly. "You might not like to get your hands dirty with physical torture, but you certainly don't have a problem torturing her mentally, do you? You've been doing that every time you've seen her for two thousand years."

"Not as much as I'd have liked," Abaddon assured him. "It was tricky with Leonius there. He's protective of his mother . . . as a loving son should be," he added with a sneer.

"Why?" Divine demanded before Marcus could respond to that. "Just tell me why the hell I earned so much antipathy from you? Why did you want me so fricking miserable all these years?"

Abaddon turned to peer at her. "The truth?"

When Divine nodded, he shrugged.

"Basically it's because I don't take rejection well."

"Rejection," she echoed with confusion, not having a clue what he was talking about.

Abaddon sighed with exasperation. "Here it's been a thorn in my side for eons and you don't even remember it?" he asked with annoyance.

"Remember what?" Divine asked with annoyance of her own. Cripes, if she'd been paying all these years for something, it would be nice to know what the hell it was.

"I offered to save you," he said heavily, and when Divine stared at him blankly, he tsked irritably and reminded her, "On the ride back to camp the night we found you? You were all tied up and on my horse in front of me. When you thought no one was paying you any attention, you started to weep. I chucked your chin and you looked up at me with these big, beautiful, sad silver-blue eyes and I was moved," he added with self-disgust. "I offered to save you from Leonius."

"You offered to save me *if I became your lover*," Divine said with remembered outrage as the memory came back to her.

"Would that have been worse than letting that animal paw and rape and cut you up?" Abaddon snapped.

"Let?" she snapped right back, leaning forward in her chair as much as the chains would allow. "I was *eleven years old*. A *child*. I had no idea what was in store for me. All I knew was some old pervert was pawing me up and demanding I be his lover or I'd be sorry."

"But you weren't, were you? You weren't sorry at all," he growled. "You enjoyed what he did to you."

Divine slammed back against her chair as if he'd slapped her. Here was the seat of her shame. The reason she'd been sure her family would have turned from her as Abaddon had repeatedly claimed. The reason she'd spent her life running and hiding, even from herself. Most of the time, her captivity had been nothing but terrifying, screaming agony. But there were occasions . . . Divine hadn't understood it at the time, but there had been sessions when she'd seemed to be experiencing Leonius's pleasure in her pain, along with her agony. At first they were brief, just snapshots really, because Leonius had quickly stopped what he was doing and backed away from her when it happened, looking shaken and confused. But after half a dozen sessions like that, he hadn't backed away, he'd continued on, raining a storm of pain and pleasure on her until she passed out.

That had shaken Divine, shaken her belief in herself. It had made her feel ashamed, dirty, unredeemable. Like there was something wrong with her. In her mind, what he did to her was abominable, inhuman. She'd been horrified and hurting. So how could she at the same time have experienced any pleasure at all?

"You can't deny it," Abaddon accused. "You enjoyed it."

Divine's gaze shot to Marcus and then quickly away when she saw him looking at her with concern. Scowling at Abaddon, she muttered. "Go to hell."

"I expect to," Abaddon said, relaxing. "In fact, I expect to like it."

"This isn't because she rejected your offer of protection all those years ago," Marcus said suddenly. "All the energy you've expended on making her miserable all these years, ensuring she never felt it was safe to turn to her family, ensuring she was always alone, lying to make her keep feeding off the hoof when you knew that was no longer allowed . . . and calling her in to whisk Leonius away when Lucian and the others had captured him . . ." Marcus shook his head, eyes narrowed on the man. "You could have done the saving yourself, but you deliberately called her in to do it because you knew it would make her rogue and ensure she would never be accepted back into the fold. Or you hoped it would."

"So?" Abaddon scowled.

"So those aren't the actions of a man who was rejected," Marcus said calmly, and then added, "Those are the actions of a jealous wife who blames a mistress for stealing a husband."

Divine's eyes widened incredulously and she glanced to Abaddon to see that his face was turning color, reddening first, and then purpling to fury.

"What happened, Abaddon?" Marcus asked. "You couldn't read Leonius and he couldn't read you? You wanted him for your life mate, and didn't even mind that he was busy with torturing his little toys so long as he let you be a part of it. But then Divine came along. How did you know he'd take to her as he did? You must have known that to offer her protection. Although I suspect you only offered that thinking that Leonius wouldn't want her if she went to you willingly."

"It was the way he looked at her," Abaddon snarled and then glared at Divine. "From the moment you ran into the clearing, it was like he was star-struck. He'd never looked at any of the other women like that. I knew . . ." His mouth set and he scowled at Divine. "So I took you up on my horse before he could, and I made that offer on the ride back to camp, but oh no, you wanted Leonius, *my* Leonius."

He turned to Marcus. "He didn't just ban me from the tent once he started on her, he wanted to stop playing with the others. Not right away, of course, it took a session or two before he started to not bother with the others. I had to remind him over and over again about our plans and the need for an army of his sons. But it was only when I said the Argeneaus would come take her away from him if he didn't have an army strong enough to hold them off that he gave his attentions to the others again. He let me watch again too, but it was obvious his heart wasn't in it anymore. All he wanted was *her*," he said with disgust.

"She was a possible life mate too," Marcus said with sudden understanding, and Divine glanced at him sharply.

Leonius Livius a life mate? The thought was unbearable. Besides—"I thought we each had only one life mate? You're my life mate."

Marcus shook his head. "Life mates are rare, but not that rare. Others have encountered more than one in a lifetime," he said gently, and then turned to Abaddon and repeated coldly, "Divine was a possible life mate for him too, and he chose her over you . . . and you hated her for it."

Divine remained silent, her mind racing. She wanted to deny what he was saying, but it explained so much. The pleasure she'd felt and fought when Leonius had raped and tortured her . . . it could have been his pleasure in the act. If so, it hadn't been a sign that she was as deviant and dirty as the things he did to her . . . and that had been her biggest fear, what had allowed her to believe his claims that her family would not want her, that she had shamed them, that she had shamed herself.

"You don't plan on keeping to the bargain and letting Divine go," Marcus said suddenly and Divine glanced to him again. He was no longer looking at her. His gaze was now firmly on Abaddon as he said, "You can't. She knows too much now, and she'll tell Damian all of it. How you've manipulated her and ensured she was alone and lonely all these years. How you kept them both from her family when his father wanted him to be raised among them. And the reason why, that she was his father's life mate."

"She shouldn't have been. She wasn't good enough for him. She was a stupid little child and—" He paused and glanced down to his pocket with surprise as it gave off the foghorn sound again. Letting his breath out on a slow sigh, he reached for his phone and stood to move away from the table as he read it.

"How will you explain killing her to Damian?" Marcus asked idly as Abaddon began to type an answer into his phone.

"I'll tell him that you convinced her he wasn't her son and told her what he's been up to. I'll tell him that she wanted to turn him in. I had no choice," Abaddon murmured, still typing away.

"If you thought he'd accept that as reason enough to kill me, you wouldn't have arranged to meet me on the sly," Divine said, pushing all other issues away for the moment. She'd learned long ago to compartmental-ize when necessary, and sitting there fretting over the fact that she had probably been a life mate to Leonius

Livius wasn't going to help them get out of there alive. When Abaddon didn't respond, she added, "Damian won't be happy I'm dead. As you said, he has mommy issues. And my knowing about him now won't be a good enough excuse for killing me when all he has to do is stop giving me his address. He already has Lucian and all of his Rogue Hunters after him; hiding from me as well would hardly be a hardship."

Abaddon heaved a long-suffering sigh and tore his gaze from the phone to glare at her. "Then I'll have to tell him your uncle caught up with and killed you both and we found you here."

"Oh, right. Well, make sure you take the chains off our bodies before he sees them then," she said dryly and followed it up with a short laugh as he returned to typing.

"What?" Abaddon asked, scowling at her.

"What what?" she asked innocently.

"You laughed as if you thought of something, but I was distracted with my phone and wasn't reading your mind. What were you thinking?"

Divine shrugged. "I was just thinking that Danny here behind me, or number Seventeen as I think I've heard Damian call him, isn't likely to keep his mouth shut about what happened here today. Neither will the others. They were always greedy little boys. Every time they want something, they'll blackmail you with this, and good Lord, don't say or do anything to piss them off or they'll tell their dad about this just to spite you."

Abaddon stared at her blankly for a minute and then shifted his gaze to the man behind her. She didn't turn to look, but if she were to hazard a guess, Divine would have said Damian's son must have been grinning and nodding or something stupid like that because Abaddon suddenly pulled a gun from the pocket of his joggers and shot Danny.

Divine did turn then, and just in time to see that he'd been hit dead center in the middle of his forehead. The young no-fanger dropped like a stone without even enough time to look surprised. He was no-fanger, however, and not dead. Given time he'd heal, his body pushing the bullet right out of his head. Or he would have except Abaddon then slid his phone in his pocket, opened one of the cupboards along the wall beside the refrigerator, pulled out an axe, hefted it, and then walked over and cut off Danny's head with one blow.

"There," he said, straightening with satisfaction. "Now Danny won't tell anyone anything, will he? I'll take care of the others later, when their usefulness has worn off. Leonius can always make more. Lord knows he works at it hard enough. He's worse than his father for rutting. He seems to actually enjoy that as much as, or more than, causing them pain. Something I was hoping he'd grow out of, but so far no luck," he muttered, pulling his phone from his pocket as it made the foghorn sound again.

Divine tore her gaze from the dead man she'd thought of as a grandson and peered at Abaddon. Danny's death had reminded her of the other boys, the ones she'd raised as grandsons, and she asked abruptly, "Who killed Luc?"

Abaddon glanced to her with surprise. Apparently

she'd caught him by surprise, but after a moment, he admitted, "No one. He didn't survive being turned."

Divine nodded. "And the others?"

"A couple died when Leonius tried to turn them, but the rest—" He grimaced. "They were edentate, weak, wouldn't hurt a fly. It made them useless to Leo, and he worried they'd tattle to you, so—" He gestured to Danny. "They went the same way he did only without the shooting part first."

Divine closed her eyes and bowed her head at the thought of all those lovely little boys, and then glanced up sharply when the phone actually rang rather than make the foghorn sound. Abaddon cursed, took a deep breath for patience, and then answered his phone.

"Hello?" he said pleasantly. "Yes, Leo. I know. I'll be there as quickly as I can, but I have some business— No, I know, but— Yes, but— Fine," he finished a little snappily and hit the button to end the call. His teeth were audibly grinding together as he announced, "It would seem I have to go for a while. The other boys will be here to watch you though, and I'll be back."

"Thanks for the warning," Marcus muttered as Abaddon left the room.

Twenty-four

"I wish you hadn't come here."

Marcus turned his attention from the door Abaddon had just walked out of and peered at Divine at those words. She looked so incredibly sad. He just wanted to take her in his arms and hold her close, kiss and hug her and tell her everything would be okay. Unfortunately, he was chained to his seat and couldn't do any of that. At least not the hugging and kissing part.

"I told you, Divine. Your fate is mine. If you're dead and buried, I may as well be rotting in the ground right next to you." He grimaced even as he said that, and then added solemnly, "But if I can save your life with mine, I will."

"And leave me to go on without you," she said dryly and then shook her head. "Abaddon would love that, then I could add horrible guilt and loss over you to my suffering for the next millennium or however long I live."

"Then I guess we'd better get out of here," he said solemnly and began pulling at his chains.

"The chairs are metal and the chains are strong," Divine said, sounding weary. "We aren't going anywhere."

"Giving up?" he chided. "I didn't think you were the sort."

"I'm not usually," she said tiredly. "But right now . . ."

When Marcus remained silent, his attention on straining against the chains, Divine said, "I don't understand why Abaddon didn't just take control of my mind and make me accept the offer to be his lover that day. I mean if he thought that would have kept Leonius from touching me—"

"It wouldn't have," Marcus assured her. "Leonius probably would have killed him and taken you back. Besides, Abaddon didn't really want you, he wanted Leonius. And at that point, I suspect it was just a throwaway offer. He saw the way Leonius looked at you, was afraid, and made it. But he didn't know at that point that you were a possible life mate to Leonius. He was just jealous of the way he looked at you, so there was no real need to push the issue."

"Oh, yes," Divine murmured and then glanced to him with surprise when one of the vertical stiles holding the back of his chair to the seat suddenly snapped.

"I noticed it was rusty when he urged me to sit in it," Marcus said with a grin as the chains around him loosened. He tipped himself over and quickly shimmied out of the chained chair, then stood and came around to her. But he didn't immediately go to work on her chains. Instead, he knelt before her and cupped her shoulders with his hands. "Divine, I saw your expression when he accused you of enjoying Leonius's . . . attention."

Flushing, she lowered her head, but he caught her chin and raised it again. "You have nothing to be ashamed of. Even child abusers and mortal rapists can make their victims experience a moment's pleasure."

"But the things he did to me, Marcus. I didn't like any of those. I don't like pain. My brain was screaming with horror at what he did, but my body—"

"He was a possible life mate," Marcus said firmly. "I'm sure of it, and that being the case, what you experienced was his pleasure. Not your own." When she just shook her head, he asked, "Didn't you feel my pleasure when you kissed and caressed me last night and then took my cock into your—"

"Yes, of course I did," she interrupted, wishing she had a Kleenex. Her eyes were beginning to tear up and her nose clogging up. She really could have used a tissue.

"Well, it's the same thing, sweetheart," he said gently. "Sucking on a banana would have given about as much pleasure to you as what you actually experienced physically when you did what you did to me last night, more actually because it tastes yummy. But the point is, what you did pleasured me, and so because we're life mates, you shared in that pleasure, experiencing it with me. And that's what you experienced with Leonius. Your body might have been in agony, but his pleasure was sent to you at the same time." He paused and then said sadly, "It must have been terribly confusing for you at that age. Hell, it would have confused an adult too, I'm sure."

"I felt so dirty," she admitted leaning her head against his chest and sniffling miserably. "I thought there was something wrong with me, that I was sick and twisted like him. Unlovable."

"No doubt that's why Abaddon found it so easy to keep you away from your family all these years," Marcus muttered, hugging her to his chest as much as he could.

Divine nodded against his T-shirt, leaving a wet trail.

Sighing, he pulled her face back and said firmly, "Well, you're not like Leonius, you're not sick and twisted, and I love you."

She blinked in surprise at that. "You do?"

He nodded.

"Why?" she asked with bewilderment. "I mean I know we have the whole life mate thing, Marcus, but—"

"Sweetheart, from what I've seen you're just like me," he said with amusement. "I've spent my whole life taking care of others, and so have you. At least, I know you've tried to help all the people you did readings for at the carnival, as well as the carnies themselves. I'm guessing you've done that your whole life. Aside from that you're brave, strong, smart, and sexy as hell."

Divine laughed at the last one. She didn't feel very brave, strong, or sexy at the moment weeping all over his chest. But God she loved this man. Any man who could make you laugh in a situation like this was a keeper, she thought.

"I hope you come to love me too," Marcus added, kissing her forehead.

Divine bit her lip, but then sighed and admitted, "As much as I hate to admit it, I'm pretty sure you sealed the deal on my loving you when you walked in here of your own free will, offering up your life for mine."

Marcus grinned and squeezed her briefly, but then eased his hold and frowned as he asked, "Why do you hate to admit it?"

"Because you're better off without me. If we get out of here and stay together, you're going to spend the rest of your life on the run," she pointed out sadly.

"I've been thinking about that," Marcus said, releasing her to move around and look over her chains and the chair she sat on. "That might not necessarily be true."

"Um, yes it is," she assured him dryly. "I rescued Leonius from Lucian. He's hardly going to just forget that."

"Yeah. But I'm thinking that Damian," he said the name firmly, "is your Jean Claude."

Divine glanced around, to peer at him with surprise. "Uncle Lucian's twin?"

"Yeah, I don't know if you know this, I mean, you haven't been in touch with the family for a while, but as it turns out, Jean Claude was a rogue. He was breaking immortal laws. As in the plural," he added dryly. "Anyway, Lucian knew he was behaving badly, but like you, not that he was actually breaking laws, and, like you, he helped him out when it would have been better if he hadn't," Marcus explained, tugging at her chair.

"Of course, once he found out, he killed Jean Claude, but only because Jean Claude asked him to."

Divine heard a snap and her chair back suddenly shifted behind her, the chains loosening.

"I'm thinking if we remind Lucian of that, he might go easier on you," Marcus finished, coming around to help her get untangled from the chains. Once he had her free, he cupped her face and smiled. "We might yet get to have a family and home and all those other things you've never had that others take for granted."

Divine closed her eyes briefly, afraid to allow the hope taking seed in her heart to grow. Opening her eyes, she asked, "But what if he doesn't?"

"Then I guess we'll be traveling a lot," Marcus said wryly. "Could be fun."

Divine gave a short laugh and shook her head. "Are you always this upbeat?"

Marcus shrugged. "In my youth, yes. Haven't been for centuries though. But I find you make me feel that way." Slipping his arms around her he said, "I feel like I could conquer the world with you at my side."

"Not if you're going to waste your time standing there in the middle of enemy territory, kissing and cuddling."

Divine and Marcus both stiffened at those words and turned to peer at the man who stood in the doorway. He was leaning against the door frame, ankles and arms crossed, and eyeing them with an expression that was hard to read.

"Lucian," Marcus breathed, releasing Divine and stepping protectively in front of her. "We need to talk."

"Do we?" Lucian asked dryly.

Divine frowned, and slipped in front of Marcus, hands on hips as she confronted the uncle who had been a bogeyman to her for so many years. "No. *We* need to talk," she said firmly, and then added grimly, "Marcus has done nothing wrong. You can arrest or kill me, but you have to let him go."

"Divine," Marcus snapped, grabbing her arm to pull her behind him. "Let me handle this. I—"

"I suggest you both shut up and let me do the talking before you piss me off," Lucian said dryly.

Marcus stopped pulling on Divine, and instead slipped his hand down to catch and squeeze hers encouragingly. Or perhaps to suggest she take the man's advice and stay quiet. Divine wasn't sure which it was, but she held her tongue and leaned back against him, accepting the support he offered.

Lucian nodded, apparently satisfied with their obedience, and then his gaze slipped to Marcus.

"When you didn't answer phone calls, we had Mortimer track the GPS for Tiny and Mirabeau's SUV and flew up here to find out what the hell was happening. We found and took out three of Leonius's sons guarding the building as we came in, are there any more?"

When Marcus hesitated, Divine glanced to him to see that he was peering down at her in question. Turning back to her uncle she said, "I only know about four of them. That guy—" She nodded to the unfortunate Danny who lay in two pieces on the floor. "Then there was his partner, and two other men who came in behind Marcus."

"They followed me from the hotel," Marcus inserted and then asked, "You didn't see Abaddon out there anywhere?"

"What is an Abaddon?" Lucian asked dryly. "It sounds like something that belongs in an outhouse."

The comment surprised a laugh out of Divine. Biting her lip, she quickly bowed her head to hide her amusement, afraid her uncle would be angry if he thought she wasn't taking this seriously.

"It's good to hear your laugh again, Basha," Lucian said quietly.

Divine glanced up with surprise at the words, but said automatically, "I'm Divine now."

For some reason that made Lucian's expression close up like a vault. His eyes also narrowed on her with concentration. He was reading her, she knew, and stayed still, not trying to close him out. After a moment, he blinked and released a long weary sigh as he rubbed his eyes with the thumb and fingers of one hand. When that hand finally dropped away, Lucian speared Marcus with a look and said, "Out."

Divine felt Marcus stiffen and glanced to him with alarm, half afraid he'd tell her uncle to go to hell and half afraid he'd obey and leave. He had come here as Lucian's spy, after all. Did that mean he had to obey?

Marcus squeezed her hand reassuringly, but didn't glance down. He looked her uncle in the eye and said, "She's my life mate, Lucian, so with all due respect . . . screw you."

Eyes wide, Divine shot her gaze back to her uncle to see his reaction. Much to her surprise, after staring at

Marcus for several tense moments, he nodded, his mouth almost forming a smile before he said, "You'll do."

Divine was still blinking in confusion, unsure what he meant by that when Lucian turned his attention back to her.

"Your name is Basha Argeneau," he said firmly. "You are not Divine, Nuri, or Naduah. You are Basha Argeneau and always will be."

"Until it's Basha Notte," Marcus said grimly from behind her.

Lucian ignored him, not even acknowledging him with a glance as he continued, "You are Basha, the daughter of my brother Felix. The girl who as a child looked like the eldest daughter I lost in Atlantis. You are the Basha who was my first favorite niece, and who I have grieved and felt guilty for not keeping safe for two and a half millennia." He moved forward to grasp her shoulders firmly. "You are Basha Argeneau. Got it?"

When she nodded reluctantly, he squeezed her shoulders and said, "Your father named you Basha. Don't refuse to use it because of something done to you as a child. You will always carry that child with you, but you aren't that child anymore. You're a survivor, strong and brave. You had the courage to survive when immortal women centuries older than you broke and took their own lives."

That made her blink as she wondered just how much he'd read of her memories from her mind in those few moments he'd searched it. But then she shifted her attention back to her uncle as he continued.

"You were a victim of Leonius. There is no shame

in what happened that belongs to you." He frowned briefly, and then added, "And while I am sorry you have suffered greatly over the years because of the confused feelings you experienced every time he attacked you, I will tell you right now that I am grateful that you were a possible life mate to him. If you hadn't been, your remains would have been among the ashes of the immortal and no-fanger women we found when we got there. I suspect your being his life mate was the only reason he let you live and I am able to talk to you now."

Divine's head went back slightly at that. It was a consideration that hadn't occurred to her and one she would definitely consider more later, if she had the opportunity.

"You're still thinking of yourself as Divine in your head," Lucian growled. "Cut it out."

"Yes, Uncle," Basha murmured, and then, unable to stand the worry for her future any longer, she blurted, "I am the woman who whisked away Leonius II when you had him at the hotel in Toronto."

"Yeah. That's a problem," Lucian said, releasing her shoulders with a grimace.

"You—" Marcus began, but Lucian cut him off.

"Do not spout your bit about my brother Jean Claude. I heard it the first time," he said sharply, and then admitted, "I was standing in the door quite a while longer than you realize, which proves that we're all useless when we find our life mates. Hell, if I'd been this A-bidet character—"

"Abaddon," Basha corrected, but couldn't help grinning at his mispronunciation.

"Whatever," Lucian muttered. "If I'd been him you'd both be dead right now."

Neither of them argued the point. He was right.

Lucian rubbed his forehead grimly, and then straightened his shoulders. "You didn't know the boy you raised as your son was a killer when you helped him. You didn't even know he was rogue."

"No," Basha assured him even though he wasn't asking.

"You also didn't know feeding off the hoof wasn't allowed anymore," he added, and she blinked, startled by just how much he did know. But he was continuing, "While that doesn't excuse your actions, it does mitigate them."

Basha stilled as he considered her briefly.

"We can forgive the feeding off the hoof so long as you stick to bagged blood in future."

"I will," she promised.

"As for the other . . ." He paused, expression unhappy, and then said solemnly, "I know this will be hard since you've thought of him as your son all these years, but you'll need to help us recapture Leonius to make up for it."

Basha was silent for a moment, her emotions in chaos. She had thought of him as her son for so long, and as such her instinct was to protect, but after all she'd learned about him . . .

Marcus squeezed her shoulders, and Basha sighed and nodded in response.

"And you'll also have to help catch this Abaddon character who has apparently scurried back to whatever hole the two of them are hiding in," he added.

There was no hesitation this time, Basha nodded firmly. She'd be happy to put an end to that bastard.

"Good," Lucian said quietly. "Then come on. I made the others wait outside until I knew what was what. I'm sure they're peeing their pants worrying over whether you're both okay or not."

Basha sagged back against Marcus's chest with relief when her uncle turned away. It was a relief she knew Marcus shared. She felt the tension slide out of his hard body as his arms slid around her.

"We're going to be okay," he assured her.

"Yes," Basha agreed, and found a smile to offer him as he turned her into his arms.

"No more running," he said with a smile. "We can make a home. We'll have family, both yours and mine, and we can have children . . . if I'm still capable," he added wryly.

"Why wouldn't you be capable?" Basha asked with concern.

"Well, after what you did to me with the mop . . ." Marcus paused and caught her wrists on a laugh as she realized he was teasing her and tried to smack his chest. Using his hold on her wrists, he tugged her against his chest and kissed her quickly before saying, "I love you, Basha Argeneau."

For once, she didn't flinch at the name, and supposed it was knowing that her father had given it to her that made the difference. She'd tried so long to deny the past and what had happened to her as a child. Denying the name had been the only way she'd known how to separate that poor abused child from the woman she wanted to be. Now though, she realized that by denying the name, she denied her father too, and everything else that connected her to the family she so dearly wanted to be a part of. Besides, little Basha had done all right. She had survived, and grown stronger. She had nothing to be ashamed of.

"I love you too, Marcus Notte," she murmured and leaned up on her tiptoes to kiss him.

"Come on you two, you're busting my balls here. Get a move on."

Divine turned sharply toward the door, just in time to see her uncle turn and walk away. "He didn't—?"

"He did," Marcus said dryly.

"But he doesn't know—"

"He knows," Marcus assured her. "He read our minds."

"Oh, damn," Basha groaned. "I'm so going to get teased about that for eternity."

"Yeah," he agreed with a grimace as he slipped his arm around her waist to steer her to the door. "We both are. I can hear it now, uniball, one-nut, half man . . ."

"No," Basha said at once. "They'll know it healed. You still have two balls."

"That won't matter," he assured her with a crooked smile.

"I guess we'll have to suffer it together," she said apologetically.

"Together we can handle anything," Marcus assured her, and risked her uncle's wrath to stop and kiss her again.

Keep reading for a peek into
the Argeneau world . . .
from the very beginning!
All available from Avon Books

A Quick Bite

That hot guy tied to Lissianna Argeneau's bed? He's Gregory Hewitt, the doctor her mother hopes will help cure her phobia of blood . . . because that's an especially annoying quirk for a vampire. But is Greg the answer to her troubles, or will he be just a good meal?

"Let's get this off you," she suggested as she worked at the bow around his neck.

He sighed as it was removed, relaxing on the bed a bit, and Lissianna decided to discard his tie as well.

"There, isn't that better?" she asked, sliding the silk cloth from around his neck.

The man started to nod, then caught himself and scowled instead as she undid the top three buttons of his shirt. "It would be better still if you untied me."

Lissianna smiled with amusement at the way he was struggling with himself, then tried to distract him by running her fingers lightly over the bit of chest she'd revealed. Much to her satisfaction, a shiver went through him as her long nails grazed gently across his naked skin. This education business was turning out to be easier than she'd feared.

"Untie me." He was trying to be firm, but it was obvious his heart was no longer wholly behind the desire to be free.

Smiling knowingly, Lissianna scraped her fingers lightly down to run along the cloth just above his belt. The provocative action sent his stomach muscles galloping and his breath came out on a little hiss of air.

"What the hell," he breathed. "There are worse things than being a sex slave."

Love Bites

Etienne Argeneau's three hundred years of bachelorhood comes to an end when, to save the woman who saved him, he turns her into an immortal. But all Rachel had really wanted was just to get off the night shift in the morgue. Now this man says she's a vampire? At least the look in his bright silver eyes said they'd be spending a lot of time together.

"Why you won't come to me?"

Rachel glanced back at the corpse. He wasn't making much sense, but then who said hallucinations had to? She tried to reason with him. "Why would I come to you? You aren't real. You aren't even sitting up."

"I'm not?"

"No, I just think you are. In reality, you're still really lying there dead. I'm just imagining you sitting up and talking."

"Hmm." He grinned suddenly. It was a nice grin. "How do you know?"

"Because dead men don't sit up and talk," she explained patiently. "Please lie back down now. My head is starting to spin."

"But what if I'm not dead?"

Single White Vampire

Editor Kate Leever was adamant that her newest vampire romance author Lucern Argeneau will attend a romance convention to meet his fans. Despite his reclusive nature, odd sleep schedule and avoidance of the sun, the handsome Luc was going to be recognized by the public. But soon Kate would learn that his novels were more biographies than bodice rippers, and it'd be her neck on the line.

In a pale blue business suit, Kate C. Leever resembled a cool glass of ice water. The image was pleasing on this unseasonably warm September evening.

The image shattered when the woman dragged her luggage up the porch steps, paused before him, offered him a bright cheerful smile that lifted her lips and sparkled in her eyes, then blurted, "Hi. I'm Kate Leever. I hope you got my letter. The mail was so slow, and you kept forgetting to send me your phone number, so I thought I'd come visit personally and talk to you about all the publicity possibilities that are opening up for us. I know you're not really interested in partaking of any of them, but I feel sure once I explain the benefits you'll reconsider."

Lucern stared at her wide, smiling lips for one mesmerized moment; then he gave himself a shake. Reconsider? Was that what she wanted? Well, that was easy enough. He reconsidered. It was a quick task.

"No." He closed the door.

Tall, Dark + Hungry

*Terri had flown from England to help plan her cousin's wed-
ding, but paying for a New York hotel room was like giving
blood! She had an alternative: the new in-laws were offering lodging. Of course, the Argeneaus were a certifiably odd
family, but then there was Bastien, the tallest, darkest and
hungriest of the bunch—and his effect on Terri was decidedly delicious.*

It was then Bastien had realized he'd forgotten the
blood. He could not believe that he had been so remiss.
He was an idiot! And that idiocy was about to see him
ruin the day. He could not continue to walk around in
this heat with the sun killing him.

Perhaps it would help if he bought a big floppy hat
and a long-sleeved shirt from one of the booths or
something. Bastien grimaced. He might as well buy
a clown nose and floppy shoes, too. This day wasn't
going at all as he'd hoped.

"Bastien?" Terri was suddenly at his side, concern
on her face. "You look a bit . . . ill. Are you feeling all
right?"

"Yes, I— It's just the heat and sun," he said finally.
He wasn't surprised he looked sick. They had been
outside for two hours, and he was really starting to
feel it.

"I think I could use a break," he admitted, and
sighed inwardly at the concern on her face. Now she'd
think he was some pitifully weak guy who couldn't
handle a little walking.

"If you like." She frowned. "You really aren't feeling
well, are you?"

"No, I just—" He sighed. "I forgot about the sun. I
have a bit of an allergy to it."

A Bite to Remember

Once bitten, twice shy, and sexy PI Jackie Morrisey wasn't going there again. Vincent Argeneau may be the hottest guy she's ever met, living or dead, but she's here to stop a killer from turning this vampire into dust, not to jump into bed with him. Okay, so Vincent does look rather tempting shirtless. He's also charming, protective. Still, Jackie needs to be on her guard, lest this little fling be . . . a bite to remember.

Vincent pulled the front door open.

"Vincent Argeneau?" the woman asked.

When he nodded, she stuck out her hand. "I'm Jackie Morrisey and this is Tiny McGraw. I believe Bastien called you about us?"

Vincent stared at her hand but—rather than take it—pushed the door closed and lifted the phone back to his ear as he turned away. "Bastien, she's *mortal*!"

"Did you just slam the door in Jackie's face?" Bastien asked with amazement. "I heard the slam, Vincent. Don't be so damned rude."

"*Hello!*" he said impatiently. "She's *mortal*. Bad enough she's female, but I need someone who knows about our 'special situation' to deal with this problem. She—"

"Jackie *does* know," Bastien said dryly. "Do you think I'd send you an uninitiated mortal? Have a little faith." A sigh traveled down the phone line. "She has a bit of an attitude when it comes to our kind, but is the best in the business. Now open the door for the woman."

"But she's mortal and . . . a girl!"

Bite Me If You Can

One minute Leigh is walking home, and the next a vampire is sinking his teeth into her neck. Turns out it was a rogue vampire marked for termination, but it does Leigh little good because the damage's already been done. She's become one of them. Lucian Argeneau has been alive for over two thousand years, and little excites him anymore. Then Leigh drops into his life. Suddenly he finds himself imagining the sassy brunette in his nice big bed . . .

"Am I really a vampire?"

Lucian's hands froze on the mop and he glanced at her with surprise. "You doubt it? You haven't noticed anything different?"

Understanding struck him when Leigh looked away, and he said, "It's tempting to deny it to yourself, but it won't change anything. It just delays your coming to grips—and learning to live—with it."

"I suppose you're right," Leigh acknowledged unhappily as he went back to mopping. He glimpsed her sitting up, straightening her shoulders, and raising her head, then she said, "Okay, so I'm a vampire."

"Yes," Lucian said solemnly, and added, "But we dislike that name."

She shrugged, then asked with a little movement of her shoulders, "I gather this means I'll now live forever and never age?"

Lucian rung out the mop again as he considered how to answer her question.

"Probably not forever," he said finally, as he slapped the mop to the floor. "But so long as you aren't decapitated or trapped in a fire, your life has been greatly prolonged and you won't age, or get sick, or even get cavities."

"Yeah?" she asked with interest. "No cavities?"

The Accidental Vampire

Ever since an accident turned her into a knockout vamp, Elvi Black knows there's more to being undead than what she saw in Dracula. *And Victor's the perfect man for a novice neck-biter like Elvi. He's willing to teach her everything he knows, but he'll have to do it fast. Someone's out to put a stake through her new vamp life, and only Victor can keep her safe—and satisfied—for all eternity.*

"So you have to give them your blood," Elvi said. "I must have missed that part of the movie."

"What movie?" Victor asked.

"*Dracula.* I don't remember seeing that."

"What? You researched by watching the movie rather than reading the damned book?"

"I wanted to learn as fast as I could. Movies are faster than books."

He rolled his eyes. "Definitely a child of your times."

"God! Sometimes you're such a . . . a . . . *man.*"

"Good of you to notice."

Several moments passed. Elvi's tongue slipped out to glide along her lips. Victor's gaze shifted there. She had the most incredible mouth. Full, red lips that begged to be caressed and kissed . . .

Vampires Are Forever

Vampires don't exist . . . do they? Inez Urso is beginning to have her doubts. Her business associate Thomas Argeneau has some interesting vampire-like traits. Not to mention, he just tried to bite her neck . . . but maybe that was a sign of passion?

There was no way she was going anywhere with this man.

"Inez? You were here all day and perfectly safe. If I'd wanted to harm you, I could have done so first thing in the morning. Instead, I drew you a bath and ordered you breakfast—"

"And then you bit me." Inez had luxuriated in that bubble bath, thinking what a wonderful, sweet man Thomas Argeneau was. She'd looked down at his sleeping face and pondered how wonderful it would be to have a handsome, thoughtful man for a mate.

She'd imagined him greeting her at the door with a kiss, the smells of scrumptious cooking drifted to her as he kissed her hello, his hands moving over her body, stripping away her clothes one at a time . . .

Right up until he woke up and bit her.

Vampire, Interrupted

After seven hundred years of life, Marguerite Argeneau finally has a career as a private investigator. It seemed a simple enough assignment, until she finds herself at the wrong end of a sword. Julius Notte wants to protect Marguerite, and not because someone just tried to take her head off. She doesn't know it yet, but she's his life mate and he's determined to woo her. Now if only he can keep her alive—so to speak—so they can have that happily-ever-after.

"We are life mates."

Marguerite choked, spitting wine out as she coughed and sputtered.

"Are you all right?" Julius asked.

She nodded.

"Not the most delicate approach, was it?"

They stared at each other, his expression assessing, hers wary.

"What are we going to do about it?"

She swallowed. "Do we have to do anything about it for now? I mean, there is no need to really do anything at all. We are immortals and appear to be life mates."

"We are life mates, Marguerite. There is no 'appear' about it," he growled.

His eyes were blazing, the silver consuming the black of his eyes.

She licked her lips nervously and paused when his gaze followed the action. The air in the room was suddenly electric. Her heart rate sped up, blood moving swiftly through her veins as her breathing became shallow.

The Rogue Hunter

*Samantha Willan is a workaholic. She's grateful for some
rest and relaxation in cottage country . . . until she meets
her irresistible new neighbor. Garrett Mortimer is a rogue
hunter here to track down a reported rogue, but fun in the
sun is every bloodsucker's nightmare. Worse, he can't seem
to get his mind off Samantha . . . After eight hundred years
as a bachelor, is he ready to turn a volatile attraction into a
lasting love affair?*

"Do you need help finding a candle?" he asked as
they mounted the steps.

Sam hesitated, tempted to say yes, invite him inside,
and see if he might try to kiss her, or . . .

She caught herself. She wasn't ready for that.

"No, that's okay. We keep the flashlights on a shelf
just inside the door. But thank you," she added, pausing by the door.

Turning back, she opened her mouth to say something.

What it would have been she didn't know, because
it slipped from her mind the moment she saw the way
his eyes were shining in the darkness.

It was as if they were soaking up the moonlight and
reflecting it back at her.

Like a night predator, she thought, and felt a shiver
run up her back under her T-shirt.

The Immortal Hunter

Danielle McGill doesn't know if she can trust the man who just rescued her . . . from vampires? But, with her sister in the hands of these dangerous men, she doesn't have much choice. Decker Argeneau is also awakening a passion beyond anything Dani's ever known. Being undead may not be half-bad . . . especially if it means spending forever with a man who would love her with his mind, body, and immortal soul.

"I'm two-hundred-and-fifty-nine, Dani."

"You're pulling my leg, right?"

"No," Decker said solemnly. "Does the age difference bother you?"

She gave a disbelieving laugh. "Decker, you've told me about life mates, and I know you think I'm yours, but—"

"I don't think, I know."

She started to slide off the bale of hay, but he caught her arm.

She wanted him to kiss her. She wanted to kiss him back. She wanted— Giving her head a shake, she pulled her arm free and started walking toward the door.

He caught her arm and spun her around. "Don't run from me, Dani. I'll just follow."

"I'm not running," she whispered, her eyes on his mouth.

"Yes," he growled, "you are." And he did exactly what she wanted and kissed her.

The Renegade Hunter

The Argeneau family has a secret—one of their own is a rogue vampire! But Nicholas Argeneau was once a hunter himself, and when he sees a woman being attacked by one of his own, he comes to her rescue. Josephine Willan never expected a gorgeous stranger to save her life . . . and gets locked up for his troubles. Now she's determined to prove that this renegade hunter is worth fighting for.

"I want you," Nicholas admitted, his eyes glowing silver.

Jo suspected that was a tell with him: molten silver meant hot and horny. Which was fine with her, as she was feeling rather hot and bothered herself.

"But I can't claim you," he added.

"Claim me?" she echoed, then gave a laugh. "You make me sound like lost luggage. No one can claim me. I have free will." She moved around the table and dropped into his lap. She slid her arms around his shoulders. "Fortunately for you, I'm free and willing."

"Jo," he said, but she didn't want to hear it and covered his mouth with her own.

She smiled, slid her lips to his ears, and nibbled briefly before whispering, "I ache for you."

He sucked in a harsh breath, then something snapped. Suddenly his head jerked around so his lips could claim hers.

Mirabeau LaRouche knew she had a job to do, but she never expected her assignment to take her through New York City's dark, dank underground—in her bridesmaid gown, no less! And when her partner turns out to be mortal private investigator Tiny McGraw, Mirabeau knows it's no ordinary Cupid's arrow that has struck her heart this Valentine's Day.

"You'll meet her soon enough, and when you do . . ." Marguerite hesitated, then sighed, and said, "Our Mirabeau is prickly. She has a lot of defenses. She lost her entire family to the greed and betrayal of a favorite uncle back during the Massacres of St. Bartholomew and finds it hard to trust and love. She's erected a lot of protective walls. You will need to be patient."

Tiny stared at Marguerite blankly. She seriously believed he would be a life mate to this Mirabeau. The idea was both exciting and scary as hell. His life would change forever. God. A life mater. It would mean his days as a bachelor were over . . . and he'd probably have to turn, become an immortal like Jackie had. He'd have to drink blood and . . .

Born to Bite

*Legend has it that Armand Argeneau is a killer in the bed-
room . . . But with all three of his late wives meeting un-
timely ends, is this sexy immortal a lover or a murderer?
As an enforcer, it's Eshe d'Aureus's job to find out and bring
rogue vampires to justice, even if the rogue in question
makes her heart race.*

"I'm going to kill her."

"Who?" Armand asked with confusion, and then
turned to glance in the direction that Lucian's gaze
now seemed fixated. He was staring past him at the
dark road outside. Armand peered at the long stretch
of dark highway for a minute, slow to recognize the
fiery vision approaching for what it was, a motorcycle
with red, yellow, and orange LED lights around the
tires and across the body that made it look like the bike
was roaring up the road aflame. It was one hell of a
magnificent sight.

"Eshe," Lucian snapped, finally answering her question. "That's her."

Hungry For You

Alexandra Willan's restaurant is due to open in two weeks, but her chef just walked out. Then a highly recommended replacement arrives, a culinary genius who sends electric tingles racing through her body . . . Except Cale Valens can't cook. In fact, as one of the most ancient of the Argeneau clan, Cale hasn't eaten real food in two thousand years. Yet he's determined to prove to Alex his prowess in the kitchen . . . and elsewhere.

He was going to kiss her, some part of her mind yelled in warning, and Alex knew she should turn her head away, or kick her legs to be set down, but found she was unwilling to. She wanted him to kiss her, wanted to know if it would be as wonderful as it had been in her dream.

Surely nothing could be that good, Alex thought faintly, and then his mouth drifted softly over hers, brushing across them as lightly as a butterfly's wings, once, then twice before settling so that his tongue could slide out to urge her lips apart. Alex wasn't aware of giving her brain the order to do it, but her mouth parted willingly enough, allowing his tongue in, and she had to revise her belief that no real kiss could compare with those from her dream. This was definitely as good or better, she decided, as his tongue swept in to tangle with hers.

Cale tasted of lemon meringue pie and coffee, the snack they'd had during the last break he'd insisted on while they'd been antiquing. But it was combined with another taste entirely his own, and Alex found herself moaning and shifting slightly in his arms so that her hands could creep up around his neck.

The Reluctant Vampire

Rogue hunter Drina Argenis (from the Spanish side of the Argeneau family) has been many things in her years as an immortal, but bodyguard/babysitter to a teenage vampire is something new. There's an incentive, however: the other vampsitter, Harper Stoyan, may be Drina's life mate. Trouble is, having just lost a life mate, Harper is resigned to being alone. Can Drina tempt this reluctant vampire to take a chance?

Gasping an apology, Drina immediately stumbled forward again to get off him, lost her footing, and started to go down. In his effort to save her from the fall, Harper managed to get his own feet tangled up with hers and found himself crashing to the icy pavement with her.

"Are you all right?"

Harper opened his eyes at that concerned query and turned his head to see that Drina had pushed herself to her hands and knees beside him and was eyeing him worriedly. Her coat was open despite the cold, revealing a low-cut silk shirt that gaped slightly thanks to her position. It left him an extraordinary view of full, round breasts encased in a lacy white bra that looked rather fetching against her olive skin.

Blinking, he tore his gaze from the delectable sight and glanced past her to Stephanie, who was nearly killing herself laughing in the SUV, and then he sighed and said dryly, "I'll live."

Teddy Brunswick is perfectly comfortable with the immortals who live among us. But he never counted on being snowed in with one over Christmas—especially not a tasty little bundle like Katricia Argeneau. She seems to really like Teddy but who can tell for sure? After all, the snowstorm has derailed Katricia's blood delivery, which makes Teddy the only available meal on the menu . . .

Katricia took her time closing bedroom doors, peering curiously into each room as she went. It was partially out of curiosity and partially to give Teddy some breathing room. She didn't need to read his mind to know that he wasn't comfortable with her. She supposed she'd come on too strong too fast, but hadn't been able to help herself. The very fact that he might be her life mate made her want to test it. She wasn't hungry yet, but then the only food around was in cans and boxes. There was nothing really to tempt her palate. Which meant the easiest way to know for sure was to kiss Teddy and see if she experienced the shared pleasure she'd heard so much about.

Unfortunately, it was looking like that might be a hard objective to achieve. Teddy didn't appear to be comfortable with what he thought was their age difference. That seemed obvious to her from the way he'd quickly removed his hat and scarf and then turned as if presenting some monstrosity to her. This was going to take some patience, which had never been Katricia's strong suit. She was already struggling with the urge to simply walk straight back out into the kitchen and jump the man's bones. The only thing stopping her was the worry that she might give the poor guy a heart attack or something. That would be just her luck—kill her life mate with a heart attack before she could woo and turn him.

Under a Vampire Moon

Christian Notte never imagined he'd let himself fall in love—until he meets the enthralling, charmingly skittish, and oh-so-mortal Carolyn. She has no desire to think about men, a vow she's determined to keep while on vacation in St. Lucia. So how will Christian reveal what he is and still convince this once-bitten mortal to trust him with her heart . . . and her forever?

The young woman stood there for a full minute, garnering the attention of everyone in the room, and then she opened her mouth and released a high pure note that pierced the silence. Her hand crashed down across the strings of the electric guitar she held and the band suddenly kicked to life, all movement and sound. Santo's body vibrated as he appeared to try to beat his drums to death. Zanipolo was working his electric guitar like a cross between a lover and a submachine gun. Raffaele was pounding on his keyboards, his head bobbing to the music. Gia was alternately making love to her own electric car with long riffs, and singing into the microphone with a clarity that Carolyn had never encountered before, and Christian . . .

Carolyn stared, watching the muscles in his arms and chest ripple under his black t-shirt as his bow scraped so quickly over the strings of his violin that she expected to see sparks flying and smoke rising. His eyes were closed, his face transported as the music moved through him. She couldn't seem to tear her gaze from him as he played song after song . . . and then his eyes suddenly opened and met hers. Carolyn felt like someone had jammed an adrenaline shot into her heart. She was sure it skipped a beat when his eyes opened, but when he caught her gaze and didn't release it, her heart started thumping again, charging ahead at a frightening rate that left her breathless and almost dizzy.

The Lady Is a Vamp

When Jeanne Louise Argeneau left work, she never thought she'd end up kidnapped by a good-looking mortal. More attracted than annoyed, she quickly realizes there is more to her abductor than meets the eye. But their time together is running out and they will need to risk everything to spend an eternity together.

"Bite me," he said grimly.

"Same to you," she muttered irritably.

Paul blinked, and then a surprised laugh slipped from his lips. "No. I wasn't—I mean, really go ahead and bite me, Jeanie. You need to feed. Feed on me."

"Oh," Jeanne Louise said on a sigh, and then frowned at him. "Not ten minutes ago you were upset with me because I was going to bite someone. Now you want me to bite you?"

He grimaced and glanced away. "Yes, well . . . I shouldn't have reacted as I did. I guess I was a little jealous when I saw you cuddled up to that hunk in the parking lot. I suppose after that kiss earlier today I feel a little possessive." Paul shrugged uncomfortably, and then rushed on. "Besides, you shouldn't have to feed on others. You're only without blood because I kidnapped you. If you have to bite anyone it should be me. No one else should have to pay."

Paul shifted a little closer and turned his head to offer her his neck.

Immortal Ever After

*Valerie Moyer doesn't believe in vampires—until she is kid-
napped by a fanged psychopath! After she escapes, she finds
herself under the protection of the darkly handsome Anders.
The Rogue Hunter felt a connection to Valerie from the
moment he cradled her bruised body in his arms. But before
he claims her, he must destroy the vampire who almost stole
her from him forever.*

Valerie glanced down at the melting sundae. It did
seem a shame for it to go to waste. It was good ice
cream. And it hadn't been cheap.

"Just give him a taste, Valerie, so he'll stop and eat
it," Leigh suggested.

Valerie hesitated, but they were pulling up to the red
light and it wouldn't interfere with his driving, so she
scooped up a healthy selection of her own ice cream
and topping and leaned over to offer her spoon to him.

Anders eyed the offering but didn't at first open his
mouth. She was just about to give up, sit back, and eat
it herself when he suddenly did. Valerie moved the
spoon between his open lips, watching silently as he
closed his mouth around the spoon and ice cream. She
could have sworn the gold flecks in his eyes flashed
bigger and brighter in the black irises, and then he
closed his eyes on a long moan that sounded almost
sexual.

Valerie stared wide-eyed as he savored the food,
then withdrew the now clean spoon and sank back in
her seat uncertainly.

One Lucky Vampire

When Nicole Phillips agreed to hire a housekeeper, she pictured someone a little frumpy and almost certainly female. Instead, she gets gorgeous, unmistakably male Jake Colson. Secretly playing bodyguard to sweet, sexy Nicole is turning out to be the wildest ride of Jake's life. First, he'll put a stop to whoever's targeting her. Then he'll prove that this kind of love, and luck, happens only once in an eternity.

"The chocolate cake is good," Jake said suddenly.

Blinking, Nicole glanced down at her cake. She hadn't even tried it yet.

"But you taste better," Jake added.

Nicole stilled, then slowly raised her head to peer at him. Oh yeah, his eyes were on fire now . . . and so was she. How the hell did that happen so fast? No kissing, touching, nothing. Just a couple of words and she was ready to go.

Jake picked up his plate and coffee and carried them to the island, then returned to stand beside her. Nicole tipped her head back, expecting him to kiss her, but instead he caught her chair and turned it so she faced him. He then scooped her up and set her on the table where his cake had been moments ago.

"These have to go," Jake announced, reaching for the button of her jeans. "You should wear skirts and dresses," he added conversationally as he slid the button free and started on the zipper. "It would make things much easier."

"I'll have to buy some," Nicole said breathlessly as he slid the zipper down.